She looked  *into his eyes and saw a silver blaze of raw, determined hunger.*

The shock of his undisguised desire as he lay in his sickbed set her heart pounding in her chest. Tristan's hand shot out and he grabbed her by the wrist. He tugged her to the edge of the bed and forced her to lean over him. "You're ill," she said.

"Not that ill." His eyes looked her over as he raised his free hand to grasp the zipper of her velour jacket. Slowly, he tugged it downward until the sides fell free.

"Stop that!" she cried. Then as suddenly as he had grasped her, he set her loose, and shakily Amanda straightened. Oh, thank God, he'd changed his mind.

Tristan had changed nothing. He skimmed his sweatshirt over his head and flung it aside. Then he rose up and grasped both sides of Amanda's jacket and whipped it down her arms, dropping it to the floor. He picked her up, swung her around and lowered her to the mattress.

"Oh, please," Amanda whispered. At first she wasn't certain whether she was begging him to stop or to continue. But soon she found herself digging her fingers into the bare, warm skin of his wide shoulders, and tossing her head back, she arched into his touch.

Shadow Dance

Susan Andersen

POPULAR LIBRARY

An Imprint of Warner Books, Inc.

A Warner Communications Company

Popular Library books are published by
Warner Books, Inc.
666 Fifth Avenue
New York, N.Y. 10103

 A Warner Communications Company

Printed in the United States of America

First Printing: October, 1989

10 9 8 7 6 5 4 3 2 1

This is for my guys
dedicated with love

To Steve
My long time lover

To Christopher
My sweet baby boy

And in memory of Dad and Uncle Harold

. . . . . Susie

PROLOGUE

Amanda Rose Charles awoke Tuesday morning with a warm feeling of well-being that lasted about forty-five seconds. Then she remembered her conversation with Charlie just before the midnight show the previous night, and a leaden weight seemed to press down upon her sternum, making it difficult to draw a really satisfying, deep breath. Struggling up on her elbow she yawned, raked her fingers through her hair, and then reached hesitantly for the telephone on the nightstand. She placed it on the mattress next to her stomach, picked up the receiver, and punched out the familiar numbers.

The phone rang ten times before she conceded defeat and hung it up. Damn.

Where was Maryanne? The idea of calling the police sure didn't appeal to her—Maryanne would be furious if it should turn out she had done so needlessly. But she and Rhonda had agreed on the way home last night to call the authorities if Maryanne didn't come home today. It had been three days since they'd had word of her. This wasn't the first time Maryanne had taken off without a word to anyone. She seemed to make a habit of it, despite the agreement the women had

made to always let one of the others know where they could
be reached and how long they would be gone. It was so
blasted inconsiderate, the way she let them worry about her
. . . but typical, vintage Maryanne.

But to not even bother calling in sick was sheer professional
suicide, and not typical of Maryanne at all. Amanda only
hoped that the guy she was with, whoever he was, turned
out to be worth it.

But she wouldn't hold her breath. They so rarely were.

Amanda didn't understand this preoccupation with men that
every single woman she had ever met seemed to harbor.
Sometimes she felt like the only grown-up in a room full of
adolescents when the conversation turned to men and sex—
as it invariably did.

Is it just me? Well, yeah, obviously it must be, since she
was the only one who ever seemed to feel the least bit out
of step. But what *was* the attraction? For the most part, it
honestly eluded her. And it wasn't because she was a man-
hater, either, as one woman had insinuated when Amanda
had been foolish enough to actually express her lack of comprehension out loud. She simply didn't understand the rougher
sex's seemingly limitless ability to turn a woman's life inside
out.

Amanda hadn't exactly appreciated being told she must
hate all men, simply because she had failed to understand the
few she had known. She was a little tired of being treated
like a heretic by people who didn't know the first thing about
her. But, looking on the bright side, at least that particular
woman hadn't also loudly concluded that Amanda must therefore be a lesbian, which had been the result another time
when she had inadvisably aired her personal confusion on the
subject of men.

On that particular occasion, Amanda had politely refrained
from spitting in the woman's eye. She had been tempted, but
lessons in deportment, drilled into her as a little girl, were
too firmly entrenched to disregard. Where did people get these

outrageous ideas? Just because her views were a little different. . . .

Amanda liked men just fine. They made great dance partners, and a couple of them even made dandy friends. It was only when they took a perfectly good friendship and tried to turn it into a sexual involvement that she grew a little bit leery.

And it wasn't as though she hadn't really given sex a fair shake, either, despite Rhonda's near-constant insistence to the contrary. She'd had experiences with three different men, but was her friend satisfied with that? Oh, no. According to Rhonda, the numbers were insufficient to render a conclusive verdict. Well, Amanda was sorry as could be if Rhonda wasn't thrilled with the numbers, but she wasn't going to go to bed with two dozen, or a hundred, or however many men it took just to satisfy her idea of fair market testing.

It wasn't as though she was standing on a street corner with a tambourine in her hand, advocating one and all to a life of celibacy, for heaven's sake. She was only saying she had weathered quite enough experiences to know that men weren't all that essential in her own life.

What her personal philosophy probably boiled down to, Amanda decided as she tried Maryanne's number again, was that men were fine, and men were fun. But it seemed to her that once a relationship was allowed to turn sexual, it grew much too complicated, with returns that were negligible, at best. It was much simpler to keep men as friends.

Amanda tossed back the blankets and climbed out of bed. She stretched luxuriously and then strolled across the carpet to rummage through her closet and drawers. She suddenly thought of Raymond, the street youth to whom she'd surrendered her virginity. She hadn't thought of him in years. They'd had such fun together, Amanda remembered as she squatted down to paw through the tangle of shoes on the closet floor—until the subject of sex had reared its ugly head.

She had been not quite nineteen years old and had arrived

in New York a few months before. Raymond had been twenty-two, and different from any of the boys she'd known. His knowledge of the city and his street savvy had impressed her immensely. Her life up until then had been sheltered, so Raymond seemed to be the epitome of worldliness.

Amanda pulled a pair of distressed-leather ankle boots out of the mess on the floor, thinking of how innocent she had been in those days, how willing to take a chance.

She had walked into that affair with her eyes wide open, knowing that when a girl made love for the first time, it wasn't likely to be a totally wonderful experience. The truth was, she hadn't been expecting much, but it hadn't been all that dreadful, either. She'd had years of dance to tone her body, so the pain of losing her virginity had been minimal.

But it had been like a good news/bad news joke, and the bad news was, she had lost it for all the wrong reasons.

Emotionally, Amanda had been at a reckless point in her life. She was on her own for the very first time, sporting some painful emotional scars that were only superficially healed. Teddy was gone; her family life was a total disaster; and all around her, in this permissive new environment, her friends, roommates, co-workers, and fellow inhabitants of the dance world had been touting the glories of sexual freedom. So she had brushed aside Teddy's teachings and had gone with the flow, simply because a dozen or so people had recommended that she do so.

And she had chosen Raymond because she liked him, because they had fun, and because he had pressured her a bit. Or maybe she had chosen him because she'd thought he was very experienced. The reasons didn't really matter much, in the final analysis. She would never forget Raymond, simply because he *was* the first. And in his hands, her initiation into the glories and wonders of sex had turned out to be not such a wonder, not so glorious, and yet, not too awful.

Unfortunately, it had never really improved after the first time, either. She hadn't expected that. She'd rather assumed that once the awkwardness of actually losing her virginity was out of the way, sex would miraculously become as spontaneous and wonderful as everyone claimed it to be.

Another erroneous assumption in the life of Amanda Charles, she reflected wryly, standing in the middle of her bedroom floor ten years after the fact, digging her toes into the plush carpeting.

Her relationship with Raymond had continued to be short on erogenous splendor, and long on self-conscious bumbling and tense frustration. That had been her fault, she was sure, not Raymond's. It wasn't as though he had changed after they had made love. And he had never once attempted to misrepresent himself. She had just somehow mistaken him for someone he was not.

But she had nevertheless found sex with him intrusive, and that couldn't help but color the rest of their relationship. After all, how much more personal could you get than to allow a part of someone else inside your body? Their encounters had always left her feeling embarrassed and uncomfortable, as if she were trying too hard to be someone she simply wasn't. He had sensed it, of course, and resentment over her failure in bed had eventually bled onto the successful aspects of their friendship. Finally, after a few months of pretending that matters would miraculously improve, Amanda had conceded that most likely they would not, and she had called it quits.

And in the process, she had lost a friend.

One of Amanda's many shoes prevented her from closing the closet door. She tried to kick it inside, but its strap caught in the crack between the edge of the door and the doorjamb. She sat on the floor, reached for the shoe, and gave it a yank, only to have the small metal buckle wedge more tightly still. She rattled the door, without noticeable results. Amanda rested her forehead on her drawn-up knees. She hated mornings.

It was a funny thing about her introduction into the wonderful world of men and women. When all was said and done, she hadn't actually been able to regret her experience with Raymond, if for no other reason than she had learned something valuable from it. She had left home at eighteen, angry and hurting, determined to forsake all the false values and pretensions of her former life, prepared to jettison every single rule Mother and Father had ever drummed into her. Only to discover that it wasn't necessary to discard it all in order to be different from them.

It was ironic, really. She had arrived in New York with a chip on her shoulder. She was going to be wild and wicked and do things that would blow her parents out of the water, if they ever found out about them—all the things her sister would have done.

Instead, after the false start with Raymond, she had learned to accept herself for the person *she* was. She was not Teddy. She could not change her reserved nature, and wild, raucous behavior was simply beyond her. Her manners had been reinforced from the cradle until now they were all but carved in stone. Her one attempt at public rowdiness had left her feeling like an idiot, and rudeness was totally beyond her. The few times she had managed to attempt to be rude, it had turned out to have been hardly worth the effort, for she possessed one of those inconvenient consciences that made her pay in spades for any unmannerly utterance.

Not that she had seen rude or insulting behavior as traits to be actively pursued. She had merely been tired of a world where the appearance of good manners seemed to count for more than a person's actions, and she had thought, if nothing else, she would be more direct and blunt in her new life away from home.

It had felt like a defeat of epic proportions at first, when she'd failed to emerge from behind her lifelong shield of frozen good manners and tell the world what she really thought of it. She had feared she was more like Mother and Father than she had thought.

One result of the hours of soul-searching she had put herself through after the aborted affair with Raymond was the realization that she couldn't buck her own nature. Her manners would most likely remain with her until the day she died.

They might be a blessing, or they might be a curse; all she knew was that she had tried to shake them and they had refused to be dislodged.

By coming to New York on her own to pursue a career in dance, she was considered by Mother and Father to be beyond the pale. But Amanda was also seen as something of an oddity in the dance world. She didn't have a bohemian bone in her body. Except when she danced, she was actually quite conservative in nature. Her personal style also differed radically from most of her fellow dancers. She dressed with a flair that was highly individualistic, but the image she unconsciously projected suggested restrained elegance rather than flamboyance. And she was quiet. She was friendly, but she didn't rush relationships.

Raising her head up off her knees, Amanda cast a baleful eye on her tangled shoe strap. Then, stifling a yawn, she decided to tackle it later, after she'd had her coffee. She dragged herself to her feet.

It was time for her morning workout. Amanda made a face, but with inbred discipline, she began a set of floor exercises.

During her preliminary stretches, she reflected how much easier it had always been for her to make friends with women. Perhaps that was because she had grown up with three sisters. For some reason, men were a different story altogether. She supposed that it was due to her lack of understanding of their basic nature that she erected fences between herself and most men. It was simply automatic—she threw up these guards without even realizing that she was doing so.

Not that it made a lick of difference to the gossips in the dance community, she acknowledged wryly, lying on her stomach and arching until her toes touched the back of her head. They couldn't have cared less what her reasons were. They simply knew what they saw, and they spread the word as they saw it. Amanda rolled to a sitting position and spread her legs until they formed a line perpendicular to her torso. Leaning forward, she rested her weight on her forearms and touched her forehead to the carpet. Tales of her tendency to be aloof, of her standoffishness with men, quickly made the rounds, and she soon began to acquire a reputation for being coolly unattainable.

Escalating the pace of her workout as she switched from stretches to more serious body strengthening exercises, Amanda decided she could live with that. She occasionally regretted her reputation, but at least she wasn't likely to be led astray and have her entire career jeopardized, like Mary-anne.

She doubted there was a man alive worth sacrificing her career for.

In the bathroom, she eyed the bathtub covetously for a moment, but decided to settle for a shower in the interests of time. She leaned into the mirror, curling her lip in disgust at her image. How charming—there were at least a dozen creases pressed into her cheek from the bed linens. Averting her eyes, she reached for her toothbrush. She wished someone would invent some sort of instant energizer for people like her—something you could plug into a socket for a few minutes to make you come alive. She wasn't at her best first thing in the morning.

Propping herself up under the flow of hot water in the shower, Amanda stood with head tilted back, sleepily blowing the water that streamed down her face out of her mouth. She wondered idly how her life would have differed if she had acquired a reputation for being wild and wicked, instead of stuffy and standoffish. The thought made her smile. One way or another, she would have still been categorized and tagged.

She'd always thought that being a member of the dance community must be a lot like growing up in a small town. Everyone knew everything there was to know about you, and what they didn't know for a fact, they invented. Labels were indiscriminately dispersed, and once you acquired a name for something, it took practically an act of God to change anyone's estimation of your character.

Amanda was pretty sure it was the challenge of overcoming her aloofness that had originally attracted Larry, with whom she had had an on-again, off-again relationship for nearly two years.

They had been the strangest two years of her life. The way that man had treated her had been so inconsistent—hot one moment and cold the next—that it had kept her perpetually off balance. Unfortunately, it had taken Amanda nearly the entire two years to realize just what a sorry specimen Larry actually was.

Amanda caught herself practically scrubbing her skin off her bones and she sagged against the wall of the tub enclosure. *Why are you doing this?* she asked the cloud of steam above her head. *You broke up with that jerk over three years ago, so forget it.*

Yeah, sure. Resolutely, she stepped under the spray again and rinsed off. She had a regrettable tendency to analyze a situation to death, and she knew it. But, knowing it and doing something about it were two different things. There was no sense in trying to avoid thinking about Larry. She knew from experience that once a thought got lodged in her mind, that portion of her subconscious became as tenacious as a pit bull. She wouldn't be able to dislodge its grip on her thoughts until she had hashed them out. She stuck her face under the full force of the shower, blowing and shaking her head like a seal pup.

It was more than likely that Larry had been manipulative from the word go, but she hadn't seen it in the beginning. Like a boxer concentrating on a left hook and missing the sucker punch that blindsides him and drops him to his knees, so had she been gulled by Larry's moments of laughter and gentleness—those rare, perfect instances when he had simply sat with her quietly, when he had held her and told her silly jokes and bestowed tender kisses upon her.

Unhappily, those moments had been few and far between, and in the final analysis, they had been heavily outweighed by the little games in which he had found such delight.

The competitions he had instigated between them had been kind of funny, at first. Amanda might be uncomfortable making a scene or responding to rudeness with rudeness, but she had never been a pushover. In her own quiet way she was stubborn and strong, and she had refused to let him treat her as a doormat.

Larry's games completely lost their ability to amuse, however, when it came to the matter of birth control. He had thought it would be entertaining to play Russian roulette with contraceptives, and he had pouted and sulked when he couldn't get her to go along. If there was one thing Amanda adamantly believed in, it was that you never gambled with a situation with consequences as serious as the potential to create a life. She had good reason to maintain that position, and she had haltingly explained it to Larry. It was painful for Amanda to reveal a confidence of a personal nature, as Larry knew perfectly well. But she had hoped that doing so would make him respect her position. Yet he had still persisted in trying to change her mind—right up to the bitter end of their relationship.

And in the end, it had been very acrimonious. It had dawned on Amanda only gradually that Larry was by nature a controller.

Turning off the water and stepping out of the tub, Amanda reflected that while she might be slow, the good Lord knew she had lived too many years with Mother and Father, who were both past masters in the art of manipulation, to subject herself to more of the same. If she hadn't learned anything else in her life, she had learned that there was usually no pleasing those who lived to control the lives of others—not unless you were willing to forgo the need to maintain a separate identity for yourself. Amanda had not been.

She hesitated in the act of vigorously drying her hair, her mouth slanting in a rueful grimace. Unfortunately, Larry had also been unwilling to allow her to be the one to say good-bye. His unwillingness to set her free until *he* was ready to say good-bye had summoned forth a stubborn streak in Amanda, which only later she had seen to have been self-defeating and unnecessary. Somehow, at the time, it had seemed utterly vital to her sense of self-worth that she be the one to sever the bonds. And so they had gone around and around, until they had finally discovered a middle ground where both of their senses of pride could be preserved.

Amanda smoothed body lotion on her arms, legs, stomach, chest, and shoulders, and stepped into her underwear. Blotting the ends of her hair, which were still dripping little streams of water down her back and over her collarbones, she walked into her bedroom. Should she dress first, or put on her makeup? Another drip trickled between her shoulder blades. Makeup definitely.

Draping the towel over her shoulders, she sat down at her dressing table and picked up her foundation. She leaned into the mirror and began applying it with a light hand. Then she blended one small dot of rouge into each of her cheekbones. By the time she had smoothed plum-colored eye shadow into her eyelids and outlined her eyes in matching liner, her stomach was beginning to growl. She hurriedly untangled her damp curls and dressed.

It was her one day off in a blue moon—hers and Rhonda's both, which was even rarer still. They had made plans to carpool to the nearest shopping center to stock up on staples and to run all those errands they hadn't had time to in the past few weeks. It was nearly noon; she had arisen earlier than usual. Being a dancer meant keeping a timetable that was different from practically everyone else in the world.

Greg had been a dancer. She stopped dead in the hall, resisting the urge to bang her head against the nearest hard surface. *What is this—the life and loves of Amanda Charles day? My God, you are just bound and determined to think about all three of those guys this morning, aren't you?*

Jeez. Apparently so. All these old memories were whirling around in her brain, and she hadn't a clue how to stop them.

Amanda's experience with Larry had been so perfectly rotten, it could easily have put her off men forever. In truth, it was about eighteen months before she had chanced another relationship. That was when she had met Greg.

Of the three relationships, Greg was the only one whose loss she had regretted—the only one she had missed when he had gone. Because he was a dancer, they had shared a solid bond from the beginning. He had been funny and cute—and in the end, unluckily, still in love with his ex-wife.

Amanda knew she had never experienced a truly deep and abiding love. The truth was, she had never even been sure such an emotion actually existed outside the pages of a novel or the larger-than-life images in the movies.

But what she had felt for Greg had been as close to romantic love as she had ever come. And she had always maintained that if the timing had been a little better, the way she had already felt about him would most likely have evolved into the real thing. Greg was the only man with whom she had ever come close to trusting with her innermost secrets and feelings.

But something had held her back, even with him. Good sense, probably. It was just not possible, she had determined without acrimony after he was gone, to nurse a man through endless postmortems of a divorce he had never wanted in the first place, and still conduct a love affair with him that you hoped to see progress. He had been fun and considerate and he had made her laugh. But it was just as well he had left when he had. For Amanda had too much pride to play second fiddle to another woman indefinitely—not if the man for whom she harbored feelings was ultimately unwilling to let go of his previous relationship.

When Greg's wife had admitted she had made a mistake and had taken him back, Amanda had been hurt for a while, but she hadn't been bitter, or even especially surprised.

It had just reinforced her unwillingness to take a chance

on another relationship. Why risk it? She didn't care what her friends said: she simply couldn't see the value in it.

In the kitchen, Amanda put on the kettle to make a pot of coffee. She snapped on the small television set on the counter to catch the noon broadcast of the news and reached for the coffee grinder. The volume was turned low on the set, so she missed the beginning of the announcement over the rattle of coffee beans pouring into the grinder and the high-pitched whir of the grinder itself as it turned the beans into a fine, fragrant powder. Without looking up from her task, she reached over to turn up the sound.

". . . woman the authorities believe to be the latest victim of the Showgirl Slayer. She is five feet eight inches tall, weighs one hundred twenty-three pounds, has dark-blond hair, hazel eyes, and a small, fine scar running through her left eyebrow. Anyone having knowledge of her identity is urged to contact Detective Joe Cash at the Reno police department, homicide division. That number again is. . . ."

Very slowly, Amanda raised her eyes to focus on the screen. She lowered the kettle, cutting off the stream of steaming water that she had been pouring through the coffee grounds into the pot below. Oh, God. It couldn't be.

Could it? Dear God, no. Please.

Amanda finished making the coffee, automatically setting the kettle back on the stove and turning off the burner beneath it. Pouring herself a cup, she placed the glass coffeepot on a wire on the back burner and turned that burner on low. Then she picked up her coffee cup and carried it into the living room. She noticed without surprise that the cup was rattling badly in its saucer. Very carefully, she set it down.

Slowly, she reached out and picked up the telephone that rested on the small, marble-topped end table. She punched out the numbers that seemed to be burned into her brain. Clutching the receiver in sweaty palms, she sat rigidly upright as she listened to the telephone ring on the other end of the line. Then it was picked up, and Amanda suddenly caved in. She felt boneless and light-headed. Slumped on her tailbone on the velvet covered cushion, she clamped the receiver to her ear.

"Reno police department," said the polite, businesslike voice.

CHAPTER
1

The flight was like no other that Tristan MacLaughlin had ever taken. Not that he considered himself a world traveler, by any means, but when he did fly, it was usually on the commuter shuttle, packed with businessmen. And regular commuters generally slept or went over papers from their leather briefcases. They were a different breed altogether from the boisterous revelers surrounding him now.

Certainly, on the average public transport, he wasn't accustomed to hearing the sound of cards being shuffled or the rattle of dice. And when the plane hit a wee bit of turbulence approaching the Reno airport and abruptly lost altitude for a stomach-dropping instant, Tristan was not amused to hear more than half the passengers whoop, as though they were on an amusement park ride. He felt, in fact, downright grim. It hammered home the frivolous nature of the city to which he had been assigned.

The muscles along Tristan's jaw bunched and relaxed rhythmically as he stared out the tiny window at the dusty green and dun landscape below. Why him? There had been at least three detectives who had begged for this assignment—who had actually considered it the opportunity

15

of a lifetime to set up a task force for a case involving show
girls in a city designed for entertainment. Tristan hadn't been
interested at all, and he had been stunned when Captain
Weller had called him into his office to discuss the temporary
transfer to Reno. He couldn't argue with Weller over the fact
that his experience on the task force for the Green River serial
murders in Seattle was exactly what Reno was looking for.
But he certainly hadn't agreed when Weller had suggested
that this would also be an opportune time for Tristan to be
absent from Seattle, in case Palmer, a man he had been
instrumental in putting behind bars, decided to make good
on his threat to see him planted six feet under. Palmer had
just escaped from prison in Denver, and Tristan was certain
he had more important matters on his mind right now than
exacting his promised retribution. He was going to have all
he could handle just to avoid recapture. Tristan hadn't bought
that particular theory when Weller had first limped it out as
an additional reason to head up this Reno case, and he didn't
buy it now.

But when it came to departmental politics, it wasn't necessary for him to buy anything, Tristan acknowledged glumly
as he waited for the majority of other passengers to finish
shuffling past him before he stepped into the center aisle to
leave the plane. A captain outranked a lieutenant every time,
and it was clear that Weller had already made the decision
to send Tristan to Reno. As far as Weller was concerned,
Tristan MacLaughlin was the best man for the job. And that
was the beginning and the end of that.

Once out on the concourse, Tristan went to retrieve his
luggage, which consisted of two suitcases and a giant, un-
wieldy box. But he was sidetracked by his amazement at
some of his fellow passengers. They hadn't even waited to
leave the bloody airport before they had begun gambling.

He shook his head as he watched his former seatmate,
a talkative little white-haired lady in a red polyester pantsuit,
as she plumped herself down on a padded stool in front of
a bank of slot machines. She wasn't talking now. She was

all business as she began feeding quarters into the machine and pulling the arm at an amazing rate, avidly watching the revolving cherries, oranges, bars, and sevens as they whirred past, finally to clunk one, two, three, into a pattern between a set of red lines. Her eyes were in constant motion, darting left and right to keep tabs on the slot machines on either side of her, as well as her own. When she felt his gaze, she threw a suspicious glance at him over her shoulder. It was as if their previous amiable conversation on the airplane had never existed. If her expression was anything to go by, she was clearly convinced he was ready to pounce on her slot machine. Personally, Tristan failed to see the attraction. He shrugged and turned away. Removing his glasses, he pulled a snowy white handkerchief from his pocket to polish the lenses.

Lieutenant MacLaughlin?''

Tristan replaced his glasses and peered down at the man in front of him. ''Aye,'' he acknowledged. ''How did you know, then, mate?''

''I'm a detective,'' the man said, grinning. When his smile was not returned, he hastened to interject, ''Actually, your captain said to look for a very large man with sandy-brown hair and horn-rimmed glasses. My name is Cash,'' he added, thrusting his hand at Tristan. ''Joe Cash.''

What Weller had actually said was, ''He's a big, dour, sonofabitchin' Scot with blondish-brownish hair and horn-rimmed glasses. You can't miss him. Look for shoulders like a linebacker and a face that doesn't exactly remind you of the life of a party.''

Which was what the detective had done, and he had spotted MacLaughlin right away. But considering he was going to have to work with the man, Cash didn't see any point in antagonizing him right off the bat by repeating the description verbatim. Besides, he had to admit he was curious about this guy. He'd wondered why Weller had called the man a Scot, since American citizenship was a prerequisite for every police officer in the United States. But when he had questioned the captain, Weller had merely laughed and said, "Sure, MacLaughlin's a citizen. But wait until you hear him speak." Then he'd added with irritated amusement that MacLaughlin was a damned brilliant detective—a man whose lack of charm was well worth putting up with in exchange for his help in organizing the type of task force that Reno so sorely needed. Cash had tried to analyze the captain's tone of voice when he'd spoken of MacLaughlin, but the closest he could come was a sort of puzzled, grudging affection and a definite, lasting impression of professional respect.

Tristan made a swift, comprehensive survey of the man in front of him as they shook hands. Cash was about six feet tall, rangy and lean, with a well-shaped head that was entirely bald. He had a luxuriant, bushy brown mustache, watchful, intelligent brown eyes, and large white teeth, which he flashed in a friendly smile. *He'll do*, Tristan thought and nodded abruptly, reaching that decision in his usual way—instantaneously.

"Sir, we have a number of choices," Joe Cash said moments later as they stored Tristan's luggage in the trunk of a nondescript car in the parking lot. Tristan pulled his attention away from the group of people he'd been watching as they piled onto a gold and brown Harrah's coach. He raised an eyebrow at Cash in question.

"We can either go straight to the station," Joe said, "or we can check you into your hotel and drop your luggage. Or," he hesitated briefly, glancing at Tristan from the corner of his eye as he turned the ignition, "we can go to the morgue. There are a couple of dancers coming in from the Cabaret Lounge who think they might be able to ID the latest victim. They're due at five; some uniforms are bringing them in. I was going to call and have someone else meet them, but if you're willing . . ." He shrugged, leaving the decision up to MacLaughlin.

Tristan didn't hesitate. "The morgue," he said with crisp decisiveness. "You can fill me in on the way."

* * *

"They're here." Rhonda turned away from the window, letting the curtain drop. She looked over at Amanda, watching as her friend rose gracefully to her feet and turned back to gather up her jacket and purse. "Are you ready?"

"No. Yes. I don't know." Amanda drew a deep breath, shrugged, and smiled weakly at her friend. The smile wobbled and died a sudden death at the sound tapping at the door. "Oh, God, Rhonda. I wish we didn't have to do this."

"Tell me about it." Rhonda checked her lipstick in a small pocket mirror and dropped it back into her purse. She looked up to meet Amanda's eyes. "But maybe it won't be Maryanne. We gotta hope. Hell, she'll probably come roaring home and threaten to skin us alive for creating all this fuss for nothing." She squared her shoulders and stood aside as Amanda reached for the doorknob.

"Miss Charles?" The uniformed officer who stood on her doorstep was young and fresh-faced, and he wore his cap at a cocky angle. Amanda glanced at him briefly, but her gaze was drawn past him to the heavyset older officer accompanying him. He had a weather-beaten face, his uniform was rumpled, and he looked as though he'd been around the track a few times in his life. But his eyes had obviously seen the world, and still they held compassion for the ordeal that lay ahead for the two women.

"Yes, I'm Amanda Charles," she said. She turned slightly so they could see the woman behind her. "This is Rhonda Smith."

"We have been sent here by the city of Reno to . . ." the younger officer began officiously, but the older man cut him off, gently grasping Amanda's arm and guiding her down the steps. He smelled strongly of tobacco.

"They know why we're here, son," he said in a smoke-roughened voice as he released her and reached for Rhonda. "This way, miss," he directed politely, and somehow he managed to ease all of them along the path, up the stairs,

and into the back of the police cruiser without creating a lot
of unnecessary fuss.

They rode in tense silence. All too soon, it seemed to
Amanda, they were pulling into the emergency entrance of
St. Mary's Hospital, and the older officer was helping her
out of the car. She quietly thanked him and turned away.
Only seconds after they stepped away from the patrol car,
the hospital door opened and two men walked out. Even from
a distance, Amanda knew they were policemen. She assumed
one of them must be the officer she had spoken to on the
phone, and her heart began to beat with painful force.

"Miss Charles? Miss Smith?" Joe Cash approached them.
"Thank you for coming. I'm Detective Cash." He indicated
Tristan. "This is Lieutenant MacLaughlin."

Amanda examined the two men. They were big. The bald
one, Detective Cash, was lean and almost adolescently loose-
limbed. He had warm brown eyes, and she was instinctively
drawn to him. He looked as though he'd try to protect them
from as much unpleasantness as was humanly possible.

She couldn't say the same of Lieutenant MacLaughlin.
Warmth and humanity didn't strike Amanda as his primary
characteristics—not with that remote expression of his. Her
immediate impression of him was one of cool, efficient control, and without uttering a word, he made her feel defensive.
There was something about the aloof and assessing way he
inspected her and Rhonda. . . .

He was an extremely large man—immense, really. She
figured he must be six foot five, and he possessed the widest
shoulders and chest she had ever seen. Standing next to the
lieutenant in the elevator moments later, she felt uncomfortably crowded and short of breath, as though his massive frame
were taking up all the space and absorbing all the available
oxygen.

His size alone was enough to intimidate, without the added
military sternness that he projected. He had thick, sandy-
brown hair that would probably have been fairly curly if it
hadn't been rigidly subdued by a short cut. It receded slightly

above his temples, leaving an M-shaped hairline that attractively set off his high, wide forehead. His skin bonded leanly to the strong bones of his face, and the hollows of his cheeks under his cheekbones looked slightly rough. He had a large, sharp blade of a Roman nose, thick eyebrows, and his eyes, as they made contact with hers, were a steady, piercing silvergray behind heavy-rimmed glasses.

Amanda was aware of Rhonda perking up next to her, drawing her shoulders back and thrusting her breasts forward, and without looking, Amanda knew that she was flashing her patented, cocky, *Hel-lo Sailor Boy*, welcoming smile. Rhonda adored men and was a shameless flirt. But Amanda had the feeling Rhonda should save her wiles in this instance, for there was an inherent austerity about the lieutenant that no amount of eyelash batting and pretty pouting was liable to affect. The clinical way he inspected the two of them chilled her. She much preferred Detective Cash's warm smile.

Tristan gazed pensively at the subtle sway of Amanda's hips as they moved down the corridor to the morgue. He hadn't missed her withdrawal from his inspection, and one corner of his mouth tilted up bitterly. She was the type of woman he had never been able to talk to without tripping all over his size-thirteen feet and making a total ass of himself. She was cool, unexpectedly elegant. Her hair was wheat-pale blonde; her makeup was subdued. She wasn't at all what he had expected.

He knew he had come into this case with some prejudices, which he had been prepared to set aside until the case was closed. Hell, half of the hookers he had booked in his long career as a cop had said they were dancers. He'd figured the Reno show girls were maybe one step above the whores he was accustomed to dealing with, but Amanda Charles's air of refinement didn't fit in with his neat, preconceived image at all.

Well, vulgar or refined, he resented being dismissed by those large, round, violet-blue eyes, which were framed by surprisingly dark eyebrows and eyelashes. *Bet she bloody well dyes her hair to get that shade*, he thought with un-characteristic antagonism. She had an olive complexion—a skin tone not generally associated with blondes. Her natural hair color was probably an ordinary mousy brown, instead of the pale Scandinavian blond it appeared to be. The idea gave Tristan a jolt of dark satisfaction.

But, God, what a figure. Miss Charles was not a flashy dresser like her more flamboyant, black-haired friend, but she had the same sort of fabulous body, recognizable even in the unzipped canvas jacket, lavender cashmere sweater, and black linen slacks. It was a figure to attract stares: fairly tall, wide shouldered, deep-chested, and wasp-waisted, with a tiny, tight butt and long, long, *long* legs. Of course, that wasn't exactly surprising. She was a show girl, even if she didn't wear spandex pants during her off-duty hours like the other, friendlier lassie.

They all halted outside the morgue doors. Cash turned to the two women, rubbed a hand over his bald head, smoothed his mustache with his thumb and index finger, and said, "Listen. There's really no reason for both of you to go in; we only need one of you to make the identification."

There was an instant of dead silence while Amanda and Rhonda stared at each other. Then, before they had a chance to decide which of them it should be, Tristan decided for them.

"You, Miss Charles," he said peremptorily and grasped Amanda's arm just above the elbow, propelling her through the doors.

The abruptness with which the decision had been taken out of her hands, plus the knowledge of what was to come, turned Amanda's knees to the consistency of warm wax. The atmosphere into which she was suddenly thrust was coldly sterile. Chemical odors permeated her senses, making her membranes sting, and she sagged slightly in Tristan's grasp. Her eyes, staring up into his, were huge and dilated, and Tristan experienced a momentary twinge of guilt. Then he shrugged it aside irritably. Bloody hell—he wasn't entirely insensitive. He knew this was not going to be a picnic for the lass. But he also knew that if he'd let the women decide between themselves, they'd be here until midnight. He ignored the small voice that whispered inside his head—the one that said if she hadn't happened to be the type of woman most designed to make him feel like the shy, awkward, oversized, under-coordinated Glasgow street urchin he'd once been, he might have allowed her more time to come to a decision on her own.

Beside him, Amanda resolutely drew a deep breath and silently straightened her shoulders. Her eyes, snagging his once again, were frigidly aloof as she pointedly withdrew her arm from his grasp. She made him feel a right proper sod without half trying, and when the door opened behind them and Joe Cash entered, flashing him a questioning glance before he turned his attention to Amanda, Tristan cursed the heat that crept up from under his collar.

Amanda stared straight ahead as an attendant pulled open a stainless steel drawer. Not until the sheet covering the body on the slab was flipped back did she glance down.

Nausea rushed up her throat and she swallowed hard, staring. Then she jerked her head up, her glance bouncing off the silver surface of Lieutenant MacLaughlin's eyes and locking with Detective Cash's. "Oh, God. It's her . . . she," she whispered, and then immediately felt foolish for worrying about correct grammar at a time like this. "That's Maryanne Farrel."

Joe nodded to the attendant to close the drawer, and Tristan gently placed an arm around Amanda's shoulders and turned her away. He wasn't unsympathetic to her horrified emotions, but he tended to forget just how traumatic death could be to the uninitiated.

Amanda Charles's face was a testament to remind him. It had turned greenish-white under the harsh overhead lights. The delicate tracery of blood vessels just below the surface of her skin stood out like a dark purple spiderweb against her bloodless complexion. Within the loose grasp of his arm, he could feel her periodic shudders, as if she were chilled to the bone, and he experienced an uncharacteristic urge to tighten his hold on her and share some of his own abundant body heat. He resisted, naturally, and escorted her out of the morgue.

Amanda drew air deep into her lungs once they were back out in the hall. She nodded curtly to Rhonda's questioning look and gratefully walked into her friend's embrace when Rhonda opened her arms to her. They clung to each other. Tristan, watching them, wondered what it would be like to have someone to hold you in your worst moments—those times of stress and grief. He had always dealt with his own problems alone.

"Which hotel are you staying at, Lieutenant?" Joe asked the big Scot, making conversation to provide time for Amanda to regain her composure. She looked ill.

"I'm not sure," Tristan replied. "I havena made a reservation anywhere." He removed his glasses and rubbed the bridge of his nose. Replacing them, he eyed Joe seriously. "I was hopin' you could recommend somewhere fairly inexpensive. The S.P.D.'s payin' a per diem until I draw my first paycheck here, and it's not the most generous in the world."

Rhonda eyed the large policeman with fascination over Amanda's shoulder as she listened to his softly spoken brogue. She eased her grip on her friend. "If you're looking for someplace nice, clean, and reasonable," she suggested, "an apartment in Amanda's triplex will soon be available." Her face tightened with emotion. "Maryanne's."

Amanda pulled out of Rhonda's arms. "Please," she said, looking around so wildly that Joe was afraid she was going to be sick on the spot. "Is there a rest room?" Grasping Rhonda's hand, she almost ran down the hall, following the detective's hurried directions.

Once through the public rest room's door, she swung Rhonda around and none too gently shoved her up against the wall, pinning her there by planting her hands on Rhonda's shoulders. Sticking her nose up next to her friend's, she hissed, "Are you crazy, Rhonda? What on earth possessed you to do that?"

Rhonda blinked her brown eyes. "What? Do what?"

Amanda growled in frustration. "Why did you offer Maryanne's apartment to Lieutenant MacLaughlin?"

"Are you serious, Mandy? Didn't you take a look at the man? Talk about prime! His feet and hands are absolutely huge, and you know what that means—he's probably endowed like a stallion."

"For crying out loud, Rhonda!" Amanda interrupted. "Haven't you ever, just once in your life, had a thought that wasn't sexual in nature?"

"Well, sure. I must have, back in kindergarten or something. But that was a long time ago, and getting back to this guy, don't you think he looks kinda like a really built *GQ* model?"

Amanda shook her head. "*GQ?* You mean *Gentlemen's Quarterly*?" She was finding this conversation incomprehensible.

"Yes! Well, okay, maybe he doesn't dress quite as hip, but with those steely eyes, and the short hair and glasses, and that *body* all buttoned down under that suit and tie . . ."

"What do his clothes have to do with . . . He can be second cousin to the Brooks Brothers, for all I care," Amanda said through clenched teeth. "That doesn't mean I want him as a tenant. I'd rather rent to Gunga Din."

"Then I say you're the one who's crazy, Amanda Charles, not me," Rhonda said as she stared at her friend with eyes that had become deadly serious. "Forget viewing him as a sex object, if you're too damn pure for that," she snapped with the barely concealed disgust that the always-on-the-prowl have for the hardly-ever-looking. "Look on it as protection. Our whole damn world is suddenly getting very hazardous. Someone out there is killing off dancers the way Jack the Ripper once went through hookers!"

"It hasn't been that many. It hasn't been nearly as many

as Jack the Ripper or any of those other serial murderers," Amanda whispered, but she knew that was a feeble, dangerous attitude to take. One violent death was too many. When one of the three recently murdered young women turned out to be someone you knew, that made the statistics a moot point. God, why would anyone want to kill Maryanne?

"Not yet." Rhonda interrupted her thoughts. "But for all we know, this guy may just be warming up." She reached out and touched Amanda, her dark eyes sober. "The fact that we're down here at all, though, having to make an identification on Maryanne, is too damn close to home to suit me, Amanda."

"Yes, I know," Amanda conceded, and she had to hug herself against the trembling that shook her body. "Oh, Rhonda, I can't believe this. This morning when I woke up, I was mad at her. I kept thinking how typical it was for her to disappear without letting anyone know where she could be reached. And now, four or five hours later, I look at Maryanne on that slab and she is *dead*, Rhonda. Suddenly, it's no longer something that could only happen to someone else. God, if it could happen to her, it could happen to you or to me." Goose bumps cropped up all over her flesh.

She was quiet for a moment, then she looked up at her friend. "But why MacLaughlin? I don't like him, Rhonda. He looks at me like I'm a bug on a pin, and he didn't even give us a chance to decide which of us should go in to identify her before he dragged me in there." She shuddered in remembrance.

Rhonda hugged her. "I know, kid. You don't like him because he grabbed you and hauled you off. I think maybe —his Hunk-of-the-Month body aside for just one moment— that's the very reason I do like him," she confessed with the ruthless honesty Amanda had always admired in her. "I didn't want to go in there any more than you did, and I was so damned relieved when he chose you instead of me, I could have sat down and bawled. But Amanda, whatever else

MacLaughlin is, he is a cop. And you gotta admit he appears to be one hell of a tough one, too.''

"Yes," Amanda concurred dryly. "I don't think anyone would argue with that.''

"Well, then?''

"I suppose, if he's interested—but he's going to have to bring it up himself, with no prompting from you, Rhonda,'' she stipulated firmly, hoping that would be the end of the matter, despite an unwelcome knowledge that everything her friend had said was true. They *were* going to have to take measures to protect themselves.

Amanda stiffened with resolution. She would simply make it a point to rent Maryanne's apartment to a man. There were any number of male dancers who could probably protect them just as effectively as that huge cop with his remote, analyzing eyes, and one or another of them was always looking for a place to rent. She relaxed by perceptible degrees. Mac-Laughlin had set her teeth on edge, but after their part in this case was over she'd never have to see him again. And, in any event, it was doubtful that he would be interested in renting her apartment. The conversation that had prompted Rhonda's impulsive offer had been about hotel accommodations, not permanent lodging.

There was no sense in letting herself get all worked up over something that would probably never come to pass.

"They're bloody well taking their own sweet time," Tristan growled as he paced the hall.

"Miss Charles looked pretty shook," Joe said mildly. "And you know women . . .''

"No, I canna say I do, precisely." Tristan stopped pacing and faced Joe. "On the whole, lassies are one big mystery I've never been able to unravel.''

Joe grinned. "You don't have any sisters, I take it."

"No, nor brothers either.''

"I've got five sisters, myself.''

"Lord, mon." Tristan tugged at his tie, eyeing Cash with an envy he would never allow to show. It must be nice, having a family. "What's that like, then? Living with that many lasses?"

"Hair-raising," Joe said, and then he laughed ruefully, rubbing his bald scalp. "Back when I had hair it was, that is. I'm a big boy now, and it's been a few years since I've lived with any of them, but it wasn't so bad, having sisters." He grinned. "That's not what I would have told you when I was a kid, of course. But I get a kick out of them these days. They've taught me a lot about females. And rule number one is that damn few women can enter a bathroom and just do their business and walk out again. There are mirrors in there, MacLaughlin, and they've got purses loaded with hair-brushes and makeup and the like. So you might as well relax. They'll be out when they're damn good and ready, and not a minute before."

"Bloody hell." Tristan resumed his pacing, then, abruptly all business, he questioned Joe extensively and made a few suggestions for immediate action. Joe left to make a phone call.

Cash was still gone when the two women returned, but he returned almost before Tristan had a chance to concur with his analysis of female grooming habits. The women's hair was impeccably styled—it shone under the fluorescent lighting—and their mouths glistened with lipstick.

"Your color's better," he said to Amanda. "Are you feelin' a wee bit stronger, then?"

"Yes . . . thank you," she replied, surprised and just slightly gratified by his show of consideration.

"I apologize for the necessity of your ordeal," he continued smoothly, and Amanda felt her jaw go slack. That was certainly not the impression she had received earlier when he had hustled her into the morgue to make the identification. She'd been under the impression that he was gaining some covert satisfaction from her ordeal. Resolutely refusing to let her confusion show, she closed her mouth, only to have her stomach drop at his next words.

"Do you possess a key to Miss Farrel's apartment?"

"Yes, of course. I own the triplex." Her heart began to pound. *Oh, God, please,* she prayed. *Don't let him say he's been considering Rhonda's suggestion. Please, don't let him say that.*

"I would appreciate it if you'd hand it over. It saves us from having to break in the door," he said with implacable briskness. "Your identification has opened up a whole new can of warr-ums, Miss Charles, and I'm afraid we have a great number of questions for you and Miss Smith."

"Oh, but . . ."

"I suggest we take you home and talk there. You'll be much more comfortable than at police headquarters." Tristan had been making a conscious effort to sound pleasant in an attempt to make amends for dragging Amanda into the morgue earlier, but even he could hear the way his voice flattened, teetering on the edge of hardness. Well, hell, he truly did believe she and Miss Smith would be less intimidated in her home. That didn't mean that he would hesitate to drag the two of them downtown if they showed signs of becoming recalcitrant, however. He had a job to do, and the sooner he began, the better.

Amanda stared into MacLaughlin's hard gray eyes and commanded herself not to cry. This had been possibly the worst afternoon of her life, since Teddy. . . . It had been a hard day, entirely, and apparently, it wasn't going to be over any time soon. Her head was pounding and her stomach felt like it might never tolerate food again. She felt lousy all over, period: shaky, sick, and ice cold. Grudgingly, Amanda put aside the fantasy she'd been harboring of soaking in a deep, hot bubble bath. She experienced something close to hatred when she looked at the lieutenant. He wasn't sorry at all. He was probably getting a real kick out of this.

Well, okay, that might not be entirely fair, and maybe,

just maybe, she was skating on the thin edge of paranoia, but she doubted it. And even if she was, she still held this oversized, cold-eyed bully with his stupid, lovely brogue personally responsible.

Eyeing him with disdainful rebellion, she told him what he expected to hear—she preferred to be interrogated in her own home.

CHAPTER
2

Tristan would have said he hadn't thought about Amanda Charles's triplex, yet its appearance somehow managed to take him by surprise. Given her own appearance and her unexpected air of refinement, he supposed he had expected something sleek and contemporary, or cool and elegant—not this rambling, cream-colored, shake-covered building planted squarely in the middle of an upper middle class residential neighborhood.

It was a big, sprawling, older house, built on three levels around a fern and flower-bedecked rockery. Its slate-blue wooden shutters and window boxes, plus the two-tone chocolate and blue wooden trim that neatly encased large expanses of small-paned windows, gave it a warm, homey appearance. Only upon closer inspection did Tristan discover that the two glossy, milk-chocolate-colored doors that faced out onto a small, enclosed yard each led to a separate complex. Next to the doors, mounted on the wall, was a highly polished brass mailbox, whose address was engraved in flowing, lowercase script, followed by a letter to distinguish each individual residence. The third door wasn't readily visible, but

Tristan assumed it was tucked into the recess at the top of a short flight of wide brick steps that led up to the middle level.

Each apartment had an individualizing feature. The one on the highest level had a small wooden deck jutting out over part of the rockery, and the lowest level residence had a ground-hugging porch, whose slender, doweled pillars looked nearly too fragile to support the floor of the third, midlevel apartment above it. That residence, in its turn, was distinguished by double French doors that led out onto a tiny, narrow wooden balcony.

The yard was sunken and surrounded by a low picket fence atop the rockery banks, lending an overall illusion of privacy. Amanda led them down wide, shallow steps, bypassing the flight of stairs that branched off to the top-level apartment. A narrow brick path wound through the rockeries and culminated in another flight of stairs down to the yard and the ground-level residence, but she turned left where the path verged and climbed the shallow set of steps to the apartment with the recessed door. Tristan looked down into the yard as they climbed the stairs to her apartment, more curious than he cared to admit. He noted that it was well kept but not meticulously maintained—the flowers and ferns had been allowed to grow wild.

Amanda took a deep breath as she unlocked her door and stood aside to let everyone enter. She didn't relish the prospect of having her private domain invaded, and she resented being powerless to prevent it. She exhaled quietly, knowing that, realistically, the best she could hope for was to get it over with as quickly as possible. *God, let them just ask their questions and go away.* She still harbored a faint hope of taking a long, hot bath this evening to soothe away the chill that seemed to have taken up permanent residence deep in her bones.

It was dark inside. Rhonda, the first one through the door, wove through the dim interior with the ease of familiarity and switched on a Tiffany-shaded lamp in the living room. It sat on a marble-topped table between two gray velvet wing-backed chairs. She flopped down on one of them and waved her hand expansively for the two policemen to sit in the remaining chair or on the facing peach and gray, chintz-covered couch. Presently, the two men were settled and Rhonda offered an array of refreshments. Amanda resolutely ignored them all and continued on to the bathroom, where she kept her aspirin.

There was a knock at the front door while Amanda was still in the bathroom, and she returned to the living room to find it crowded with men. Tristan detached himself from the group and came over to her.

"May we have the key to Miss Farrel's apartment, Miss Charles? The lads from the lab are here, ready to go to work." Tristan felt pretty grim, observing her. She had lost a great deal of the color she had regained earlier, and he realized with uncharacteristic concern that she was probably both hungry and fatigued.

His sympathy for her state of mind both surprised and disturbed him. It was an ironclad rule of his never to become personally involved with individuals in a case. He had seen several of his fellow officers do it, and it was his observation that it invariably led to nothing but trouble. Against his better judgment, he followed her into the kitchen, and when she she handed him a key from the hook on the wall, on impulse he reached out and grasped one of her wrists in his hand. The bones felt fragile beneath his fingers.

Amanda stared up at him silently. "Make yourself a spot of tea or some coffee, lass," he rumbled, absentmindedly running his thumb over the smooth-textured skin on the inside of her wrist. "We'll try to be as brief as possible this evening, so you can get some rest. We canna have you droppin' from exhaustion." Releasing her wrist, he turned on his heel and left the room.

Amanda stared at his back until he disappeared from view. Then she shook her head and moved to put the kettle on. Would wonders never cease? Perhaps the man was human after all.

Quickly she assembled a tray, using the time it took the kettle to boil to resurrect some old techniques for relaxation. The deep-breathing exercises made her feel marginally calmer, and she carried the tray out into the living room, where, she noticed with relief, the crowd had dispersed. Setting the tray on the small oak coffee table, Amanda sank onto the soft cushions of the couch. Her brow furrowed as she looked around.

"Where's Rhonda?"

"She ran upstairs to feed her cat," Joe replied, leaning forward to accept a cup of coffee. He consulted his notebook. "She lives in apartment A?"

"Yes." Amanda cupped her fragile china teacup in both hands, appreciating the warmth that sank into her chilled flesh. "Rhonda lives in A; I live in B; and Maryanne lives . . . lived . . . in C."

"Did Miss Farrel have family, Miss Charles?" Tristan asked. "Someone we should contact?"

"No." Amanda stared into her cup. "At least, none that I know of. She once said that she was originally from Ohio, but there was nobody left back home."

"Miss Charles, what prompted you to call the station?" Tristan regarded her with eyes as cool as winter rain.

"Maryanne hadn't been home for three days." She took a sip of her coffee, set the cup down, and looked at him. "It's not that we live in each other's pockets. But when one of us planned to be away, we generally let one of the others know about it. It served a couple of purposes: it saved us from worrying unnecessarily, and we could keep an eye on her apartment while she was away. You know what I mean: bring in the paper and mail, switch the lights around, that sort of thing." Amanda leaned forward to take a sip of her coffee, gazing at the two policemen over the rim of her cup. "But it didn't always work out the way it was intended. Once or twice before, Maryanne had simply taken off without letting anyone know. So, when she didn't come home this time,

I just assumed she had met a man and was spending some time with him, you know?''

Rhonda returned, slipping into the wing-backed chair and helping herself to a cup of coffee. ''Maryanne was always falling in love,'' she contributed, leaning back in her chair and crossing her long, spandexed legs. ''It was kind of a standing joke with us. Maryanne was always 'in love.' '' Her fingers sketched quotation marks in the air. ''I'm always in heat.'' She gave an unrepentant grin. Then she jerked her thumb at Amanda, and her voice registered disapproval. ''And Mandy Rose here is so damn selective, she rarely goes out with anyone.''

Amanda smiled thinly. ''Right,'' she agreed drily. ''So, at first, I didn't worry about her. I talked it over with Rhonda and we decided she'd probably met someone—again—and she'd be back when she was ready. But that was before Charlie asked me if she was sick.''

''Who's Charlie?'' Tristan swept his eyes up and down Amanda before focusing once again on her eyes. So she was selective, was she? He wouldn't have thought it.

''Charlie,'' Amanda repeated emphatically, as though that one name said it all. When Tristan continued to eye her levelly, she elaborated. ''Charles Bagotta at the Cabaret. He's . . . oh, I don't know how you'd describe Charlie's position, exactly.''

''Try slave driver,'' Rhonda suggested with a cynical smile.

''Charlie is . . . in charge. He shows us our numbers and puts us through our paces,'' Amanda said slowly.

''Charlie yells, screams, humiliates us, and drives us beyond human endurance,'' Rhonda said with flat finality. ''If we aren't sweating buckets, Charlie is one unhappy man.'' The two women stumbled over each other as they took turns trying to explain.

''If you need a day off,'' Amanda said, ''you see Charlie . . .''

"If you have a problem with a stage door Johnnie, you see Charlie . . ."

"If you think you can improve a set in the routine, you see . . ."

"If you screwed up in the high kick, you better hope Charlie didn't see you . . ."

"Lord, yes, that's the truth. You definitely want not to be seen then by Charl . . ."

"So this Charlie," Joe interrupted. "He asked you if Miss Farrel was ill?"

"Yes." Amanda stared soberly first at Joe and then at Tristan, but saw neither of them. Instead, she saw Maryanne's lifeless body on a stainless steel slab at the morgue. Hugging her arms, she rubbed her hands up and down, attempting to smooth away the goose bumps that had cropped up beneath her warm sweater. "And that's when I started to really worry. You see, you don't have unexplained absences at the Cabaret. Not if you want to continue working there. You can get away with playing sick occasionally, but never without calling in. And Maryanne—no matter how deeply in love she suddenly perceived herself to be—knew that. She might be an incurable romantic when it came to men, but she was totally practical when it came to her career and livelihood." Amanda's voice trailed away and she sat staring at the flawless, French-manicured oval nails of her long fingers as they nervously twisted together in her lap.

Joe gave her a second and then prompted, "So that's when you called us?"

"Not immediately." Amanda looked up, frowning.

"It was right before the midnight show last night when Charlie asked Amanda about Maryanne," Rhonda contributed. "And afterward, she came to me . . ."

"We didn't know what to do," Amanda took up. "If she was just off with some man and we called in the police, she'd never forgive us. Yet, if she were in serious trouble and we didn't call the police, we'd never forgive ourselves. We talked about it in the dressing room and all the way home, and we finally decided to give her just one more day before we made any calls. But when I woke up this morning, I turned on the news, and there was a story about an unidentified woman whom the police believed to be the latest victim of the Show Girl Slayer. Her description fit Maryanne. And that's when I called."

"Didn't it occur to you before then that she might be this guy's latest victim?"

"No. Not once." One corner of Amanda's mouth pulled up in a bitter, self-accusing smile. "That must sound incredibly stupid to you. We had all heard of him, of course. There's been a regular media blitz ever since the second murder. But it was the sort of thing you see on the news or read about in the papers, not something that happens to you or to anyone you know. It simply never occurred to me . . ."

"Yeah," Rhonda said. "Take the first one—the Morgan girl? Well, at the time of her murder, no one knew she was going to be the first of many, and the news originally made it sound as if a jealous lover had done her in. Somebody she knew—you know?—not some loony-tunes freak off the street. And since she *was* the first, we didn't relate the murder to what she did for a living so much as to the type of woman she was reputed to be. One of the guys in our troupe mentioned having worked with her at Bally's for a brief period when it was still MGM, and he said she'd had something of a reputation as a tease. He said that unless she had changed dramatically, most likely one of the guys she'd dated had finally just flipped out from the frustration."

"What's this dancer's name?" Tristan asked, and Rhonda looked stricken.

"Oh, it couldn't be Pete," she hastened to assure him. "He's gay."

Tristan merely regarded her with steady gray eyes, coolly waiting for her to quit editorializing and answer his question, and Rhonda looked to Amanda for guidance. Amanda just shrugged. As far as she was concerned, Rhonda might as well tell him. She had a feeling if MacLaughlin wanted specific information, he wouldn't rest until he got it.

"Schriber," Rhonda supplied reluctantly. "Pete Schriber."

Tristan scribbled the name down; then he glanced up at Rhonda, noting her distress. "We're not plannin' to arrest the mon, lass," he said and smiled. "But he might be able to furnish information about the victim that we don't already have. You can never tell what might be important."

Both Rhonda and Amanda stared at Tristan, momentarily transfixed by his smile. His teeth were crooked and white, and his smile was quirky and totally, devastatingly masculine. It changed his entire appearance, transforming him from a stern, forbidding cop to a warm, accessible man. It made Amanda wonder if she hadn't been too hasty in her unflattering assessment of him. It made Rhonda itch to jump into his bed.

The two women's abrupt regard, unexpected and intense, made Tristan's smile fade, and he began to feel flustered. He could feel scorching waves of blood wash up from beneath the sudden constriction of his collar and tie, and for an instant, he had to struggle against the temptation to reach up, jerk the knot in his tie loose and undo the top button of his shirt.

What the bloody hell were they looking at? Their scrutiny dredged forth his latent shyness. In a professional situation, he never had these sort of problems. He could converse with anyone, anytime. He was in charge and he never had to worry about where a conversation was leading. He bloody well directed it. But there was something abruptly personal about the way these two were regarding him. And on a personal level, Tristan never had a word to say for himself. Now, if a lass wanted a bit of action, on the other hand, he could think of one or two very personal things he wouldn't mind doing to the Charles lassie.

Jolted by the sheer lack of professionalism of that last thought, Tristan's questions became even crisper and more coldly impersonal than before. Finally, he snapped his notebook shut and stuffed it into the inside breast pocket of his brown wool suit jacket. He nodded to Joe, and the two men surged to their feet.

"Do you have a card you can give the lasses, Detective?" he inquired, and when Joe produced two and passed them to the women, he directed his instructions aloofly, glad to be in command once again. "Call if you have any questions or if you think of anything you'd like to add—anything at all. If something occurs to you, don't talk yourself into believing it's not significant. As I said before, you never can tell what might be important. Call that number and ask for Detective Cash or me." He hesitated briefly, then smiled at the women again. "We appreciate your cooperation this evening, and we will be talking to you both again."

He turned to Amanda. "Miss Charles, you were a brave lass entirely this afternoon. I'm right sorry about the necessity of putting you through that ordeal. I realize it was traumatic, but you can be proud of the way you handled the situation." Then he included Rhonda in his look. It was somehow simpler to talk to her. She didn't summon forth an awareness he was uncomfortable feeling. "And Miss Smith, you're not to worry about your friend, Mr. Schriber. You had no choice but to give us his name, and he willna be learnin' from us where it came from. Actually, we'll be talking with the entire cast, or troupe, or whatever it is you call your co-workers. So, he'll have the chance, himself, to tell us that he worked with Miss Morgan. If he doesn't, then we'll simply mention we understand that he worked with her, as well as with Miss Farrel. There is no need for your name to be brought into it."

Joe observed Tristan closely. The lieutenant employed a lot more diplomacy than Joe had been led to expect. MacLaughlin was a good cop—Joe had felt it in his bones from the moment Tristan had opted to accompany him to the morgue instead of checking in at the precinct or settling himself into a hotel. A damn good cop—Joe would put money on it. His gut reaction said MacLaughlin had the stuff to teach them what they needed to know about dealing with this type of serial killer.

But Captain Tweedt was sure going to be knocked on his butt. He was expecting a bureaucrat to direct the rest of them—someone to stay behind at headquarters, setting up the logistics and instructing others for the street work. It was quite obvious to Joe, however, that MacLaughlin was a field cop, and damned if there wasn't bound to be some butting of heads down at the station house before MacLaughlin ultimately got his way—which, in Joe's mind, seemed to be a foregone conclusion. Somehow, he didn't doubt for an instant that MacLaughlin inevitably would emerge triumphant. He hid a grin. The fireworks that occurred before that happened should make for a damn fine show, and he, for one, didn't plan to miss them.

They left shortly after that. Tristan stepped out into the early spring chill and shivered. "Let's go downstairs and see how the lab lads are doin'," he suggested, but before he reached the landing, Joe grabbed him by the arm.

"Don't you ever eat, MacLaughlin?" he demanded. "I don't know about you, but I'm hungry, and I work a helluva lot more efficiently on a full stomach." Jesus, he'd never seen a guy with so much focused energy. He gave the impression of being entirely single-minded.

"I'm sorry, Joe," Tristan replied contritely. "Have you got a family, then, holdin' up a meal for you?"

"No, I'm divorced. And I'm more than willing to come back and check out Farrel's apartment. But let's go over to the Comstock and grab one of their six-buck New York steaks first, okay?" His voice turned persuasive. "Sixteen ounces of U.S. prime, MacLaughlin."

"You get that much steak, and a flamin' good cut of meat to boot, for six dollars?"

"Damn tootin'. With potatoes and salad and maybe a veggie or a roll thrown in. For peanuts, MacLaughlin, you can eat like a king in Reno." He grinned at Tristan. "Lieutenant,

I ain't denyin' we might have a lot of problems in this town, what with the highest suicide rate in the nation and a dispro-portionately large violent-crimes ratio. But eating poorly is not one of them. This here's the best metro area in the country for dining out, bar none. Won't put much of a dent in your per diem at all. Most of the time I find it's just as cheap, not to mention a whole lot easier, than doing for myself.''

It was a short drive downtown from Amanda's. The quiet neighborhood where the two dancers lived gradually gave way to an industrialized area, dimly lit at this time of night. A few blocks beyond, the bright lights of downtown glowed against the inky clouds hanging low in the night sky. As Joe drove into the heart of Reno's downtown entertainment district, Tristan tried to absorb a sudden onslaught of impressions.

He had been downtown earlier when they had gone to the morgue, but the city's impact wasn't as immediate during the day. Miles of light bulbs and neon tubing of every imaginable color lit up the darkness, gaudy and vulgar and vivid against the night sky. Some of the lights were stationary, while others incessantly blinked, flashed, or rolled in frenetic patterns designed to catch the eye and lure you off the street. Some of the casinos were wide open, their entire front walls rolled up to display the banks of slot machines and crap tables nearest the street. Other casinos teased, giving the merest glimpses of the activity within as their smoked-glass doors opened and closed, admitting and disgorging patrons. The sidewalks filled and emptied as people came and went. Hawk-ers stood in front of establishments, handing out coupons and bawling the advantages of their casino over all the others. And on every street corner, it seemed to Tristan, there was an establishment offering loans. You could hock nearly any-thing, apparently, for one more chance to spin the wheel, roll the dice, turn the card.

Tristan shook his head. What a flamin' crazy town.

But just as Joe had promised, the Comstock served up a

good, substantial meal at an absurdly reasonable price. It wasn't often Tristan found a full-service restaurant that was capable of satisfying his large appetite for less than ten dollars. But when he finally pushed his plate away and leaned back in his chair, he was pleasantly stuffed. By the time the two men headed back to the murdered woman's apartment, he was feeling downright optimistic about his assignment in Reno. Maybe it wouldn't be so bloody awful after all.

The crowd of lab men and detectives was thinning out when Joe and Tristan arrived back at the triplex. There was a thin film of black dust coating all the surfaces, but the man dusting for prints was in the process of packing his case, preparing to leave.

"Hey, Cash, you want me to get prints tonight from the other two broads who live here?" he asked Joe, and Tristan looked up from his study of the deceased's address book, which he had flipped open with a pen he'd pulled from his breast pocket. A slight frown puckered his heavy eyebrows.

"You'll refer to them as women," he instructed in a soft but clipped tone of voice. "Or ladies. Not broads."

"Hey, they're just a couple of sweet-assed bimbos, not the Queen Mother and Princess Di. And who the hell are you, anyway, Jack?" the man demanded belligerently.

Joe had never seen a man of Tristan's size move quite so swiftly. He was across the room in a flash, dwarfing Johnson with his sheer size as he leaned down to stand eyeball to eyeball with the forensic man. "I'm the mon who willna hesitate to hang your butt out to dry if you don't learn to show some respect," he growled. "These women are not suspects, Detective. The victim was their friend. She has been murdered in a most brutal way, and they have spent a grueling afternoon down at the morgue, identifying her body and assisting us in our investigation. I wouldna be surprised if they're not spendin' the evening wondering if it's going to happen to them next. The last person they need to be seein' tonight is some snot-nosed, arrogant cop who thinks his badge gives him license to be discourteous. So, to answer your question: no, we do not want you to get prints tonight from the other two women in this complex. Leave it for tomorrow." Tristan backed up and gave the man, who was a few shades paler than he'd been moments ago, room to breathe. "As for your other question, my name isna Jack. I am Lieutenant MacLaughlin. And as of today, I head this case."

"Shee-it, Mack," a black detective in the corner murmured, and he slowly shook his head in disbelief. "Smooth career move."

Johnson glanced over at him, obviously sharing his opinion. He was sweating lightly, but he straightened up and faced Tristan squarely. "Sorry, sir," he said. "I'm Sergeant Mack Johnson. I . . . uh . . . didn't know who you were."

"Who I am isn't the point, Johnson. The badge you wear carries a responsibility, and the taxpayer who pays your wage is due courteous treatment, at the verra least. You don't have to like what someone does for a living; that's your right. I've thought a great many disrespectful thoughts m'self." Tristan's eyes were level and cool on the man in front of him. "But as long as you're on the job, you keep your thoughts to yourself, Sergeant. Because the public has rights also, and one of them is the right to be treated equally under the law, regardless of your private opinion."

Johnson wiped sweat from his forehead with a beefy forearm. "Yes, sir," he repeated.

"Good." Tristan stuck out his hand. "Joe tells me you're verra good at what you do. Have you gotten a set of Miss Farrel's prints yet, so you can start eliminating?"

Johnson shook Tristan's proffered hand and relaxed fractionally. "Yes, sir. The morgue supplied them."

Tristan nodded. "Call Miss Charles and Miss Smith late tomorrow morning and, if possible, find a time that's convenient for everyone."

"Yes, sir."

"Verra well. Were you on your way out?"

"Yes, sir."

"Take off then, mon." Tristan smiled slightly as Johnson turned away with visible relief. "Oh, and Johnson?"

The forensic man turned back, his face wary. "Sir?"

"You dinna have to call me sir, Sergeant."

Johnson grinned. "Gotcha, Lieutenant."

Joe sidled up to Tristan. "You lie through your teeth, Lieutenant," he murmured.

Tristan turned cool eyes on him. "How's that?"

"I never told you Mack was very good at his job."

"Oh." Joe was amused to see Tristan shift uncomfortably. He'd just raked Mack's butt over the coals without turning a hair, yet he appeared embarrassed to be caught restoring Johnson's pride. "That," Tristan mumbled. "Well, I don't like to take something away from a mon without givin' him back something in return." He smiled crookedly. "You're not gonna be tellin' me he's not worth shit, I hope."

"No. You erred on the side of the angels this time, Lieutenant." Joe's teeth gleamed whitely. "He's damn good at what he does."

Shortly thereafter, the rest of the lab crew finished. Tristan ordered a seal placed on the apartment and pocketed the keys after they locked up. Then Joe drove him to an inexpensive motel not far from the police station.

The room was like a thousand others in every city in every state, decorated in oranges and golds, furnished in nondescript blond laminated Danish modern, and it was overheated. Tristan stripped down to his shorts, meticulously hung up his clothes, and neatly lined his shoes on the floor next to the bed. He hung his gun, in its leather shoulder holster, on the back of a desk chair within reach of the bed.

Lying on his back on the bed, one arm crooked behind his head, Tristan reflected on the past ten hours. It seemed longer, somehow, since he had left Seattle. He had a whole host of impressions and reactions crowding his mind. He thought of the new town, the case . . . the Charles woman.

Hell of a day, he decided as he watched the impersonal, plasticized room glow red and grow dim, glow red and grow dim, as the motel sign outside his window blinked on and off.

Hell of a day.

CHAPTER
3

A manda's first reaction when she finally had her apartment to herself once again was a sagging feeling of relief, as if every rigid muscle and nerve in her body had suddenly unclenched and responded to the force of gravity.

After the two policemen had left, Rhonda had remained, settling in, ready and willing to dissect the day's events. Amanda couldn't imagine a single activity she had felt less like doing. She loved Rhonda dearly, but her curiosity and her desire to probe into the whys and wherefores of Maryanne's murder had made Amanda feel as though she were about to jump out of her skin. She had felt, in fact, just like JoJo Malone used to act before she'd been fired from the Cabaret last year for a major cocaine dependency problem. She was shaky and sick, all raw nerves and restlessness, and she'd found it impossible to sit still for any length of time. She had kept hopping up to straighten this and tidy that, until Rhonda had finally snapped at her to plant her butt in the chair, sit still, and listen up.

She had tried, but quite honestly, she hadn't noticed how tight Detective Cash's cute little tush was. Neither had she observed that if Lieutenant MacLaughlin peeled out of his conservative suit and tie and put on a pair of jeans, his body would probably look just like the guy in the Soloflex ad, only hairier. And she didn't want to even *think* about what Mary-anne's body had looked like on that slab in the morgue, let alone discuss it with Rhonda. Her nerve endings had felt as though they were right on the surface of her skin, making her foot tap, her hands fidget, and her bottom shift in agitation against the velvet covering of the chair, and she was afraid if she opened her mouth, she would begin to scream and not be able to stop.

Rhonda had stopped chatting quite suddenly and had looked at Amanda with concern. She'd popped up out of her chair and had come to squat in front of her, reaching out to fold Amanda's hands in her own. The cool, calming grip had gradually penetrated, soothing the perturbed movements of her fingers.

"I'm sorry, Amanda," Rhonda had whispered. "I can be such an insensitive boob sometimes." She'd stroked Amanda's wrists and waited until she was ready to meet her eyes. "This entire situation has me wired, and you already know how a really built man gets my motor running. Well, jeez, Mandy, I truly couldn't help but notice that both Cash and MacLaughlin have bodies designed to keep it revving in high gear for a week. But that's no excuse for being such a horse's ass." She squeezed Amanda's hands. "What would you like? Can I get you a Valium?"

"No," Amanda whispered. "I want a hot bath."

"You and your baths." Rhonda rose to her feet. "I'll go run one. Why don't you make yourself something to eat? You haven't had a bite since lunch . . . and we were both so nervous we only picked at that."

"Maybe after my bath."

"Okay, hon, whatever. At least pour yourself a glass of wine, though, will you? You look like a ghost."

"All right. You want some?"

Rhonda looked at her closely. "No thanks," she replied

slowly. "I'm going to run your bath and then leave you alone." She smiled slightly at the barely suppressed relief that scudded across Amanda's violet-blue eyes. Moments later she was ushering Amanda into the bathroom, helping her out of her clothes and into the tub. She lighted a number of candles and handed Amanda a goblet of wine. Promising to lock the front door on her way out, she snapped off the overhead light, smiled at the picture Amanda made, sitting in her fragrant bubble bath in the candles' glow, and then she was gone.

Limp with relief at finally attaining a measure of privacy, Amanda slumped bonelessly, but then thought better of it when the tips of her hair touched the water. She set her wineglass down on the tile ledge that encircled the tub. Twisting her hair up, she reached into the pottery jar sitting next to the fern in the corner where the ledge met the wall. She extracted a handful of pins, which were used to skewer the French twist into place. Sighing, she leaned back, resting her head on the inflatable, shell-shaped cushion. She picked up her wineglass and drained it in one gulp. Not very ladylike behavior, she decided. Wouldn't Mother be appalled?

She snorted, yet another unladylike mannerism. The hell with Mother. Her parents were certain she was going to hell in a hand basket anyway. And Amanda appreciated the warmth the wine provided as it coursed through her bloodstream. Resolutely, she put her mind in neutral and simply enjoyed soaking up the heat of the water, listening to the hiss and whisper of the bubbles as they shifted, sliding and popping, against her skin.

The bubbles slowly began to dissipate and Amanda glanced down at her breasts. Even in the flickering candlelight she could see they were flushed from the water, exposed from their full top curve to their pale tan nipples. She smiled for the first time that day, remembering when she had first developed. God, how she had hated it. She had been a late bloomer, and at the time, she would have been perfectly content never to have bloomed at all. All she had wanted to do was dance. And up until she was seventeen, she had possessed what she'd considered to be a perfect dancer's body: long, lean, strong, and flat-planed. Then, suddenly, it had begun to change.

She hadn't minded the changes in her hips and bottom too much. They weren't all that different from what they used to be, actually, just a little rounder, a little fuller. Nothing she couldn't learn to live with. But the newly lush breasts were an abomination. She couldn't even run across a studio floor anymore without her chest aching from the bouncing weight of her full breasts. And in the course of a routine her arms no longer wrapped unimpeded around her torso. All the graceful arm movements of dance, which until then had been second nature to her, had needed to be relearned to accommodate the hated new protuberances. It was her opinion, at age seventeen, that tits were the pits.

Amanda smiled again, ruefully. Where in the world had those particular memories come from? Talk about out of left field; she hadn't thought about that for years. But somehow, seeing her breasts floating amid the dissipating soap bubbles just now had dredged forth memories of a long-dead adolescent outrage. She shrugged impatiently and stretched out her toes to snag the bathtub plug, releasing it and rinsing the last of the clinging bubbles from her skin as the water gurgled down the drain.

Wrapped in a warm robe, her hair shook loose and curling wildly above her shoulders as a result of the steamy air, Amanda carried her empty wineglass into the kitchen and set it on the counter. She made herself a scrambled egg but then pushed it away before she had scarcely eaten half. Her mind refused to remain a blank, and thinking about Maryanne's murder made her stomach churn. What if Maryanne had been killed by someone she had known?

Amanda hadn't said so to Lieutenant MacLaughlin, but Maryanne hadn't always picked wisely when it came to men. She was always searching for a romantic ideal, and every time she fell in love, she was convinced that it was for real.

But Maryanne had had a definite penchant for the most un-suitable men, often troubled ones, the most notable of whom had been a porno star suffering from job burnout. Even Rhonda, who didn't always agree with Amanda that a woman had to set some kind of standards, had admitted that the king of the blue movies was not a guy you'd automatically cate-gorize as a desirable catch. That relationship had been short-lived and had dissolved long ago, but in all honesty, Amanda couldn't truthfully state that she had observed Maryanne's more recent lovers to have been a noticeable improvement. Maryanne had simply been one of those women who seemed destined to pick men most likely to hurt her.

Amanda knew she should have mentioned at least some of this to Lieutenant MacLaughlin. But she'd known if she had, he'd be around even longer than he had been, and she had taken about all she could handle of those probing, rain-cold eyes of his for one evening. There was something totally unnerving about that man. He was too damn big, for one thing—big and hard . . . powerful. She was accustomed to dancers, who were generally slender and wiry. They were also strong, but not so massively built, not so palpably suf-fused with raw energy. It was a more subtle strength.

There was certainly nothing subtle about MacLaughlin's physique. The body that Rhonda so admired looked like it would be more at home in jeans and boots and a flannel shirt. But the conservative suit he had worn, with its starched white shirt and tightly knotted, subtly striped tie, hadn't diminished his aura of toughness one iota. He had still looked capable of being mean as hell. When he had touched her, she'd felt frail and helpless, which she most definitely was not, and she had detested the sensation. He'd been able to just tow her along, and there hadn't been a damn thing she could do to prevent him. You'd think he would realize that, given the situation with Maryanne, being manhandled and dragged around against her will was precisely the worst sensation he could inflict on a woman. Apparently it hadn't occurred to him, however, for he sure hadn't hesitated to lay hands on her whenever he had felt the urge, and she resented him hotly for it. It had driven home the fact to Amanda that no matter how fit she was, and she was very fit indeed, men were still bigger and stronger. And, to top it off, every time he had focused his attention on her, she had felt as though she were being assessed and found wanting. She had always thought glasses softened the impact of a person's eyes, but not MacLaughlin's. Even behind the slightly smudged lenses, his eyes had been laser sharp, and they'd had a way of looking at her that had made her feel insignificant. About the only good thing she could think to say about the man was that at least he'd had the sensitivity not to mention Rhonda's offer to rent Maryanne's apartment.

Oh hell. Her assessment of him wasn't altogether fair, she supposed. She was exhausted and scared spitless. MacLaughlin hadn't been a total ogre—not all the time, anyhow. He was doing a job at which he was quite obviously competent, and there had been moments when he had even shown flashes of compassion and gentleness. His smile that one time had been surprisingly sweet—attractive, even. But somehow, he was all mixed up in her mind with the way she felt: shaken and sick, with ragged, jumpy nerves. She couldn't get her hands to quit trembling, and in her mind, MacLaughlin symbolized this whole horrifying situation. Damn him—he shouldn't have taken away her freedom of choice; he shouldn't have dragged her in to identify Maryanne's body without allowing her time to prepare herself.

The little bit of food Amanda had been able to eat, and the wine she had drunk earlier while sitting in the bathtub, rose in a sour tide up her throat. She swallowed repeatedly and wrapped her robe tightly around her body, shivering with the cold sweat that flowed from her pores. She kept seeing Maryanne's lifeless body beneath the sheet in that cold, stainless steel drawer.

Despite the numerous discussions she and her fellow Cabaret dancers had had about the gruesome details of the most recent murder, and the grisly abundance of facts presented in the papers and on the news, Amanda hadn't been prepared for seeing Maryanne's corpse. Talking and reading about a madman who brutalized his victims in no way compared with seeing the final result of that brutality. Amanda had only seen Maryanne's face, but it had been enough. God, what an understatement: it had been too much, and she just couldn't shake off the memory of what she had witnessed. It was the primary reason she refused to forgive MacLaughlin for his part in forcing the identification.

Maryanne's face had been sort of a waxen yellowish-gray on those areas of flesh where it hadn't been grossly distorted by ugly, multicolored contusions. Amanda shivered. God. Maryanne had been all scratched and battered and misshapen, and if she had been merely a casual acquaintance, Amanda probably wouldn't have recognized her at all. Her mouth had been hideously swollen, her nose flattened, and the shape of her face distorted, but nonetheless, Amanda had known it was Maryanne immediately. The little scar that bisected her left eyebrow had been visible, and Maryanne had distinctive earlobes. They were sort of fiddle-shaped, dipping in excessively on the perimeter just below the whorls of her ears and flaring extra wide and flat on the lobes. Maryanne had hated them. She'd called them her Dumbo flaps and had always made sure that her hair was cut in short, wispy curls at the temples to disguise them when she was forced to pull the rest of her hair back to suit some of the headpieces that were a part of their costumes. She had also favored large, clip-on earrings to conceal their shape.

Amanda wished she could quit visualizing it, but it kept replaying itself in her mind's eye. She paced her apartment, prowling from kitchen to living room to the dining room that doubled as studio space. She came to a halt at the French doors, pressing her forehead against the cool panes as she peered out into the yard. Except for weak pools of illumination from the three porch lights, it was dark down there. There was an absence of light splashing out into the yard, which indicated that Maryanne's lights had been turned off

and her curtains drawn. The police must have finished for
the night and left.

Amanda lowered pleated fabric blinds over the French
doors and turned away. She hesitated a moment, then drew
a deep breath and began to move furniture out of the dining
room. She wasn't going to be able to sleep; that was a cinch,
so she might as well dance.

The conversion from dining area to dance studio was one
she had made so often, it had become second nature to her
and took only moments to complete. She put the chairs into
the living room, rolled the drop-leaf table and antique sideboard down against the north wall, and placed the Oriental
rug atop the sideboard. She removed her two-part wooden
barre, custom built for her by one of the Cabaret's carpenters,
from the coat closet, screwed it together, and placed it into
the brackets permanently affixed to the mirrored wall where
the sideboard normally resided.

She stripped out of her robe on the way to her bedroom,
dropping the discarded garment on a chair and reaching for
her worn leotard, slouch socks, and scuffed, soft, kid-leather
ballet slippers. She scraped her hair into a haphazard pony-
tail atop her head and returned to the studio. Heart thudding,
she grasped the barre and took a deep breath. Exhaling
slowly, she looked at herself in the mirror, drew her frame
up to its full height until all her muscles aligned correctly
from an erect skeletal structure, and executed a deep plié.
From there she moved through her daily repertoire of exercises.

Very well, she thought as the coils of tension in her stomach
began to ease and the jumpy restlessness drained away, *maybe
I can't sleep or eat. I'd settle for a good cry*, but the tears
wouldn't come. *Well, dammit, I can dance. I've always been
able to dance—even right after Teddy. . .*

Amanda stopped, staring at her damp, flushed image in
the mirror. She watched her reflection's jaw firm, chin lifting
slightly, and slowly she resumed her exercises.

In her life to date, always, she could dance.

* * *

Amanda had built a life for herself around dance. It was
her passion and her refuge.

She'd had her first dance lesson when she was seven years
old, and it was a case of love at first instruction. In the society
in which she had been raised, instruction in piano, dance,
and the arts was considered de rigueur. Like her sisters before
her, Amanda had been enrolled from a tender age in lessons
in social deportment. That the lessons were designed to de-
velop a polished and poised young woman who would ultimately be marriageable was tacitly understood.

At seven, one didn't care about such things. For Amanda,
piano was a necessary evil to be endured, art was minimally
interesting, but dance—dance was everything. From her first
lesson, Amanda was enthralled. She loved everything about
it: the big mirrored hall; her willowy, graceful teacher; the
music; her pretty new pink tights, leotard, and slippers—
everything. She walked through the big mahogany door on
her first day of instruction, and it was like entering another
world—one that was exciting and warm and endlessly fas-
cinating. And it was a world that quickly came to mean home
to her in a way the elegant mansion where she resided never
had.

Amanda wasn't very old before she realized her home
wasn't anything like the one on the only program Nanny
Campbell allowed her to watch on television before dinner.
It wasn't loving like the Beaver's, and Mother and Father
certainly didn't bear the slightest resemblance to June and
Ward Cleaver. She had often tried to imagine getting into
mischief and having warm, understanding conversations with
her parents about her transgressions, but her imagination simply couldn't make the stretch. She couldn't even imagine
calling them Mom and Pop.

Her parents were not warm, understanding people. Father
was an investment broker who spent long hours in the city,
and Mother—well, Mother was on all the right committees.

Between them, they conducted an ongoing, civilized warfare in well-bred, carefully modulated tones of voice—strictly in private, of course; one quite naturally did not air one's differences in public.

When she was still quite young, Amanda regularly expected to hear of her parents' imminent intention to divorce. Heaven knew, many of her classmates' parents went that route, with subsequent remarriages and second and sometimes even third divorces. Amanda had observed so many stepparents come and go in some of her classmates' lives that at times she felt a scorecard should be supplied, just to keep track of who was currently related to whom.

But as she grew older she came to realize her parents had no intention of seeking a divorce. From their point of view divorce was a chump's game, although neither Mother nor Father would be caught dead using that particular phrase. However crassly put, it expressed exactly their opinion of the dissolution of a marriage. Fortunes were lost through divorce, blown to the four corners of the earth by alimony payments, child support, and the high cost of maintaining separate residences and multiple club dues. And modern mores notwithstanding, in certain circles, reputations were quite often still tainted by it. In Robert and Arlene Charles's opinion, it wasn't necessary to like one's partner in order to sustain a viable marriage. Lack of affection wasn't excuse enough to squander family fortune and reputation by dissolving a union that was mutually advantageous. Naturally, if one wanted to break the rules, one could always do so—discreetly.

Always discreetly.

Discretion was her parents' forte. There were few people outside the immediate family who knew of the Charleses' own discord behind closed doors. It was, in fact, one of life's little ironies, Amanda had always thought, that, contrarily select members of the revered, blue-blooded Old Guard often held up the Charleses' marriage to the younger generation as a model to be admired in a world gone mad. That appealed

strongly to Bob and Arlene Charles's esoteric sense of what
was important. And in public, Amanda had to admit, they
put on an extremely convincing display of marital harmony.

Bending over the leg up on the barre, Amanda sighed.
Lord, but Mother and Father were big on appearances. And
the absolute hypocrisy of it all failed to even register, let
alone disturb them. In private, the cold war was allowed to
rage on, in carefully couched words and cool tones. It was
very civilized . . . and deadly, for all of that. The reality of
a situation wasn't important, as long as it projected an illusion
of propriety and social correctness.

It could have been emotionally stunting to grow up in an
atmosphere where one was expected to behave properly in
public at all costs, regardless of the battles one constantly
witnessed in the privacy of one's home. And in truth, Amanda
thought her two oldest sisters were extremely neurotic, but
prudently discreet about it in the venerable Charles tradition.
Proper clones of their parents, they kept their messes out of
public view and felt righteous for doing so.

Amanda escaped the emotional vacuum Mother and Father
called home through her dedication to and love for dance.
And through her relationship with her third sister, Teddy.

Teddy. Theodora Marie. Impulsive, bright, and beautiful,
she had been the bane of her parents' existence and the delight
of Amanda's heart. Teddy broke every rule Mother and Father
lived by, blithely living her life in accordance with what felt
right to her, unconcerned with how correct it appeared to
others. She was rowdy and flashy, scandalizing her parents
time and again with her conduct; the volume of her voice,
which dared to rise above the accepted level of the truly well-
bred; the clothes she wore; and the vast, inappropriate group
of friends she attracted like heat to a solar panel.

Amanda adored her. They were total opposites, and as
such, the laws of nature that govern these things said they
shouldn't have had enough common interests to form a bond.
It made Amanda uncomfortable to hear swearing and dirty
jokes; Teddy used language and told stories that could make

a trucker blush. Amanda was dedicated to fitness; Teddy thought taking care of oneself meant smoking low-tar cigarettes and drinking diet beer. But Teddy was big-hearted, warm, and generous, and she showered Amanda with attention. In a house where physical contact was minimal, Teddy was like a roaring fire on a cold winter's night. She was tactile and spontaneous, and she made Amanda laugh over things that, had they come from another, would have made her uncomfortable.

Teddy was a toucher. It was probably one of Amanda's favorite things about her. She loved the way it made her feel inside when she was the recipient of all Teddy's attention and enthusiasm. It didn't have to be anything major. In fact, it was usually the small moments that meant the most, like when Teddy insisted on fussing with Amanda's hair, torturing it into all kinds of outrageous shapes. And then there were the "Theodora Charles Patented Preparation for Hollywood" sessions, where she sat Amanda down to experiment with makeup. It didn't matter that Amanda wouldn't be caught dead outside her bedroom door in most of the results of Teddy's efforts. What was important to both of them was the contact and the time spent together.

It was usually Teddy who initiated their furious tussles across the floor. Inevitably, it was also Teddy who cried uncle, since years of dance had made Amanda strong, and she always won—but never before first faking Teddy into thinking that maybe this time she was finally going to come out on top. Even sitting quietly, Teddy maintained contact with her younger sister, casually nudging her with a toe or a finger while she discussed or debated a subject, using touch to emphasize a point.

Surprisingly, she also stimulated Amanda intellectually. Although emotionally impulsive, Teddy had an inquisitive mind, and she loved to debate the merits of any issue that popped into her mind at a given moment. She could be silly and frivolous, but she had a serious side also, and often she and Amanda would argue heatedly over something they had

read about or had seen on the news. Some of their obser-
vations and opinions were ludicrous and some were not entirely thought out. But just as often, they could be
disconcertingly astute, and their opinions were always their
own, not judgments passed along secondhand, which was all
that Amanda ever heard when she occasionally tried to elicit
an original point of view from one of her other sisters.

So, it could have been stifling, growing up in that mau-
soleum of a mansion, but it wasn't. Between the discipline
of years of dance classes and her exchanges with Teddy,
Amanda developed a quiet confidence in her own ability to
make decisions. She discovered alternate options to the way
their parents insisted they should live their lives, and she
pursued those options with unobtrusive diligence. And because she was naturally quieter and her methods were so
different from Teddy's flamboyant rebellion, most of the time
her parents believed Amanda to be doing exactly what was
expected of her. Their styles may have varied, but both sisters
managed to arrange their lives to suit their individual needs.

Then, shortly before Amanda's eighteenth birthday, Teddy
ran into trouble. She was nearly twenty years old, and as
trouble went, it wasn't at all unique. Always afterward,
Amanda would believe it could have been resolved to Teddy's
satisfaction, if only outside influences hadn't intervened.

It would have been.

Dammit, weren't she and Teddy in the process of working
it out when their parents found out about it and decided to
take a hand in its solution?

Caught up in old memories, Amanda didn't realize she had
stopped dancing. She stared unseeingly at her reflection and
remembered another time.

God, how many times had it exploded full-blown in her
mind, sneaking up unexpectedly? It had been a long dry spell,
though, since the last time. Amanda had thought it was finally
behind her.

It was never recollected in its entirety, all tidy and pat, a nice little scene such as you'd see on television, squeezed between commercials. Rather, it flashed through her mind in vignettes, blurred at the corners, colors faded and indistinct. It was recalled as an elusive aroma, snatches of remembered conversations, tableaux from the past, frozen in time.

Her sister Elenore, flipping through a glossy magazine as she openly eavesdropped on Amanda's argument with their parents.

The smell of cherry wood crackling in the fireplace; the rain as it ran down the library windows. The soft pool of illumination from the antique lamp spilling across the highly polished fruit-wood desk.

Echoes of the passion in her voice as she defended her decision to go to New York after graduation: "I *am* going to dance professionally. I *need* advanced classes that I simply cannot get here!"

The cool distaste in her mother's voice as she explained how unsuitable it would be for a Charles to become what she termed a "dancing girl"—in the same tone of voice another mother might use to describe a child molester.

Elenore's mouth curled up in a mocking smile. And her supercilious tone of voice. "Oh, Mother. Let her go. After all, it could be worse. She could be pregnant, like Theodora."

The quiet—so thick you could hear the ancient manor house creak as its timbers settled. Then the pandemonium, subdued on her parents' part, her own strident shrillness.

"How do you know?"

"You bitch!"

". . . difficult to miss with Teddy tossing her cookies in our bathroom every morning."

Teddy summarily summoned.

And then afterward—Oh, God, afterward. . . .

Amanda blinked, reemerging in the present with a physical jolt. She picked up her towel and blotted the cooling perspiration off her brow. "Shit," she whispered wearily. "Shit, shit, shit."

That was all she needed to round out her day. Here she'd been attempting to exhaust herself so she could still catch a few hours of sleep tonight, and instead, she had dredged up the one sure memory guaranteed to keep her awake.

As she restored the studio back to a dining room once again, she reflected with bitter resignation that she might as well kiss good-bye all thoughts of sleep tonight. Her chances would have been a good deal more sporting if she had just continued to dwell on the image of murderers who liked to brutalize dancers, and big, cold-eyed cops who apparently got their jollies out of dragging helpless women in to view the results.

CHAPTER
4

Tristan was ready to snarl with frustration by the time he finally pried himself loose from Reno police headquarters. He climbed into the passenger side of Joe Cash's car and slammed the door. "Get us to the Cabaret, Joe," he directed in a clipped voice. Then his temper slipped its leash and he growled in disgust, "We'll be damned lucky if we can catch anyone still there. Bloody police brass— they're the same wherever you go." He drew a calming breath and whispered to himself, "Bugger 'em all."

Joe, who heard, grinned and pretended he hadn't. He gunned the motor, shooting out into traffic.

Tristan stared out the window at the garish lights flashing by. Damn Captain Tweedt and his demands that he chain himself to a desk while the new task force was being put into effect! He wasn't a desk cop, never had been, and the purpose of his transfer here sure as hell was not to turn him into one. But it had taken wasted hours of argument before Captain Tweedt had finally seen the light.

Although Tristan had no way of knowing it, as he stared impassively out the window at the passing scenery, the decisive argument on which the captain's determination had

been based had been Tristan's own heated assertion that the
ultimate objective should be to catch this killer as quickly as
possible. And the best way to do so, he had insisted, was
not with a one-man task force but by utilizing all the personnel
at Tweedt's disposal, maximizing each individual's strength
in an area best suited for him.

Gory murder headlines were not popular in a town with
an economy that was dependent to a large degree upon the
tourist trade, and Tweedt had everyone from the mayor to
the chief of police breathing down his neck, demanding a
quick solution. Also, being an intrinsically fair man, Tweedt
couldn't fault Lieutenant MacLaughlin's claim that he had
been assigned here to train and assist, not to single-handedly
do Reno's bloody work for them. With a feeling of sheep-
ishness, which he kept well hidden, Tweedt belatedly remembered his conversation with MacLaughlin's superior in
Seattle. He had been advised to give MacLaughlin his head,
wryly informed he'd get maximum results out of the stubborn
Scot if he was left alone to do the job his own way. And so,
in the end, Tweedt had somewhat gracelessly acceded. It
wasn't the easiest thing he had ever done. For, despite the
fact that MacLaughlin appeared to be extremely well-prepared
and had a reputation for being damn good at his job, he was
an abrasive son of a bitch to deal with, all the same.

More hours had been used up in finding the best men within
the precinct for utilization on the task force. Joe had been a
big help in that respect, and so had Tweedt, Tristan grudgingly had to admit, once the captain had warmed to the project. When all pertinent personnel had finally been assembled,
Tristan had held a meeting to brief his new task force. And
it was off to a smooth start, for although Tristan was often
impatient with police superiors when he felt they were trying
to prevent him from doing his job in the quickest and most
efficient way possible, he was excellent with the rank and
file. He had a knack for pinpointing a man's—or, in some
cases, a woman's—primary strength and making use of it,
which in turn imbued enthusiasm in his men for the work at

hand. And he had done his research well before he'd left Seattle. By the time he and Joe had left the precinct, the gears that would make this task force go around had already begun to mesh.

Joe pulled over to the curb and Tristan studied the glitzy facade of the hotel that housed the showroom where the murdered lass had worked. It was deep in the heart of Reno's gambling district. The two men climbed out of the car and went inside.

The Cabaret was located off the main casino on the ground level of the hotel. Blinking yellow lights spelled out the name of the lounge in a glittering arch above the drawn gold velvet draperies that guarded the entrance. Two free-standing brass poles stood guard in front of the drapes, connected by a velvet rope that sagged gently beneath the weight of a sign that read: Lounge Closed. Open at Eight.

The casino was bright with lights that reflected off the myriad mirrored surfaces, and it roared with sound. Bells rang, and the loud metallic clank of silver dollars hitting the trays of nearby slot machines, most of which were manned by white-haired ladies, assaulted Tristan's ears as he hesitated outside the Cabaret's entrance to skim the lobby card. He leaned down to peer at the eight-by-ten glossy of the Cabaret's dancers in the lower left-hand corner, his gaze moving quickly from face to face. His eyes paused just once, hesitating for the merest fraction of an instant. His heart began to pound with inexplicable force, and he straightened. He must have drunk too many cups of coffee at the precinct earlier. Rolling his shoulders impatiently, he swung a long leg up over the velvet rope with an easy sidestep and slipped between the draperies. Joe followed.

As the velvet curtains fell back into place behind them, the obtrusive casino noises faded to an indistinct murmur, and a small corner of Tristan's mind noted the well-planned quality of the acoustics. He and Joe paused a moment to let their eyes make the transition from the casino's glare to the dimness of the empty lobby before they crossed the narrow expanse. A piano tinkled somewhere behind the closed double doors leading to the lounge proper. Tristan eased the doors open just wide enough for the two of them to slip through.

They entered a world of confusing sensory impressions. The lounge itself was dark, but lights flooded the raised stage, bathing it in a strong white blaze that eliminated even the smallest of shadows as far back as the wings. The large room smelled of stale tobacco, perfume, and sweat. A piano player banged out a jazzy tune. A dictatorial voice called out commands, and the stage floor thudded rhythmically beneath a dozen pairs of feet as the dancers ran through their routine.

Tristan tripped over a chair, and he swore softly. It had been a mistake to stare into the glare of white lights illuminating the stage, but for just an instant, his attention had been riveted by the dancers. They were damned good—bloody excellent, in fact. He stood very still, waiting once again until his eyes adjusted properly. Almost simultaneously, the number on the stage came to an end and it was abruptly silent, except for the uneven sound of dancers loudly sucking in oxygen, dragging it deep into their diaphragms and then harshly expelling it. They stood or milled about in small, shifting groups, flexing arms and legs to keep limber, the exposed portions of their skin glistening with perspiration. Their eclectic dance garb provided the only bright splashes of color on the dun-colored stage.

''I've seen better dancing at a first-year recital, people,'' a voice called out. Using the sound for direction, Tristan located a short, slender man, with the unnaturally pale complexion of a person who never sees the light of day. He was seated at a table directly in front of center stage. The man's foot jiggled rapidly on the end of a crossed leg, and he puffed furiously on a white filtered cigarette, giving the overall impression of a man with more than his share of energy to burn. ''Let's take it once more, from the top. And this time, people, I wanna see some professionalism. Hit it, Lennie.''

The piano began again. The seated man snapped his fingers

in time to the music and called out, "and five, six, seven, eight . . ."

The dancers had lined up as he talked and on the count of eight they burst into motion. To Tristan's eye they looked professional in the extreme, and for the first time, it hit him that there were actually dancers who were dead serious about their craft and put as much effort into it as he put into his own career. But the man with the arrogant, authoritative voice—Charlie?—apparently felt otherwise, for he kept up a shouted, running critique, and it was rarely favorable.

"Keep your head up, David," he bellowed. "Rhonda, you're slacking off on the kick. Good, nice turn, Kelly." He was silent for three beats, then he roared, "Who the hell ever told ya you could dance, June? Get in step! David! Head up, dammit! You, Amanda, you're snapping your head back again, hold it still. Goddammit, David, keep your fuckin' eyes off your feet and bring that chin up! And side, side, cross over, chorus line kick! This ain't no friggin' solo, Amanda; bring your kick down to match everyone else."

"Let's go," Tristan muttered, and he and Joe cautiously wove between the close-packed ranks of tables supporting tipped up chairs until they flanked the seated man. When their combined shadows fell across the table where he sat, blotting out what little light had illuminated it, Charlie dragged his attention from the dancers, glancing up in annoyance.

"How did you get in here?" he snapped. "This ain't no goddamn peep show." The action on the stage grabbed his attention. "Pete! Pick up your feet—you look like a friggin' logger." He turned back to the two men still towering over him and looked straight into Tristan's gold shield, which he had flipped open and was holding at eye level. Pushing his chair away from the table, he stubbed out his cigarette in an overflowing ashtray and lit a new one, his attitude changing only slightly. He exhaled a plume of smoke through his nostrils. "What the hell is this all about? I'm a busy man, and as far as I know, I haven't done anything illegal."

"You Charlie Bagotta?" Joe asked, and the man nodded. Tristan glanced up at the stage, locating Amanda. Sweat lent a sheen to the bare portions of her honey-toned flesh, and her deep purple leotard and white tights stuck to her in damp patches as she danced with unsmiling vigor and grace. There was something about her . . . something both coolly competent and heatedly sexual—impressions at odds with each other.

Tristan's eyebrows snapped together. Bagotta didn't know what this was about? Bloody hell, hadn't she even mentioned to this clown that one of his dancers was recently murdered? He felt a curiously strong disappointment in her. She had appeared torn up about it yesterday, but maybe she only allotted one day's time to grieve for a friend before it was back to the business at hand. Yesterday he had admired her ability to remain cool in a tight situation, but he sure hadn't pegged her for a totally cold bitch, devoid of normal feelings. He hadn't been able to pin down precisely what type of woman he thought she was, but "cold" sure as bloody hell hadn't been the word to enter his mind. He knew he had felt an unwilling sort of admiration for the strength she had displayed.

But he didn't admire this, not at all. He didn't care for this flamin' little sod, Charlie, or the manner in which he bullied his dancers. Even less did he like the idea of a lass who was so lacking in emotion it enabled her to identify her dead friend one day, and then turn around the next and not even bother to mention to her fellow dancers that one of their number had died a slow and painful death. She must live one hell of a fast-paced life if she didn't find something like that worth mentioning. Just what did these people consider important? He was beginning to think that dancers were a selfish and cold-blooded lot, a breed that set itself apart from the rest of the human race.

"We're here in regard to Maryanne Farrel," Tristan said with a frigid control that did not allow his personal feelings to show.

"Yeah, what'd she do? I ain't hiring her back, and you can tell her that from me. No one just walks outta one of Charlie Bagotta's productions without an explanation and then expects . . ."

"She's dead, mon," Tristan interrupted, and he received a savage sort of pleasure seeing the color drain out of the officious little bastard's face, leaving Bagotta's complexion dead white. *Verra unprofessional attitude, MacLaughlin,* Tristan admonished himself dispassionately. Then, immediately upon the heels of the admonishment, he shrugged. Tough shit. He noticed that Joe wasn't above rubbing it in a little, either.

"We suspect Miss Farrel's the latest victim of the Show Girl Slayer," he said. "I'm a bit surprised Amanda Charles or Rhonda Smith didn't tell you, since Miss Charles identified the body for us yesterday, and Miss Smith was at the morgue also, to lend her moral support."

Charlie rubbed his hands against his scalp, making the thinning hair on the top of his head stand up untidily. "Amanda and Rhonda had last night off," he muttered distractedly. "And they were late this morning. They came running in here at the last minute, wanting to talk about something, but I told 'em to get their butts up on stage. They had already interrupted practice, and they damn well know my policy regarding tardiness." His hand slid to the back of his neck and he gouged his fingers into the muscles there. "Dead. Jesus Christ."

The music had come to an end, and the dancers shifted about in puzzled silence, hands shielding eyes from the glare as they peered out into the gloom of the lounge. Why wasn't Charlie screaming abuse at them? Maybe he'd had a heart attack, someone speculated in a hopeful voice, but someone else whispered that she thought there were people out there talking to him. Everyone immediately strained harder to see, since Charlie's attitude about interruptions during rehearsal was notorious. However, there did appear to be two large, shadowy figures standing over him at his table, just barely discernible from the stage, and when the troupe tacitly fell silent again and moved a little closer to the edge of the stage, they could also hear the quiet murmur of voices, although whoever it was out there was speaking in tones too low to be overheard. Rhonda was the one who recognized, by its sheer size and bulk, one of the dark images intercepting the light. Solemnly, she turned to look at Amanda. "Mac-Laughlin."

Amanda's mouth went dry and her heart throbbed in her throat. It had been early morning before she had finally fallen asleep, and then she had slept until Rhonda had pounded on the door. It had been a rude awakening in more ways than one. She had been disoriented, forgetting for a moment where she was and what had happened yesterday. She'd picked up the bedside clock and swore, yelling at the person pounding at the door that she was coming. Then, as she had thrown back the covers to leap out of bed, she had practically been poleaxed by a rush of mental images—images of Maryanne, of the morgue, of MacLaughlin and his unreadable, assessing gray eyes, and of Teddy—the way she had looked the last time Amanda had seen her. It had all come crashing down around her like a truckload of clammy gray cement, threatening to overwhelm her.

The timing could not have been worse, for she hadn't had so much as a minute to pull herself together and try to make some sense of it. She had barely had time to do more than brush her teeth, scrape her hair into a banana clip, and throw a coat over her dance clothes before she and Rhonda had raced out the door. Then, in a town that didn't have all that many streetlights, they had somehow managed to hit every red one there was between home and the Cabaret. They had talked very little—just enough to decide between them that, as little as they relished the prospect, they were going to have to break the news of Maryanne's murder to Charlie and the dance troupe.

As it had turned out, however, there hadn't been time. Charlie had been foaming at the mouth by the time they had raced in ten minutes late, and he had refused to let them say a word.

Amanda heard the whispers and the startled exclamations around her as Rhonda told someone of yesterday's events, and word of it spread across the stage faster than a grass fire across an arid prairie. She stood silently in the midst of the subdued, horrified babble, staring out at that big shadow bent over Charlie's table. For too brief a moment while they had rehearsed, she had been able to put Maryanne's murder in the back of her mind. She didn't particularly like herself for that pretend-it-didn't-happen-and-maybe-it-will-go-away attitude, but she couldn't seem to help it. She had never been in a position like this before, and frankly, it shook her right down to the ground. She didn't honestly know what she was supposed to think or feel or do, but somehow, this whole situation was getting mixed up in her mind with Teddy, and she was beginning to feel more than a little out of control.

Conversations dwindled away one by one as the three shadows in the lounge detached themselves from the table and headed for the stage. By the time Charlie led the way up the steps from the orchestra pit, the dancers had fallen silent. They eyed the two big cops accompanying him warily.

"I take it you've heard the news," Charlie said, and he shot an accusing glance at Rhonda and Amanda. "Good of you to let me know, ladies."

"Hey, we tried, Charlie," Rhonda protested with some heat. "If you recall, you didn't have the time to listen."

"Yeah. I know, Rhonda," he admitted and rolled his shoulders in a quick, guilty movement. "I'm sorry." The glance he directed at Amanda was curiously tender. "You okay?"

His unexpected concern was nearly Amanda's undoing. "Umm," she replied and turned her head away, hoping he'd accept that as an affirmative and not ask her to elaborate. She felt hopelessly fragile all of a sudden. She was deathly afraid it wouldn't take much to make her lose her grip entirely. Her chin and bottom lip wobbled precariously, and she compressed her lips in a tight line, ordering herself not to cry. She stared blindly into the wings until she regained control of herself. "I'm fine," she finally managed to reply in a croaky little voice. Her eyes were caught by MacLaughlin's, and for a fleeting instant, they stared at each other.

It was yesterday all over again. Amanda hadn't the first idea what MacLaughlin was thinking, but once again she felt at a distinct disadvantage, as though whatever it was, it was not exactly flattering to her. She shrugged and looked away. Why did she care? Let him examine her like a virulent disease on a slide; she was hardly going to lose any sleep worrying about his opinion of her. And perhaps she was overreacting anyway; it was difficult to read his expression.

Amanda nearly snorted. Difficult? God, that was rich: it was downright impossible. She had never encountered anyone quite so adept at disguising his every thought, which accounted in part for his ability to unnerve her. Usually she could get at least an inkling of a person's thoughts and beliefs by observing his facial reactions, but MacLaughlin's didn't give away clue one. The man was a study in Olympian detachedness. His eyes were cool and shuttered, and on a face where flesh bonded leanly to muscle and bone, no tiny movements marred the creased skin near his gray eyes; no muscles clenched along his strong jaw. The corners of his mouth were relaxed and so were his thick, sandy eyebrows.

Never before had such a lack of expression on a man's face possessed the ability to make her feel so small and insignificant.

Amanda had always prided herself on her own self-discipline. It was a necessary part of dance, but not something easily attained, for all its necessity. She had worked hard to achieve a level of self-regimentation, but as she studied MacLaughlin's noncommittal, blank expression, it occurred to her for the first time that perhaps self-regimentation wasn't the same thing as self-control. Amanda could force herself to complete any task, no matter how unpleasant it might be. But she had never possessed the ability to disguise the effect that unpleasantness might have on her. MacLaughlin, on the other hand, would also deal with unpleasantness. But his cold, cynical eyes said he'd damn well control his responses to it, as well. No one would ever, from looking at Lieutenant MacLaughlin, know exactly what—if, indeed, anything—it had cost him.

Well, goody for you, she thought with forced cockiness. Big deal. So she was plagued with insecurities at the moment. So the current situation was rapidly turning her into a nervous wreck. At least her reactions were human. MacLaughlin, on the other hand, reminded her of an android in a science fiction movie—the looks of a human, the emotions of a robot. Amanda glanced at Tristan again, and although she tried to match his lack of expression, she was afraid she was less than successful. She had often been advised not to depend on her poker-playing abilities to earn a living.

She was not wrong; her attempt was less than successful. Amanda had a whole battery of social defenses, but her face was very expressive, nevertheless. She might find it impossible to read Tristan's reactions, but he had no such problem reading hers. Her disdain for him was clear as crystal upon her face, and it annoyed him. It antagonized him. Bloody hell—it aroused him. God, he'd love to. . . . Abruptly, he turned away. In his burred, soft-spoken voice, he began to address the gathering, and conversations immediately halted as the dancers gathered around him to listen. Within minutes, he had the names of everyone in the troupe and was beginning to sort them out in his mind.

Amanda was left alone by the other dancers as they milled about, covertly or openly observing the two policemen at work. She didn't feel like talking to anyone anyway, but as she sat on the floor, she felt isolated—a feeling that was reinforced by the glances that were cast her way as the rest of the troupe gave her a wide berth. She wished she knew if it were consideration that held them apart, or if they simply wanted to avoid the identifier of Maryanne's corpse. For the past three years this group had been more of a family to her than her own family had ever been, but right this moment, she was feeling like a disinherited stepchild.

The sheer melodrama of that thought stiffened Amanda's spine.

You can't have it both ways, Amanda Rose, she lectured herself with determined sternness. *Either you want comfort or you want privacy. But, for God's sake, don't go throwing yourself a one-woman pity party just because life refuses to be perfect and give you both.*

Besides, for the life of her, she couldn't decide whether she was relieved or hurt by the distance the other dancers were keeping. In her present state of mind, she felt she was in a no-win situation, where kind word or cruel, she was going to burst into embarrassing tears at any moment.

One of the first things Lieutenant MacLaughlin requested was for anyone who knew both of the previous victims to come forward. Amanda exchanged a relieved glance with Rhonda across the stage when Pete Schriber approached the large cop. At least they wouldn't have that on their conscience.

A hand squeezed Amanda's shoulder and she jumped, her head snapping around. June, the newest dancer in the troupe, stood over her and smiled at her sympathetically. "Ah'm sorry y'all had to be the one to identify Maryanne," she whispered, bending down. "Y'all've always been so nice to me, helpin' me with my steps when Ah've been so klutzy and all."

Quick tears of gratitude rose in Amanda's eyes, and she smiled tremulously as she reached up and gave June's hand on her shoulder a quick squeeze in return. "Thanks," she whispered in reply, and she smiled to herself as the dancer moved away. June was so sweet. She was a Georgia transplant and was actually a very good dancer—not nearly as clumsy as she made herself out to be. She was just easily rattled by

Charlie's harsh indictments. Amanda had invited her over to her apartment a few times, and they had moved out the furniture and gone over the routines in Amanda's converted studio. There, June danced beautifully. During actual performances, she also danced beautifully. It was only when Charlie began one of his harangues that she stiffened up and made mistakes. Her gesture and words warmed Amanda, restoring a little bit of her battered confidence.

Several other dancers drifted past Amanda after that, pausing just long enough to whisper words of encouragement or to touch her lightly and smile before moving along once again. Even Randy, whom she didn't like, stopped long enough to say something encouraging, and for once he even kept his busy little hands to himself. The dancers' quiet show of support helped steady her nerves, and she was feeling almost normal, nearly in control of her emotions for the first time in more than twenty-four hours, when she glanced up and found Lieutenant MacLaughlin's eyes on her.

There was no sympathy or encouragement there, only an opaque silver gaze, coolly assessing her, and Amanda's stomach clenched. Bitter resentment clamped her throat closed when he raised one large hand and arrogantly crooked his finger at her, indicating her presence was required. Whipping the towel from around her neck, Amanda surged to her feet.

As she was making her way across the stage, she was halted midstride when a hand reached out of nowhere and brought her up short. It clamped around the back of her neck and whirled her in a half circle. She bumped up against a strong male body, and the sheer unexpectedness of it made her eyes widen with surprise. Backing away a step, she looked up into the admiring gaze of one of the male dancers.

"Jeez, David," Amanda breathed. "You scared ten years off my life."

"Sorry, sugar," he murmured. "I just wanted to let you know I think you're one gutsy lady."

"Ah, me." Gratitude made her shoulders slump for just

an instant and she rested her forehead against his chin. Then she raised her head and tilted it back to look at him, a slight smile on her lips. "Thank you."

He grinned and kissed her on the forehead, running his hands down her bare arms from her shoulders to her fingertips. He held her hands wide of her body and squeezed them in a friendly salutation before he stepped back and released her.

Tristan, watching from across the stage, had half risen from his chair when the muscular dancer first grabbed Amanda around the neck. Given his reason for being here, he had automatically assumed the gesture to be a prelude to violence, although serial killers generally displayed more wile than to fly off the handle within sight of several policemen. Still, stranger things had happened. Watching the two dancers, male and female, however, his hand slid away from the shoulder holster inside his jacket and he dropped back into his chair, disgruntled. The man was obviously one of Miss Charles's lovers. Undoubtedly, just one of many.

He didn't know why the thought should bother him. It had nothing to do with him.

The slight smile that David's words had brought to Amanda's eyes was nowhere to be seen when she stopped in front of the chair he straddled. She regarded him without favor and her voice was ironic when she drawled, "You beckoned?"

"Aye," he replied, and his voice was just as cool as hers. "That mon at the table over there is Sergeant Johnson. He's here to take your fingerprints." Tristan waved his hand in Sergeant Johnson's direction and glanced back down at the papers in his hand, dismissing her.

He'd had Joe call the forensic man earlier to request that Johnson meet them here to speed up the elimination process. They had dusted Miss Farrel's apartment on the off chance the killer may have been there, even though her body had been found by the golf course, miles away. But it was senseless to check the two or three good sets of latents that they had managed to lift from various surfaces in her apartment against the extensive files of known felons, before they had first verified they weren't simply the fingerprints of a regular visitor of Miss Farrel's. Working together and living in the same complex, Miss Charles and Miss Smith were obvious candidates for immediate elimination. But they were by no means the only candidates. He and Detective Cash were also checking with each dancer they questioned, trying to weed out anyone who had recently visited Farrel's apartment.

Tristan was aware that Amanda hadn't moved away, but he studiously ignored her until the sheer horror of her hoarsely whispered "My God!" snapped his head up. She was staring at him incredulously, her eyes a violet-hued smudge in her white face. "You can't seriously believe I had anything to do with Maryanne's death," she said hoarsely. All the blood rushed from her head as she swayed weakly in front of him. "You can't."

Tristan swore violently and surged to his feet. He whirled his chair around and shoved Amanda into it, pushing her head down between her knees. The back of her neck was as cold as ice, and squatting in front of her, Tristan pulled off his own warm wool Donegal tweed jacket and dropped it over her shoulders. He tugged it closed around her and bracketed her thighs with his forearms, lending some much-needed body heat. Chagrin over his failure to adequately prepare her made his voice brusque as he slowly detailed the need for her prints.

The warmth of his jacket and of his big hands splayed over her hips began to seep through the cold layer of shock mantling Amanda. One small corner of her mind registered surprise that so much heat and scent could come out of a man whom she wasn't convinced was entirely human, but all she heard was the impersonal coolness of his voice as it spoke close to her ear. Slowly, Amanda raised her head. She braced her elbows on her knees and shoveled unsteady hands through her hair to hold it off her forehead. The action brought her face close to Tristan's.

"You bastard," she said wearily. "You could have said that straight out and spared me this." Her hands flopped away from her hair and rested limply in her lap as she straightened in the chair. "You know what I think, Lieutenant MacLaughlin? I think you get a real kick out of terrorizing me."

Tristan's fingers momentarily clenched around her hips, squeezing them, his thumbs digging painfully into the high arch of her pelvic bones. But almost instantaneously his hands loosened and slid away as he rocked back on his heels and stood up, making Amanda decide that the action wasn't in reaction to her words so much as an involuntary push off as he had risen to his feet. His face was as militarily stern and noncommittal as ever as he looked down his nose at her from his great height. Shaken and angry and unwilling to grant him even so slight a psychological edge over her, Amanda also rose to her feet. She shrugged out of his warm jacket, regretting the loss of its warmth but unwilling to accept even secondhand body heat from him at this point. Silently, she held it out to him.

"I'm sorry you feel that way," Tristan said stiffly as he took his jacket back, slinging it over his shoulder with a crooked finger. His level gray eyes regarded her impassively from behind the slightly smudged lenses of his dark-rimmed glasses. "It was insensitive of me not to explain the reason we needed the prints, but it was certainly not my intention to be scarin' you, lass."

Amanda's chin tilted up. "My mistake," she said with patent disbelief. She longed to tell him to keep his distance, that she would deal exclusively with Detective Cash in the future, but she didn't want to give the man the opportunity to tell her the choice was not hers to make. So she held his gaze for a moment longer to let him know he couldn't intimidate her, then she turned away.

Even after he could no longer see them, Tristan thought about her eyes, so big and round and such an incredible color, willing him to drop dead. He felt a tug of regret as he watched her cross to the table where Sergeant Johnson had set up his forensic paraphernalia, but he shrugged it aside irritably. Stonily, he turned his attention back to the next job on his list.

Life was just full of regrets. But there was sure as hell always work to be done.

CHAPTER
5

Amanda found herself temporarily alone in the middle of what Pete Schriber claimed was *the* party to end all parties. It was four o'clock in the morning, and she was tired, but not so tired that she was willing to forgo the company of her fellow dancers. Not yet, at any rate.

Pete had said his impromptu party was to be, in part, a wake for Maryanne. But, primarily, he had claimed, it was a celebration of life for the rest of them. It was his personally held philosophy that those who have departed should be commemorated with a toast and a fond remembrance. But he also felt quite strongly that to be among the living in the midst of death was in itself a cause for celebration. And so, earlier in the evening, when the police had finally run out of questions and had packed up their paraphernalia and left, Pete Schriber had proposed a party that would honor the dead and fete the living, to be held in his current lover's little rental house, following the culmination of the midnight show.

Sitting momentarily alone in the midst of Pete's party, Amanda experienced a vivid sense of déjà vu. It was so reminiscent of her early years in New York—years when time was of the essence, when every waking moment was

spent rushing from a job that was consequential only because
it paid the rent, to dance classes, to open gypsy auditions for
that coveted position in the chorus line, or—less often—to
singing lessons, which had never truly paid off, due to a voice
that would never be more than adequate and a decided lack
of interest, as well.

And as the days had drawn to a close, back then, there
had been parties like this one, with plastic cups of beer or
wine, a thin, hazy, permeating layer of smoke, a portion of
which was suspiciously acrid, and the same inescapable group
over in the corner or perpetually slipping in and out of the
bathroom to indulge in controlled substances from a mirrored
surface. Parties like this, with the same inevitable mix of
people, most of whom were enjoyable, with the same exotic
fashions, the same loud voices, whispered conversations,
boisterous laughter. Sleep in those days had been a negligible
thing, but she had been eighteen, nineteen, twenty years old
back then, and it hadn't seemed to matter.

She wasn't quite as resilient at twenty-eight. It didn't seem
possible that a measly little decade, particularly one that had
passed as swiftly as the past ten years had, could make such
a difference. But the years between then and now had managed to exact a price—she was no longer tireless, and she
had lost her unquestioning fearlessness. She used to be able
to just pick herself up, pat herself back into shape, kiss the
bruises better, and move on when she had sustained a blow.

Somehow, it wasn't quite that simple anymore. And Maryanne's murder had taken an even greater toll on Amanda's
ability to bounce back. Closing her eyes for a brief rest,
Amanda cradled her wineglass to her chest and snuggled into
a stack of pillows on the floor.

And she smiled.

Okay, sure. It was a fact that her life wasn't as simple now
as it had been ten years ago. Or maybe her relative innocence
back then had only made the world *appear* a simpler place.
But once again she was attempting to overanalyze the situation, for she had grown during that ten-year period. And

despite the changes—the loss of innocence, the recently acquired fears—she still had to smile. Hadn't she just been thinking that these parties never varied? Some things did remain the same. Neither time nor the murder of a friend had the ability to alter at least two aspects of every single party she had ever attended—not if it was hosted or attended by dancers. The topic of conversation at one of these shindigs and the main mode of entertainment remained constant.

Dancing.

It never changed; it never varied. Always, these parties boiled down to one thing: dance.

The current name of *the* production in which it was most desirable to land a part, or the name of the production that currently offered the best potential for employment, was the only difference that Amanda could discern between a conversation overheard ten years ago and the two or three separate conversations into which she had inadvertently eavesdropped when she had closed her eyes just now. The names of the musicals, revues, and follies might change from year to year, but the text of the conversation did not differ at all. All around her, everyone was still talking about what roles were available, who had attended what auditions, who had the best chance of landing a plum role, who had blown their chances in the most dramatic fashion.

And then there was the favored entertainment at one of these parties. Opening her eyes, Amanda took a sip of warm wine and smiled anew as she watched the press of dancers on the small, hastily cleared area that served as a dance floor. In what other profession could you find so many people spending the best part of their recreational hours practicing the same craft at which they made a living?

Pete materialized in front of her. "Why is it, I wonder, that the prettiest women can usually be found grinnin' all by their lonesome in a dark corner somewhere?" he asked as he bounced up and down on his toes in front of her. "Aren't you feelin' social, Amanda Rose?"

Amanda's smile grew wider as she looked up at him.

"Why, Peter, my fine host, I'm not being antisocial. I was just sitting here in awe, marveling over your party-throwing abilities. It's a rare, God-given talent that I, myself, have never possessed." She laughed and then assured him, "But I *was* planning on getting up and joining in the festivities any moment now. Honest, I was."

Pete's return grin was white as he squatted down in front of her.

"Have you ever noticed, Pete," Amanda asked, sitting a little straighter on her pile of cushions, "how absolutely, certifiably *fanatic* most dancers are when it comes to dance? It's quite irrational. They live it, talk it, and breathe it. Don't these people know there are other interests out there in the big, bad world?"

"We can't all be as multidimensional as you are, sweet-cheeks."

"Indeed, no. I suppose that would be too much to ask," Amanda agreed in an affected tone of voice that she borrowed from countless remembered arguments with her mother over this very subject. "Well, what can I say? I'm certainly pleased to announce that *I*, for one, am much more well-rounded. I find it quite distressing to see this many otherwise rational adults lose all sense of proportion over a subject as trifling as dance."

"I guess that means you wouldn't be interested in learning how to shag, then, huh, Amanda? It's just a dumb little dance that June taught me." Pete stood up and looked down at her, shaking his head sorrowfully. "Nah, forget I even mentioned it. I can see it wouldn't interest a genuine blue-blooded, Yankee type like yourself."

Amanda immediately set aside her plastic cup of warm wine and extended her hand for Pete to pull her to her feet. "Show me."

Pete refrained from smiling. Instead, he said mildly, "Yes indeedy-do, I am certainly glad to see there's still *someone* around here who can remain dispassionate when the subject of dance rears its ugly head."

"Oh, hush up, Pete," she mumbled and smiled at him sheepishly, deciding it really was a pity that he was gay. A man who was as funny and decent and just plain nice as Pete Schriber was could almost make a woman forget her policy of noninvolvement.

Yeah, right, a little voice whispered in her brain. *You don't mind if a little honesty is shed into this sweet little fantasy, do you? Because the simple truth is, Amanda Rose Charles, if Pete Schriber were both straight and available, you wouldn't feel as free and easy with him as you do at this moment. Consequently, you would be busy as a beaver in dam-building season, erecting barriers between the two of you for all you were worth, just to keep him at a safe distance. Come on, girl; admit it.*

But there was a portion of her ego that disliked facing the unpalatable little truths periodically tossed out by her conscience. She had been raised to project an image of perfection at all times. Day after day, as a child and a young adult, her obligation to uphold the family image had been drilled into her, and it was a hard habit to reverse. She sometimes feared that no matter how much she had abhorred her parents' hypocrisy when it came to the subject of public versus private behavior, some of it must have rubbed off—it was still extremely difficult for Amanda to admit that there were fragments of her personality that might be viewed as a little less than faultless. She hated to admit it, but she would catch herself occasionally in the midst of building elaborate rationales in her own mind, strictly for her own benefit—rationales that allowed her to dodge giving any thought to her less pleasant personality traits and her tendency to avoid commitments with men.

It was hard to admit, so she didn't; she put the entire dilemma out of her mind. This was a party, for heaven's sake. It was neither the time nor the place for deep introspection into her tender psyche or the possibility that scars had been inflicted on it at a young age. The subject under discussion had been dance; how on earth had her thoughts gone off on such a tangent? Besides, she'd said it before, and she'd say it again: she liked men. She didn't have a problem with the idea of committing to one. She had just never met one special enough to be worth the effort.

Ignoring everything but the desire to learn the shag, Amanda smiled up at Pete. "Never make fun of a woman with a longing to learn a new dance, Pete. Didn't your mother ever explain to you about the really important issues in life?"

"You mean, like world peace and an end to homelessness and hunger in our time?"

"Well . . . yeah. Those are imperative problems, for sure. Not the one I was thinking of, but important, Pete—no doubt about it. But the absolutely definitive topic, important issue number one, is . . ."

"Finding that one perfect love, and having him turn out to be great in the sack," Pete interrupted.

What *was* it with everyone? Why did love and sex seem to have so much significance for everyone but her? She was beginning to feel like she was really missing the boat here. Was something vital missing in her? Or was this some sort of conspiracy?

"*Dance*, Peter. *The* number one important issue is *dance*."

"I knew that. I was just testing ya."

"Yeah, sure you were. As usual, a woman tries to talk to a man and it lands her in a heap of trouble. Well, that's okay, dear." She patted him on the cheek. "We don't have to make conversation. I won't ask you to say a word, as long as you show me how to shag."

"Duh . . . thank you, Amanda." He crossed his eyes and gave her an idiotic smile and they both laughed.

For the next twenty minutes, they were both absorbed as he showed her how to shag.

•

It was nearly 7:00 A.M. when Amanda's concentration on the number that she and a fellow dancer were trying out was broken by a feeling of being watched. She broke eye contact with her partner and looked across the room, straight into a pair of rain-gray eyes, laser-sharp behind freshly washed, dark-rimmed lenses.

Unfortunately, in the split second before she had caught his eye, she had already begun the process of bending backward from the support of the masculine arm clamping her lower body to her partner's. Once arched in a back bend, she was supposed to sway languorously. The unexpectedness of seeing MacLaughlin, however, made her go stiff where she was supposed to be loose-limbed, and consequently she was off balance. Her uncentered weight nearly knocked both herself and her partner to the floor.

"What the hell?" Her partner did some fancy footwork to save them from sprawling in a graceless heap on the ground. He squatted slightly to compensate for her uncharacteristic awkwardness, braced himself, and planted a muscular thigh between Amanda's legs, tightening his hold on her waist with an abrupt tug that pulled her hips flush against his. Amanda quickly planted her right foot and completed her back bend. Her left knee rode up the outside of his leg to his hip as she swung in a sinuous side-to-side motion in his hold, but as soon as she could, she completed the movement and brought her foot back to the floor, arching and lifting her upper body until she was upright again.

"I'm sorry," she murmured, wishing the music would come to an end even as she moved with automatic sensuousness to its rhythm. She couldn't think over the tiny panicked voice in her brain that kept asking with frantic repetition, "What is *he* doing here? What is *he* doing here?"

Tristan was wondering the same thing. It had seemed like a good idea when he had received the phone call from Rhonda Smith inviting him, but now he almost wished he had stayed in bed and gotten an extra hour's sleep instead. He felt utterly out of place, and he had no business being here when there was real police work waiting to be done—more work than he could realistically hope to accomplish in his normal ten- to fourteen-hour day. So, not only did he stick out like a bloody sore thumb in his conservative suit and tie, he didn't even have the authority of being here in an official capacity to back up his uncharacteristically impulsive decision to crash this affair.

Tristan rolled his shoulders uncomfortably, eyeing the rainbow flamboyance of gold and silver lamé, multicolored sequins, and glitter spandex as it caught the light with the crowd's perpetual movement. Outfits flashed with fire as the dancers wearing them moved in and out of light and shadow. Next to him stood a woman with a friendly smile, moving in time to the music blasting from the stereo speakers and humming along with the song between sips of wine. She wore a purple wig that looked like nothing so much as a dandelion gone to seed—a pinkish-purple explosion of synthetic fibers. Her breasts were barely contained by the sparkling little matching tube top she wore. Tristan decided he must have been out of his mind to have thought he could blend into this crowd.

He hadn't passed unnoticed, that was for damn sure. He watched drugs quietly disappear, a roach pinched out and pocketed here, a line of coke hastily scraped into a minuscule bottle and palmed there. He could bust the whole damn party if he was of a mind to do so.

But that wasn't why he was here.

Shit, he wasn't exactly sure why he *was* here. Rhonda had rousted him out of a sound sleep and had suggested he come over. He had told himself at the time that it was only the opportunity to satisfy a purely professional curiosity that had made the invitation sound so appealing. But it was more than that, and if he were to be the least bit honest with himself, he would have to admit he had known it all along. It was curiosity, all right, but not necessarily related to the case.

He watched the way the dancers at this party related with one another, as they talked and gossiped and laughed and argued, and he wondered if that was something one had to be born knowing how to do. Or maybe one was taught social interaction as a child by one's family. It was not a subject on which the orphanage where he had been raised had spent a great deal of time, that was for damn sure. The orphanage had been more concerned that the children under their supervision learn obedience and a healthy respect for the rules of society. It had most likely assumed that if a child wished to have friends, he would make them on his own initiative on his own time.

Only, Tristan never had.

Institutional life had not been the Dickensian horror that it was often portrayed to be—at least, it hadn't been in Tristan's experience. The staff, as he remembered it, had been nice enough; they had seemed to care about the children. But the employees of the orphanage had also been overworked and underpaid, and there hadn't been a great deal of time or money for the little niceties that make the difference between a home and an institution.

Tristan had been painfully shy as a boy, and the intermittent need to be paraded before prospective adoptive parents— men and women with regretful eyes who had rejected him time and again as a candidate for adoption—had merely served to reinforce his shyness. More than anything as a very young boy, he had desired a real home. But, the day had finally come when he had known in his gut that he would never again be told to clean himself and report to the musty-smelling visitor's room to endure another inspection. He had become too old to be considered a desirable candidate, and he was too big. It was common knowledge that only the smallest, cutest children—and preferably babies, at that— were in demand in the adoption market. Nobody had a need for a boy with poor vision who had grown too large too quickly.

From that day of realization on, he had taught himself not to care. He had learned to guard what was his, to trust no one, and to assume a mask of indifference to disguise and protect his feelings. If he didn't expect anything, he had figured, he couldn't be disappointed. He had also given up what had only been a halfhearted attempt in the first place to make friends with the other boys in the orphanage, because it was too disruptive when they moved on, as they often did. The orphanage's population was a fluctuating, transitional one. He had never really had the knack, anyhow, and he had always figured that the ability to make friends must be one that you either possessed or did not.

So, why was he suddenly questioning that decision now? He had spent most of the afternoon and part of the early evening yesterday at the Cabaret, and in the course of his investigation, he hadn't failed to observe the way the members of the dance troupe had interrelated with one another.

He couldn't fail to notice it now.

And it tugged with near-painful insistence at something deep inside of him.

Tristan had found it difficult to fall asleep when he had finally gone back to his overheated motel room last night. He had lain there for what seemed like hours, mulling it over in his mind, moodily watching the red glow that tinted his room and then faded as the neon sign outside his window blinked on and off. He didn't know what it was, but there was something about the way these dancers kidded and talked and supported one another that had made him want to re-evaluate his way of looking at friendships.

Perhaps it wasn't something that came naturally to a lucky few, after all. Watching the give and take, it had been his reluctant observation that it appeared to take some effort on everyone's part.

Unfortunately, he also had a sinking feeling it had something to do with trust—not an emotion with which he felt at home. Trust was not a commodity he had dealt in as a child or young adult, and in his line of work, it was generally considered more of a liability than an asset. Just contemplating the dangers inherent in opening himself up to another person made him edgy and irritable. Bugger it. He didn't belong here.

Actually, he was beginning to establish a tentative friendship with Joe Cash. Why couldn't he just be satisfied with that? It was sure as bloody hell more than he had ever managed in the past, even if he couldn't claim much credit for it. Joe was actually the one who was actively pursuing a friendship both in and outside of regular working hours.

He had thought that these dancers would be a bunch of dilettantes, only to discover that they worked hard at their craft. And Tristan admired hard work perhaps more than any other virtue.

He had thought they would shun his company. He had certainly run into that a hundred times before in the course of an investigation: victims or witnesses who seemed to confuse him in their minds with the crime in which they were involuntarily involved. Yet many of these dancers, rather than scurry away to the safety of unsullied territory the minute he was through with them, had stayed to talk to him about his line of work and to ask him personal questions.

He should hold himself separate from them, Tristan knew, if for no other reason than to maintain a professional objectivity.

But, dammit, he harbored an urge to know more about them.

He harbored an urge to know more about *her*.

That cut right to the heart of the matter. Tristan closed his eyes and swore beneath his breath. Reopening them, his gaze was drawn straight back to Amanda Charles, just as it had been from the very instant he had walked through the door.

Flamin' lot of good it would do him. He had taught himself a long time ago not to want those things he could never have. So what the bloody hell was he doing here when he should be downtown mapping out the specifics that would set his investigation in motion? It sure wasn't to get a professional perspective on the world of dance.

He had never in his life been stimulated by a woman's antagonism, and God knows, in his profession, he was subject to a lot of it. So, why was it different with her? Why did even her hostility strike a responsive chord in him?

Why was he standing here like a lonesome puppy, watching her, when he knew that even if he did catch her eye, all he would see there would be dislike and disdain? She was one of the ones who seemed to have trouble separating him from his work, and she had already made it clear that she believed he was enjoying the spectacle of seeing her turned inside out by this investigation.

Tristan straightened his shoulders. This had been a mistake, and it was getting him nowhere. It was definitely time to leave. There weren't enough hours in the day as it was, and he couldn't afford to waste his time in a make-believe world.

Two things happened simultaneously. Amanda looked up just as Tristan was about to turn away, and Rhonda arrived at his side, reaching out to touch his right arm. "Hi, there. I didn't know if you would come."

Accustomed to always keeping his right arm and hand free in case the need arose to reach for his gun, Tristan automatically clamped a hand over Rhonda's to remove it from his forearm. Still watching Amanda, he failed to see the signs of her unusual awkwardness after she had spotted him. He only saw the sexual overtones in the climatic finish of the dance she was performing.

His fist tightened around Rhonda's hand, preventing the blood from reaching her fingertips. She looked up in surprise as the painful grip intensified, automatically reaching out with her free hand to peel his fingers away from her knuckles, which were being painfully ground together in his grip. His face was smooth and calm, free from expression, but his grasp was unrelenting, and Rhonda followed his unblinking gaze straight to Amanda. My God, he was breaking her fingers. "Lieutenant, please, you're hurting me." Rhonda's knees started to buckle.

Tristan's head whipped around at the unmistakable sound of pain in her voice and the gravitational tug against his hand as she sagged in his hold. He released her immediately, but unfortunately not before Amanda chanced a peek in his direction once again, only to see him turning away and what appeared to be him forcing Rhonda to her knees.

"Ah, God, Miss Smith, I'm that sorry," Tristan apolo-

gized and put a large hand under her elbow to help her
straighten. He picked up her abused hand and held it as
tenderly as a wounded bird in his own large palm, rubbing
his thumb gently over her reddened knuckles. "Are you all
right, then, lass? I'm ever so sorry."

"Yes, I'm fine. I realize it wasn't intentional . . ."

"Leave her alone, you bastard!"

Tristan released Rhonda's hand and turned to face an outraged Amanda. "What?"

"I said, leave her alone! What are you doing here, anyway,
MacLaughlin? You don't belong here."

Her words struck so close to what he had been thinking
himself that Tristan felt himself reddening. "Nice of you to
point that out," he said stiffly. "I was just leaving."

"No, you're not." Rhonda moved out from behind Tristan's bulk, which had been blocking her from her friend's
view. "Mandy, it's okay. I invited him here."

Rhonda observed Amanda with interest. Although her
voice was pitched low, it was clear she was upset—extremely
upset. And she was being impolite, which was a rarity indeed
from this woman who had been raised to always present
impeccable manners, regardless of provocation. Even as she
watched, Rhonda could see Tristan's quiet reprimand had
registered with Amanda. Her pale, creamed-honey complexion became suffused with the hot rush of blood that swept
just beneath the surface of her skin as a result of having been
caught in a rudeness. Rhonda smiled to herself as she turned
to Tristan. "Care to dance, Lieutenant?"

If it had been Amanda who had asked him, Tristan knew
he would have been too self-conscious to comply. But he felt
at ease with Rhonda, or at least as at ease as it was possible
for him to feel with any woman. She reminded him, in fact,
of the women he dated. They were free and easy, sexually
uninhibited women, with whom one never had to watch one's
language—women who were filled with light, effortless conversation that bridged over the gaps of his own silences.

Breezy lasses with wary, knowledgeable eyes, just like the girls with whom he'd grown up.

"Lass, you might just be takin' your life in your hands, riskin' a dance with a nonprofessional," he replied after a moment's consideration. "But I think I could manage to do that with no problem . . ." He indicated a couple performing the same style of dance he had watched Amanda and her partner perform and gave Rhonda a slow smile that almost held a suggestion of wicked amusement.

"Goody." Rhonda grabbed his hand and tugged him toward the dance floor. "It's called dirty dancing, MacLaughlin."

Tristan stopped dead, pulling Rhonda to a halt also. "Dirty?" He tossed back his head and roared with rare, unrestrained laughter. "Perfect. Oh, that is just too bloody perfect. I watched a couple of the dancers and thought to myself it looked less like dancing than it did like a vertical fuck . . . oh, beg pardon, lass."

"No problem." Rhonda noticed that he carefully didn't mention Amanda's name as one of the dancers, and being nobody's fool, she relinquished all of her half-formed plans to attempt a seduction of the good lieutenant. She experienced only a momentary twinge of regret. No one had to hit Rhonda Smith over the head for her to see the big picture. She had pretty much abandoned any nebulous plans already when he had watched Amanda dirty dancing and failed to realize he was grinding her knuckles to dust. "But, be warned, Lieutenant," she told him with a breezy grin. "This style of dance requires a little more skill than it might appear. Follow my lead."

Amanda thought she was probably the only one at Pete's party who didn't automatically smile at the infectious quality in MacLaughlin's brief burst of laughter. She watched Rhonda lead him through a dance, and she experienced a confusing rush of emotions. One of them felt suspiciously like jealousy, but Amanda knew it was only a momentary envy of Rhonda's ability to take the best components out of any situation that came her way, without first trying to diagnose it to death the way she, herself, sometimes did. She also felt anxious and angry and ashamed. It was pretty clear she had misinterpreted what she'd thought she had seen, for if the lieutenant had indeed hurt her, Rhonda would most emphatically not be shy about informing the world.

So, you jumped to an erroneous conclusion. Amanda tried to silently put it into its proper perspective. *You reacted with unwarranted rudeness, and now you feel like a fool. Big deal. You know damn well that anyone else would just shrug it off or chalk it up to frayed nerves as the result of a couple of truly horrendous days.*

Anyone who hadn't been programmed from childhood to feel ten kinds of guilt when she committed a social faux pas. Dammit, when was she going to let go of the past? It was at times like this that she missed Teddy the most, for Teddy had always had the ability to provoke her little sister into a little rash rebellion, the aftermath of which had left Amanda's pristine manners just the tiniest bit tarnished. It seemed to Amanda that she had possessed a more mature attitude when she was seventeen than she did right this minute.

Maybe she ought to leave. She was too tired to deal with all this.

But before she could make good her escape, her impeccable manners once again backed her into a corner. She had gathered her jacket and purse and should have left right then. Instead, she'd had to track down Pete to thank him for the party and let him know she was leaving. She was in the middle of her excuses when he said, "Just a minute, love," and, instead of relinquishing her, dragged her along with him to intercept Rhonda and Tristan as they left the dance floor.

"Hey there, Lieutenant," he greeted Tristan. "Good to see you. Did you get a glass of wine?"

"Actually, I was just leaving," Tristan replied. "I've got to get to work. Thanks again for invitin' me, lass," he said to Rhonda. "And for the dance." He smiled slightly. "It was most instructive."

"Amanda's leaving, too," Pete informed them. "Maybe you could walk her to her car."

"Oh, no, really," Amanda protested. "That's not necessary. I wouldn't want the lieutenant to have to go out of his way."

"I insist," MacLaughlin said. "It's not smart for a young woman to be out on the streets alone these days, Miss Charles—particularly a dancer."

Amanda gave Rhonda an imploring look, but she merely smirked. Pete removed any further options when he grabbed Rhonda's arm and said, "There's this guy who's been driving me crazy, insisting he has to meet you. Why don't you come along with me and let me introduce you, so I can get him off my back."

"Ooh," was all she replied, and she wiggled once all over in anticipation. She smoothed an eyebrow, grinned indiscriminately at all of them, hooked an arm through Pete's, and strolled away without a backward glance. Tristan and Amanda exchanged uncomfortable glances, and neither one could think of a word to say.

Tristan cleared his throat. "Are you ready, then?"

"Yes." Amanda hitched her purse strap more securely onto her shoulder. "We can leave by the kitchen door. It's closer to where I parked."

The short walk to her car was accomplished in absolute silence. A small frown dug a groove between Tristan's thick eyebrows when Amanda opened her car door without using a key. He stopped her from entering the automobile by placing a hand on her arm. "You didna bother to lock it?"

"I forgot." And the one time she had done so *would* have to have been when he was around.

"Of all the careless . . ." Tristan moved her aside and leaned inside the driver's door to check the interior of the car. He noticed that it smelled like leather and some light, elusive perfume. Backing out once again, he leveled clear gray eyes on her. They were carefully free of all expression. "Every time you go out alone, Miss Charles," he said in a carefully neutral voice, "you put yourself at risk. It's necessary to be more cautious than you have ever been before. Your life may depend on it."

"Yes, sir," she said stiffly, staring at the rigidly knotted tie beneath his white starched collar. She knew he was right, of course; she had been inexcusably careless. But the last person she needed a lecture from this morning was this man. "May I go now?"

Tristan felt like spitting nails, although with his mask of cool indifference firmly in place, Amanda never would have guessed it. *Damn her. She takes every single thing I say to her the wrong way. Every flamin' time.* With reluctance, he stood back and held the door for her. "Aye. Drive carefully." Chances were, she would most likely find exception in that, too.

But it was not for nothing that Amanda had had acceptable behavior drilled into her from the time she was old enough to string two words together. "I will," she said softly, and she extended her hand. When the lieutenant's large grasp swallowed it up, she fought a panicked urge to snatch it back. She was surprised anew at how warm his skin was. He had such a cool attitude, it never failed to amaze her that he radiated as much heat as ordinary men, if not more. It amazed her, too, that he didn't just pump her hand once and release her. Really, wasn't he holding it just a little bit longer than was strictly necessary? "Um . . . thank you for walking me to my car. You may not think so, but I do appreciate it."

Tristan released her hand and stepped back from the car. "It was no problem. Be sure to lock your door." Once her legs were pulled in, he closed the door behind her.

"Yes," she replied through the rolled-up window, and immediately did so. The corner of her lips turned upward in just the tiniest of smiles.

And then she drove away.

CHAPTER
6

In the following weeks, Amanda's life slowly returned to normal. Lieutenant MacLaughlin eventually ran out of questions, and the police ultimately directed their attentions elsewhere. As far as she knew no real progress was being made in the hunt for Maryanne's killer, but at least she was no longer in the thick of it. Nothing was exactly the same as it had been before, of course. Everyone she knew had been affected by Maryanne's death in one way or another, and they'd all learned to adopt a new wariness.

Her apartment was a case in point. The seal across the door had finally come down last week, and after cleaning up the mess the police had left behind and sorting and packing away Maryanne's more personal possessions, Amanda was now free to rent it. The problem was to whom.

The only male dancer she knew who was currently looking for a place to live was Pete Schriber, and although he expressed a strong interest in Maryanne's apartment, Amanda did not want to rent it to him. He was gay. Amanda had no particular problem with that; she liked Pete. But he was also extremely promiscuous, and while Amanda didn't care to judge another's life-style, the truth of the matter was that the last thing she needed right now was a parade of strange men constantly coming and going. It simply didn't strike her as an intelligent idea, in view of the present circumstances. If this entire ordeal had taught her anything, it was the crucial need for caution. She had to be able to look at any unidentified male who entered the premises and know whether or not he belonged there. With Pete's life-style, she would never know if a stranger on the grounds was a friend of his or someone who had no business being there.

But even with the new knowledge of danger that made such considerations a necessity, it was still good to reestablish some normalcy into her routine. And each day that passed without incident—and particularly without further contact with the large, unyieldingly stern lieutenant—she relaxed a bit further. Slowly, she felt her life begin to regain its former steady footing.

Tristan was beginning to settle into a routine also. He set about erecting his new division in his usual manner—with cool, methodical competence. In all honesty, he believed any halfway intelligent police officer could have done as much; it was merely a matter of instituting routine procedures. But he suspected the reason that Reno had specifically requested a Seattle policeman to head its new task force was because law enforcement agencies from the Pacific Northwest had unfortunately had more encounters in that field than they cared to think about. Thus they were more sensitive to the patterns of mass murderers than almost any other police department in the nation. In recent years they'd had extensive experience in cases involving serial killers of such notoriety as Ted Bundy, Kenneth Bianchi, Gary Addison Taylor, and Randy Woodfield—names that had gone down in the annals of crime for the sheer grisly proliferation of their victims.

But experienced or not, Tristan warned his division against expecting an early solution. "You know as well as I," he addressed the officers gathered in his office one morning, "that most murders committed in the United States involve people who know one another, usually spouses, relatives, or neighbors. A smaller percentage represents murders committed in the course of another crime, generally robbery. Either category ordinarily generates a large amount of evidence.''

He sat facing his task force in his favorite position, straddling a turned-around, straight-backed wooden chair. He rested his chin on his stacked hands and regarded them glumly. ''Mass murderers are a different proposition altogether. The verra randomness of a serial killer, coupled with the premeditation, which nearly always is involved, drastically reduce the clues that point to the killer's identity. And as much as I'd like to be able to tell you that you can recognize one of these bloody butchers by the mad gleam in his eye, I cannot.'' One corner of Tristan's mouth quirked up briefly at the momentary swell of appreciative laughter, but then he sobered. ''They're bloody hard to pinpoint. In just about every respect, the killer is someone who blends in extremely well. He is of above-average intelligence, and he can—and usually will—project an air of superiority. Historically, he dresses conventionally and well; he's considered a good employee; easily adopts middle class behavior; and invariably there's a neighbor willing to say, 'But he was so quiet and nice.' '' Tristan snorted. ''If and when we do catch the bugger, you can bet he will tend to try to control any interrogation. They're at their best in an interview situation, for they lie easily and well.''

''Sounds like a real charmer, Lieutenant,'' a detective said sarcastically from the back of the room.

''Aye, he can be that, too,'' Tristan replied with complete seriousness. ''When it suits him. But he's a predator and a killer, and his personality is not yet clearly understood by either criminologists or psychiatrists.''

''That's quite a profile you've given us,'' said a black detective with a degree of skepticism coloring his tone. ''So, tell us, is this a brother we're talkin' about here or your average white bread?''

''Most probably he is white,'' Tristan replied. ''With the

exception of Wayne Williams in Atlanta, every serial killer to date has been Caucasian." He smiled faintly. "It tends to send statisticians around the bloody bend, since blacks ordinarily have a murder rate nine times that of whites." He regarded his subordinate levelly. If there was going to be racial tension in his squad, now was the time to address it.

But the black detective merely shrugged, rolled his toothpick to the other side of his mouth, and murmured, "I guess you white folks really do it up right when you decide to play catch-up, though, don't ya?" Tristan laughed and turned back to the subject at hand.

"These buggers are generally caught when they suddenly change their M.O.," he informed his task force, and he looked up from his notes to see an almost uniform puzzlement on the faces of his men.

"Whataya talkin' about?" one of the detectives asked.

"Well, take Ted Bundy, for instance. He was considered to be a neat, methodically organized killer when he was operating in Washington State and Colorado. He was caught when he suddenly changed his methods and broke into a sorority house in Florida, where he clubbed two women with a piece of firewood in a rather random, unplanned attack."

Tristan riffled through his notes and glanced up at his men again. "I have a few more pieces of psychological trivia to pass along, which may help you get an idea of the type of mon we're hunting. A typical trait of a serial killer is to see a woman as all good or all evil. There are no shades of gray to him; in his eyes, she's either a saintly madonna or a sinful whore, and woe be it to the woman he once thought of as pure, if something occurs to make him see her as a whore.

"Much as they appear normal, we're not lookin' for a rational human being here. And just to make our job real interesting, they're highly mobile. One of the questions we'd like answered is whether or not he's a resident of this area or operating across the border. If he's drivin' in and out of the area, then he's going to be that much more difficult to track down. His penchant for mobility can be a definite hindrance to doing our job effectively. So, to see if we can't counteract that somewhat . . .'' He hesitated, then pointed a blunt forefinger at an extraordinarily handsome, muscle-bound blonde in skin-tight jeans and leather jacket, who sported a Hollywood-style punk-rocker haircut. "You, Edwards. Put a request in to Las Vegas, Atlantic City, New York, Tahoe—any place you can think of that employs dancers in a major way. Ask them if they've had similar crimes. If they have, get all the particulars. What we really need here is a central computer and better coordination and co-operation between police departments. Damned if you canna have a crime with the same M.O. being committed within the jurisdiction of two police departments no more than fifty miles apart, and still have one not know what the bloody hell is goin' on in the other. Put in a request first with the FBI's National Center for Analysis of Violent Crimes. It's the closest thing we've got to a clearinghouse—see if they've got anything that corresponds. Meanwhile, we dig up as much background as we can. The more information we have at our disposal, the better this investigation is gonna proceed.''

"Gotcha,'' Edwards said.

"How many men are available this mornin'?'' Tristan asked, well aware that like any other police station the world over, Reno was understaffed. The size of his force could fluctuate from one day to the next, depending on the needs of the entire precinct. Other crimes didn't grind to a halt just because they had a special case in the works.

"What you see is what you got, boss man,'' said Lavander Mason, the black detective. "There's eight of us today.''

Tristan assigned their duties. In the early days of the investigation he concentrated on pinpointing where the victims had lived, where they had worked and were last seen. He and his men talked to scores of people in the victims' neighborhoods, the surrounding vicinities, and their places of employment. They searched the entire area where the bodies had been found, although that was rather unprofitable, since the trail had been cold before Tristan had been assigned to the department. He had to rely on the written reports of the officers who had been on call and on the slides that had been taken. But that didn't stop him from going over the areas himself, if for no other reason than to try and get a feel for the killer. He directed his force to talk to anyone involved with the victims, no matter how remote the connection may have been. And if new information should arise, he expected them to go back and talk to everyone again.

The department lacked a sophisticated computer system, but the task force was given a MacIntosh, into which information was fed. It was then charted to avoid duplication of effort. Tristan met every day with his key investigators and task force supervisors to discuss the previous day's work and evaluate tips from the public. Files were pulled on known offenders of every type, not only rapists and murderers. They were perused with an eye toward discerning suspects with an unnatural prejudice toward women. It was a long, tedious, and so far fruitless endeavor.

More frustrating still was the interference of the news media. Most police probes of this nature had a grace period between the first murder and the consecutive related cases before the media spotted the connection and turned the crimes into the sensation of the moment. More often than not, the police were lucky enough to have made some headway on the relationship between cases before this happened, for media attention often hampered, if not outright harmed, an ongoing investigation.

Unfortunately, Reno's news network started a media blitz earlier than most task forces were forced to deal with. It was simply bad luck that on the day the second dancer's body was found, there was no other real news. It was the kind of day that produces nightmares for newsroom and network editors. Not a natural disaster to be found; not a single politician caught committing the same crime for which he was currently prosecuting another; not one dope ring, large or small, headed by an Ivy League yuppie of sterling reputation to be exposed.

And so, nearly before the police department itself had made the connection between the violent deaths of the two blond dancers, headlines were screaming Show Girl Slayer in bold-face type, and anchors on the evening news were questioning how safe it was to be a dancer in Reno.

Much to his disgust, Tristan found himself a favorite media target. Much was made of the fact that an out-of-state officer had been brought in to head the task force. He would have been much happier without the publicity, for it wasn't unheard of for a serial killer to gradually come to feel he is locked into a contest with the police. There had been more than one recorded case where a mass murderer had felt he was in competition with the law in a deadly game of wits, and consequently, his ego had turned it into something intensely personal. Too often, it had resulted in the killer using the lives of his victims as stakes. Tristan didn't want to see that happen here.

But in the newsmongers' eyes, Tristan was copy too good to be ignored. They loved his size and his accent; they wanted to know every detail of his life, be it professional or private. The only thing about Tristan MacLaughlin that they didn't love was his hard-line attitude toward reporters, which he had established unmistakably in his first confrontation with the media.

It occurred the day following the identification of Maryanne Farrel's body. When Tristan stepped out of the precinct he was immediately surrounded by reporters. Microphones were thrust in his face; strobe lights flashed in his eyes; and he had to squint against the glare of the hand-held spotlight that was used to facilitate the television cameraman's job. A dozen voices spoke at once.

"Lieutenant MacLaughlin! Are we dealing with another Hillside Strangler?"

"No. The mon responsible for that has been in custody for some time now."

"But isn't it true that someone is out to kill Reno's dancers in a very brutal manner?"

"It's true there have been three deaths that share similar characteristics."

"And all of the victims were dancers?"

"Aye."

"What kind of person picks up a dancer, kills her, then goes out and repeats himself?"

Tristan leveled cool, noncommittal gray eyes on the speaker. "You havena been a reporter for long, I assume?"

The young woman bristled. "I've been with the paper three years."

"Then you should be familiar with policy by now. We do not deal in speculation or opinion."

"Then how about some cold, hard facts," another demanded. "All three women were blondes, weren't they?"

"Aye."

"What does the coroner say was the ultimate cause of death for those three dancers?"

"No comment."

"Who made the identification?"

"No comment."

"Come on, Lieutenant! Give us a name."

"Not bloody likely, mon. The verra last thing the identifier needs is to be hounded by the likes of you."

"The public has a right to know!"

Tristan narrowed his eyes on the speaker. "The public has a right to know that their police department is working day and night to locate hard evidence that will help find the killer and that will eventually stand up in a court of law. Period. They havena got the right to invade the privacy of a person whom they suddenly decide belongs in the limelight, simply because he or she was unfortunate enough to have known the victim well enough to establish an identification for us."

It was too much to hope that the media wouldn't get around to interviewing Amanda Charles eventually, but Tristan had done his best to keep her out of it, nevertheless. The fact that she had been Farrel's landlady, however, and a dancer herself, not to mention her looks and bearing, soon had them nipping at her heels. Tristan saw her on the late news one evening shortly after his own initial brush with the press. The mention of her name made him look up from cleaning his gun as he sat on the bed in his overheated motel room.

One of the more persistent newshounds, a woman with dark-brown hair and an overbite, apparently had run Amanda to earth in the dancers' dressing room at the Cabaret. Amanda was seated on a stool with her back to a well-lighted mirror, an array of makeup pots and brushes cluttering the counter behind her. A sequined costume draped over the corner of the mirror kept appearing and disappearing at the periphery of the television screen as the cameraperson made subtle adjustments with his equipment. Amanda was dressed in street clothes, her stage makeup scrubbed off and her pale hair brushed away from her face in loose waves. Tristan gave her his undivided, critical attention.

He couldn't help but admire the poise with which she handled the interview. And it made him smile with grim pleasure to see that she was nearly as reticent with information as he himself had been, a fact which seemed to irritate the interviewer. Perhaps in retaliation, the reporter began to slant her line of questioning in a manner designed to make Amanda appear the stereotypical dumb blond show girl. As a tactic, it turned out to be less than successful.

Amanda did't attempt to defend her intelligence. Her violet blue eyes, which on television came across as a rather ordinary dark blue, did it for her. They were level as she stared solemnly out of the screen, and she sat quietly without fidgeting. The reporter's voice, coming from offscreen, rushed to fill in the silences that Amanda allowed to stretch out between them, stammering slightly over her words. Amanda answered each question concisely and intelligently, but she refused to be drawn into speculation.

"Well, isn't it true that a fact that needs to be considered in the police department's search for the killer is that all three victims led rather . . . active . . . sex lives?" asked the reporter at one point.

"I'm hardly qualified to answer that," replied Amanda coolly. "I know nothing about police work. I don't even know that it is a fact, since the only victim I knew personally was Maryanne."

"And her private life was . . . ?"

"Exactly that. Private."

"You didn't consider her promiscuous?"

"No."

"Isn't it true she dated quite a few men?"

"What do you consider quite a few?" For the first time, Amanda's irritation surfaced. "Twenty? Ten? How many men have you dated in the past year? Perhaps you can supply me with a frame of reference by which to judge."

The interview terminated shortly after that, and Tristan got up and snapped off the television. He removed a squat motel glass from its sanitary bag, poured himself a shot of whiskey, and went to stand at the window. Pulling the curtain aside, he sipped his drink and watched the neon lights outside his window blink on and off, creating wavery, intermittent reflections in the rain-dappled puddles that dotted the parking lot.

It was a long time that evening before he finally returned to the bed, sat down on the edge, and picked up his gun once again.

"Charlie's auditioning a male dancer."

Surprise rippled through the dancers making their way down the drafty back hall to the dressing rooms, and their footsteps faltered and came to a full stop, thoughts of hot showers, medicinal rubs for sore, overworked muscles, and the donning of dry, warm clothes temporarily forgotten. An audition? Most of those present turned around and drifted back to the wings to watch. It was unusual for Charlie to hold an open audition, let alone a private one, unless he had a position to fill. More than one of the dancers crowding the wings wondered if someone had given their notice. The males who were present hoped so, because the alternative was that

Charlie was so dissatisfied that he was planning to replace one of them.

Charlie finished giving the auditioner the combination of steps he wanted to see, then stepped back and nodded to Lennie, the piano player. Amanda studied the dancer. He was average height and on the lean side, with soft ash-blond hair and an intense air of confidence about him. As music filled the lounge, Charlie counted out the meter. With loose-limbed grace, the dancer launched into the prescribed routine.

"Oh, hell, wouldn't you know it? He's good."

Amanda glanced up at the speaker. It was David, and his face was rather strained as he watched the audition in progress. She reached over and squeezed his arm, but her eyes were drawn back to the dancer on the stage.

He was good—very good. But so were the four men in their troupe, and she couldn't imagine Charlie just arbitrarily releasing one of them without a warning. Despite his less than lovable personality, Charlie was usually fair with the dancers. The few times he had fired a member of the troupe, it had always been preceded by several warnings, so by the time he had gotten around to the actual firing it had come as no big surprise to anyone.

The music came to an end, and the auditioner stood panting lightly, head tossed back in the sure knowledge of his superior performance. The troupe looked from him to Charlie and held its collective breath.

"Well, as I told you before, I'm not hiring at the moment," Charlie called out from his table out front. "But give Lennie your name and a number where you can be reached just in case an opening comes up. I'd like to be able to use you. You're a damn fine dancer."

"Well, son of a bitch. I'd guess we've been put on notice," David muttered, and Amanda grinned. The guy who auditioned must have been one hell of a fast talker to get Charlie to agree to the audition in the first place. But once he had acquiesced, Charlie had probably looked upon it as a golden opportunity to let the male members of his troupe see that they were not irreplaceable. You could bet the men were going to be giving all future rehearsals and performances their best effort from this point on. "I wonder if he has a female waiting in the wings to get the rest of us to shake the lead out," she whispered, and David returned her grin.

Amanda and Rhonda talked about the mystery dancer again on their way home, after the conclusion of the midnight show. They tried to imagine what the man could possibly have said to Charlie to convince him to grant the audition at all. As the hour was late and they both were giddy with fatigue, their suggestions began to border on the absurd.

"Maybe it was a threat," Amanda said and dropped her voice, trying to sound like a tough guy. "We've got your wife," she growled. "If you don't audition me this minute, my accomplice will put her to death."

Rhonda giggled, but then said, "Don't be ridiculous, Mandy. Charlie'd just say, 'Barbara? That useless bitch? Why, just last night I told her I'd be home at five, and do you know that when I arrived at seven-thirty, with only minutes to spare before I had to be back to work, the silly broad had let my dinner dry out? She never was reliable. But make it painless for her, won't you?' " Hands relaxed on the wheel, she glanced over at Amanda. "Nah, it was more likely something that appealed to his greed."

"Okay, then, how about this?" Amanda pulled her heels up on the seat and hugged her knees to her chest. "He told Charlie he was a personal friend of the angels backing the show, and if Charlie auditioned him today, he would see to it that Charlie got a bigger budget for costumes and back-drops."

"Yeah, I like that one," Rhonda decided as she pulled up to the curb outside their yard. "That, I can definitely picture." She looked at Amanda over the car's roof as they climbed out and locked the doors. "He was good, though, wasn't he? Did you catch his name?"

"No. I mean, no, I didn't hear his name. He was good."

"And he looked straight, too." Rhonda sighed. "Ah, well. He was probably married, anyway, with three kids."

Amanda laughed. "Rhonda, I adore you. You never change. But it makes me cringe to visualize Charlie's reaction if he had hired the guy and then caught you coming on to him."

Rhonda smiled unrepentantly. She had an unabashed sexuality and charm that attracted men by the droves, but she was easily bored once their attention was captured. And after two consecutive if brief affairs with co-workers, both of which had resulted in sulks and diminished performances on the part of the men when she had said good-bye, Charlie had taken her aside and had told her in no uncertain terms that the next time he saw her dallying with one of his dancers he would personally bounce her down the figurative front steps of the Cabaret on her pretty little tail. In addition, he had declared furiously, he would see to it that she never worked another club in Reno.

And Charlie had enough clout to follow through on his threats.

"Amanda, you can be a real mood buster," Rhonda replied cheerfully. "I mean, a girl can still dream, can't she?"

"Well, sure, I suppose so. But, what about the love of your life?" Amanda asked. "What about Chad?" She fluttered her eyes up to heaven. Chad was the man who had wanted to meet Rhonda the night of Pete's party. He and Rhonda had been conducting a hot and heavy affair ever since.

Rhonda inhaled slowly and deeply and her eyes closed. She bit her lip, licked it, and smiled. When her eyes opened again, they were only at half mast. "Um . . . yes, Chad. Perhaps you're right, Amanda." She turned at the stairs that led up to her apartment. "Well, g'night, kiddo. See you tomorrow."

If there was one thing you could count on, Amanda decided humorously, it was that Rhonda would never, ever change. Amanda was still smiling when she let herself into her apartment, and reflectively, she touched her fingers to her lips, feeling the upward curve as though it were something rare and precious. How long had it been since she had last felt so carefree? Thinking about it as she pushed away from the door she had closed behind her and leaned against, she realized that this was the first time since she had identified Maryanne's body that an entire twenty-four hours had passed without her harboring one single thought of murder; blunt-spoken, unyielding cops with unreadable eyes; the potential for personal danger; or bitchy newswomen full of questions heavily laced with nasty innuendo.

She could even smile over the latter, and that was saying something. She hadn't gone looking for that interview, but she had hoped that if she gave an exclusive, the rest of the press and television people who had been hounding her would finally leave her alone.

She wasn't exactly sure what she had expected the experience to be like, but she certainly had never dreamed it would turn out the way it had. Lord, she had itched to smack that woman! But it was the very fact that she had managed to subdue that impulse that contributed to her good feeling. Having held on to her composure was something of a personal triumph for her, and overall, she was quite proud of the manner in which she had handled that interview.

Her impeccable manners and natural inclination for passive resistance rather than outright rebellion usually enabled her to control her outward reaction to provocation. Like everyone, however, she had her tolerance threshold, and nothing irritated her quite so quickly as an unwarranted lack of justness, or people who dealt in malicious insinuations based on pure, unadulterated speculation. Faced with a situation laden with those properties, she had been known to react first and think second. That she had controlled herself in this particular instance was a victory important to no one but herself, but one in which she took pride.

And obviously she had done something right, for the press hadn't bothered her since her interview. Then, too, there was that additional little bonus: she had escaped suffering the guilt that always plagued her when she failed to be mannerly.

She was smiling when she went to bed that evening, and happy still when she dragged her weary body out of bed the next day at noon. Throwing on old clothes, Amanda hummed as she buzzed around her apartment, cleaning. Life was getting back on track, and she reveled in it.

It was therefore all the more disconcerting when her doorbell rang at one-thirty that afternoon and she opened it to Lieutenant MacLaughlin. He was standing on her threshold, Buddy Holly glasses gleaming with a fresh cleaning, dressed in his usual suit of Scottish wool, pristine starched shirt, and a tightly knotted tie, but incongruously supporting the plump belly of a small brown-and-black dog in his big hand.

"Is your apartment still available, lass?" he asked without preamble. "Ace and I want to rent it."

CHAPTER
7

Amanda stared at the large man and little dog on her doorstep as though they were from another planet. Her feeling of well-being deflated like a balloon with a slow leak, and she shivered in the blustery wind blowing through her open doorway.

"I didn't know you had a dog."

"I didna set out to," he replied and glanced down at the dog lying trustingly in his grasp. "It just sort of happened." He scratched the dog between the ears with his free hand.

"Oh?" She watched the blissful expression on the dog's face at the treatment; then, slowly, she raised her eyes to Tristan's. "How does one 'just sort of' acquire a pet?"

"May we come in, lass? You're losing all your heat."

"What? Oh! Yes, sure, I guess so." Amanda stepped back, feeling a little less than brilliant. Nothing like a nice, decisive statement to get your day rolling right, she decided in self-derision. Lord protect the inarticulate.

She led the way into the living room and gestured for Tristan to sit down. He did, resting the dog on his knee. The mutt sprawled happily, shedding short black and brown hairs indiscriminately on the fine wool of Tristan's slacks.

Amanda remained standing and stared at them, trying to reconcile Tristan's apparent lack of concern to the type of man she thought he was. Why, the dog wasn't even cute. She could picture the stern, humorless man she imagined Lieutenant MacLaughlin to be with a handsome breed of dog like a German shepherd or a Doberman pinscher, but this little mutt wasn't any breed that she recognized. His biggest distinction was his complete lack of eminence. He was just short and fat and kind of homely, except for his coloring, which was quite lovely. His coat was a rich, deep brown with clearly defined markings of black on three of his chubby feet, in a saddle across his back, and in a circle around his left eye.

The rest of him was like something out of Dr. Seuss.

Amanda smiled suddenly and stepped closer. She collapsed cross-legged in front of Tristan's chair and reached out to chuck the dog under his chin. Ace opened one eye and rotated his neck to allow her greater access. He wasn't really ugly at all, Amanda decided. "He's what Teddy used to call a D.A.W.G. kinda dog," she said and grinned. "How did you end up with him?"

Tristan wondered who Teddy was. Damned nancy name for a bloke with the slightest shred of masculinity, if you asked him. He tried to imagine letting someone call him Tristy and had to suppress a snort. Not bloody likely.

Tristan noticed Amanda looking at him quizzically and realized he hadn't answered her. What was the question, then? Oh, yes, how he had come to acquire the wee pup.

"It was outside a building where we were conducting our investigation," he began, and Amanda felt the warmth that the dog's presence had imbued on the moment turn to chill at the unwelcome reminder of this man's profession. Watching him with the pup, she had forgotten for a moment that Lieutenant MacLaughlin was actually a ruthless individual.

"We came out and found a man abusin' the poor mite," the ruthless individual said, and then added with some heat, "You can see he's just a wee little bugger, and the great sod was kicking him and knockin' him about the head. Well, lass, I must say I don't care for bullies much, so I objected. Seems the mon was attempting to teach the wee doggie some tricks, and when Ace didna catch on promptly, the bloke threw a bloody bloomin' fit. Joe Cash pointed out nice and calmly that whipping was no way to teach anything to anyone, and I pointed out less than calmly that if the bloke kept it up I could slam his arse in jail, and dead happy it would make me, too." His voice was flat with remembered anger.

"And did you?" She would have liked to have been there to see the unflappable, enigmatic lieutenant lose his temper. She hadn't thought he did such things. He was so controlled, it hadn't even occurred to her he might have a temper to lose.

"No. The mon slapped the pup's leash in my hand and said if I thought I was such an effin' expert then I was effin' well welcome to try my hand with Ace. He was a right charmer, that one. Then he bloody scarpered. Mind if I take my jacket off, lass?"

Amanda didn't want him to make himself at home, but social politeness was too firmly ingrained for her to say so. She rose to take his jacket, then stared with horrified fascination at the smooth butt of his gun nestled in its underarm shoulder holster. He was a policeman, so she supposed she should not have been surprised to see that he carried a firearm. In truth, she couldn't have been more shocked if she had suddenly spied a rat peeking out from under his armpit.

Tristan saw the repugnance she couldn't hide, and he could have punched a hole in the nearest wall. Damn it to bloody hell. For once in his misbegotten life he was in the presence of a woman of her sort—not a barfly or a whore, but a woman an entire world removed—and he'd had something to say. He hadn't even had to search for the words; they had just appeared, with surprising ease. She was the type of elegant, self-assured woman with whom he was generally at his worst, yet he had actually been sitting here conversing with her about subjects other than business, and his tongue hadn't tied itself into a dozen knots in the process.

Well, they said a picture was worth a thousand words, and he couldn't disagree. He had been talking right along like he'd had flamin' good sense, thinking he was getting somewhere. Then he had taken off his damn coat.

Hell, yes. Worth a thousand words.

Tristan ground his teeth in bitter frustration, feeling defensive. Well, how was he supposed to know? The type of women he didn't have a problem talking to, usually those in bars, always loved his gun. They seemed to find it highly erotic. But the Charles lassie was regarding him as though he'd suddenly unzipped his fly and exposed more than a piece of hardware.

Amanda further distanced herself by backing to the chair farthest from where Tristan was sitting and slowly sinking down on the edge of it, her back ramrod straight, ankles neatly crossed, and hands resting palms up in her lap, as prim as a little girl at her first grown-up function. "Why do you want to rent my apartment?"

"I'm being bounced from my motel," he replied. "Ace took a day or two to adjust to his new surroundings, and he cried a wee bit late at night." Tristan looked fondly at the mutt slumbering on his lap. "He didna know just what was going on in his life, did he, then? The poor mite's had more than his share of knocks, I'm afraid, but verra soon he settled right in."

"But?" Amanda asked drily. In spite of herself, she was slightly charmed by this tough man's obvious affection for the homely little dog. Whoever would have guessed? She would have sworn he didn't have one human emotion in his entire body.

"But they took exception all the same, Miss Charles. And they want us out, lass. Tonight."

Amanda's heart dropped. So he had a soft spot for the mutt. So what? He was still ninety-nine percent robot. And she didn't want him around as a constant reminder of the vicious deaths of three of her fellow dancers. Not now, when she was finally starting to put it all behind her.

Still . . .

She had promised Rhonda. "Have you tried other motels?"
she asked hopefully. "There are several that accommodate
pets."

"Oh, aye, lass, that there are." Tristan's gray eyes were
unreadable behind his clear lenses. "But a dog needs a yard
to stretch his legs." He extended Ace's right rear leg to its
full three inches. "Such as they may be." His eyes raised
and impaled her. "And you have a perfect yard, fenced and
all."

"How is he with cats? Rhonda has a cat, you know, and
she wouldn't like it if your dog terrorized it." Rhonda,
Amanda knew, would give the damn cat away, even if she
had owned it for six years and loved it dearly, if it would
mean having Lieutenant MacLaughlin move in.

"Oh, Ace is a proper gent with cats. Actually, he's right
cowardly," Tristan said, and he grinned. "You may have
noticed he's not overly large, and just this morning I took
him to the park and a good-sized tom crossed our path. My
brave laddie here cowered behind my feet until the cat went
on his way."

Amanda stared at him, immobilized. She had forgotten his
smile. God, it made him look different. And momentarily,
it chased all further objections from her mind. "Very well,"
she said. "The rent's four hundred a month. The first and
last month's rent, plus a two-hundred-dollar damage deposit,
are due before you move in." She rose.

Tristan's Scottish frugality cringed at paying out a thousand
dollars all at once, but his dismay didn't show as he stood.
They made arrangements for him to move in at four, which
would give him time to check out of his motel and go to the
bank. Moments after the transaction was finalized, he bid her
good-bye and left.

Amanda closed the door behind him and sagged back
against it, running a hand through her hair.

She assured herself she hadn't just made a big mistake.
Then, why, oh why, did the thought lack conviction?

* * *

Tristan stopped by the station after vacating his motel room and withdrawing the rent money from his account at the bank. Joe Cash was there, working at a desk. He looked up as Tristan walked in.

"Hey there, Lieutenant. Got a number of messages for you." He handed the pink slips across the cluttered desk. "One guy musta called nine or ten times, wanting to talk to no one but you. But he refused to leave a name or number." Joe shrugged.

So did Tristan. Cases of this nature frequently generated a great deal of unsubstantiated rumor, gossip, and misinformation. Quite often what it generated was simple out-and-out troublemaking that was aimed at a disfavored acquaintance or spouse. There were days, particularly when the moon was full, when their phones rang off the hooks. Information of all types found its way to the police, where it became part of the chaff of the investigatory process. Occasionally, it was important. More often, it was not. And because Tristan's name was mentioned frequently on television or in the papers in connection with the case, a large percentage of the information was directed to him personally.

"How's the search for a new place coming?" asked Joe, and once he heard about Tristan's new living arrangements, he promptly offered to help him move.

"There's not much to move," Tristan said, and then he surprised himself by adding, "but you're welcome to come along. I'd appreciate the company."

He was finding it a little easier every day to make the effort with Joe. The more time he spent around him, the more he came to realize that Joe was a man in whom he could place his trust, both professionally and, more amazing still, personally.

This type of friendship was new to Tristan. His wasn't an outgoing personality at the best of times. The most he had usually managed in the past was an occasional drink with coworkers after a long day's labor, and even those occasions hadn't always been the greatest of successes. The men with whom he drank generally ended up talking about their families or their women, and as he had neither, he never had much to contribute. Oh, aye, he had sexual encounters, but they were short-lived affairs, containing no real commitment. It wasn't quite the same thing.

By putting into his career the time he might otherwise have spent with others, he had quickly advanced, and loneliness had become an established fact of life never closely examined. He didn't want to analyze it now. But he didn't mind getting to know Joe Cash; not at all. He was a comfortable man to be around, and easy to talk to, as well.

"Well, hey there, Ace," Joe said as they stopped in front of Tristan's recently issued car in the parking lot moments later. He tapped on the passenger window to attract the dog's attention. In the time it took Tristan to walk around the car, climb into the driver's seat, and then lean across to unlock the door and push it open, Joe directed nonsensical kissing sounds through the window at Ace and produced a patter of sweet talk that almost, but not quite, induced the dog to raise his head up off the upholstery. Climbing in, Joe edged Ace over to make room for himself on the front seat, talking all the while. "This here's gotta be the sleepin'est dog I've ever met. So, Acer, what's this I hear about you goin' to live with a whole bevy of beauties?" He scratched the mutt's head and Ace rolled over on his back, ecstatic. "You're a sly ole dog, aren't you?"

Tristan glanced over at Joe. He smiled slightly. "Do two women constitute a bevy?"

"Lord, yes, Lieutenant. They do when they come packaged like the Misses Charles and Smith," Joe replied. "Man, those pretty, pretty little rear ends. It gives me palpitations just thinking about it." He grinned comfortably at Tristan's raised eyebrows. "I guess you would have had to have met my ex-wife to appreciate my appreciation. When Carol walked, her butt just sorta rolled around in those polyester pants she favored, like two angry tomcats in a burlap bag. And when

Carol ran . . .'' Joe shook his head as though it simply defied description. Then he sighed happily. "I tell ya true, Mac-Laughlin, I could just sit by the hour and do nothin' but eyeball a dancer's buns.''

Tristan considered it for a moment and decided he was more of a leg man, himself, but invited Joe to drop by, whenever, to enjoy the view. He listened to Joe's easy banter until they pulled up in front of the triplex.

Without being asked, Joe reached into the trunk and dragged out the large box he had seen Tristan effortlessly heft on his shoulder at the airport the day of his arrival. "Jesus, MacLaughlin, what've you got in here?"

"My weights.''

"Weights?'' Joe deposited the box on the car's fender. "As in barbells and whatnot?'' he asked. Then he shook his head. "Naah! Nobody drags their barbells from one city to the next." He peered inside the container to see what was really there. "Well, I'll be damned—it *is* weights!''

"Aye, did I not just say so?'' Tristan was slightly irritated, unused to being the recipient of sarcastic male give and take. "Do you not work out yourself, then, mon? How can you hope to keep up with the bloody buggers on the street if you don't stay in shape?''

"Well, sure, I work out,'' Joe replied and stooped down to get his shoulder beneath the box. With a grunt, he rose. "I just can't quite imagine dragging this shit with me everywhere I go. I guess if it were me, I'da probably just stored it and bought myself some more in the next town.''

Heat crept up Tristan's neck. He had a definite problem when it came to spending his hard-earned money. He knew it. Privately, he was even somewhat embarrassed by the tendency, but he couldn't seem to do anything about it. It was probably the result of going too long without any money at all. For years, he had scrimped and cut corners and taught himself not to want. He had forced himself to save every last penny, setting goals and slowly attaining them. He was dead proud of how far he'd come, too. Yet, now that he was free to loosen some of the restraints he had imposed on himself, he found it was a difficult habit to reverse. He had a respectable bank balance now, but he still didn't know how to spend his money simply for the sheer bloody enjoyment of it.

Tristan rolled his shoulders uncomfortably as he followed Joe down the stairs. No, that wasn't exactly true. He liked suits of fine Scottish wool, so he'd bought himself a few. And, hell, yes, he had bought . . .

Nothing. That was it, basically—just the suits. The rest of his wardrobe was certainly nothing to brag about, and his car was a rust bucket, which was why he hadn't bothered to drive it to Reno. He had feared it wouldn't make the trip. And his apartment in Seattle . . . Tristan sighed. *Oh, bloody hell, mon, admit it. The Union Gospel Mission for the homeless is probably furnished with more style than my apartment.*

Well, then. He'd have to stop being such a miser, is all. But he would bloody well not apologize for the thriftiness that was too ingrained for him to discard a perfectly good set of weights in one town, when he knew damn well he would be needing them in another.

Packing Ace in one hand and his cases in the other, Tristan nearly tromped on Joe's heels, lost in a fog of angry confusion. What the hell was this town doing to him? He had never felt a need to apologize for himself before he'd come here. He had always figured he was who he bloody well was, and if others didn't like it, then that was their problem. It was much the same attitude that had prevented him from correcting his speech to sound more Americanized. As long as people could understand him well enough without straining themselves, he didn't see the point in trying to sound like someone he bloody well wasn't.

But since his arrival in Reno, he could feel himself changing. He suddenly wanted things he had never wanted before—things he had never allowed himself to want. And he was suddenly discontented with other aspects of his life that had never before upset him. Worst of all, his career was no longer enough in itself to occupy his mind day and night. He didn't like this new turn of events at all.

Amanda met the two policemen at her front door. Between the time she had agreed to rent the apartment to Lieutenant MacLaughlin and his reappearance with his possessions, she had done some thinking, and she had decided to make the best of the situation. Rhonda was undoubtedly right when she had stated that they would all be much safer with the very large MacLaughlin in residence—gun and all, Amanda admitted grudgingly. And maybe once she had gotten to know him a bit, he wouldn't seem so remote and cold. After all, he had acted pretty human with the puppy, hadn't he? And anyone with a smile like his couldn't be totally robotic.

Twenty minutes later, Amanda was convinced Mac-Laughlin's smile had been nothing more than a figment of her imagination. With sheer force of will, she prevented herself from slamming the door behind her when she left Maryanne's—MacLaughlin's—apartment. Her heart was thumping. She knew her color was high—she could feel the heat pulsating in her cheeks—and she felt as wrung out as if she had just completed a brand new routine.

The man didn't have one human emotion in his entire body. He was aloof, and uncommunicative, and cold, and hard, and unfriendly, and . . . and a giant pain in the butt! Amanda let herself into her own apartment, stalked over to the couch, and flopped down in a huff, picking up a pillow, which she clutched to her chest.

She had really gone out of her way to be cordial—fat lot of good it had done her. "Huh!" Amanda snorted. When she had smiled at him, had he smiled back?

He had not.

She had pointed out features in his new apartment, and he had just looked at her with those cool, analytical eyes of his. He hadn't indicated by so much as a word or a look whether or not he was pleased with them. He had ripped off his jacket and hung it neatly in the closet, then he'd looked at her as if he dared her to say something about the ugly gun snugged up under his armpit. Damn the man. That look—God, she could see it still. He had all but put his hands on his head and spread his elbows wide to flaunt the deadly weapon in her face. She didn't understand why he had suddenly seemed so determined to irritate her, but the temptation had been sugar-sweet for a brief moment to make use of the hassock to Maryanne's leather chair, which had been positioned right behind MacLaughlin's knees. Every old Three Stooges episode she had ever seen had flashed through her mind, and that old hassock had beckoned madly. She could almost swear she had heard a little voice whispering, "Do it, do it: push him over."

Somehow, she had managed to resist the impulse, mostly because she'd figured MacLaughlin was just cold-bloodedly mean enough to retaliate in a way she wouldn't like. Charlie would skin her alive if she went and got herself shot.

But she would sure like to know what made him so damn wonderful that he couldn't even respond to a simple, friendly overture. She'd tried. No one could say she hadn't tried. But obviously, the big, dumb cop didn't care to be neighborly, and that was his less-than-subtle way of telling her to keep her distance.

Well, that was just dandy with her. It wasn't as though she'd had any burning desire to be his good buddy in the first place.

Except, dammit, for a brief space of time this afternoon, she had sort of hoped it would be different. Lord help her, but there was something about the way he smiled—like a window suddenly opening to shed light into what had been unpenetrable darkness.

Amanda tossed the pillow aside and stood up. *Well, snap out of it, girl,* she told herself. *Obviously, you were dreaming, and that's not like you. The much-vaunted smile is plainly a fluke, totally wasted on a man with all the fire and emotion of a computer.*

* * *

The man had discovered that it was not that difficult to glean important information from the abundance of current gossip. The dimly lighted downtown bar was a favored gathering place for the dancers from most of the main lounges in the larger surrounding hotels, and all that was required of him was to spend a portion of each day in it. All he needed to do was slouch in his chair or on a stool at the bar, curve his mouth up in an easy smile, stand a round of drinks occasionally, and keep his mouth shut and his ears open.

On occasion he had to vary his routine. During those rare incidents when he had to do some talking of his own, however, it was only to pass along a little gossip he had heard from a source other than the one to whom he was currently speaking, and then it was only to maintain an even keel. After all, it wouldn't do for someone to notice that he never contributed, merely listened.

For the most part, however, he lingered on the edges of small groups or gatherings. He had perfected the ability to appear a natural part of nearly any crowd he had chosen. It had only failed him once, when he had tried to blend into the fringes of a party made up of a group of long-time friends celebrating one of their number's last days of freedom as an unmarried man. Nobody knew him, and a few had wondered out loud who he was and what he was doing hanging around, before he had quickly moved on.

But this afternoon, most of the men who were gathered around the bar were just your usual mix of dancers from several different lounges. Most of them were casually acquainted with one another, but no one seemed to know anyone else real well. The man gazed at the television mounted on the wall behind the bar, pretending an interest in the early news. So far, nothing had been said that was remotely useful. Mostly there was a lot of talk about women, and which ones would do what.

Suddenly, his eyes focused in on the screen and he grew

more alert. He had to concentrate to recapture his indolent slouch. He picked up his drink, and his elbows spread wide on the bar as he cradled it in both hands, holding it before his face. He reached for the battered pack of cigarettes on the bar and fished one out. It was a rare occasion when he befouled the temple that was his body with noxious fumes. Mostly, he just carried them as a prop. They came in handy as an icebreaker to be offered to whomever he was sitting closest, or to ask for a light for himself as a means of opening a conversation. But at this moment he felt in need of the camouflage that the cloud of smoke would provide.

It was *him*, up there on the screen. His adversary. The media liked to make a big production out of his coming to Reno, but the man at the bar knew that in the final analysis, it wouldn't make a bit of difference. *He* was invincible.

"Say, isn't that MacLaughlin?" asked a dancer two stools down. "Harry, turn that up for a minute, will ya?"

The bartender turned up the volume, and the conversations in the bar petered out for the few moments the broadcast was on. When it was finished, the television's volume was decreased once again and conversations resumed.

"I saw him at a party at Pete Schriber's once," the dancer two stools down said. "A few weeks back. Heard he was invited there by Rhonda Smith. Leastwise, he was dirty dancing with her." He took a sip of his drink. "Wasn't half bad, either . . . for a cop."

"Hell, man," said a man farther down the bar. "Rhonda Smith'd make anyone look good. Wouldn't mind a little horizontal dirty dancin' with that one, myself. Heard she's *real* good."

"Isn't she the blonde," the man asked, "dances at . . ."

"Nah, you're probably thinking of Amanda Charles," the dancer down at the end of the bar replied. "They're friends. But ya might as well roll up your tongue and tuck it back in your mouth, cuz they're about as different as night and day. Amanda's savin' it. Nobody knows quite what for, but there's about a hundred guys out there wouldn't mind finding out.

Rhonda's got dark hair, about yea long. They both dance for the Cabaret, which I wouldn't mind doin' myself, I can tell ya. Lately Rhonda's been dating Chad Steerwhiler, who dances for Bally's. I've got a buddy who's a friend of his, and according to him, Chad says that Rhonda . . .''

The conversation died a natural death about five minutes later. The man at the bar ostensibly maintained his end of the next few exchanges to eliminate the possibility of someone, somewhere down the road, linking him with the names Rhonda Smith and Amanda Charles.

He was smiling triumphantly when he finally scooped up his change, picked up his cigarettes and stuffed them into a jacket pocket, then turned to walk away.

''Stop the music, Lennie! Now, dammit! Stop the friggin' music!''

Lennie raised his fingers from the keys midnote, and silence descended over the rehearsal hall as the dancers stumbled to a halt. Charlie strode up to the stage and stood, hands on hips, glaring up across the footlights.

''Amanda, are you having trouble staying awake?''

''No.''

''Well, you coulda fooled me, sister,'' he snarled. ''Dammit to hell, Amanda! What's the matter with you? If this is just too, too boring for you, if dancing is just too much work, then go find yourself a nice waitressing job! Do something, because you're screwing up the rest of the line!'' He turned and stomped back to his table, arrogantly snapping his fingers over his shoulder to resume the music.

Amanda blinked back tears. This was the third time in less than half an hour that Charlie had screamed at her. Her energy level was zilch today and her extensions had been halfhearted at best, so she could understand his exasperation. But that didn't necessarily make it any easier to accept the verbal abuse he seemed to take such delight in heaping upon anyone foolish enough to make mistakes on his time.

June, standing next to her in line, surreptitiously touched

her arm in sympathy, and Amanda grimaced ruefully before she doggedly directed all her concentration toward getting through rehearsal with her job intact. It felt like hours before Charlie finally called it a day.

The dressing room was steamy with the sudden preponderance of sweaty, overheated bodies. Rhonda slumped down on the stool next to where Amanda stood stuffing her exercise clothes into her bag. She rested her elbows back on the dressing table shelf and swung her hips gently from side to side on the plastic-upholstered stool anchored in front of the mirror. "You really stunk today, kiddo."

"What a rotten thing to say!" June protested hotly from three places down. She set down her eyeliner brush and glared at Rhonda. "Amanda's the best darn dancer in the troupe!"

"Usually," Rhonda amended. "Usually she is, June. But she wasn't today. You know it, too, even if you don't want to admit it. But just ask Mandy Rose here if she thought she was any good."

"Rhonda's right," Amanda admitted. "I was really lousy today, June. A first-year student could've danced rings around me."

"You're damn straight they could've," Rhonda agreed. "And I want to know why, Amanda. I've seen you dance when you have your period and your iron level is next to nonexistent. I've seen you dance when you're sick, when you're blue, when you're dead on your feet from being without sleep for too long. Kiddo, all you gotta do is name it. You've had it and still danced better than most of us do on our best days. So, what the hell gives today?"

Amanda had been pulling on her clothes during Rhonda's tirade. She was aware that everyone but June had drifted out of the dressing room singly or in pairs, and, avoiding the eyes of the two remaining women, she sat on the floor and fiddled with the soft leather straps of her skimpy red shoes. One refused to button properly, and finally she gave up and looked up at Rhonda. Her eyes were bleak. "I haven't been sleeping too well lately."

"Do tell," Rhonda snapped. "A blind idiot could see that. Tell me something I don't already know, Amanda Rose. Tell me how come?"

"I guess because lately I've been thinking a lot about Teddy, and it's hard to get to sleep. Then, when I do sleep, I dream all the time."

"Oh, hell. I should've known," Rhonda snarled, and June asked, "Who's Teddy?"

"My sister," Amanda replied.

"Her goddamn albatross is more like it," Rhonda stated flatly.

Amanda surged to her feet. "You take that back, Rhonda Smith. That's a lousy thing to say!"

"Yeah? Well, maybe it is, Amanda, but the way I see it, it's nothing short of the truth! The only times I have ever seen you blue enough to just chuck aside every damn thing you have ever worked for is when you've been thinking of Teddy. When are you going to let yourself off the hook and admit that nothing you could've said or done at the time would have changed a damn thing?"

Like a spectator at a tennis match, June's head turned from one protagonist to the other. "Ah'm confused," she murmured.

"So's Amanda," Rhonda snapped. "Let's go get us a drink and I'll set you both straight."

"I don't want a drink," Amanda replied belligerently. "And who the hell are you to set anyone straight, anyway? Were you there?" Rhonda opened her mouth to speak, but Amanda poked her in the chest with her finger and continued, "Well, I was, and I know I should've tried harder to find the right words to change her mind. If I had just tried a little bit harder, I could have made a difference, Rhonda. I could have."

"Bullshit!" Rhonda roared. "Bullshit, bullshit, *bullshit*! Once your parents messed in her affairs, and once Teddy made up her mind and set things in motion, you had about as much chance of patching things up as I have of joining a nunnery. You did every damn thing you possibly could have, Mandy. And I sure as hell refuse to stand here and watch you beat yourself black and blue over something you had about a snowball's chance in hell of controlling. Now, fix your damn shoe, and let's go get that drink!''

Amanda stood fast, glaring at Rhonda. Then that tiny corner of her brain that harbored a love of the absurd got the best of her. She had a sudden flash of the picture they'd present if anyone peeked into the room. She and Rhonda standing nose to nose, yelling at each other, while poor June stood by, completely bewildered. Rhonda's chest was heaving with indignation. Her brown eyes were shooting sparks, her cheeks were flushed, and she looked like a warrior in spandex armor. Poor June looked like she was wondering how she had happened to fall down this particular rabbit hole, and she herself probably looked like a not-too-bright schoolgirl, with her flopping shoe strap and her uncombed, tangled hair.

''Okay, you win,'' she said with a small half smile of surrender. ''We'll go get a drink and hash this out.'' She picked up a brush and started working out the snarls.

''Oh, goody,'' June said. ''Does this mean someone's gonna tell me what the hell's goin' on heah?''

''Yeah, sure.'' Amanda eyed June's reflection in the mirror. ''Why not? I'm not real big on spilling my guts, but maybe it'll help to go over the whole sorry saga of the Charles sisters.'' She sent a sour look Rhonda's way. ''Although I don't see how, since I regret the last time I opened my big mouth.''

''No you don't, kid,'' Rhonda replied confidently. ''I refuse to let you wallow in your masochistic depression and become self-destructive, and deep down, in your heart of hearts, you love me for it.''

Deep down in her heart of hearts, Amanda did, but she was still too irritated with Rhonda to admit it out loud. She hated it when she felt Rhonda was attacking Teddy. But in a weird sort of way, it was almost like hearing *Teddy* speak.

The very first thing that had attracted her to Rhonda had been her striking similarity to her sister. Oh, not in looks. Physically, they were nothing alike. But when it came to personality, they were practically twins. Rhonda was so much like Teddy had been. She was exuberant and rowdy, outspoken and affectionate. She was sometimes crass beyond belief, but always totally unafraid to speak her mind. And in a crazy way, Amanda knew that if the roles had somehow been reversed today, Teddy would have stood nose to nose with her in the exact same manner that Rhonda had.

It was a scary thought.

But comforting.

CHAPTER
8

B uy you ladies a drink?''
     The three women glanced up from their conversation. Standing next to the table was an attractive man in a pin-striped suit. Rhonda declined for all of them, but it was with a trace of regret that she watched him walk away. He was just her type—male.

"So, what happened when youah folks found out Teddy was pregnant?" June delicately poked through the ice cubes in her glass to fish out the cherry. She popped it in her mouth and looked up at Amanda. "Ah imagine they pitched quite a fit, huh?"

"To put it mildly." Amanda drained the last sip from her glass and, catching the waitress's eye, raised it to indicate she wanted a refill. She knew she shouldn't; she wasn't much of a drinker, and as a result, her tolerance was very low. She shrugged. Well, what the hell. She was off tonight. In fact, if she had been halfway smart, she would have avoided today's rehearsal entirely. If she had just stayed at home, she wouldn't be sitting here now, searching for a way to explain events from so far in her past she couldn't figure out why

they had chosen this particular time in her life to resurrect
themselves.

Well, no, in all honesty, that wasn't exactly true. She had
been battling a mild depression off and on ever since she had
viewed Maryanne's body at the morgue, and it had grown
harder to ignore once MacLaughlin had moved in. Because
of his size, he was highly visible, and he served as a constant
visual reminder of something she would desperately like to
forget. The current situation tended to resurrect feelings from
an old one. Which was why, despite the Cabaret not requiring
its dancers to attend rehearsals on their days off, Amanda
had found it easier to attend than to remain in the apartment
where recently she had been spending too many sleepless
nights and restless days.

June and Rhonda were sitting quietly, patiently allowing
Amanda the necessary time to sort through her feelings. She
knew they wouldn't press if she decided not to tell June the
rest of the story. But she also knew she needed to talk it out
of her system. This recently escalated mental funk was not
healthy.

Finally, she looked across the table at June and said, "You
have to understand that my parents' anger with Teddy was
nothing new. As far as they were concerned, there was little
she did that was right. Naturally, she would have liked a little
more time to make some decisions about her pregnancy before
she had to face them, but . . ." Amanda shrugged. "Teddy
was really crazy about the guy who . . . Tim was his name,
Tim Walters. She had never made the class distinctions that
were so important to Mother and Father, so she couldn't
understand why they were so appalled to discover that Tim
was a mechanic whose dream was to own his own shop."
Amanda laughed cynically. "I really think they were more
disturbed about his lack of social standing than Teddy's pregnancy. They really pitched a fit, as you call it, when she and
Tim announced their plans to get married and keep the baby.
They had wanted her to have an abortion."

Amanda's voice trailed away and June reached across the table to touch her hand. "But they didn't get married?"

"No." Amanda drained her drink and signaled for another. She laughed bitterly. "Oh, no. My parents decided to take a hand—for Theodora's own good." Her voice took on a fluting intonation that June assumed was an imitation of her mother. "So, a week before the wedding was to take place, Mother and Father took Tim into the library, where they told him that if he married Teddy, they would cut her off without a penny. But if he walked away that day, without any further contact with their daughter, they would give him the twenty-five thousand dollars he still needed for the shop that he and Teddy were saving to buy." She looked at June and her eyes were bleak. "My parents are not kind people, June. And they took great delight in informing Teddy that the Neanderthal with the grease under his fingernails, whom she so foolishly had planned to marry, was so blessed dumb he just snapped up their offer without bothering to discover that Teddy would be worth ten times that when her trust fund became available on her twenty-fifth birthday."

"Charmin'."

"Yeah, that's Mother and Father."

"Is youah sista still alive, Amanda?"

"No." Amanda's eyes filled with tears, and the drinks that she had belted back so ill-advisedly threatened to climb back up her throat. She pushed her glass away and used both hands to massage her temples. Looking up, she met Rhonda's eyes. "Dammit, I want to let it rest, Rhonda. I do. But it keeps returning to haunt me." She turned her head to look at June. "When Teddy heard how easy it had been to buy off Tim, she was bitter—*very* bitter. And she, um, she decided on the spot to have an abortion."

Amanda coughed, trying to clear the huge knot from her throat. "We sat up in her room all that night and talked— at least, I talked. Teddy didn't have much to say. I begged her not to rush into a decision of such serious consequence until she'd had a chance to calm down and think things

through. I said . . . Oh, God, I said she was in no condition
to make such an important decision and that I knew she would
regret it if she got rid of her baby, especially if she did it
before she gave herself time to calm down and view everything rationally. Frankly, I couldn't see her doing it at all.
She had actually been excited about having a baby, and abortion had never even been one of the options before Mother
and Father had gotten involved. But the point was, she
couldn't make that kind of decision in her present state of
mind. I mean, anyone could see she was in an absolute state
of shock. And she agreed. I thought she'd agreed. But when
I got home from my recital the next day, I found out she had
gone ahead and had the abortion anyway.'' Amanda reached
into her purse and pulled out a Kleenex. ''All alone, dammit,
with no one there to support her.'' Surreptitiously, she wiped
at her eyes, then blew her nose.

''And they botched it?''

''No.'' Amanda shook her head so vigorously her pale hair
flew around her head like a storm-blown cloud. ''No, it was
all very nice and safe and clinical. But as soon as she'd gone
through with it, Teddy realized she had made a dreadful
mistake. She grieved something awful. I sat with her for the
longest time, and it just broke my heart when she told me I
had been right. I didn't want to be right, June; I just didn't
want to see her hurt. I didn't want to see her do something
she wouldn't be able to live with.'' Amanda sat silently for
several moments. Finally, she looked up. ''That night when
she went to bed, she took an entire bottle of Mother's sleeping
pills.''

''Oh, shit,'' June whispered.

''I found her the next morning.'' Amanda's eyes were
totally lacking in expression. She was silent for a moment.
Then she looked at the woman across the table, and she smiled
bitterly. ''You want to know what upset my parents the most,
June? They wanted to know what on earth they were going
to tell their friends. They had encouraged Teddy to have that
abortion; then, they wanted to know what to tell their stinking

friends." Amanda pinched the bridge of her nose between her thumb and forefinger. "I stayed for Teddy's funeral. And I finished my school year so I could graduate. But then I left home, and I've never been back. God, it's been ten years now." She reached for her glass again. "Can't say that I've missed them at all. Not my parents or either of my other sisters, both of whom are regular little clones of dear old Mother and Father anyway."

"But you're still letting it affect your entire life," Rhonda pointed out.

"How do you come to that conclusion?" Amanda demanded with cool composure. "This is—what?—the second time you've seen it affect me, Rhonda. The first time was the first year we met when I was depressed on the anniversary of Teddy's death, and now, seeing Maryanne's corpse and everything, it's just sort of dredged it all up again. That's hardly my entire life."

"Okay, I'll admit that except for today, it hasn't had much of an effect on your professional life. But what about your sex life?"

"What about it?"

"You don't have one!"

"Well, excuse me. Not all of us live for sex the way you do, Rhonda. But I'm hardly a virgin."

"You might as well be. You go so long between men, I'm surprised your cherry doesn't keep growing back." Rhonda raised her glass in a mock toast. "To Amanda Charles, born-again virgin."

Amanda laughed, and she realized it had been quite a while since the last time she'd done so. It felt good. "Look, Rhonda, don't lose any sleep over it. I'm just not the passionate type, okay? I guess all the passion in the Charles family was passed out to Teddy."

Unexpectedly, June disagreed. "Ah don't believe that, sugah."

Rhonda grinned. "Me either, June-bug, but what's your reasoning?"

"Her dancin'. No one can dance like that and still be lackin' in passion."

"You give my ability to dance more credit than it deserves, June." Amanda sat straighter in her chair and signaled the waitress once again. She wouldn't have believed it, but the absurdity of this conversation was making her feel much, much better. "It certainly isn't superior to anyone else in the troupe."

"The heck it's not," June disagreed. "You always seem to catch on to everything quicker than anyone else. Youah kicks are higher, youah jetés are longer, and youah always suggestin' new routines. Why Charlie has even been known to actually listen to youah opinions!"

"Yeah, Charlie's got a tender spot for Amanda," Rhonda agreed.

Amanda ignored Rhonda's comment and addressed herself to June. "That is really nice of you to say, June, although I can't say I agree. But even if it were true, that doesn't have anything to do with passion," she argued. "It just means I'm a competent technician."

"Bull," Rhonda said, and June nodded her head vigorously in agreement. "To anyone who has ever seen you dance, Mandy, that just won't wash. I think Teddy's experience reinforced your own natural reserve, and you've gotten into the habit of pushing men away. You throw up fences, you're friendly but distant with all the guys, and you've got yourself all convinced that hot blood doesn't run in your veins. But you're passionate, all right. You just haven't tapped into the right guy to bring it out in you. Which is hardly surprising, since the few men you do date are the easily managed type. You can deny it to yourself all you want, Amanda, but when you dance you give yourself away. All that sexuality you're repressing is out there for the world to see. Why do you think the guys love partnering you? Sure, you're one of the best dancers in the troupe, but it's more than that, sweetie. And why do you think they've got that pool going about when you will tum-

ble?'' Rhonda hardened her heart against Amanda's wince.
"They know. You can't sublimate it into dance forever,
though, kiddo. What you really need, more than anything
else, Mandy Rose, is a good, raunchy roll in the hay, and
I know just the man to give you one, too.''

"Oh, yeah? And who might that be?"

"Your new tenant, the good lieutenant.''

Amanda's body went icy in shock. "You're joking!"

"No, ma'am, I'm dead serious. I bet Lieutenant Mac-
Laughlin could bounce you around a bed like nobody's business.'' Her eyes grew dreamy. "Umm, that man. What you
wanna bet he knows just how to make the girls scream for
more?"

Amanda's nose tilted disdainfully. "You take him, then."

"Don't think I wouldn't, Mandy Rose . . . if Chad wasn't
in the picture. Hell, maybe even then, if MacLaughlin showed
the slightest bit of interest. Chad is beginning to lose his
charm anyway. But MacLaughlin's not interested in me,
kiddo. You're the one he's simply dying to love up.''

"You're crazy," Amanda whispered, appalled at the vivid
imagery that had sprung full-blown in her mind, yet surprisingly, a little excited by it, too. What would it be like to see
him come alive, to see all that icy control ripped away?

"Okay, if you say so," Rhonda said and shrugged. "But
that cutie he hangs out with, the bald guy with the big
mustache—Detective Cash? I know he agrees with me. I've
seen him eyeballing the lieutenant, then you, and then the
lieutenant again. And he isn't fooled by that aloof act
MacLaughlin puts on when he's around you any more than
I am. He's hot for you, all right. Trust me. I have radar when
it comes to these sorta things.''

"The thought of MacLaughlin and me in bed would be
funny, if it wasn't so pathetic,'' Amanda said disparagingly.
"I don't think he's ever had an emotion in his life that wasn't
preprogrammed, and goodness knows, sex isn't at the top of
my list of essentials. Not exactly my idea of the sizzler of
the century, Rhonda. I can see the headlines now, though."

Her fingers fanned wide in front of her face. "*RoboCop Meets Indifferent Woman: Millions Yawn.* You couldn't even sell it to the Inquirer."

"Ooh, I think you're seriously underestimating the man, Amanda," Rhonda disagreed. "And I know damn well you're underestimating yourself. Listen. Let me set up a little scenario for you. Just suspend your disbelief and your inhibitions for a moment and use your imagination. Okay, here we have two perfect physical specimens . . ."

Amanda blushed, and Rhonda almost hooted with delight. She *knew* it! Yes, yes, yes, she *knew* it! Despite her protests, little Mandy Rose hadn't failed to notice the good lieutenant. Exerting a great deal of self-control, Rhonda managed not to gloat, continuing in an even tone, "We put them together in a room. Add a little wine . . ."

"Rhonda, please . . ."

"And maybe a few strategically placed candles . . ."

"Rhon-da . . ."

"Quit interrupting. You'll definitely need a place that will lend itself to lovemaking. Doesn't have to be a bed, necessarily."

Amanda rolled her eyes.

"Stop that," Rhonda commanded. "Did I mention you're naked? He removed your clothes, because he knew if he didn't strip you down fast, you'd cut and run. Okay, kid. I've set the stage. Now, voyeurism isn't my thing, so this is where I fade out and the two of you take over."

"In that case, we're already in trouble, because I sure don't know what to do next."

"He's the blunt-spoken, forceful type, Mandy, so you don't have to sweat it. Ooh, kiddo, I can hear him now, telling you exactly how he likes it."

"How ducky. And if I don't follow his instructions explicitly, he'll probably whip out his gun and blow me away."

"Interesting choice of words, Amanda."

Amanda shivered. "Could we change the subject, please? This one's making me nervous."

Rhonda grinned knowingly at the red bloom on Amanda's cheeks, but mercifully, she didn't pursue it and the conversation moved on to less personal matters. The talk was inconsequential, but they laughed a great deal and Amanda's mood was worlds removed from the one with which she had started the day by the time Rhonda and June had to leave to return to the Cabaret.

Amanda was half convinced her depression would return if she went straight home with nothing better to occupy herself than an aimless wander around her apartment. She decided to risk twenty dollars at a blackjack table. By the time she called a cab at midnight, she had somehow beat the odds and made herself a thirty-seven-dollar profit. It wasn't a fortune, she knew, but she was still elated. She was also decidedly tipsy, thanks in part to the additional free drinks the casino had supplied as she had played cards. When the cab pulled up to her curb, she decided to take a short walk around the yard to clear her head.

Amanda heard the faint sound of Ace barking from inside MacLaughlin's apartment as she picked her way through the deeper shadows cast by the high rockery that bordered her yard. She shivered in the chill night air. As usual, the only predictable element of Reno's climate was its complete unpredictability. It had been sunny and mild when she had left home this afternoon and she hadn't thought to grab a jacket. And naturally, since she wasn't prepared, the temperature must have dropped nearly forty degrees. That wasn't at all unusual for this town, of course, but it was still a nuisance. Oh well, she decided philosophically, at least there were side benefits. Her head, as a case in point, seemed to be clearing quite satisfactorily as a result of the chill air. She would simply complete the process indoors with a nice, hot bath. Ooh, yes. She smiled in anticipation. A deep, hot bath with a generous handful of scented bath beads tossed in for good measure.

Turning away from the dense pools of darkness that comprised the areas away from the lighted walks, Amanda took a cautious step forward and bumped up against a large, hard body. A hand clamped down on her arm, and she felt a warm trickle down the inside of her thighs as the shock of discovering she wasn't alone loosened her bladder. Humiliated at her body's loss of control, furious and scared, she struck out wildly and opened her mouth to scream, hoping against hope that MacLaughlin was home and would hear her in time. But although she felt her fist connect, a tough-skinned hand clamped over her mouth before she could utter a sound.

Panicked, Amanda went crazy. She bit at the hand covering her mouth; she slammed her knee up between her assailant's legs in an attempt to disable him; she struck at him with fists and fingernails. But he was big—so big. He whirled her around and pulled her back against his body. She kicked backward and bucked wildly against the arms restraining her. Her eyes strained in the darkness. Oh, God, was she going to die like Maryanne and those other two dancers? Her assailant's breath whistled harshly and it was a moment before Amanda realized she recognized the voice growling in her ear.

"It's MacLaughlin, Miss Charles; it's MacLaughlin." Tristan loosened the hand over her mouth, but he wasn't prepared to take it away entirely until he was satisfied she knew who he was. The way she was still struggling made it evident it hadn't yet sunk in. He gave her a small shake. "Amanda! Settle down, darlin'; it's only me. It's Mac-Laughlin."

"Mcmmphlin?" It was MacLaughlin? Here she'd been trying to scream for his help, and it was *he* from whom she had needed rescuing? God, she'd nearly had a heart attack! One of Tristan's fingers had slid into the moist recess of Amanda's mouth when his grip on her relaxed, and with vicious intent she bit down hard.

"Ow! Bloody hell!" Tristan released her. "What'd you do that for?"

Amanda whirled around in fury. She took a swing at him, but, sucking on his injured finger, he ducked. The ease with

which he evaded her blow made her livid and she waded in
with all ten fingernails bared, prepared to strip the skin from
his face. "You bastard! You lousy, lousy bastard!" Tears of
fright and relief and rage splashed down her cheeks.

Tristan caught both her wrists in his hands and forced them
down to her sides. "What the bloody hell were you doing
skulking out in the garden at this time of night?" he demanded
violently. He clasped both wrists in one hand and clumsily
wiped the tears from her cheeks with the other. Dammit, he
had planned to apologize for scaring her so badly, but the
more he thought about how easily she could have been taken
had he actually been the killer they sought, the angrier he
became. His usual and accustomed objectivity had disappeared somewhere during their scuffle. Cautiously, he loosened her wrists, and she yanked them free.

"It's my bloody yard and I'll walk in it if I damn well
please," Amanda spit out furiously, whipping her hair back
from her face. "How dare you scare me like that—how dare
you!"

"I'll dare more than that if I ever see you put yourself at
risk like that again, lassie! I'll bloody well turn you over my
knee and beat your pretty little arse until you canna sit down!"

"Ooh!" Amanda stared at him, maddened by his ego.
"I'm sick to death of you manhandling me whenever you get
the urge . . ."

"Tough!" he roared. "If you don't like bein' manhandled,
stay out of dark corners! And another thing—why the
bloomin' hell are there no floodlights out in the corners of
this yard? There's a bloody murderer on the loose and, except
for the sidewalk, it's dark as a peat bog out here. I want that
rectified immediately."

"You want? *You want!* Just who the hell do you think you
are, MacLaughlin, my daddy?"

Tristan was outraged. "Your daddy?" he snarled. Quick
as a cat, he reached forward and buried his fingers in her
hair, gripping her skull in his large hands and tilting it back
until her throat arched. *"Your daddy?"* He'd give her a

demonstration that ought to prove he wasn't some old man bawling out his daughter. "Lass, did your daddy ever do this?" His head lowered with obvious intent.

Did he think he was going to kiss her? Just like that, after scaring ten years off her life and making her wet her pants? The hell!

"Get your hands off me, MacLaughlin!" Amanda demanded fiercely, reaching up and grasping his wrists, trying to pry his hands away from her head. It was like wrestling with warm, hairy granite; they didn't budge. She took a quick step backward, attempting to throw him off balance, but it was a less than successful tactic, as he simply took a step forward. She could feel his breath hot on her mouth. "Damn you, let me go!"

"Tristan?" The voice from the sidewalk was breathy and feminine. "Are you out there? Who are you talking to?"

Tristan released Amanda so quickly she staggered. While she was still reeling, off balance, he swore under his breath and turned toward the lighted walk. "Go back inside, Bunny," he growled. "I'll be right in."

Amanda peered around him and watched as a pretty brunette in a pink frilly dress whirled on her stiletto heels and walked back toward Tristan's apartment. "Obedient, isn't she," she muttered. "Does she come when you whistle, too?"

"Verra funny," Tristan snapped.

"Bunny, huh?" Amanda edged her way around his large body, moving closer to the lighted walks and safety. "Cute name."

Tristan took a threatening step toward her. The light from the porch glinted off the lenses of his glasses, turning them opaque, obscuring his eyes. "And what sort of name is Teddy, then? At least Bunny's name suits her gender."

Up to that point, Amanda had been cautiously edging away, but Teddy's name stopped her in her tracks, and her chin shot up to a mutinous angle. "What the hell do you know about Teddy?" she demanded belligerently. "Have you been talking to Rhonda?"

"No." But he might. He might.

"Good. Teddy is none of your damn business." Amanda whirled around and stalked to her apartment. "Go back to your bunny rabbit, Lieutenant," she flung over her shoulder. "I'm going in."

He was right on her heels. "I'll see you to your door."

"Oh, for . . ." Amanda bit off her words and picked up her pace. There was no sense arguing, so she would just save her breath. She had her key out by the time she reached her door and she unlocked and opened it, stepped inside and whirled to face him. With one hand on the door frame and the other holding the door partly ajar, she leaned out, tilting her head up to catch his eyes. "Don't go grabbing me again, cowboy," she snarled. "I refuse to put up with it." Then she slammed the door in his face.

"*Blood-y* hell!" Tristan slapped his open palm against the door frame in frustration. He glared at the closed portal with its glossy, chocolate-colored paint. He certainly didn't care for his physical reaction to this night's encounter, not by a long shot. What had happened to his usual cool detachment? He couldn't seem to summon it. His heart was thumping up against his rib cage, and his blood was racing hot and heavy through his veins. And, facing it squarely, he acknowledged that his behavior had been far from professional when she had made that crack about being her daddy. If Bunny hadn't interrupted . . . oh, shit, Bunny! Swinging away from Amanda's door, he loped down the stairs to his own apartment.

Bunny looked up from her seat on the couch as Tristan barreled through the door. She had been left alone quite a while—long enough to feel less than thrilled by his tardy reappearance. Snapping her compact closed she tossed it, along with her hairbrush, into her purse and regarded him petulantly. "It's about time you got back."

Ace tried to climb up into her lap, but she brushed him aside, fastidiously picking off the hairs he left on the skirt of her dress with his customary, uncaring abandon.

"Aye, I'm sorry I was so long." Tristan stopped just inside

the door and stared at her helplessly. Hell. Now what should he do?

Ace tumbled from the couch in a graceless heap, picked himself up, and came over to his master. He balanced precariously on his hind legs until he could plant his fat front paws on Tristan's shins, wagging his tail so furiously his entire hind section was a dark blur. Tristan bent down and picked him up, absently rubbing his head.

From Bunny's baleful expression, Tristan could see it was going to take a great deal of sweet-talking on his part to reestablish the malleable mood she'd been in before Ace had commenced barking at the window. The dog's abrupt howls had interrupted a situation that had shown every indication of becoming an evening of serious sexual enjoyment. But the fluffy pink dress that he had rearranged earlier was pulled back tidily into place. Her hair was combed and her lipstick was freshly reapplied, and it didn't take a genius to see that the mood had definitely been broken. Shit. After he'd spent the best part of the evening, too, culling her from the crowd of cop groupies at a bar not far from the precinct. He had been enjoying her company, and not only for the prospect of a little sexual relief. They had danced a little and drunk a little. She had talked a lot, mostly about fashion, of which he wasn't particularly interested. But still, that had meant he hadn't had to rack his brain trying to come up with a subject of conversation that might interest her, and that was a good thing, since the world knew that light conversation was not his strong suit. Also a definite plus, she, as opposed to some women he could name, thought his gun was extremely sexy.

Tristan set Ace down in his basket and walked over to the couch. His body throbbed with unspent needs and aggressions. *Verra well*, he decided, heaving an inward sigh as he sat down next to Bunny. There was no point in moaning and groaning then, was there? He would just have to start over again. Running a finger down her cheek, he bent over her and murmured, "I really am sorry I left you alone so long." He lowered his head.

"Who was that woman, Tristan?"

The descent of Tristan's head abruptly halted. "Who?" He pulled back fractionally to look into her face. "Oh, out in the yard, you mean?" Bunny nodded. "Uh, that was just my landlady." Rubbing the edge of his thumb over her cheek, he lowered his head again. Almost there. Only, suddenly he found himself just going through the motions, for it was starting to feel all wrong.

"Do you always kiss your landlady good night when you have another woman waiting in your apartment?"

With a whispered curse, Tristan pushed away, throwing himself next to her on the couch. His head flopped to the back of the davenport and he stared at the ceiling. "I didna kiss her."

"Well, excuse me." Bunny dug through her purse and pulled out a pack of cigarettes. She lighted one and looked around for an ashtray for the spent match. Not finding one, she placed it in a saucer on the coffee table. "From my vantage point it looked like you were preparing to pull her down on the cold, hard ground and give her the hottest fucking of her life." She blew a stream of smoke at him. "I guess it slipped your mind that you had already brought someone home for that express purpose."

"You're daft," he muttered, knowing she was right. He hadn't acknowledged it consciously before, but he supposed he had picked up Bunny in the first place because he'd been having trouble sleeping nights, thinking about Amanda Charles lying in her bed practically right above his head. He had tortured himself night after night, wondering about the kinds of things he hadn't thought of since he had gone through puberty. Wondering about the color and size of her nipples, what she wore to bed—did she wear anything at all? It was only a sexual attraction, he repeatedly told himself, and he kept waiting for it to burn itself out on the altar of her indifference. But it was bloody well stronger than anything he had ever experienced before.

Damn that blond witch—damn her! She kept intruding

into his life where she had no right to be. She had never so much as given him one miserly little smile, and still, he thought about her all the time. So tonight he had decided if he couldn't have what he wanted, he would just damn well take what he could get. He had been disgusted with his half-assed fantasies of Amanda and tired of the frustration. In a buried corner of his mind, he had been determined to find himself a woman. He wanted the warmth of a real body, not the feel of his own hand as his mind churned out a raft of unrealistic dreams.

Bunny stubbed out her cigarette and stood up. "Like hell, I'm crazy," she snapped. Looking down at him coldly, she stated without mercy, "Listen, buddy boy, I stood there and watched you with your 'landlady' for some time before I finally called your name. And let me tell you, you'd have to go some to find a more desperate individual. You ask me, you got the hots for that bitch so bad you can taste it. But you're afraid to try for her, aren't you? Big, strong cop," she sneered. "Well, listen, honey, I think you're probably right to keep your big mitts off that one. She looks like the type who'd faint dead away if you ever suggested trying something other than the missionary position."

Tristan regarded her levelly, his face expressionless. The malleable femininity that had first attracted him to Bunny was stripped away, exposing a woman who was older than he had originally assumed and worlds harder. The last of her innocent facade evaporated as she vented her scorn toward what she assumed was Amanda's lack of sexual prowess. Damn, but he wished the evening had turned out differently. He had been so damn lonely lately. He really needed a woman's sweet warmth tonight, and if she had just kept that foul mouth of hers shut . . .

Even now, he knew he could talk her around if he wanted to. A few sweetly worded phrases, one denigrating remark about Amanda . . .

Abruptly, he surged to his feet. There was no sweetness to be found with this one. He had either been blinded by his own needs, or it had been nothing more than a facade from the beginning.

"Here, put this on," he commanded coolly as he picked up her coat and handed it to her. "Put it on," he repeated as she stood, hands at her sides, staring up at him. "I'll take you home."

Bunny's jaw sagged. "You're taking me home?"

"Aye. That I am." He hustled her into her coat and out of his apartment. "In truth, Bunny, you can't be all that surprised. I liked you, lass, and I thought we'd do well together. But you can't walk into a mon's home and start sneering at him, pointing out his weaknesses and making remarks that defame a woman you do not even know, and expect him just to put up with it."

"But I thought . . ."

"That I was desperate. Aye, I know."

He opened the car door and ushered her in. Still holding the door ajar, he looked down at her. They stared at each other in silence, and Tristan knew he had reached a turning point in his life. He wanted Amanda Charles. She was ruining him for other women; she was becoming even more important in his life than his career. There. He'd admitted it, instead of dancing around the fact like he had been doing ever since he'd clamped eyes on her.

Well, the fact was, he might never get what he really wanted. But he would never again settle merely for what he could get. It had to have *some* meaning; otherwise, what was the point?

"I'm lonely, lass. I can't deny it," he finally said quietly. "But, Bunny, I'm not nearly as desperate as you may like to believe."

And he gently closed the door.

CHAPTER
9

Rhonda received a flower by messenger early that same morning.

For several moments after the delivery boy had left, she could only stand and stare down at the rose through its green wax-paper florist covering. Eventually, she reached out hesitant fingertips to trace its outline through the paper, and finally picked it up.

The faint echo of a door closing down the hall underscored the silence in the dressing room and she glanced over her shoulder, surprised to find the room empty. When had everyone left? Of all the evenings for Amanda to have her night off, it would have to be now, just when Rhonda was most in need of her company.

She peeled off the wrapping, ripping the paper in several places where it had been stapled together, and gently lifted a single, perfect, long-stemmed red rose out of the resultant shreds of green waxed tissue. The discarded paper drifted unchecked to the floor, already forgotten as Rhonda raised the flower to her nose and inhaled reverently. Her eyelids slid closed as though weighted down by the sudden rush of bittersweet emotion that assailed her.

Oh, hell. Her eyes were prickling like she was going to cry.

Which was too asinine for words. It was only a flower, for God's sake.

Only . . .

She was twenty-seven years old, and she had never in her life received a flower before this night.

Wasn't that odd? Men had bought her meals and drinks and had paid for her tickets to shows and events; they had sent her chocolates and wine and champagne. One man had once bought her a darling stuffed animal; two had offered to buy her jewels, and many had offered to buy her clothing. The offers of clothing and jewelry she had been quick to discourage—and not always as gently as she might have—because it was simply too reminiscent of the manner in which a good many of the women in her old neighborhood had earned their living.

But never in her life had a man bought her a flower.

She slipped the stiff white card from its minuscule envelope and read it.

Well. Rhonda just looked at it for a moment.

It was from Chad, and wasn't that peculiar? She had been under the distinct impression that the situation between them was cooling. At least, she knew her feelings for him had been losing their intense edge, and she could have sworn that his desire for her was also diminishing.

She had given it some thought in the past few days—no, the truth was, she had given it a great deal of thought. And it seemed to her that they were too much alike—each living for the moment, occasionally to the detriment of the future; both of them exchanging sex as a sometimes satisfying, sometimes inadequate, substitute for love. He was her male equivalent. They were butterflies, constitutionally unable to settle down. She didn't know why, but invariably she was attracted to men she knew would move on.

It was admittedly rare, but she'd had occasion to privately question a few of her own less than positive personality quirks. She thought it was kind of funny, in an ironic sort of way, therefore, that as a general rule, she still found such questionable shared traits rather exciting when she came across them in a man.

At first.

But then, inevitably, they began to irritate her—the need to live for the moment. The restlessness. The sleeping around as a means of finding approval—perhaps even as a means of finding love. The way the men she dated almost invariably came to feel that it was their God-given right to criticize her.

She would like to think that somewhere out there, there was a man with the ability to hold her attention forever and a day—one who would accept her exactly the way she was and love her in spite of her faults. But those were just occasional fantasies. In reality, she doubted that such a man existed.

And in the meantime, firmly entrenched in the real world, she was always afraid she was going to miss out on something if she didn't keep moving on.

But what she felt for Chad at this moment, as she brushed the velvet-smooth petals of the flower across her lips and inhaled its rich, unmistakable fragrance, were emotions singularly soft and sweet. It didn't matter how transient in her life he might be, because for one brief instant in time, as the man who had sent her this perfect gift, the emotions she experienced very nearly equaled love.

The enclosed card requested her presence at an address she did not recognize, and it was signed, simply, *Chad*. Rhonda glanced at the clock on the dressing room wall—2:27 A.M. The invitation was for three.

She was awfully tired. But, still . . .

A woman didn't stand up the only man to have ever sent her a flower, did she? That seemed like a perfectly tacky thing to do. It really was too bad Amanda wasn't here. She probably knew all about the etiquette involved in this type of situation.

Oh, what the hell. She wasn't *that* tired.

Rhonda used the stage doorman's map of the city to look up the route she would need to take to the address indicated on the card. She wondered what kind of restaurant or hotel could possibly be in that area. It wasn't possible to be certain, of course, using only a map for reference, but if the address on this card was in the same locality she was thinking of, she could swear it was mostly a light industrial district.

And so it turned out to be.

Well, kid, Rhonda told herself sarcastically as she sat in her car in a dimly lighted parking lot at two minutes to three in the morning, looking up at the corrugated tin warehouse door of a computer manufacturer, *it's good to know that you haven't lost your instincts. When you're right, you're right.*

She picked up the card once again and double-checked the address against the one painted on the glass office door that was situated near the loading dock. Nothing had changed since she had checked it a moment ago; the two addresses still matched.

What the hell was going on here? The ambience of this place didn't exactly jibe with the romance of the flower. She would give Chad exactly five minutes to present himself and explain, and then she was leaving.

Rhonda rolled up the car window and checked the locks on the doors to be sure they were secure. A girl didn't grow up navigating the streets of a Chicago housing project without learning a thing or two. She didn't like the feel of this at all, and her instincts were urging her to get the hell out of here.

He appeared out of nowhere, approaching the car from the passenger side. The first that Rhonda saw of him, he was striding up to the car, and from her seated vantage point, all she could see clearly was his torso from midchest to thigh, and even that view shrank the closer he got to the car. Relief surged through Rhonda that he was finally here and could explain the reason for picking this bizarre location to meet. His explanation had better be good, too, for there was something about this place that was giving her the creeps. She leaned across the seat to unlock the passenger door for him, expecting him to squat down and greet her through the window.

It was his unnatural stillness that initially caused her to hesitate with her hand on the lock button. She had grown up in a neighborhood where one learned not to take any situation at face value. Growing up under the auspice of the Housing Authority taught one an intrinsic wariness, and hers was screaming Red Alert now. Why was he just standing there so quietly, instead of leaning down to say hello, which would be the natural thing to do and which would have given her a look at his face?

Unless he didn't want her to see his face. Rhonda went cold all over. Slowly, she straightened back into the driver's seat and reached for the ignition key.

"Come on, Rhonda," he said, and his voice was indistinct and muffled through the glass of the window. "Open the door." He reached out and rattled the handle.

And she saw that he was wearing surgical gloves.

"Oh, no! Oh, shit! Oh, God . . ." Rhonda put the car in reverse, removed the safety brake, and hit the gas. The man's gloved hands slid along the fender as she roared backward. She traveled in reverse about fifteen feet before hitting the brakes, and the sudden stop bounced her forward against the steering wheel and then snapped her back against the seat. For an instant she just sat there gripping the wheel, and stared at him in the headlights' glare.

Who the hell was that guy? He looked vaguely familiar, but the way he kept smiling was far from natural. It was downright eerie.

He took a step toward the car, and Rhonda interpreted a world of menace from his body language. She gripped the wheel in sweaty hands as her survival instincts snapped into place. Putting the car in gear, she floored it . . . straight at him.

The man whirled aside with amazing agility and ran swiftly at an oblique angle to the car. He leaped into the air, soaring the remaining feet to the short set of steps that led up to the

office entrance and loading platform. Grasping the tubular
metal handrail, he vaulted over it with athletic dexterity. He
raced up the stairs and was up and over the warehouse roof
in seconds flat. Close on his heels, Rhonda nearly crashed
into the solid stairs. She fought the wheel, wrenching it hard
to the right, and stood on the brakes, shaking as the car
screeched sideways and rocked to a standstill inches from the
concrete stairwell. It took her about one instant to gather her
wits.

And then she turned the car around and drove it out of
there like a proverbial bat out of hell.

Amanda was in bed but still wide awake after her confrontation with MacLaughlin when the pounding on the door
commenced. For crying out loud, what now? She threw back
the covers and grabbed her robe. This had been the craziest
damn night.

She hesitated at the door and drew a deep breath. "Who
is it?"

"Amanda, please, let me in," Rhonda's voice pleaded
through the door.

"Rhonda?" Amanda fumbled with the chain and dead bolts
and threw the door open. Rhonda immediately stumbled in,
slamming the door behind her. She slumped against the now-
closed portal, chest heaving, and stared wild-eyed at Amanda.

"What is it—what's going on?" Amanda demanded, and
she reached out to touch her friend's arm. "Are you okay?"

"Yeah. Give me a minute." Rhonda took several deep
breaths, holding them for as long as she was able before
exhaling gustily. "It was a mask," she finally said.

"What? What on earth is going on here, Rhonda?"

"A mask," Rhonda replied. "One of those rubber, whole-
head ones, with hair and everything." She shook her head
slowly, as if bemused. "Of course. I couldn't figure out what
was different about him. His head was a little bit bigger than
normal. And that smile. But it was a goddamn mask."

Then she told Amanda everything.

Amanda stared at Rhonda in horror, momentarily robbed of speech. "Are you crazy?" she finally demanded in a fierce whisper. "You went to meet a man in a deserted industrial park at three o'clock in the morning when there's a killer on the loose? You've done some asinine things in your life, Rhonda, but of all the feeble-brained . . ."

"Mandy, please," Rhonda said wearily. "Don't, for God's sake, lecture me. I have just been scared out of my few remaining wits, and I'm not exactly thrilled by my own stupidity. The last thing I need is a lec . . . a lect . . ." She couldn't finish her sentence as reaction set in with a vengeance and she began to shake.

"Oh, God, I'm sorry, Rhonda. I'm sorry," Amanda wailed and she lurched forward to wrap her arms around her friend, holding her in a grip that drove the blood from her own fingertips. "It's just that you're my best friend in the whole world and I couldn't bear to lose you, too, and . . ." She pulled back far enough to look into Rhonda's face as a thought struck her. "Oh, jeez, Rhonda, we've got to call Mac-Laughlin right away."

"He's not home. I tried there first."

It was childish and mean-spirited, Amanda knew, to be hurt by the knowledge that Rhonda had turned to him first, but somehow . . .

No. She refused to entertain any such thought. Of course Rhonda was going to contact a policeman before she came to her friend. "He had a woman at his apartment earlier," she informed Rhonda. "Maybe he's just not answering the door."

"I pounded long and hard, kiddo," Rhonda informed her wryly and gently disentangled herself from Amanda's hug. She led them both into the kitchen. "He couldn't have failed to hear me, and you know MacLaughlin—he's the responsible type. Believe me, with all the racket I made, not even the greatest orgasm of his life would have prevented the good lieutenant from coming to investigate. Trust me. He's not home."

Amanda really wished Rhonda hadn't mentioned the possibility of Lieutenant MacLaughlin's sexual satisfaction. Had the Bunny woman, with her soft and feminine voice and her fluffy dress . . . "Well, then, Detective Cash. We'll call Detective Cash."

"Good idea. But, Mandy, do you think you could make me some coffee first? God, I'm so cold, and my hands keep shaking."

"Oh, Rhonda. Yes, of course." Amanda turned on the burner under the teakettle and went to place her call to Joe Cash. Back in the kitchen, she ground some coffee beans and poured them into the drip basket. "I cranked the heat up," she told Rhonda, picking up the kettle and pouring steaming water over the grounds. "Between that and this, you should warm up pretty soon." She poured a cup of coffee and handed it to her friend.

"Thanks, kiddo." As Rhonda sipped cautiously at the steaming drink, the significance of Amanda's earlier words suddenly sank in with delayed meaning. So MacLaughlin had had another woman in his apartment tonight, had he? Somehow, that surprised Rhonda. Boy, she would sure like to know how Mandy felt about it, but she knew better than to ask. All Mandy would say was that MacLaughlin's life is his own and what he does with it is his business; it has nothing whatsoever to do with me. Or some equally polite drivel.

Rhonda really wished he had been home. But failing that, Lord, she hoped Detective Cash got here soon. She had been taking care of herself for what seemed like all of her life, but she didn't feel safe tonight. And her entire body trembled with a lack of confidence over her ability to see to her own protection for what was left of the night. She was angry and hurt and scared. And what really hit her the hardest was knowing that this deranged person had managed to expose something in her that was deeply buried and painfully vulnerable when he had used a lousy flower to get to her.

She began to chatter and couldn't seem to stop. Even after Joe Cash finally arrived and she thought she would begin to unwind, her conversation retained its tendency to wander off on tangents. He kept trying to gently guide her back on track, but her concentration would waver with a word or a stray thought or a look, and she would find herself taking a whole new conversational tack. Part of her wanted to curl around herself and be very quiet. But her body was humming with nerves, and she found it difficult merely to sit still as she talked on and on.

"Receiving that flower was kinda like getting an invitation to the senior prom," she said at one point. "Did you go to your senior prom, Mandy?"

"No. It was right after Teddy died."

"Me either. Not many girls from my old neighborhood were invited to a senior prom. We were mostly invited to share the backseat of some guy's car—an invitation, as you know, that I regularly accepted. But getting that flower was almost like being invited to the prom by the captain of the football team and getting to wear organdy and a wrist corsage and have your mom say 'be in by midnight.' For like twenty minutes, it made me feel all innocent and young, in a way I most likely never even was. It made me feel special. And I could kill him for ruining that for me."

Rhonda noticed Joe watching her speculatively and she experienced a rare moment of embarrassment. God, he must think she was a first-class idiot, whining about a stupid flower when she could have been killed tonight. There was just no way to explain why the spoiled symbolism of a single flower hurt far worse than anything else that had gone on this night, or in practically her entire life. She couldn't expect people who hadn't grown up in an area where poverty was rife, where welfare was a perpetual way of life, to understand.

And yet Amanda, who had grown up in a neighborhood that was about ten worlds removed from the one that had nurtured Rhonda, seemed to possess an instinctive affinity for what Rhonda was feeling. She sat down next to her on the couch and put her arm around her. "It hurts, doesn't it?" she murmured. "What that bastard did to you with that flower is kind of like what my parents did to Teddy when they told her about her boyfriend. I'm truly sorry, Rhonda. You don't deserve any of this.''

Rhonda very nearly cried then, something she hadn't done in . . . she couldn't remember how long. Instead, she squeezed Amanda tightly in return and then straightened away from her. Amanda's empathy helped to ground her. It made her feel a little less disconnected. She faced Joe Cash squarely, her face composed. ''I'm ready to answer your questions now,'' she informed him with what she sincerely hoped was cool composure.

Joe reached for his notebook, but there was a knock at the door before he could begin his prepared inquisition. ''That's probably the lieutenant,'' he informed the women gently after watching both of them start nervously at the sound. He got up to answer it.

Tristan burst through the door the instant Joe opened it. ''Amanda?'' he asked in a low voice.

''Rhonda,'' Joe replied.

''Jesus,'' Tristan breathed and ran a hand through his thick, short hair. ''I knew something was up when I saw your car on the street and all the lights on in here, and I thought . . .'' His voice trailed away and he snatched his glasses off, rubbing the bridge of his nose. Reseating them, he asked, ''Is she okay?''

''Yeah. Come on in. She was just going to give me the details.'' Quickly, he filled Tristan in on the bare bones of Rhonda's story.

Upon entering the living room, Tristan crossed straight over to Rhonda. ''Are you all right, lass?'' he asked her gently.

''Yes. I'm a little shook, but all right.''

''Good. Can you tell me what happened?'' Tristan spared a quick glance for Amanda, who was seated beside her friend. She was wearing a warm navy-blue, wrapped-waist robe over a puritanical white cotton nightgown, and it was hard to look

at her without remembering what he had felt for her earlier
this evening, or this morning, or whenever the hell it had
been. And that he could not do. He couldn't afford to think
of anything but the investigation. He pulled his eyes away
and listened to Rhonda repeat her story.

"You say he was wearing a mask?"

"Yes. I didn't realize it until I got here. I told you I saw
him in the headlights. And he looked familiar . . . but odd.
His head was kinda big, for one thing. He had one of those
long, droopy mustaches, his hair was blond and receding in
front but long in the back, and he had a big nose and this
great big white grin and a big dimpled chin. And . . ." She
swallowed hard. "I thought, who *is* that guy? Why does he
look like someone I've seen before? But it wasn't until I got
here that I realized it was one of those rubber masks you pull
over your entire head, and the one he wore was of some
football player or something. No. Wait. It was that wrestler
guy, Hunk Holgen or something like that?"

"Hulk Hogan?" Joe asked.

"Yeah, that's the one. Not that it does you much good,
does it? He was still masked, and he wore surgical gloves
on his hands, so there won't be any prints on my car."

"Don't worry yourself about that," Tristan said and smiled
at her. "What about his hands? Can you remember anything
about them? Were his fingers long, short? Thin, stubby?"

"Oh, God, I'm not sure. You know what flashed through
my mind when I saw he was wearing surgical gloves? The
Hook. Remember him? We used to scare ourselves silly with
stories of the Hook when we were kids."

Tristan was perplexed. "Who's the Hook?"

"Are you kidding me? You've never heard of him?"
Rhonda turned to Joe. "Tell him, Detective."

"The Hook is a favorite, modern-day American ghost
story, Lieutenant," Joe said. "It's about this couple out necking in their car in a deserted area, who hear a news flash on
the radio about an escaped killer from a nearby insane asylum.

The killer can be identified by a metal hook on his right hand. Well, they get a little nervous and decide maybe they had better go on home, so the guy starts up the car and they roar on out of there. Then, when they get home, he gets out of the car and comes around to help his girlfriend out. And there, dangling from the door handle, is . . .''

"The Hook!'' Rhonda and Amanda chimed in with the end of Joe's tale, and Rhonda rubbed her arms.

"It still gives me goose pimples,'' she said, and then grew grave as she turned to Tristan, who obviously didn't see how three supposedly mature adults could get sidetracked from the seriousness of Rhonda's near attack by a corny, old-time story. "Anyhow, the point is, Lieutenant, when I saw those gloves on his hands, that's what flashed into my mind. I mean, there can only be one reason for a man to wear surgical gloves in a deserted parking lot at three o'clock in the morning, right? He clearly wasn't there to do brain surgery, and I got the same all-over chill that the story of the Hook always gives me. And, I truly am sorry, MacLaughlin, but I didn't notice anything about their shape or size or anything else.''

"Can you tell us anything about his height? His build?''

"Yes. He was average height—maybe five-ten, five-eleven. And he was athletic, but in a real lean way, you know? Not big and muscular like you, Lieutenant; more like a dancer. In fact . . .'' Her voice trailed away. "No, it can't be.''

"What?'' Three voices demanded to know.

Rhonda's eyes were closed, as if reliving something in her mind. "My God. He did.'' She opened them again and stared at them all blankly. She looked stunned.

"What, Miss Smith?''

"He jetéd.''

"*What?!*'' Amanda jerked upright.

"When I tried to run him down with my car, he jetéd.''

"What the bloody hell is a jet-tay?'' Tristan demanded, and at the same time, Rhonda said to Amanda, "He's gotta be a dancer.''

There was an instant of dead silence. Then Tristan asked again, "What is a jet-tay, Miss Smith?"

"Show him, Amanda."

"I beg your pardon?" Amanda looked at her friend as if she had lost her mind.

"Amanda has one of the longest jetés in the nonballet world," Rhonda said. She turned to Amanda. "Show him."

"I can't jeté in my nightie."

"Then go put on your damn leotard. It'll be quicker than trying to explain."

"Oh, for . . ." Amanda got up and stomped to her room.

Tristan thought he heard her mumble something about this being ridiculous, but he couldn't be sure. More quickly than he would have thought possible, she was back, her long legs bare, wearing only an old threadbare leotard, a pair of socks that sagged around her ankles, and a pair of scuffed, black kid ballet slippers.

"Ready?" she asked. When the men nodded, she indicated the path that Rhonda had hastily cleared up the middle of the room and said coolly, "Would you mind sitting down? I'm going to need the room."

They sat.

Amanda ran lightly for several steps and then launched herself into the air. She soared effortlessly, right leg extended in front of her, left leg extended behind her, like an elevated splits, both legs in a perfect horizontal line three feet above the floor. She landed lightly on the ball of her forward foot nearly eight feet from where she had leapt into the air.

"You see?" Rhonda asked, but Tristan had a difficult time seeing anything but the long, bare expanse of Amanda's legs as she walked out of the room without a backward glance. He had to force his eyes away. Bloody hell. It was this very thing he had to guard against—these lapses of professionalism. Grimly, he turned to Rhonda.

"The guy in the parking lot jetéd just like that before he reached the railing," she said. "Then, when he touched down, he used his momentum to vault himself over. I've seen so many jetés in my life, it didn't even register at the time, and it sure as hell wasn't done with the same finesse and grace Mandy Rose just displayed, but all the same, that is definitely what he did.''

"Steerwhiler is a dancer," Tristan said slowly, feeling her out, watching for her initial, intuitive reaction. So many times, that was the one that told them the most. "Maybe he was playing some esoteric kind of joke on you."

A frown puckered her forehead. "There is always the possibility, I suppose," she slowly acknowledged. "And his build is right. But somehow . . . I don't know, Lieutenant. At this point, I just don't know."

"Has your relationship with him changed at all recently?"

"Well, that was the thing, you see. I really was kind of surprised that the flower was from him, because I had thought we were sort of . . . mutually cooling off."

"We will check him for an alibi," Tristan said. "And I guess we'll just have to go from there." Bloody hell. This case was getting stranger by the minute.

"Let's go back to the beginning," he said. "Can you tell me the name of the florist?"

"No. I'm sorry."

"How about the delivery boy? Was he wearing a uniform?"

"No. Just jeans and a sweater, an unzipped jacket and a baseball cap. I'm sorry, Lieutenant. Once I saw that flower, I didn't see anything else. You might check with the security guard at the stage door, though, because the kid probably parked the delivery van in the alley, and he would have had to sign in."

"Verra good, lass. What about the card?"

"Oh! I still have that. It's on the seat of my car."

"Joe?" Tristan said.

"I'm on it," Joe affirmed. He collected Rhonda's car keys from her and let himself out of Amanda's apartment.

Amanda returned to the living room, holding aloft a plastic baggie. "Detective Cash said he needed one of these, but then he left without taking it."

"Put it on the table, Miss Charles," Tristan directed crisply, keeping his eyes trained on his notebook. "He'll be back directly."

"Yes, sir," she murmured. She sat down next to Rhonda and yawned widely behind a politely raised hand. Her head rolled wearily against the back of the couch until she was looking directly at Rhonda's profile. "You wanna stay here for what's left of the night?"

Rhonda turned to look at Amanda, and she gave her a small, close-lipped smile. "Thanks, kiddo. I'd appreciate that a lot."

"Would it hurt your feelings if I went to bed? I can stay up with you if you'd rather."

"Don't be silly; you go ahead. I'll come crawl in myself when MacLaughlin is done with me."

Amanda raised her eyes from Rhonda's face and glanced across the room to where Tristan was seated, scribbling busily in a battered spiral notebook. She leaned over and gave Rhonda a kiss. " 'Night, Rhonda."

"G'night."

Tristan waited until Amanda had left the room, then looked up from his notebook and asked Rhonda casually, "Where's she off to this time, then?"

"To bed."

For a brief moment, he went very still as his gray eyes locked with Rhonda's. Then he looked at the doorway by which Amanda had exited, back down at his notebook, and said something that sounded like "huh!"—something that was more an exhalation of breath than an actual word.

Joe came in and they slid the small card into the plastic baggie. Unfortunately, it didn't carry the name of the florist upon it. It was a white piece of bonded cardboard with a minuscule flower in one corner, and the hand that had penned the message was probably not that of the sender. But it gave them a place to start. They spent an additional twenty minutes going over Rhonda's story, trying to coerce bits and pieces of added information from her memory. Finally, the policemen put away their notebooks and rose to their feet.

"We may need to contact you for further information, lass," Tristan said. "But for now, why don't you go to bed and try to put it out of your mind. Want us to walk you up to your apartment?"

"No, thanks," Rhonda replied. "I'm going to go crawl in with Amanda tonight. I don't particularly want to be alone."

"Aye, I can understand that. Be sure to lock up behind us then."

"I will. G'night, Lieutenant, Detective." She closed the door behind them.

Tristan listened for the sound of the locks being tumbled into place before he started down the steps. "What a bugger," he sighed. "Want to come down for a drink?"

"Yeah, sure, sounds good."

A few moments later they were both slumped on their spines on Tristan's couch, stocking feet up on the coffee table, Ace sprawled on his back between them. Each man held a stubby glass in his hand, the bottle of bonded on the table in front of them. "So, whataya think?" Joe asked. He inhaled one of his rare cigarettes, blowing a stream of smoke at the ceiling.

"Hell, who knows? Why Rhonda Smith? The mon's targeted blondes exclusively up to this point. So, why all of a sudden has he gone after a brunette? And how did he find out so much about her? He knew her name, that she was dating Steerwhiler . . ."

". . . her most vulnerable spot when he sent her that flower, although that might have been sheer luck," Joe added.

"What do you mean by her most vulnerable spot?" Tristan

asked, and Joe told him of Rhonda's hurt and betrayal over the flower.

Tristan went very still for a moment, but what he was thinking, he kept to himself, murmuring only, "That flamin' sod."

They were both quiet for a moment. Eventually, Tristan raised his glass, took a sip of his neat whiskey and asked, "Do you get the impression that Rhonda Smith has something of a reputation for sleepin' around?"

"Yeah. She flat came out and said as much, and she's not apologizing for it, either."

"No reason that she should," Tristan said coolly. "But, if she's the kind of woman men talk about, then our mon could have overheard a conversation about her damn near anywhere. Dammit. This case grows more fuckin' wonderful by the day. Because, the trouble is, it might not even be him. She's the kind of woman who has known a lot of men, and she has probably managed to piss off one or two of them along the way. Hell, Joe, it could verra well be our mon, going off on some tangent understood only by himself, or it could be any one of a legion of others."

"Yeah, ain't police work grand?"

"Hell, yes." They exchanged weary smiles.

"You know what the irony is, Joe?" Tristan said. "If Rhonda wasn't the kind of woman she is, our mon, if it was even him who arranged tonight's entertainment, probably never would have heard of her in the first place. Yet, it was being exactly the kind of streetwise woman she is that most likely saved her butt out there tonight in a computer manufacturer's parking lot. That lass is nobody's fool."

"That's for damn sure. I gotta admit, I kind of admire her. The woman thinks mighty fast on her feet. So, what's your immediate gut reaction?"

"I say it's him. Tonight's escapade had that slickness to it that I'm coming to associate with our killer. It was obviously well planned and it was sure as bloody hell boldly executed, and he didna panic when it fell apart on him. It just seems to me that it has his mark stamped all over it. What's your own opinion, then?''

Joe tipped up his glass. ''I don't have your experience in this kind of case, MacLaughlin. But I get the same gut re-action as any other halfway decent cop and I gotta agree. I sure as hell wish I knew what singling out Rhonda Smith is suppose to signify, though.''

''Aye, so do I, Joe. So do I.'' Tristan sat up straighter. ''I guess our next step should be running a check on all the male dancers. God, there's probably hundreds of them all over the city.'' He raked both hands through his hair. ''But I suppose the logical place to start is with the ones at the Cabaret, using the list we compiled the day we were there. We can at least run a make on them to be sure none of them has a record. Miss Smith seems convinced that her man in the parking lot was a dancer.''

Joe left shortly after that. Tristan sat in his darkened living room, rubbing his dog's stomach and thinking about the events of the past twenty-four hours. Finally, reluctant to go out again, but following a compulsion he could not explain, Tristan put his shoes back on, shrugged into his jacket, and left his apartment. He was about to violate his long-held policy of noninvolvement, and the surprising thing was it wasn't even for the woman for whom he had thought he would perhaps break all of his own rules.

He drove downtown to an all-night flower shop.

He was still torn about whether or not he was doing the right thing when he picked out a small spring bouquet to be sent to Rhonda Smith. On the one hand there was his flagrant disregard for a lifetime of professionalism. As a veteran career cop, he was certain he was making a mistake. He *knew* better than to involve himself in the lives of the people on any case of his.

But, hell, to be honest, there was a lot more at stake here than just keeping his professional distance. By making this one gesture, he was about to negate an entire lifetime of withholding himself. It wouldn't gain him a thing. In the process, in fact, he stood to lose a few of his own hard-earned protective layers.

But he felt compelled to do it, nevertheless. Somewhere deep inside of him, he had an intrinsic understanding of Rhonda Smith's sense of betrayal. He knew what it was like to grow up in an area where you were counted fortunate if you were able to scrape together the bare essentials. She had been handed something tonight that had given her a chance to experience, for a brief moment, all the wonders that had been lacking in her youth. It had laid open her deepest and innermost vulnerabilities, exposing the core that she had probably learned at an early age to protect for the sake of her own survival.

And if it had simply been left at that, it wouldn't necessarily have been a bad thing. If nothing else, it had presented her with a special memory to make up for the lack that had gone before.

But it hadn't been left at that. She had walked away unharmed from what was quite probably a practiced killer. But, whether by intention or sheer blind luck, the sender of that flower had seen to it that she had not walked away unscathed.

Hunched over the little counter that held all the cards, Tristan saw that it was going to be close to impossible to track down the man who had sent Rhonda her flower. Every flower shop in Reno probably carried tags identical to these, and if every shop also had these private little counters where the buyer could fill out his own card, all the man would have had to do was fill out his card ahead of time, and then pick a busy time to make his purchase, or better yet, find a bored teenager hanging around some mall and pay him to go in and do it for him. He wouldn't hold his breath, waiting for something to come of it from the lab. Tristan reached for one of the cards that read "To Someone Special."

He hesitated before he wrote anything, pen hovering over the little white card, his natural reticence fighting one last battle with his need to make this gesture. Finally, he compromised.

He allowed himself to get personal when he wrote: "A lass's first flower shouldn't be defiled by a man who doesn't appreciate the importance of a special memory."

But he preserved his need to maintain a formal distance when he signed it "Lieutenant T. MacLaughlin."

CHAPTER
10

Dance rehearsals were generally held only when a new headliner started at the Cabaret. It wasn't necessary to hold them on a daily basis, for the dancers had a set number of routines that Charlie only changed three or four times a year. But every few weeks the headliner changed, and for a few days thereafter, the dancers worked with the new star. Then, depending on his or her needs, their rehearsals might continue for an additional day or two to practice new placement or timing, or sometimes to learn entire new routines to be implemented into the headliner's show.

If there was one thing guaranteed to put Charlie in a particularly foul mood, it was an unexcused absence by one of his dancers. He wasn't an unreasonable man. He knew they occasionally had other plans that couldn't be worked around the schedule, and certain illnesses had a way of striking without warning. But his people knew the rules. There were phones all over town, and his dancers knew they had better pick one up and use it. He could adjust the routines for a day or two. But you never simply shined it on and failed to show—not if you wanted to continue working for the Cabaret.

165

Charlie had a great deal of clout in Reno, and it was professional suicide to thumb your nose at his rules.

When Pete Schriber didn't come in for Friday rehearsal and didn't call to say why, Charlie blew sky high. He ranted and raved at the dancers about their innate unreliability for a solid fifteen minutes. There was no pleasing him. He ran them through routine after routine, picking up on the minutest errors and using them to verbally browbeat the offender. When a stagehand handed him a note and he told the dancers to take five, there wasn't a dry leotard left on stage. He unfolded the slip of paper, read its contents, and then swore roundly.

"People," he called up to the stage. "I owe you all an apology."

Rhonda stuck her little finger in her ear and wiggled it. Pulling it out, she examined its clean tip and mumbled, "I must have wax buildup on my eardrums. I could have sworn I just heard Charlie say he owes us an apology."

June giggled and Amanda smiled wearily, rubbing the back of her knee. She'd pulled a hamstring. She had felt it go ten minutes ago, but she hadn't dared favor that leg for fear of bringing Charlie's wrath down upon her head. Better to live with the pain now, and baby it with rest and ice packs later, than to bring yourself to Charlie's attention when he was on the warpath. Straightening, she watched him climb the stairs to the stage. His expression was grim.

"Pete's in the hospital," he announced. "And it doesn't sound good. He was hit by a truck on his way to rehearsal, and from the sound of things, his left leg from shin to ankle is smashed to pieces."

"Oh, God," Amanda whispered. "Can they fix him up so he can dance?"

"Preliminary prognosis doesn't sound good," Charlie replied, and they stared at one another in shared horror. It was every dancer's nightmare.

"Dammit!" Charlie's fist smacked into his palm. "I was ready to kill him, fire him, or at the very least, rake his degenerate ass over the coals. And the nurse who left the message said he refused to even let them treat him until they agreed to get a message to me. He wanted to be sure I had time to find someone to fill in for him.'' His voice dropped to a whisper and he shook his head. ''Shit.''

Rehearsal broke up early, and Amanda and Rhonda decided to stop by the hospital to visit Pete before going back to the Cabaret for the evening show. He looked up groggily as they walked through the hospital room door, his left leg in a cast and his eyes heavy-lidded from anesthetics that were just now wearing off from earlier surgery. '' 'Lo,'' he mumbled, and then grimaced at the effort, running a thickened tongue over dry, cracked lips.

''How are you, Pete?'' Rhonda leaned down and kissed his forehead while Amanda placed the flowers they had brought him on the stand next to his bed.

''Thirsty.''

''Want some water?'' At Pete's nod, Amanda picked up the blue plastic pitcher and poured ice water into a glass. Placing a bent straw in the glass, she held it to his mouth. He took a few small sips, ran his tongue across his lips again, and sank back weakly into his pillows.

''What happened, Pete?'' Rhonda inquired gently.

''Dunno, exactly.'' He closed his eyes briefly. Opening them again, he said, ''I was standing on the corner of Virginia and Whatchamacallit? Outside Harrah's?'' When they nodded their understanding, he continued, ''There were a lot of tourists all bunched up, waiting for the light to change . . . and I was in front at the curb. You know how it is in this town —only the tourists wait for the lights.'' He gestured for another sip of water. ''I was running late, and I was gonna jaywalk, but there was a semi without the trailer comin' kind of fast down the street, so I waited. Then . . . don't know . . . I heard someone say, 'Watch it, Mac,' like someone fell against them, and somebody, something, hit me between the shoulder blades, pretty hard, and I got shoved into the street just before the truck got there.'' He licked his dry lips.

"Driver tried to stop. Too damn close." Tears filled his eyes. "Someone else grabbed me and tried to pull me back, but my left leg was still in the street. Have you ever taken a look at the tires on those rigs?" A tear trickled over his bottom eyelid. "Fuckin' monster smashed my ankle like one of those splintery little chicken-bone candies my Mom used to buy me when I was a kid. Oh, God." His control broke and he stared at them in agony as tears ran down his cheeks. "What am I gonna do? They put three pins in it, and they said eventually I could walk on it again and pro'bly even regain about ninety-eight percent mobility. But I ain't never gonna be able to dance on it. What the hell am I suppose to do if I can't ever dance again?"

"Don't worry about that now," Rhonda advised softly. "You just concentrate on getting well."

"If I can't dance, I don't know if I wanna get well."

"Don't talk like that!" Amanda squeezed Pete's hand, but she found it hard to meet his eyes. She didn't have the first idea what to say to make him feel better. On the one hand, with her family history, it was difficult for her to hear someone say anything that sounded even remotely suicidal. But, on the other hand, she was a dancer, and she could most definitely identify with his despair. What on earth would she do if she were in Pete's shoes—if she suddenly couldn't dance anymore? She had no family, no lover, nothing at all to fill such an enormous void. Dancing was all she had, and if it were suddenly taken away . . .

"How the hell should I talk, then, Amanda? Can you tell me it's gonna be all right? God!" He laughed bitterly. "Can you even tell me that if, by some miracle, I was able to dance on it eventually, Charlie would still hold my place for me?"

Amanda and Rhonda exchanged uneasy glances. As they had left the lounge after the aborted rehearsal, they had both heard Charlie telling Lennie to get on the phone and try to locate that guy who had auditioned for him.

"Listen," Rhonda said sternly. "Nobody expects you to act like Pollyanna. It's a rotten thing that happened to you. But the only way you're going to get through this is to take it one step at a time. You can't just blow it all off before you know exactly what you've got to deal with. Maybe the doctors . . ."

"What?" Pete demanded as her voice trailed off. "Maybe the doctors what?"

"Well, maybe you should get a second opinion, is all. They probably want to see how it heals before they hold out any encouragement. I don't know, Pete! Just don't give up on yourself."

"Yeah, okay," he agreed. He took a deep breath and wiped at his cheeks with the back of his wrist. "I'm sorry. I didn't mean to fall apart on you like that. It's just . . ." His eyes filled up with tears again, and impatiently he shook his head. "No. I'm not going to worry about it tonight—at least, I'll try not to."

Pete's current lover came rushing in at that moment. He fussed around the bed, straightening and touching and exclaiming, and after a few moments of watching his solicitous ministrations, Amanda and Rhonda excused themselves.

They avoided catching each other's eyes in the elevator, and the ride to the Cabaret was made in strained silence. It wasn't until Amanda was already dressed in her costume for the first number, bending forward to the lighted mirror to put the finishing touches on her makeup, that she raised her head and met Rhonda's eyes for the first time since leaving Pete's hospital room.

"What would you do?" she inquired softly beneath the babble of the other dancers' voices.

"I don't know." Rhonda didn't pretend to misunderstand. "I've been asking myself that very question ever since we saw him." She put down her lipstick and swiveled to face Amanda directly. "Mandy, I feel so damn guilty at the relief I experienced, knowing it wasn't me that it happened to."

Amanda stared at her in astonishment. "God, you, too? I thought it was only me." She picked up the elaborate headdress and secured it over her hair. "You know, it's sort of ironic, but when I think of that guy who's killing the dancers,

I can't imagine that happening to me. Well, I did briefly when MacLaughlin scared me half to death out in the yard, but not ordinarily, you know? Not even with Maryanne's death and what happened to you last week in that parking lot. It doesn't seem quite real. But something like this—the idea of having your entire life go down the tubes due to some stupid, freak accident—that I can imagine, and it scares me to death.''

''Yeah, it could happen.''

''Rhonda, I don't know what I would do if that happened to me. Dance has been my entire life since I was seven years old. It's all I know. My friends are all dancers. My social life is built almost entirely around dance. God, here I am, twenty-eight years old, and I've only had three lovers my entire life, and one of them was a dancer, too.'' She closed her eyes briefly. Opening them, she shuddered lightly. ''Lord, if I couldn't dance . . .''

She watched Rhonda put one high-heeled foot up on a stool and straighten the sheer tights of her costume by cupping her hands around her trim ankle and smoothing upward over calf, knee, and thigh. Rhonda dropped her leg and hooked a finger beneath the G-string of her costume where it rode up the division of her buttocks, squatting slightly to adjust it to a more comfortable fit. ''I'll tell you one thing,'' Amanda continued, handing Rhonda her headdress. ''Feeling that flash of triumph that it hadn't happened to me might make me feel like a selfish bitch, but I'm going to enjoy dancing tonight. My brain might feel sadness for Pete's situation and guilt for my own duplicity, but my body feels alive and rarin' to go. It wants to celebrate its healthy condition.''

''I understand what you're saying, Mandy Rose—believe me, I do.'' Rhonda faced her, and a slight smile curved one corner of her mouth. ''But just once in your life, why don't you celebrate your body's healthy condition by finding yourself a man after the last show. Pick out some healthy stud, take him home, close the doors, and don't come out again until you're both too worn out to think. After all, kid, there's celebrating and then there is *celebrating*.''

"Rhonda, that just isn't me."

"Well, that's what I'm gonna do." The discordant notes of the orchestra tuning up faded away, and moments later it began to play in earnest. Rhonda had to raise her voice slightly to be heard over it. The other dancers began to drift out of the dressing room to assemble according to height out in the wings. "And let me tell you, kid, for sheer relaxation, nothing can beat it."

At Amanda's skeptically raised dark eyebrows, Rhonda said heatedly, "Don't you dare tell me again that you're cold, or sexually indifferent, or whatever it is you think you are. Some intellectual type once said there are no frigid women, only inept men. And I say hallelujah. If you aren't impressed with the benefits of a little sexual therapy, it's probably because your previous lovers were all bumbling turkeys, whose only interest was in taking care of themselves."

"Rhonda! Amanda!" Charlie's voice roared down the corridor. "Get your butts out here. Pronto!"

They trotted for the wings. "Hell, Mandy, you said it yourself," Rhonda continued with determination. She detested seeing someone as sweet as Amanda go to waste. "You've only ever had three lovers. I don't know about the first two, but I know for a fact that the last one lasted for less than three months before he reconciled with the ex-wife. And if you're too shy to try your hand with a stranger, you don't even have to go looking for someone. You've got the perfect candidate living right below you. Just knock on MacLaughlin's door. I bet he could change your mind in a hurry about the therapeutic benefits of sex."

"Why do you keep trying to link me with MacLaughlin? I'm not the one to whom he sent flowers." The truth was, it was those flowers MacLaughlin had sent to Rhonda that had made Amanda begin to look at him differently. It was such a . . . well, human thing to do.

"I don't know. There's just something there. I told ya, kid, I've got radar when it comes to this sorta thing. It could have something to do with the fact that when he's around, you hardly look at anyone else. And you're sure not your usual polite but reserved self. You let yourself get mad at him, and that's an improvement over indifference.'' Rhonda winked and left Amanda to take her place in the lineup two dancers down. Amanda drew a deep breath and did some preliminary leg exercises to warm up.

"Okay, people, thirty seconds.''

"Hey, Amanda!''

Amanda leaned backward, disturbing the clean line the dancers made as they stood an exact arm's length apart. Rhonda was doing the same, and she grinned at Amanda and gave her a thumbs-up. The music in the orchestra pit swelled.

"Five seconds to go, people. Four . . . three . . . two . . .''

"Break a leg, kid,'' Rhonda called softly and straightened back into line. Her voice drifted back as the dancers began to run lightly toward the stage, smiles lighting their faces the moment the stage lights touched thém. "Break a leg.''

"Yo, Lieutenant!''

Tristan looked up from the pile of papers on his desk. God, he hated this bloody paperwork. "Line two's for you, sir,'' one of his men said, waving a hand at the blinking light on the telephone in front of him. "Insists you're the only one who can help him.''

Tristan picked up the receiver, tossed down his pencil, and leaned back in his chair. "MacLaughlin.''

"Well, sure and begor-rrra,'' a whispering voice said. "You sounded more like a Scot on the tube.''

Tristan straightened. "Who's callin', please.'' He stuck a finger in his free ear to block out the sounds of loud voices, slamming file drawers, erratic typing, and ringing telephones in the squad room. The voice coming through the receiver was little more than a scratchy rasp, barely audible over the racket.

"Ach, Scotty, I am disappointed in you. Why, if the papers and the news on TV are to be believed, you're Reno's Great White Hope, come to rescue our fair-haired damsels in distress. I thought for sure you were gonna arrive on my doorstep any day now, complete with flashing blue lights and wailing sirens, to slap me in irons. But here you don't even know who you're talking to. Major disappointment, bud.''

''Are you the mon who's been killin' the dancers?'' All around him the men fell silent. Someone left the room to search for the call-tracing equipment.

''Bull's-eye.'' The laugh that followed was self-satisfied. ''I've been such a good boy lately, too, MacPrick, and let me tell you, it ain't been easy. I'm startin' to feel a real need for a little action. Yeah, I'm gettin' a definite itch. You got a special lady I can scratch it with?''

''No.'' Tristan ignored the cold sweat that trickled down his backbone.

''Too bad. That could've made things more interesting.'' There was a short, dead pause, during which Tristan was afraid his man had hung up. Then the raspy voice chuckled. ''I did get a tad tired of being such a choirboy, though, so I entertained myself with a little diversion. It was strictly bush league, you understand, and not nearly as much fun as boppin' the bitches, but still . . .''

''What did you do?''

''Hey, who's the detecative around here, bud, you or me? Come on, genius, you're the answer to all the dancers' prayers . . . or so they say. Let's see you figure it out.'' A distinctly disdainful snort traveled down the telephone wires. ''Not that you've got a snowball's chance in hell. When it comes to intelligence, I can run rings right around all you law-abiding bozo types.''

''I'm sure you can,'' Tristan agreed and glanced over at the man with the call-tracer. The man shook his head.

''Damn right. Well, listen there, Scotty, beam me up. I'm afraid I gotta run. Give my love to all the dancers.'' The man's laugh made Tristan's skin crawl. ''Tell them to watch their tails. I have been, and I'm startin' to get a little antsy.''

''Wait! I don't even know what to call you.''

''You can call me Duke, bud. Get it? Pretty fittin', eh?

You already know how good I am with my fists." The voice
laughed again. "Ta, ta, mate. We'll talk again."

The line went dead.

"Sorry, Lieutenant," the technician on the tracer said. "I
didn't have enough time to run him down. I didn't even get
the lousy first digits."

"It couldna be helped, mon. If the bleedin' sod is half as
smart as he claims to be, he was calling from a pay phone
anyhow—and not one close to his home. Shit!" Tristan's
huge hand slammed down on the desk. "He's competitive.
That makes the situation about as bad as it can get."

"Will you go public with this, Lieutenant?" Joe asked.

"No. I'm afraid that's exactly what the mon wants. If the
media gets wind of this, Duke might go on a spree just to
show the world how incompetent we are." Tristan ran his
hand through his hair. "I wonder what his side diversion
was? Not a murder, obviously. Anything unusual come over
the wires lately?"

Nobody knew of anything. "Hell," Lavander Mason muttered in disgust. "It could be damn near anything—rape, a
beating. Those would still be within his M.O., even if he
stopped short of murder this time. And if he decided to
diversify—shee-it." He shook his head. "The mind simply
boggles."

"You think he could have been talking about his encounter
with the Smith woman?" one of the detectives asked.

"Hell, who knows? I kinda doubt it, though. Rhonda Smith
outsmarted the lad, and Duke doesna strike me as the type
to brag about his failures. He must know we've come up
empty at the florist shops and dusting her car, but he never
said a word, and I get the impression he'd leap at any opportunity to rub our noses in it. No, I'm afraid we're going
to have to search elsewhere."

Tristan assigned a detail to review the records of recent
complaints. His civilian force called the ER at each of the
local hospitals and every out-clinic in the city that dealt with
emergency situations. They requested any reports pertaining

to victims of violence where the police had not been notified. That eliminated all gunshot wounds and other injuries caused by a lethal weapon. But it still left a number of incidents, ranging from a wino beaten senseless for no apparent reason to a homosexual who was beaten and robbed for either monetary gain or because the perpetrator had taken a violent dislike to the man's sexual preference, to a severely beaten young woman who had insisted to the skeptical emergency room doctor on duty that her injuries had been obtained by falling down a flight of stairs.

As Mason had stated, they were looking for the proverbial needle in a haystack. And they were searching blind. They didn't know in what manner the violence that Duke had visited upon his victim had manifested itself, or when, or even if the victim had been a woman. Historically, offenders of Duke's ilk repeated a pattern with one specific type of prey. But there weren't any hard-and-fast rules that guaranteed it. They were dealing with the actions of a sociopath, and if it had been him that night in the parking lot with Rhonda, he had already altered the pattern by deliberately selecting a dark-haired woman when all of his previous victims had been blondes. Hell, not knowing the nature of the assault, they couldn't even be reasonably certain that the victim hadn't either taken care of her own injuries or sought out medical attention from her private doctor.

It was work that promised to return negligible results, but Tristan knew that even the least likely prospects needed to be checked out thoroughly. If they could track down the proper victim, they would have their first eyewitness. And Tristan wanted that badly, before Duke decided to allow his competitive urges free reign.

Never one to give orders and then go home himself and put his feet up, Tristan worked alongside his task force. He worked double shifts, putting in eighteen-hour days, then went home and fell into a deep sleep for four hours. When he dragged himself out of bed, he worked out with his weights, ran three to five miles, showered, dressed, ate his one meal of the day that didn't originate in a fast-food emporium. Then he went back to work. On the job, he fortified himself with gallons of acidic coffee, ate greasy convenience food when somebody shoved it under his nose, and breathed the stale cloud of smoke that hung over the squad room when he was forced to spend time in the precinct. Each day, Duke called to taunt Tristan with his lack of progress, and Tristan could only be grateful that thus far, the killer was satisfied to merely bait him with words. It was stressful enough, listening to the murderous bugger brag about how much smarter he was than Tristan and the rest of the police probe. At least Duke hadn't presented him with another body, as well. Tristan decided to count it as a blessing. Everything else about this case was turning to shit.

The aggravation of his fruitless search and Duke's daily taunts, plus his lousy diet and lack of proper sleep, culminated in an explosion of uncontrolled aggression a week later. At least, that was what he assumed caused his loss of control—a loss that was more shattering to him than anything he had experienced in years. He was a man who prided himself on maintaining an iron discipline over his actions. He had learned at a tender age never to let his emotions surface for the world to see and take advantage of, and if he hadn't awakened with that damned headache pounding in his temples, he never would have . . .

Oh, hell. Maybe he would have. But he wished to hell, if he'd had to lose his bloody temper, it could have been in front of anyone other than Amanda Charles. Which was truly laughable, since she was the only person in the world who could make him lose control of his emotions with what was becoming monotonous regularity. It aggravated the hell out of him.

On the other hand, momentarily looking the fool wasn't necessarily the worst thing a man could do.

Not when you considered that just moments later he had come this close to making love to her. Up against the wall.

In broad daylight. In that bonny little alcove outside her front door.

The day after Pete's accident, Charlie brought in a replacement. His name was Dean Eggars, and he was the same dancer for whom Charlie had held the unprecedented audition a few weeks earlier.

Disgruntled by the swiftness with which a substitute had been found for one of their rank, the other dancers held themselves aloof from the new man for the first few days. At least Charlie had had the decency to wait a week to hire a replacement for Maryanne.

But the rampant speculation that Eggars must be one hell of a charmer to have convinced Charlie to audition him in the first place soon proved to be true. He went out of his way to be agreeable to everyone, even at the risk of occasionally incurring Charlie's wrath. One by one, the dancers succumbed to his considerable charms. Rhonda was one of the first, which Amanda, with unaccustomed cynicism, hadn't found surprising. After all, she decided with some irony, if Rhonda could find something to admire in MacLaughlin, whose charm quotient was zero, succumbing to Eggars, whose desire to please was unquestionable, was easy to accept. He was an attractive man. That had always been reason enough for Rhonda to be friendly in the past. Amanda could hardly deem it shocking to discover her friend's criterion hadn't changed in this instance.

Amanda wasn't as quick to capitulate to his charm. In a way, she found Dean Eggars almost too agreeable. Was it really necessary that everybody like him? In a group the size of theirs, which contained as many diverse personalities as there were souls to house them, she had never yet managed to be everybody's best friend. There was one dancer, actually, that she downright disliked, although so far, she had managed to disguise it well enough not to be out-and-out rude. Okay, so she'd admit it made her feel a little bit ridiculous to stand aloof from someone because he struck her as almost too accommodating to be true. But for a short time, she kept her distance for that very reason.

Besides, she couldn't quite reconcile his friendliness with her first impression of him. When she had observed him during his audition, he had displayed a confidence that had nearly bordered on arrogance. Yet, up close and personal, he didn't appear to have even half the overblown ego she had expected. It confused her.

Dean Eggars was one hell of a dancer, though, and if there was one thing that Amanda admired above anything else, it was inspired dancing. Watching him over a period of several days, she thawed by perceptible degrees. And when he asked for her help with the steps of a new routine that he was having a difficult time mastering, she decided it was time to quit acting like a suspicious old maid and give the poor man the benefit of the doubt. She invited him to come to her place the following day to practice the routine with her.

June and Rhonda, standing nearby, overheard and immediately invited themselves to join the rehearsal. June wanted to attend because she always felt in need of extra practice. Rhonda insisted on joining because her fear of being bounced from the troupe had prevented her from initiating a hot and heavy flirtation with Dean thus far, and she wanted a chance to get to know him away from Charlie's all-seeing eyes.

Word spread, and by the time Amanda left the casino that evening she had been approached by three other dancers, each of whom had expressed an interest in joining the impromptu practice. One of them, to her disgust, was the fourth male in the troupe, the one dancer she didn't like at all—Randy Baker.

Amanda was too polite to say so, but privately, she thought Randy was a sneaky creep, and in her opinion he was aptly named. He was as randy as a teenager riding the first raging crest of his hormones, and about as mature—more boy than man. Randy had a sly way of intimately touching the females in the troupe and then looking innocent and amazed, pretending it was an accident that his hand had just happened to skim across their buttocks or brush the sides of their breasts. Amanda disliked being touched intimately by strangers. She particularly disliked having someone take advantage of what was supposed to be a professional situation. The few times Randy had pulled his little stunt on her, it had left her almost sick with frustrated anger, for dancers did touch each other in the course of a routine, and invariably, he had managed to touch her in such a way that the only person who would look foolish if she made a fuss was herself. He had a high school stud's attitude and opinion of himself, apparently convinced he was God's gift to the female population. She would just as soon he didn't even know where she lived.

She merely shrugged, however, and said anyone who would care to come would be welcome. Most of these people were her family. She might not like Randy, but she identified with his desire to dance at any opportunity.

Dancers all shared a common addiction. They lived to dance.

CHAPTER
11

By the time Amanda's alarm rang the next day, the morning sun had been steadily shining through the French doors and the windows. The dining room was stifling when she stumbled in sleepily to arrange it for her expected arrivals. She threw open the doors and windows to air the room and hopefully cool it down, grumbling to herself all the while. Dammit. She had dancers coming at any minute, the number of whom was anybody's guess, and if there was one thing most dancers hated, it was trying to work out in an overheated, stuffy room. Of all the times to forget to drop the shades over the French doors, she wished she hadn't picked last night. Rapidly, she converted the room to a studio, then ran to the front door and swung it back and forth to create a draft. She had to cool this place down.

Amanda halted her frenzied activity in midmovement. With an ironic, crooked smile, she lifted her face to catch the cool breeze that wafted through the open doorway. She couldn't believe she was running around working herself into a sweat over a slightly stuffy room that was already cooling down nicely. Lord above, if that wasn't an indication of the state of her nerves these days, she didn't know what was. Sure, most dancers preferred a cool room in which to practice. But there wasn't one of them who hadn't danced in halls and lounges that were either hot enough to bake a chicken or so frigid you could see the icy vapor of your own breath as it formed in front of your face. Truth was, if it was comfort they wanted, most dancers would have picked a different profession.

Around ten the dancers began to arrive, shuffling their feet and grumbling about the ungodly hour. Energetic wasn't exactly the word she would use to describe them, but Amanda, not a morning person herself, had prepared a large pot of coffee, and she watched them pour cup after cup down their throats until the caffeine kicked in and they began to come alive. Like her, none of them had gotten to bed before three in the morning. And, for those who found it necessary to unwind a while after a late performance in order to sleep at all, it had been even later yet. One by one, however, they pried themselves away from the coffeepot in the kitchen and moved on to the studio, where they began warming up. Soon there was no one left in the kitchen except Amanda and Randy.

"Nice place," he murmured, watching Amanda as she moved around the room, putting the cream back in the refrigerator and wiping the spills off the tile counter.

"Thanks." She tossed the sponge in the sink. Something about the way he watched her filled her with tension. "Well, we'd better join the others if we're ever going to get this show on the road." Without being obvious, Amanda skirted the area where Randy lounged, giving him a wide berth. Good manners be damned, if he so much as laid one finger on her this morning . . .

Everyone was in the process of warming up when Amanda entered the room with Randy so close upon her heels she could feel the warmth of his breath on the back of her neck. Rhonda, Kelly, and David were squabbling good-naturedly over the best method for loosening tight muscles. Rhonda and David declared with stubborn insistence that the most efficient course was through floor exercises, while Kelly maintained that stretches at the barre were the only sensible way to begin a warm-up. June and Dean were ignoring the debate and every effort made by the others to draw them into it. They obviously preferred action to argument, as they steadfastly completed a series of rigorous exercises designed to warm up their muscles.

"I don't want to talk about it," Dean panted when Rhonda once again solicited his opinion. "I just want to get it over with." Rhonda laughed and agreed it was probably time she did less talking and more exerting.

The practice began slowly. At first they merely walked through the steps, repeatedly going over the combination that had been causing Dean difficulty. While the dancers were still largely uncertain of their ability to perform the routine, their feet were placed with hesitant lightness upon the wooden floor. But as their confidence increased, their feet began striking the floor with more firmness and strength. When David's flew out from under him and he crashed to the floor, they laughed, picked him up, and started from the top once again, this time attempting to run through it from beginning to end. They were determined not to give Charlie an excuse to berate them at this afternoon's rehearsal.

During the actual performance, the curtain opened on four of the women held aloft above the men's heads while the remaining four women were arranged at their feet as supplicants: on their knees, backs bowed and heads bent. As there were only three men at this practice and Kelly's usual role was one of the women on the floor, Amanda found herself partnered with Randy.

In this particular number, the women were suspended aloft in a forward-facing splits position, except the right leg was bent at the knee with the heel tucked into the crotch, toes pointed toward the left leg, which extended straight out on the opposite side at a right angle to the torso. Their partner's right hand cupped their crotch to support the majority of their weight while his left hand, primarily for balance, steadied the extended leg near the knee. Amanda had been hoisted over a male partner's head in this manner innumerable times, and except for the first few incidents when she was very young and still easily embarrassed, she never gave much thought to the intimate placement of her partner's hand. Within seconds of being boosted in the air that morning, however, it was evident that Randy wanted her to be totally aware of his sexuality.

The weight of her body pressing down on his hand limited his mobility, but nevertheless, his fingers managed to clumsily trace the shape of her, nudging into private hollows through her damp leotard. One finger stretched out to insinuate its tip between the division of her buttocks, while his palm cupped and flattened itself over her mound. Stealthily, his thumb caressed the tender area where her thigh joined her body.

Amanda seethed with frustration. There wasn't a damn thing she could do to stop Randy while she was suspended over his head—at least, not without upsetting her balance and probably crashing to the floor. But, my God, he was enjoying himself, wasn't he? She could practically feel the waves of smug triumph that emanated from him.

She clenched her teeth furiously. Well, the hell with that. She was tired of always displaying her pretty, impeccable manners when what she really longed to do was put a halt to something that she knew in her heart was just not right.

"Put me down!" Amanda didn't care that everyone stumbled to a confused halt at the sound of her loud and angry demand. The minute her feet touched the floor, she whirled to face Randy.

"If you ever," she said, emphasizing each word she spoke with a furious poke of her forefinger to his chest, "I mean *ever*, pull something like that again, I'll break your chops, Randy Baker."

"Hey," he said, shrugging with feigned innocence. "I don't know what the hell you're talking about."

"Oh, no?" Amanda's chest heaved with fury. "Well, let

me spell it out for you then, you slimy little grabby-fingered bastard. I've had it with your sly feelies. If you think the women in this troupe were put on earth to provide you with a cheap thrill, think again. I'm a dancer, dammit, not some two-bit bimbo. You aren't going to use my vulnerability in the air to get yourself off, and if you ever try it again, buster, I'll simply dive for the floor.'' She stared at him with contempt. ''And believe me, Randy, I'll figure out a way to break your neck on my way down.''

''You're certifiable, girl.''

''No, she's not,'' Kelly said, stepping forward. ''Every female in the group has had a run-in with your hands. Just because no one's ever called you on it before doesn't mean we aren't wise to you.''

Breathing heavily, Amanda looked around, becoming aware of the rest of the dancers for the first time. Dean was studying her with interest; David was trying hard not to smile; and Rhonda and June were nodding in agreement.

''I take it you were less subtle than usual, Randy,'' Rhonda said. ''You must be losing your touch—or getting desperate.''

Amanda snorted. ''Subtle? God, you can't imagine how rich that is. He was copping feels for all he was worth. But then, with his punk kid attitude, I suppose that's the only way he can get within touching range of a woman.''

''You bitch.'' Color high, Randy stepped forward, his body language promising retribution.

The outside door crashed back against the wall, and everyone jumped in shock. ''What the bloody hell is going on here?''

Amanda's head snapped around. Standing in the open doorway was Lieutenant MacLaughlin. She stared at him in openmouthed amazement, for it was a Lieutenant MacLaughlin she had never seen before. The man was practically naked.

Well, not really naked, but compared with his usual neat suit and tie, which was the only apparel she had ever seen him wear, the worn gray sweatpants riding low on his hipbones seemed barely decent. His thick, wiry hair was flattened on one side, his normally smooth-shaven jawline was dark with stubble, and his feet and chest were bare. All that exposed skin, stretched tautly over clearly defined muscle and lightly covered with feathery hair darker in shade than the sandy-brown on his head, made him appear larger than ever. Amanda took a reflexive step backward when he strode into the room. Even without the gun that he had hastily withdrawn from a firing stance, letting the hand that held it fall to his side, he projected a definite air of menace.

"I want to know what's goin' on," he repeated in a deceptively quiet voice. "And I want to know now. It sounded like a bloody war zone up here." Tristan felt anger climbing perilously close to the surface and tried to tamp it down. God, his head was pounding. He'd been jerked out of a restless sleep by a tremendous crash overhead, and by pure reflex he had snatched up his gun, jumped into his sweats, and raced up here, certain the killer with whom he'd been matching wits for the past week was mutilating Amanda. Now he felt like a flamin' idiot, and seeing the expressions on this group of dancers as they stood rooted in place, gawking at him, wasn't improving his mood any. They were all regarding him as if he were Rambo, come to life.

"We were dancing, Lieutenant." Amanda felt the anger that had been directed toward Randy transfer itself to the big cop. She dragged her eyes away from his bare chest, and dropped them pointedly to the gun in Tristan's hand. "Is that a shooting offense?"

Tristan swore under his breath. Dancing? God, it was hard to think straight with this splitting headache. Exerting the force of his considerable will, he managed to say in a neutral voice, "I was sleepin', lass. Do you have any idea what *dancing*"—the word came out between clenched teeth, but he quickly regained control—"sounds like over the head of someone who's sound asleep?"

"Like a herd of elephants, I should imagine, especially when David hit the floor," Rhonda said and grinned unrepentantly. She stared at Tristan's body with undisguised interest, cataloging each separate feature. Tristan failed to notice, having not more than glanced at anyone other than Amanda.

"I'm sorry we woke you, Lieutenant," Amanda said softly, trying to be reasonable. After all, no one liked to be awakened by loud noises, and he was being fairly amenable about it, not yelling at them like a lot of people would do. "But, honestly," she couldn't refrain from adding, staring with loathing at the gun he held at his side, "there's really no need to come up here brandishing your gun. All you have to do is ask us to stop."

Oh, sweet mother of God, give me patience. "Excuse us a moment," Tristan growled at the interested group, grabbed Amanda by the arm, and dragged her out the front door. Closing it softly behind them, he maneuvered Amanda into the small alcove to the left of her front door.

Angry all over again, Amanda twisted her arm from his grasp. "I've told you before, cowboy, I don't like being manhandled."

The front door opened again and Randy stepped out, his dance bag flung over one shoulder. Tristan half turned to see who it was, and Amanda peered past the smooth, rounded expanse of his shoulder at the disgruntled dancer. She smiled sweetly. "Leaving so soon, Randy?" she inquired. "Don't you go running away mad, now." He glared at her and she added, "Just as long as you go away."

The look he directed her way was pure malevolence. "You're a real ball-busting bitch, Amanda," he snarled and stomped down the stairs. Then he was blocked from sight when Tristan abruptly turned back to her. All she could see for a moment was the pattern of hair that lightly furred his chest. Amanda drew a deep breath and slowly exhaled. She felt hemmed in by his huge body, trapped in the small alcove. He peered down at her quizzically through his dark-rimmed glasses.

"What was that all about?"

"Nothing that need concern you, Lieutenant," Amanda replied. "Randy and I simply had a disagreement." She glared at the gun in his hand and then raised her violet-blue eyes to meet his. "We don't need you and your gun to mediate."

Tristan stared down at her delicate dark eyebrows, furrowed in distaste over her long, slim nose; at her blond hair curling wildly away from her face; and at her flushed cheeks and full mouth; and he felt weeks of accumulated aggravation and frustration rise up and threaten to explode in the face of her transparent antagonism. Stonily, he clamped a lid on his temper, and his voice became cold and level from the effort. "I wasna offerin' myself or my gun for mediation," he said dispassionately. He tucked the weapon that she found so offensive into the waistband of his sweatpants at the small of his back and tightened the drawstring. Bracing his hands on the walls on either side of the small passageway, he leaned over her. "You've made your opinion of my profession and my gun quite flamin' apparent several times now, and frankly, it's beginnin' to bore me." Anger flared in Amanda's eyes, but Tristan ignored it. He was angry himself, even if he refused to let it show. He might be reserved by nature, a loner by circumstance, but he wasn't some freaked-out commando with a gun in one hand and a grenade in the other, looking for an excuse to pull the soddin' pin with his teeth and the trigger with his finger, the way she apparently viewed him. "I didna coom runnin' up to your apartment, brandishin' my gun, as you say, because you were makin' a great deal of noise." He could feel his grasp on his accent slipping away, but he didn't care. "I thoght y' might be in trouble, then, dinna I. And I thoght I could be of assistance. You seem to make it a point to forget there's a killer oot there stalkin' dancers." His silver-gray eyes narrowed behind his lenses. "The gun is anoother matter. You have some serious misconceptions about a policeman's need to carry a weapon. I'll be havin' you know, lassie, that in the sixteen years I've been on the force, I have fired my gun exactly once in the line of duty. One soddin' time, lass. As a rule, I keep it oiled and I keep it ready, but it only ever gets fired at the range. That doesna mean I wouldna point it at someone and pull the trigger if I felt the situation merited it. And I'll no' be bloody well apologizin' to you or anyone else for carryin' it or for bein' fully prepared to use it, if I moost.''

Amanda stared up at him, feeling utterly foolish and in the wrong. He was right, of course; she knew that. She was unreasonably antagonistic with this man, looking for obstacles to throw in his path the instant he came near her. Amanda edged back a step. She wished he wouldn't stand so close. There was something about him that made her feel the way she used to feel back in high school when the boys had first began flirting with her, and her way of dealing with her sexual inexperience and uncertainties had been to lapse into hostile sarcasm.

Amanda's head tilted proudly. This was insane. She wasn't seventeen, and she wasn't inexperienced anymore. And she certainly didn't have to stand here with her heart pounding, being made to feel the fool. So, she'd misjudged him this once; so what? The thing to do was to apologize gracefully, and then walk the hell away. But it sure aggravated her that his face lacked all expression. Didn't the man ever mess up or do dumb things—say dumb things—like the rest of the world? It infuriated her that he could read her like a Dick and Jane primer while she couldn't tell the first thing about what went on in his mind.

Opening her mouth to say "I'm sorry; I've been unpardonably presumptuous; forgive me," Amanda was appalled to instead hear herself ask, "What do they do, MacLaughlin? Program you down at the station? I mean, how do you stay so detached? You're like a damned robot. Nothing ever gets to you."

Amanda's words died in her throat at the pure fury that twisted MacLaughlin's face. His hands gripped her shoulders with brutal force, and all the anger he had managed to suppress earlier was there in his voice now. "You just have to

keep pushin', do ya not? You dinna like my detachedness?
Fine. This should prove to you once and for all that I'm not
your bleedin' father and I'm not a damn robot either.''

That's when he yanked her forward and kissed her. And,
if before that instant she had thought he stood aloofly by and
observed life from the sidelines, she discovered then that she
was mistaken. For there was nothing detached about his hungry mouth moving over hers, nothing aloof about the powerful
grip of his arms on her back as they pressed her forward into
the heat of his body, or in his blunt fingers, tangled in her
hair, grasping her skull. There was nothing detached at all,
and his intensity laid to waste her powers of reasoning.

His unexpected anger had stunned her, and he had pulled
her to him so quickly, she had hardly had time to react.
Automatically, she raised her hands to push him away. But,
for just an instant, she was caught up in the contrast of how
things as they appeared to be and as they actually were could
be so devastatingly different.

For instance, MacLaughlin's mouth appeared hard and
stern, but, Lord help her . . . it was soft. Strong. Hot. But
not hard—not hard at all. The only remotely harsh element
of his kiss was the heavy morning beard of his unshaven jaw,
abrading the tender skin of her face.

Having hesitated for even that brief an instant, she forgot
exactly to which it was she had been going to object. Being
manhandled again, maybe? Um. Something like that. She
didn't remember and she didn't care. Any objection she might
have raised was swamped beneath a wave of sensation. And
when her hands came into contact with the texture and temperature of his skin, her fingers, which had arrived with every
intention of fighting him off, spread instead across his chest,
burrowing beneath the light fan of hair, rubbing and sliding
up over his collarbones to dig into the warm, resilient flesh
that covered his rounded shoulder muscles. Her eyes remained
wide open and dazed.

Tristan's mouth kept opening over Amanda's. Restlessly,
he slanted his lips over the fullness of hers, pulling at her

mouth with a soft, hungry suction. When she didn't open to
him immediately, he raised his head, stared into her eyes for
a moment, and then came at her from another direction, using
the hand in her hair to tilt her face to accommodate him. He
widened his mouth around her lips and then slowly dragged
it closed, tugging at her lips.

She didn't even think twice. Amanda's lips simply parted
beneath his, and Tristan made a wordless sound of satisfaction
deep in his throat.

His tongue was slow and thorough. It slid along her bottom
lip and explored the serrated edges of her teeth. Releasing
his grip on her head, Tristan pulled her closer into the heat
of his body, moving his pelvis against her with suggestive
need. His tongue rubbed along hers with mobile aggression,
and nerves Amanda hadn't even known she possessed flamed
to acute, throbbing life. Her tongue surged up to challenge
his and she arched against him, sliding her arms up to wrap
tightly around the strong column of his neck, plunging her
fingers into his crisp hair. She was aware of every muscle in
his body as he pressed against her, and she could feel him,
hard and hot and erect against her stomach. Murmuring soft
sounds of excitement, she raised up on tiptoe, lifting her left
leg with an agility borne of years of dancing, to hook the
back of her knee behind his hard buttocks and press his hips
forward with her calf until that hot rigidity was aligned to a
pulsing hollow that throbbed with the need to be filled.

Very slowly, her eyelids slid closed.

Tristan groaned and kissed her harder, aroused nearly to
a frenzy. Meaning only to lean her against a support, but
misjudging the distance from where they stood, he slammed
her up against the wall of the apartment and rocked against
her with slow, mindless insistence. One large hand slid slowly
up the leg locked around his hip, stroking from knee to thigh,
pulling her closer into him before it eased beneath the high-
cut leg of her leotard to grip her firm, tights-covered bottom
with wide splayed fingers. "Oh, lass," he breathed into her
mouth, and then, unable to bear even that slight separation,

he kissed her harder, his mouth hungry and a little rough against hers.

Amanda tightened her grip around his neck and kissed him back, following his lead exactly.

Tristan eased his chest back enough to wedge his free hand between their tightly compressed bodies. Palm pressed flatly against the warm skin over her ribs, his thumb spread wide of the rest of his fingers, he slid his hand up until it covered her breast. They both inhaled sharply, simultaneously. Amanda's back arched, pushing her breast more fully into his hand. Tristan's hand kneaded and rotated, pressing the resilient fullness back against the wall of her chest, his fingers curving to capture the overflow.

He was frustrated by the tights and the one-piece leotard she wore. She looked so bloody smashing in it, but it protected her flesh from invasion like a high-security alarm system. He wanted to sink his fingers into her, skin on skin; feel the pebbled texture of her nipple against his palm; pluck it with his fingertips; taste it on his tongue.

But the bloody outfit had no buttons; the scoop of the neckline was too high to slide his hand into; there was no flamin' hem to raise. God, it looked so bleedin' promising, but it was a tease, a bloody iron maiden.

"Help me, lass," he breathed and then gripped her head in both hands to hold it erect while he sank his mouth into the side of her throat.

Amanda was obediently reaching up to do just that when the front door opened. Rhonda stuck her head out and called softly, "Lieutenant MacLaughlin?" She was peering directly into the sun and didn't immediately see Tristan and Amanda in the shadows of the alcove. "Lieutenant? Are you out here?"

Tristan ripped his mouth free and pushed himself away from Amanda, blinking lazily at first and then with deliberation as the world began to focus around him again. Drawing air deep into his lungs, he stared down at her in amazement.

Good God. He had never, never found himself in a predicament quite like this. It was broad-bloody-daylight and he, a man who was always aware of where he was and what was going on around him, had been moments away from taking her out here on her own front porch, in a recess that was only minimally shadowed.

Staring intently at her heavy-lidded plum-dark eyes, her bruised mouth, and the abrasions caused by his heavy beard, Tristan was shook to the core as he cleared his throat and said, "Here, Miss Smith."

"Oh, there you are . . ." Rhonda's voice trailed away as she spied Amanda with the lieutenant and noticed her condition. Her eyes dropped to the front of Tristan's sweats and then immediately raised to look into his eyes. "Uh, there's a phone call for you. It's Detective Cash, and he says it's urgent."

"I'll be right there." Tristan leaned close to Amanda for an instant, dipping his head until their eyes were on a level. "I'm not a flamin' robot," he whispered harshly. "Dinna insinuate I am, ever again." He turned on his heel and padded away on bare feet, disappearing into the apartment. Amanda's dazed eyes followed the departing sight of rounded shoulder and arm muscles; long, smooth back; and the tight bunch and flex of his hard buttocks as he walked away from her. For once, she didn't even notice the gun tucked into the back of his waistband.

Momentarily docile, she remained where he had left her, slumped against the wall, lethargically searching for orientation in a disoriented mind. All of her nerve endings felt close to the surface of her skin, and they were highly sensitive to outward stimuli. She throbbed with frustration. Her breasts felt heavy and full and unbearably tender; her nipples were pinpoints of pain. Her skin burned with dry heat all over her body, and between her thighs there was an empty, pulpy void that ached with deprivation. Oh, dear God. How had he brought her to this?

"Interesting morning," Rhonda murmured, stepping close and observing Amanda with relish. "First, you expose Randy for copping a feel.'' She paused. ''Then you get down and dirty in the front yard with MacLaughlin. You're a mighty busy girl, Mandy Rose.'' A warm gurgle of laughter escaped Rhonda's throat, and Amanda winced.

''Please,'' she whispered. ''Don't make fun of me, Rhonda.''

''Sure.'' Rhonda was immediately compassionate as she studied the look of shattered confusion in Amanda's eyes. ''Oh, kid, he really shook you right down to your poor abused toes, didn't he?''

Amanda nodded weakly.

''There's always been something sorta . . . untouched about you. I knew none of those clowns you dated had ever shown you what it was all about—sex, I mean. How good it can be.'' Rhonda peered at Amanda, studying her intently. ''Mandy, I gotta ask you. Do you still think it's all just a waste of time?''

''No,'' Amanda whispered.

''I didn't hear you screaming for help, so I gotta believe you were a willing participant. So, tell me, kiddo, on a scale of one to ten, would you still rate your sexuality as a three? D'ya still believe you're not the passionate type?''

Eyes closed, Amanda slowly shook her head no. My God, no; she had just never realized. This, then, was what everybody was always talking about. She never believed it was possible to feel such things. Limply, her hand lifted to touch her swollen mouth and the patches of abraded skin surrounding it. ''God, I must look a mess.''

Her eyes snapped open, locking with incipient panic on Rhonda's. ''How am I going to face everyone? They'll all know exactly what MacLaughlin and I were doing out here for so long.''

''Does it really matter?''

''Yes! It does. To me, it does. Oh, Rhonda, I know it shouldn't. I know that I am supposedly grown up and therefore shouldn't have to apologize for my actions. But I hardly understand what I think about this myself. I need time to sort

194 Susan Andersen

it out in my own mind. What I do know is that I'm not up to facing that bunch in there. God, they'll be merciless if they know I was out here necking with MacLaughlin. Especially after the way I jumped all over Randy . . ."

"Who was begging to be jumped all over."

"Yeah." Amanda looked Rhonda in the eye. "Please don't discuss this with anyone, Rhonda."

"Honey, one look at your face and no discussion is going to be necessary."

Amanda moaned.

"Don't panic." Rhonda brushed a light curl away from Amanda's dark eyebrow. "Listen, kiddo. You know I won't discuss your private business with anyone if you don't want me to. And you weren't actually gone that long, anyhow." She couldn't prevent a grin from escaping. "It probably just felt like an eternity once MacLaughlin got you in his clutches. But you're talking to an old pro here, kid. We'll go in now and you just walk straight back to the bathroom. Close the door, run yourself one of your eternal bubble baths, and I'll take care of the rest. I'll ease them out so smoothly, they won't know what hit 'em. It's a pity you have to miss my performance, though. You're one of the few people who would really appreciate it."

"Oh, God, Rhonda, I love you."

"Hey." Rhonda shrugged, but she warmed with delight. Amanda was very special in her life. She was the first really close woman friend she'd had since she and Doris Prodecavich had drifted apart back in high school, following Rhonda's decision to seriously apply herself to dance. It wasn't through lack of interest that she'd never found another girlfriend to take Doris's place; her schedule simply precluded the time to make friends with women in other professions, and the dance world was a transient one. It wasn't for nothing that chorus dancers were called gypsies. And, unfortunately, the few women with whom she had hit it off had soon moved on.

That had left her with a host of friendly acquaintants but

no real friends, and she had missed that. There were certain things you could talk about only to another woman—shared experiences only another female could ever understand. The thing she had missed most was being able to confide in someone without the worry of hearing her secrets broadcast about town the next morning. The trouble with the dance community was you had to be careful who you told your innermost desires to sometimes, for it was gossip-minded in the extreme, and news traveled fast.

When they had first met, Rhonda had thought Amanda Charles was probably the last woman she would ever feel close to. They were poles apart, both physically and in their personalities.

For a woman her age, who had been kicking around on her own as long as she had, Amanda had had such incredible innocence when they had first met. Hell, she had it still. It had taken Rhonda a while to realize it, however, because the image Amanda projected was one of smiling but reserved elegance. If one went strictly by looks, she seemed aloof and sophisticated and cool. Rhonda herself was anything but innocent, and she didn't have the energy or inclination to pretend otherwise—an attitude that had put off more than one potential girlfriend.

With a detached, cynical amusement, Rhonda had watched Amanda operate when she had first joined the troupe. Mandy was so unfailingly polite, so agreeable and friendly, that before they'd had time to realize what she was doing, she had already managed to distance herself from the male members of the troupe and crew. She had turned them into pals with an easy, humorous deflection of all but the most persistent of sexual advances. And once a man discovered himself to be Amanda's good buddy, he also discovered it was impossible to introduce any form of intimacy into the relationship.

It hadn't been hard to guess, from her speech and her manners, that Amanda's background had been sheltered and moneyed. Rhonda had watched the men automatically curb the worst of their tendency to curse in Amanda's presence or break off the telling of a dirty joke when she appeared. And Rhonda's initial reaction had been that she was the ultimate little Miss Priss. She had assumed their basic differences would make it impossible to tolerate each other. Amanda was a "good" girl. Rhonda believed in living up to her own reputation of raunchy rowdiness whenever possible.

But it hadn't been that way. As with everyone, Amanda had quietly observed Rhonda for a while. But her smile had been friendly enough, and she had actually initiated brief conversations that Rhonda could respond to effortlessly. And despite the determination with which Amanda brushed off any topics of a sexual nature that the men might try to introduce, Rhonda had noticed that rather than poking that narrow nose of hers in the air and acting offended when she overheard one of Rhonda's off-color remarks, Amanda had seemed to be secretly amused by them. At first Rhonda had thought she must be imagining it, for although she would catch Amanda smiling, her chin would be tucked down in her neck and her eyes would be lowered. But before long Amanda had been catching Rhonda's eye and giving her a wicked, appreciative grin. With increasing regularity, she had begun to gravitate in Rhonda's direction.

Later, Rhonda had learned about Teddy, and it didn't take a genius to know that what had first drawn Amanda to her was a personality that must be strongly reminiscent of Amanda's dead sister. But whatever it was that had initially pulled Amanda into her orbit, Rhonda was just grateful she'd had it. She had expected Amanda to make her feel promiscuous and trashy, defensive about the way she lived her life. Instead, Amanda laughed at her jokes with genuine amusement when other people didn't even get them, and she really listened when Rhonda talked. She made her feel witty and special and loved. Amanda liked her just the way she was. She didn't seem to feel this compulsion that so many people did to try to change Rhonda's basic personality.

So when Amanda expressed her appreciation, her love,

Rhonda shrugged her shoulders and said, "Forget it; nothing to it." But although her voice was light, she was dead serious when she inquired, "After all, kiddo, what are friends for?"

Aside from an automatic perusal that placed everyone's position firmly in his brain, Tristan ignored the dancers milling around when he entered the apartment. His headache was back worse than before, but now he had an aching, angry body to match it. He couldn't believe he'd let himself get so caught up in the taste and feel of her that he had actually lost sight of where the hell he was. Angry with his unprecedented lapse, he snatched up the phone and growled, "MacLaughlin here." His only consolation was the fact that she had looked just as stunned as he'd felt. Not as bloody frustrated, though. Tristan's eyebrows gathered in a grim line above his nose. Nobody could feel as bloody frustrated.

"Lieutenant?" Joe Cash's voice was tired and angry. He rattled off an address. "You'd better come right down. We've got us a new victim."

CHAPTER
12

The address Joe Cash had given Tristan belonged to a small mom-and-pop-style grocery store downtown. The newest victim had been discovered in a dumpster behind the store.

Tristan was grateful the press had not as yet been alerted, but judging by the activity in and around the store—the roped-off areas, the crackling radios and flashing lights—he thought it wouldn't be long before they heard the news. His shoulders hunched. He would just have to deal with that particular problem when the time came. Right now he had other priorities.

The medical examiner was bent over a corpse with long blond hair. That's all Tristan could see—the swath of pale hair and the dancer's long legs, bruised and muddied. The rest was blocked from view by the wide backside of the examiner as he squatted alongside the body. Until he was finished there was no use approaching, for in police procedure, the medical examiner's job took precedence.

"Lieutenant." Joe stuck his head out a door at the back of the narrow store and hailed Tristan. Edging his way past policemen and their paraphernalia, he had to turn sideways to navigate the narrow, can-laden aisles. The room turned out to be a storeroom, piled high with empty boxes and several unopened cases of vodka. Joe was quietly talking to a shaken middle-aged woman when Tristan walked in. "Terrible business," she was moaning, as she pulled a damp handkerchief between her fingers. "Terrible."

"Lieutenant, this is Mrs. Schultz. She and her husband own the store, and she discovered the body." Joe gently touched one of the woman's hands to direct her attention. "Mrs. Schultz, this is Lieutenant MacLaughlin. He'll be in charge of the investigation."

"We don't even use the dumpster during the day—not very often," she said in such a way that Tristan suspected it wasn't the first time she had uttered those words today. She mumbled them like an incantation: said often enough, maybe the words could erase the horror of what she had discovered. "We jest throw ever'thing in the trash can behind the counter and take it out before we close up. But we got in a big shipment of vodka, and with all them boxes and stuff, I figured I'd better clear out some space. You kin see there's not much room in here."

"Yes, ma'am," Tristan murmured.

"Harry's been sick. That's my husband—Harry." Mrs. Schultz let go of her handkerchief with one hand and ran stubby, work-worn fingers through her bouffant salt-and-pepper hair. "His back's been acting up somethin' awful, so I tol' him to stay home today. Then, when the vodka come in, I thought I'd surprise him by putting it all away myself. But it got so crowded back here, I had to clear out some space jest to move around. So I took a pile of the empties out to the dumpster. And . . . and . . . oh, jeez . . ." She turned away, embarrassed to let the two big detectives see her tears. The knuckles of one heavily veined hand pressed hard against her lips to stop them from trembling, and the handkerchief clenched in her fist vibrated visibly. "Where's Harry?" she whispered. "I need Harry."

"Your husband is on his way, Mrs. Schultz," Joe assured

her, reaching over to give her an awkward pat on her plump shoulder. ''I called him myself, and he's on his way.'' Moments later a tall, thin, gray-haired man rushed in, making a beeline for the plump little woman sitting on the vodka cases.

Tristan beckoned Joe to the far end of the storeroom. ''What's the story?''

''Doc's not done out there yet, but even without the coroner's report, there's very little doubt it's the same guy. Same exact M.O.: she was sexually molested and apparently beaten to death.''

''You doing my job for me now, Joey?'' Tristan and Joe looked up as the medical examiner walked into the storeroom. He was just under average height, with a girth that made him appear nearly as wide as he was tall. His black hair was heavily streaked with gray, but he had a childlike, plump roundness of cheek and rosy coloring. He signaled them to step outside.

Out behind the store, the medical examiner pulled a cigar from the breast pocket of his sport shirt and struck a match, holding it to the tip and puffing until it glowed red. Shaking out the match, he turned to the two policemen. ''Joe's pretty much hit the nail on the head,'' he said. ''Superficial exam leads me to believe we're dealing with the same perpetrator. There's a pattern of tears and contusions that's consistent with the previous victims. I'll take samples of semen and the saliva where he bit her and run it through the lab, of course, but five'll get you ten, if we're dealing with the same man —and I'd put money on it—then he's not a secretor, so we won't make blood type that way. There appear to be minute skin particles under her nails, so it's probable she scratched him. Maybe we'll luck out there.'' He puffed furiously on his cigar, wreathing his face in a cloud of blue smoke. ''This is a fuckin' animal we're dealing with here, gentlemen.'' Nodding to where two men were clumsily placing the body in a bag, he said, ''She was probably a real looker. But he worked her over so systematically, you couldn't tell it by me."

"Aye," Tristan agreed. "It's bolder he's gettin', then. I don't like the sounds of that. First the calls, and now this. If he's gearin' up for a rampage, there's going to be bloody hell to pay." He caught a last glimpse of the victim's hair as they closed the bag around her body, and the floor of his stomach rippled uneasily. It was almost the exact same shade as Amanda's. "How long you estimate she's been dead?"

"If you won't hold me to it until I've had a chance to run 'er through the lab, I'd guess around ten to twelve hours. Call me about five this afternoon, and I'll have a full report."

"Aye, thanks, Doc," Tristan replied and watched the man walk away, trailing a plume of pungent smoke behind him. Tristan turned to Joe. "She have any ID on her?"

"Nothing that was readily visible," Joe answered. He indicated two men sifting through the dumpster. "They're checking now to make sure nothing worked its way down to the bottom." As they looked on, one of the men stiffened slightly and, using both hands, dug through the refuse. Still draped half in and half out of the dumpster, he raised his upper torso and turned his head in their direction. "Lieutenant?"

Tristan walked over, reaching the dumpster as the man slid off the container to his feet. "What have you got there?"

"Trouble, Lieutenant." Holding it by means of a ballpoint pen thrust under the flap, he turned it so Tristan could see. It was a navy-blue leather clutch bag, and there was a small envelope paper-clipped to the flap. The man's partner held open a plastic bag and he slipped the purse into it, then handed it to Tristan.

Tristan squinted to read the jagged line of letters. They had obviously been clipped from a magazine. As he made sense of them, a chill slid down his spine.

It was addressed to him.

* * *

Long after she had heard the last of the dancers being ushered out by Rhonda, Amanda remained in the bathtub, trying to understand her encounter with MacLaughlin. Unconsciously, her hand kept rising up out of the water to touch her tender mouth. She had never felt like this before.

Never.

One simple kiss shouldn't drive a woman to such unaccustomed lengths, should it? Somehow, though, simple didn't seem to adequately describe it; he'd involved much more of himself than just his mouth.

Oh, God, she couldn't understand this. She didn't even like MacLaughlin—except for his smile, and that was seen with about the same frequency as an entertaining commercial. How could you like someone whose expression hardly ever changed? He was aloof, cool-eyed, and distant, and as far as she could tell, he totally lacked the primary asset that always before had attracted her to a man—a sense of humor.

He wasn't so cool-eyed and distant twenty minutes ago, Amanda Rose.

Her sudden laughter in the empty bathroom was tinged with hysteria. She didn't even know his first name. That Bunny woman had said it when she'd called to him out in the yard that night, but Amanda had been too wrapped up in her anger and fear at the time to pay attention. How could she harbor an attraction for a man whose first name she didn't even know?

Yeah, you're a regular Miss Manners. Notice it didn't seem to slow you down any out there in the alcove.

Where had all that emotion come from, and where had all his icy self-control gone? What else was under that disciplined exterior? She would have sworn he was colder than an arctic wind, but it was going to be difficult to maintain that theory now. God, she'd never felt so much heat enveloping her, and it had all originated from MacLaughlin's mouth and hands and body. Did he always kiss like that? Had MacLaughlin gone back to his apartment that night and kissed Bunny with the same single-minded concentration? With the same intensity? Had he pushed her up against a wall and . . .

Not that she'd care, of course. She wouldn't . . . she didn't. She was merely curious to know if the expertise he'd displayed this morning was the result of years of practice. She'd assumed she had been kissed by experts before, but no one else had ever kissed her quite like that. No one else had ever made her feel that every atom of his awareness was focused exclusively on her.

She rolled her shoulders uneasily, not liking the manner in which her body responded to the mere memory. So, MacLaughlin had somehow unearthed her hot button—so what? It was blind luck.

Amanda sat up abruptly, causing her bathwater to slosh from one end of the tub to the other in a gathering wave. *Is there somebody else in this room that I don't know about? Just who do you think you're kidding?*

No one had ever elicited that response from her before— no one. When it came to the passion department, she'd always assumed she was—well, not deficient, exactly—just sort of inured. She had always secretly believed she was more like Mother and Father than she cared to admit. Sexual urges usually seemed so . . . extraneous. Now, thanks to that assumption, she was left nakedly unprepared for the barrage of sensations that remained with her long after MacLaughlin had jerked himself away and stomped off—sensations that made her feel raw and exposed. Yesterday, she would have scoffed if someone had told her it was possible to feel this aching, greedy need.

Yesterday, she hadn't stood on tiptoe and wrapped her leg around some guy's rear end to yank him into her waiting heat.

With uncharacteristically awkward movements, Amanda climbed out of the bath and toweled herself dry. Crossing to the mirror, she untucked a corner of the towel from between her breasts and used it to clear a circle in the middle of the steamed-over glass. Curiously, she leaned forward and peered at her image.

She looked the same as always. Her fingers touched her lips again. Her mouth was a tiny bit swollen, and there were one or two red patches from the scratchy abrasion of his beard, but other than that, no one would probably guess that just a short while ago they'd been all over each other like . . . She straightened defensively. Not that there was any real reason to look different. It was a kiss, dammit. Just a kiss.

Yeah, sure.

So, what was she supposed to do the next time she saw him? Pretend it never happened? Is that what he would do? She knew he'd been as affected by their encounter as she had been; she'd been practically glued to the rigid length of his arousal, so it was hard to miss. But he hadn't looked too happy about it.

Dinna call me robot, ever again. She could hear his voice, saying that; see the look in his eyes. *Oh, MacLaughlin, robot is no longer the word that comes to mind when I think of you.*

She didn't think she was capable of pretending it hadn't happened. At the very least, she wasn't going to be able to view him as she had before. God help her, she hadn't chosen to be attracted to him. But it was her first genuine encounter with passion, and she knew she was going to remember his hands and mouth and the heat he had generated every time she looked at him. It had been a lot simpler when she had been half convinced he was an android.

She suddenly shivered in the warm room. What if he expected to take up where they had left off? Would she be allowed to say yes or no? She had left him in very little doubt as to her willingness, but that was then. As for now . . . She didn't know what she wanted now.

She really, really wished she did.

For once in her life, Amanda didn't look forward to rehearsal. And, as luck would have it, the first person she saw when she and Rhonda walked onto the stage was Randy, the next-to-last person she wanted to see. He was examining a welt on his right wrist that looked wickedly painful, and didn't notice them immediately. He hastily dropped his sleeve over the injury as soon as he spotted them, obviously in no mood to welcome questions, but it was too late. Rhonda's curiosity was aroused.

"What happened to you?" she demanded, crossing to where he stood. Despite his attempt to stop her, she pushed up his sleeve and peered at the red, raw-looking welts that criss-crossed his arm nearly to his elbow. "God, Randy, that's ugly."

"Tell me about it." He snatched his arm away and pulled down the sleeve, glaring at Rhonda and altogether avoiding eye contact with Amanda. "All I tried to do was pet a damn cat. You woulda thought I was friggin' made out of catnip, the way it attached itself to my arm."

"Whose cat was it?"

"How the hell do I know whose cat? One outside my apartment, is all. It was black and pretty and I just wanted to pet it."

One of Rhonda's eyebrows rose. "Maybe this is just God's way of telling you not to go around snatching yourself an uninvited handful of pussy whenever you feel the urge." She stared at him with large, guileless eyes. "D'you suppose?"

An unexpected snort of pure, undiluted laughter caught sideways in Amanda's throat and threatened to blow it apart. She attempted to quell it, which hurt, and wondered why she was bothering to try to spare Randy's feelings. He had never stopped to consider hers in his attempts to grab a handful of whatever portion of her anatomy caught his fancy. Giving up the effort, she laughed uninhibitedly.

Randy pinned them both with a killing glare, then stomped off toward the dressing rooms. He brushed roughly past David and Dean when they crossed paths in the wings, and they were still darting puzzled glances at him over their shoulders as they approached the two women.

"What's with him?" David jerked a thumb at the now-empty wings.

"I dunno, Davey," Rhonda said innocently. "We were just discussing lessons to be learned from the animal kingdom and he turned sulky." She met Amanda's eye and they both grinned. It flashed through Amanda's mind that Rhonda's remark wasn't far off the mark, actually. Randy's cat had displayed more intelligence than Amanda had when it came to dealing with unwanted handling. It had registered a protest by tearing some strips off its antagonist's hide. Unlike Amanda, it obviously hadn't seen any reason to wait to take a stand.

She looked up and caught Dean regarding her closely. By the speculative gleam in his eye, she deduced David had been discussing her. Undoubtedly, her confrontation with Randy earlier had dredged up stories of her general standoffishness with men. More to divert his attention than from a real desire to know, she asked, "Aren't you going to be warm in that get-up, Dean?"

Ask ten different dancers what they considered appropriate to wear to rehearsal and you'd get ten different answers. The only reason she had mentioned Dean's apparel—aside from averting his attention—was that in some subliminal corner of her mind, she had thought he was one of those who preferred to dance stripped down. Come to think of it, however, these were the same clothes he'd had on this morning. Hell, maybe it was a new fashion trend she hadn't yet tumbled to. Randy had also been wearing cover-up togs today, and he usually practiced in the bare minimum, too.

Dean glanced down at his long-sleeved T-shirt and gray sweats. "I'm keeping my muscles warm." He flashed her a charming smile. "I'll probably pull off a few layers once we get going."

Whether he did or not, Amanda never noticed. The morning's events kept distracting her. It was all she could do to focus her wandering concentration on each separate movement of the dance and thus avoid calling down Charlie's wrath on her head.

The phone was ringing in her apartment when she dashed in between rehearsal and show, but she ignored it. MacLaughlin wasn't home. She told herself it didn't matter to her, one way or the other, yet almost involuntarily she had felt compelled to check. His blinds were pulled, however, and Ace was in the yard, disconsolately nosing a red ball between his fat paws. Seeing Amanda, he snatched it up in his jaws and followed her up the stairs and into her apartment. He trotted after her into her bedroom, dropping the ball between her feet and damn near tripping her in the process.

"Not now, Ace," she muttered, dropping her purchases on the bed. When she glanced down at him, though, he managed to look so crestfallen that she relented slightly. She scooped him up and sat on the edge of the bed, plunking the pup in her lap. "Want to see what I bought?"

She still wasn't sure what had gotten into her. After rehearsal, she had followed an irresistible urge to go shopping, and the frothy, colorful bits of satin, silk, and lace that she poured out of the bags onto the bed were the result of her spree.

Ace appeared less than impressed as he dozed off in her lap, but Amanda was enthralled with the cobweb-fine lingerie. She had spent an almost indecent amount of money on the panties, bras, teddies, and nightgowns, but as she picked each item up to admire it anew, she decided it was worth every penny. For some reason, she'd never owned really pretty underwear before. She'd always worn functional cottons that were practical and plain. But today she had suddenly decided she was tired of wearing Girl Scout undies. Ridiculously pleased with herself, she grinned as she set Ace aside and rose to put her new purchases in a drawer. She carried her old underwear out to the kitchen and unceremoniously dumped it in the garbage can under the sink. Good-bye, cottons. She had discovered the near-sinful pleasure of wearing insubstantial bits of satin and lace, and she wasn't going back, ever.

The phone rang again, just as she glanced at the clock, and Amanda swore. She was going to be late if she didn't leave immediately. Racing back to the bedroom, she snatched up a sleepy Ace, scooped his ball off the floor, grabbed her purse, and ran from the apartment. Depositing dog and toy in the yard, she took the steps two at a time, and seconds later pulled away from the curb in a squeal of tires.

Tristan hung up the phone and swore. Then he stabbed his forefinger at the bridge of his glasses, settling them back in place, and told himself it was just as well she didn't answer. He didn't know why the bloody hell he was calling her, anyway. Oh, he'd told himself it was only to request she feed Ace for him, since it looked as though he would be working very late tonight. But it was more than that, and since he didn't make it a practice to lie to himself, he had to face it squarely.

He needed to hear her voice—to make some kind of contact.

Tristan's face was impassive as he answered a question put to him by one of his men. He signed a form shoved under his nose. But when there was a lull a few moments later, he stared down at the floor without really seeing it, berating himself.

He should stay the hell away from her. She was a threat to everything he had ever worked for. Tristan MacLaughlin didn't get involved with women on a case. The truth was, he didn't get more than superficially involved with any woman, period. Needing other people only got you hurt; he'd learned that lesson years ago.

But you want her. And you need to know she's safe.

That's what truly disturbed him. Oh, not the wanting; there was nothing new there. He had wanted other women before—temporarily. It would pass with her, too, once he'd had her—and after this morning, he *would* have her, come hell or high water. But this need to have a connection, this urge to protect . . .

He was afraid of losing his objectivity. He couldn't allow himself to be concerned about one dancer—not when there was a whole city of them in peril. And so he broke his own golden rule and, blocking out the truth, told himself it was only because the newest victim had had pale blond hair almost the exact shade as Amanda's that made him anxious for her safety.

The latest victim's name was Joy Frede. They had learned today that she had been twenty-seven, single, and in debt up to her shell-pink ears when she died. From talking to her roommate, they had learned one other fact that might have a bearing on her case. Joy Frede had received at least two phone calls prior to her murder. They didn't know whether the calls had been placed by the killer. All the roommate knew was that Frede had been very disturbed by two calls, but had refused to discuss them. At the time, the roommate had assumed they had something to do with Frede's escalating debts. She'd also suspected Frede of prostituting herself to earn extra money.

In one corner of his mind, Tristan divorced himself from the facts at hand and hoped to hell Amanda was staying out of dark, deserted areas. She seemed to possess a blind faith that nothing could happen to her, and it made him nervous.

Damn it to bloody hell, he thought. *There I go again. I have a soddin' job to do here, and I can't afford to let my mind wander*. He decided he wasn't going to think about her again.

But he sure as hell wished she were in another profession.

The phone was ringing again when Amanda unlocked the door to her apartment in the early hours of the morning after the last show. "For the love of God," she exclaimed in exasperation. Who on earth wanted to talk to her so badly that they had to call at two-thirty in the morning? She plunged into the dark hall, having forgotten to leave a light on earlier in her rush to get to the Cabaret on time, but she turned back to stare at the open door behind her.

Forsaking the ringing phone for the moment, she went back and retrieved her dangling keys from the outside lock and closed the door securely behind her, locking up and placing the chain across the door. When MacLaughlin had been lambasting her in his cool, authoritative manner this morning—God, was that only this morning?—about policemen and their guns, he had also said something about her making it a point to forget there was a killer out there stalking dancers.

As much as he infuriated her, he was partially correct. She did want to pretend everything was the same as it used to be, so as much as possible, she conducted her life in its accustomed manner.

But at the same time, regardless of what he might believe, she wasn't taking foolish risks. She might wish things were different, but she wasn't blind to reality. She made it a point to park her car in a well-lighted area near the casino. She was usually with Rhonda, but if Rhonda had other plans, like she did this evening, then Amanda walked in a group to and from the casino. And there was no denying that her life had changed to the extent that she was aware of everyone around her these days. She wasn't so dumb as to place herself in a potentially dangerous situation, no matter what he might think. She had even had floodlights installed in all the dark corners of her property. You had to look hard to find a shadow out there these days.

The phone stopped ringing an instant before she reached it. Amanda uttered a word she didn't normally use and went to take a quick shower. She thought she heard the phone ringing underneath the roar of water, but when she stuck her head out to listen, it was quiet. The idea of someone trying to reach her at this hour of the morning made her uneasy, and her heart began to beat unevenly with apprehension. She wished Rhonda or MacLaughlin were home. She probably wouldn't call either one of them, but it would be nice to know that she wasn't entirely alone in this rambling old triplex.

She had thought she knew every creak and moan the building made, but tonight the house seemed foreign and rather threatening.

Amanda poured herself a glass of wine and spent longer than usual brushing her hair and her teeth and preparing for bed. Finally beginning to relax, she stood in front of the full-length mirror and admired her slinky new nightgown of midnight-blue silk with matching insets of lace. She loved the way it made her skin glow all golden in contrast. On sudden impulse, she hummed a little tune and began easing the nightie off again. Dropping the shoulder straps and inching the hem up her thighs, she executed a little bump and grind and saucily smiled at her image, deciding she wasn't half bad. If Charlie ever bumped her from the Cabaret, maybe she'd look for work as a stripper. Easing the fragile shoulder straps back into place, she decided she'd be effective as all get-out with rip-away clothing.

Blushing only a very little, she met her eye in the mirror. *Think you're pretty hot stuff, don't you?* she demanded half sheepishly of her image. *Having MacLaughlin slam you up against a wall and kiss you like you're the hottest woman on earth has gone to your head.*

Damn straight, toots.

Her image obviously had no shame. It kept dancing seductively, hands skimming up its sides, rubbing lightly over the fullness of its breasts, fingertips trailing over collarbone and neck, gathering up a handful of hair, and then letting it go to stretch lazily in the air. Amanda smiled. Maybe she had been missing out on something all these years after all. Maybe, as Rhonda had repeatedly insisted, she'd been too particular. Wouldn't it be ironic if, having only just discovered her passionate, sexy side, she found she couldn't live without . . . It?

It? Amanda laughed out loud, despite the faint throbbing of awareness that plagued her body. *It? Amanda Rose, it's doubtful you have to worry about not being able to live without it, when you can't even say the word!* She climbed into bed and turned out the light. The way MacLaughlin's face had looked this morning just after he had pulled away from her flashed across her mind.

"Sex," she whispered. "Sex." Oh, she could do much more than say the words, she decided. She'd learned exactly what she was capable of this morning. And what was truly shocking was that, after only a few hours, she didn't even have the grace to be shocked by it at all. "Sex," she said again, and she smiled, rolling over on her side.

Into the peaceful darkness, the bedside phone suddenly rang, cutting through her relaxation with the shrillness of a dentist's drill.

CHAPTER
13

Heart pounding, Amanda rolled back toward the nightstand and turned on the light. She stared at the phone for a moment as if it had turned into something incomprehensible. Then, hesitantly, she reached out and picked up the receiver.

"Hello?"

"Amanda?" The voice was low, scratchy sounding, and not one she recognized.

"Who is this?" she demanded. "Do you have any idea what time it is?"

"I'm sorry if I woke you," the voice said gently. "I did try earlier, but there was no answer, and I suppose I lost track of the time."

"Who are you?"

"A friend." The voice was not threatening, but it was also not one she recognized. "Just a friend who wanted to let you know how much I admire you."

Amanda controlled her impatience and replied levelly, "Thank you. That's very nice to hear, but it is really very late and I need to get my sleep. So, if you'll excuse me, Mr.—er . . ."

"Good night, Amanda." There was a soft click, and the phone went dead.

Slowly, Amanda replaced the receiver. That was odd—and disturbing. She picked up the phone again and punched out Maryanne's old number. It rang three times before she broke the connection. What was she going to tell him—that someone knew her name and had called to say he admired her? That he'd spoken pleasantly and had promptly hung up when she'd said she was tired and it was late? After this morning, MacLaughlin was more likely to think she was just reaching for an excuse to contact him. Forget it. She'd mention it to Rhonda tomorrow.

But it was a long time before she finally relaxed enough to fall asleep.

Three nights later, Amanda heard a crash from Mac-Laughlin's apartment shortly after she went to bed. The silence that followed seemed to beat in her eardrums. Then, faintly, from a distance, she heard Ace whine anxiously.

Heart tripping over itself, she climbed out of bed and picked up her robe. She got as far as the front door before she hesitated, looking down at her night apparel. She couldn't go down there like this. Showing up at this hour was bad enough without doing so in her bathrobe and nightie. She didn't want him to get the wrong idea, but she did need his advice—desperately.

It had been three days since the first telephone call—three long days of watching for MacLaughlin to come home so she could ask him what to do. Pulling velour sweatpants over her panties and zipping a matching sweatshirt over her silk chemise, she thought of Rhonda's advice and knew she probably should have followed it. When Amanda's caller had phoned again the second night, Rhonda had urged her to quit waiting for MacLaughlin to come home and immediately call the work number on the business card Joe Cash had given them the night they had identified Maryanne's body.

"What am I supposed to tell him?" Amanda had demanded. "That some man keeps calling me to pay me compliments? That he says I'm a virtuous woman in an unvirtuous profession?"

"Yes, dammit! This is not natural, Mandy."

She knew that. The calls were beginning to unnerve her. It had reached the point where she jumped every time the phone rang. But the man had in no way threatened her, and she couldn't bring herself to call the police station to file a report. So she had kept a close lookout on MacLaughlin's apartment, instead.

It was amazing how hard it was to pin him down. She knew he was in and out, but she kept missing him. For such a big man, he moved very quietly. Tonight was the first time she had ever heard a sound from his apartment, which was why she was going down there in the middle of the night to talk to him. She was afraid if she waited, he might not be there in the morning. Either she would toss and turn all night for fear of not waking up on time, or she would actually do something stupid like sleep late or take too long in the shower and miss him entirely.

Ace's whining grew louder, the closer she got to MacLaughlin's front door. The door was slightly ajar, and Amanda hesitated, hand raised to knock. What was going on here? It wasn't like MacLaughlin to be lax, or to make noise, and Ace sounded as if something were very wrong indeed. She retreated a step.

"Ah, bloody hell, Ace," she heard MacLaughlin's voice rumble. "Would you get your soddin' tongue outta my ear then, mate? I'm okay; I'm okay. I'll get up in a minute."

Amanda knocked and cautiously stuck her head inside the door. "Lieutenant?"

Claws scrabbled on the hardwood floor, and Ace came charging around the corner. Amanda closed the door behind her and leaned down to pat the dog reassuringly. She advanced into the apartment. "Lieutenant? Are you all right?"

Tristan fumbled for his glasses and dragged himself into a half-sitting position against the couch. Pain blurred his vision, but he'd recognize that voice anywhere. He reached out an unsteady hand to right the coffee table he had over-turned when the pounding in his head had dropped him first to his knees, then flat on his face, but the effort brought about an upsurge of nausea, and his normally powerful arm dropped uselessly to his side. The pain was almost manageable if he remained very, very still.

God, make her go away, he thought. Never, in his adult life, had anyone seen him in the midst of one of these, and he didn't want her to be the first. He could barely hold his own with Amanda Charles when he was one hundred percent well. The idea of watching the contempt she was bound to feel when she saw him was more than he could handle.

Amanda forgot why she had come when she saw Mac-Laughlin on the other side of the dimly lighted room, sprawled on the floor. His head and one massive shoulder were braced against the front of the couch, and his color was pasty. Beads of sweat stood out on his high forehead and upper lip, trickling down from his temples. His jacket was on the floor, and sweat ringed the underarms of his limp white shirt, plastering it in a large, damp patch to his chest. Underneath the straps of his leather shoulder holster, the shirt's material was transparent with moisture. Amanda dropped to her knees in front of him and laid a concerned hand on his forehead. It surprised her to find it cool.

"What's the matter with you?"

"Go home, Miss Charles."

"MacLaughlin, what is the matter?"

He was in no shape to battle her persistence. "Migraine," he said through clenched teeth. He peered at her through slitted lashes. Even allowing in the dimmest light was like having needles rammed through his eyes. "Havena had one in over a year, and I thought maybe I'd finally outgrown them." The effort of being stoic under the pressure of such pain proved too much for him. His eyes slammed shut and he gripped his head in both hands. "Oh, God, lass, my head feels like it's gettin' ready to blow off my shoulders."

"Have you taken anything?" Amanda loosened his tie and pulled it off. She unbuttoned his shirt and cuffs and pulled the tails from his slacks.

"No. Got myself home, then fell. Makes me sick, tryin' to move. Used to have a prescription for it, but like I said . . ."

"Okay. Hang on, I'll see what I can find." She left for the medicine cabinet in the bathroom, but paused in the doorway. "Where can I find your pajamas?"

"Havena got any."

That figured. Amanda detoured into his bedroom before collecting every article she felt might be useful from the bathroom. She carted her items back to where he was slumped, eyes closed, by the couch. Dropping down beside him, she popped a thermometer in his mouth and instructed him to hold it under his tongue.

"I havena got a temperature," he mumbled around it. "It's the pain makes me sweat. Happens every time."

"It doesn't hurt to check," she informed him with quiet firmness, and he decided it was easier to let her do as she wished than to argue with her.

Amanda unlatched the buckle securing his shoulder holster and eased it off, handling it gingerly as she set it on the couch. She worked the limp cotton over his shoulders and off his arms, tipping him forward to remove it. He groaned in protest, but then sighed with almost inaudible appreciation as she mopped the sweat from his chest and arms with a bath towel.

She hesitated over his slacks, but finally reached for his belt and unzipped his fly, instructing him to raise his hips so she could ease the pants down his legs. She didn't want to be, but she was highly aware of the scratchy texture of his body hair as she wiped the dampness from his hard, long-muscled legs.

Setting the towel aside, Amanda reached for a pair of gray sweats and manhandled them over his feet and up his calves to his thighs. When her request that he raise up was met with silence, Amanda glanced up at his face. His lips were folded in on themselves, clamping the thermometer tightly, and his skin was tinged green. His eyes, normally so cool and laser-sharp, were dull, clouded with pain as he stared blankly at the ceiling. No help there. She was clearly going to have to wing it on her own.

Straddling him on her knees, Amanda had to hunch awkwardly to slide the flat of her hands over his hard buttocks. She reached downward until her fingers curled around the soft cotton knit of the sweatpants' waistband, which was bunched around and under his thighs. Without his help it took her a while, but she finally inched it up into place and tied the strings at his waist. She was sweating with the effort and, resisting the desire to slump onto his chest for a rest, she contented herself with unzipping her velour sweatshirt and flapping the sides to create a breeze. Climbing off him, she rezipped with one hand and pulled the thermometer out of his mouth with the other. She raised up on her knees and snapped on the light.

"Turn the damn light off!" he howled, and she twisted around to stare at him in surprise.

"What?"

"Lass, please, have mercy," he said with what he thought was commendable restraint. What he really wanted to do was rip the light out of the wall and swat her across the room like a pesky fly. "I dinna have a temperature. The light is killing me. Turn it off!"

She turned it off. For a couple of quiet moments, she sat on the floor next to MacLaughlin, her knees pulled up and hugged to her chest, watching him. You could tell just by looking at him that he was in acute pain. "MacLaughlin?"

"Tristan," he mumbled.

"What?"

"You keep callin' me MacLaughlin. Or Lieutenant. My bloody name is Tristan."

"If I call you MacLaughlin or Lieutenant, Lieutenant," Amanda replied with some exasperation, "it's because I didn't have a clue what your first name was." Of all the exasperating, ungrateful . . .

"You do now," he growled, and for a moment his eyes focused sharply on her. "Say it."

"Tristan," she snapped, and a small smile eased the pinched white line around his mouth. His eyes closed.

"Tristan," Amanda continued in a softer tone. She never thought she would see the day, but he actually looked vulnerable. "Can you sit up?"

"No."

"Yes, you can. I'll help you." She reached out to grasp his bare shoulders, but he shrugged her off irritably, and then moaned softly, deep in his throat.

"I said no, dammit," he snarled, and let loose a string of obscenities. When he ran out of combinations, he ended with, "Will you fuckin' leave me in peace?"

Amanda surged to her feet. "I'll leave you, period, you filthy-mouthed, arrogant creep." When she whirled to go, however, she found her left ankle manacled in his large hand. She looked down her nose at him.

"I'm sorry," he mumbled. "I shouldna have said that, then. But every time I move, lass, I feel like I'm goin' to throw up." He shivered as a stray draft blew across his bare shoulders.

Amanda squatted in front of him again. Picking up a sweat-shirt with its sleeves ripped off—the only garment she'd been able to find that wasn't a starched white dress shirt—she pulled the neck opening over his head and worked his arms through the armholes. When she realized how much pleasure she was gaining by smoothing the warm, fleecy knit over the firm ridges of his muscular stomach, she snatched her hand back and became all cool efficiency. "That's what this pan is for," she said briskly. "You can't spend the night on the floor, Tristan, so let me help you into bed."

"Aye," he said wearily, knowing if he didn't agree, she would probably go home. And as much as he dreaded the possibility of disgracing himself in front of her, he didn't want her to leave.

By leaning heavily on her and marshaling all the willpower at his disposal, Tristan managed to make it to the bedroom without getting sick. He was shaky from the effort, however, and burrowed beneath the covers, both hands clutching his skull in an attempt to contain the pain. "Soddin' head feels like it's goin' to explode," he said between clenched teeth.

"Here." Cool fingers removed his glasses and set them aside, before slipping behind his head to lend support, and Amanda held out three aspirin. When he washed them down thirstily with a glass of cold water, she hesitated for a moment and then almost reluctantly said, "Let me try something. Sit up for just a moment."

"Ah, Lord, Amanda, you dinna know what you're askin'," he said, but then he struggled up on one elbow, just the same.

Amanda held his shoulders and helped him raise up. Then she squeezed behind him and, bracing herself against the headboard, slid her legs around him to bracket his hips. She eased him back until his weight rested on her, his head supported against her breasts. "I used to do this for Teddy sometimes. It always seemed to help."

Him again. A rude epithet that graphically described Tristan's opinion of Amanda's precious little Teddy rose to his lips, but he forced himself to swallow it unsaid. If he cursed again, she was going to remove that gloriously comfortable body, which was cushioning him in a way that no pillow could ever hope to emulate. And not even the warmth of an electric blanket could replace the penetration of her body heat into his chilled flesh. He closed his eyes and sighed. Then her fingers went to work and he groaned.

Tristan had never experienced anything quite like what she was doing to him. He had never been mothered in his life, but he imagined this was what it must be like. Amanda murmured low, soothing words as her fingers massaged his aching head and the taut tendons in his neck, and her thumbs dug deep to relieve the tension bunching his shoulders. The firm motion of her hands rocked his head ever so gently against her breasts, and he felt like a babe in arms, cared-for and comforted. While her ministrations didn't make the pain go away appreciably, he could feel all the accumulated stress of the past few weeks slowly drain out of him, and gradually, he relinquished the last tenuous hold he'd retained on his control. His body grew heavier against her as he slipped into sleep.

For nearly twenty minutes after his even breathing indicated he was sleeping soundly, Amanda sat with her head tilted back against the headboard, her hands still idly soothing Tristan's neck and shoulders. Not until numbness set into her hips and slowly began prevading her legs did she try to extricate herself from her wedged-in position behind him. Cautiously, she eased him down onto a pillow and slid one leg out from around him, swinging it over his head and shoulders as she tipped over on her side and rolled away. He stirred and mumbled in his sleep and she froze, perched on the side of the bed. She turned back and rested a hand on his forehead before she remembered that it was only in her own mind that he had ever had a temperature. She pulled covers up over him instead.

She felt him roll over at the same time she started to rise, but she wasn't prepared for the strong arm that snaked around her waist and tumbled her back on the bed next to him. He mumbled her name, and before she could divine his intention, he had rolled to partially cover her, one thigh flung over her legs, his cheek cushioned against the silk-covered rise of her breasts and one arm a diagonal bond, pinning her to the sheets from diaphragm to hip. He snuggled in and sighed, still asleep.

For several moments, Amanda held herself rigid within his embrace, hands flung overhead to keep from touching him. Then, slowly, she relaxed. She patted the mattress above her head for the extra pillow, futilely. She tilted her head back against the mattress and spotted it, then arched up to snag it with her left hand.

"Ah, Jesus, lass," Tristan said clearly as her motions thrust her breasts more firmly into his cheek. The hand holding her hip came up and cupped her left breast, stroking it slowly for a moment and then stilling. A second later it slid heavily to the bed, fingertips resting in the smooth hollow of her armpit. Amanda slowly pulled the pillow down and stuffed it under her head. She stared through the darkness at a ceiling she couldn't see.

There was no way to deny her attraction to this man. He might seem cold and hard in a lot of ways, but where her body was concerned, it didn't seem to matter, for he possessed an insidious sexuality that had worked its way under her skin. Oh God, one touch, delivered in his sleep, and she was as warm and malleable as soft candle wax.

If she were the tiniest bit intelligent, she'd go while the going was good. She would put as much space between herself and this man as she possibly could, and avoid him at all costs in the future.

But she knew, even as the thought crossed her mind, that she wasn't going anywhere. She wanted to stay exactly where she was.

There were depths to him that Amanda couldn't quite figure. Just when she had been convinced that Tristan was utterly cold and unfeeling, he had sent Rhonda those flowers and that compassionate note with its funny, formal signature. It would be a long time before Amanda forgot the look on Rhonda's face when she had received them. It had meant a great deal to her. And, Amanda had to face it, she reveled in this opportunity to be near MacLaughlin when he wasn't in cool command.

Cautiously, Amanda threaded her fingers through his short hair. It was wiry on the surface but satin-smooth the deeper she burrowed, near the roots of the hair shafts.

And besides, she further rationalized, she still hadn't talked to him about her caller. If she left, there was simply no telling if she would be able to catch him in the morning before he pulled another of his famous disappearing acts.

Amanda smiled wryly in the darkness. When it came right down to it, she could debate the pros and cons until the cows came home and it wasn't going to change a thing. Because, right or wrong, she was tired of trying to outrun her chaotic emotions. And for what remained of the night, she had no intention of budging from this bed.

Unfamiliar noises within his apartment woke Tristan the next morning. He automatically reached for his gun, but it wasn't where he always kept it at night, on the stand next to the bed. Even as he picked up his glasses and turned back onto his pillow, snatches of memory filtered through his consciousness. He'd been rendered helpless by a killer of a headache last night. Traces of it throbbed in his temples yet, but by peering cautiously at the uncurtained window, he discovered it was no longer a migraine.

Then—he thought—Amanda had mysteriously turned up and taken care of him. She had changed his clothes, given him aspirin, and bullied him into bed. Then she'd climbed in with him, gathered him into her arms, and done something with her hands that had knocked him for a bloody loop, and he'd slept better than he had in weeks.

Or maybe that part was a pain-induced fantasy.

The door to his room opened, and Tristan cautiously turned his head. Ace raced into the room, scrambling up onto the bed and then into Tristan's lap, wiggling in ecstasy. Tristan rested a hand on the sleek fur of the dog's back, but then ignored him as he watched Amanda back the door more fully open with her hip and swing into the room bearing a tray.

"You're awake," she whispered, crossing the room to set the tray on the nightstand next to the bed. She bent down and felt his forehead. "How are you feeling?" Self-consciously, she pulled her fingers back. She didn't know why she kept doing that.

Tristan stared at her pale, tumbled hair and her face, scrubbed clean and free of makeup. She was wearing the same outfit he recalled from the night before—a plush banana-colored thing with black edging—so she must have been here all night. "Fine."

"Good. Head better?"

"Aye."

What was the matter with him? He was looking at her as if he'd never seen her before. "Um . . . would you like a little breakfast?"

Tristan looked over at the tray she'd prepared. It held a glass of orange juice, two pieces of toast, and a soft-boiled egg in a dish. He recalled her concern of the night before, when he had been expecting her disdain. "Aye. Thanks."

Is this what families did then, when one of their members was sick? Did they massage each other's heads and bring them breakfast in bed? He looked into her wide, violet-blue eyes with their thick fringe of deep-brown lashes as she bent over to place the tray in his lap. "Who the bloody hell is Teddy?" Even as the words left his lips, he regretted the belligerence with which he asked the question. He picked up a fork and carried a bite of egg to his mouth. God, it tasted bloody marvelous.

Amanda straightened. Why did he sound so upset? Was she supposed to have discreetly disappeared this morning? "Teddy was my sister," she muttered. Well, he'd simply have to excuse her all to hell and gone if she didn't understand the rules. This was a bit outside her normal sphere of experience. She wasn't used to playing nursemaid to irritable men.

Tristan halted his hungry shoveling of the egg midway between mouth and plate and stared at her. "Your sister?" *Teddy is a woman's name?* He grinned. *Who woulda bleedin' thought?*

Amanda was fully prepared to stomp off in a huff and leave him to his own devices before he smiled. When he flashed that rare, marvelous grin that made white, slightly crooked teeth seem a much more attractive proposition altogether than the straightest of smiles, it did something to her. It was a pity it was so fleeting. Even as she stared, he grew sober.

"You said she was your sister, lass? Is she your sister no longer?"

"Teddy's dead."

"Ach, that's rough, lass. I'm that sorry. How did it happen, then?"

He watched the shutters drop over her eyes, and when she replied she would rather not talk about it, his curiosity soared. Why not? He wanted to hear about it. He wanted to know about everything that pertained to her. But then, his own defenses rose up when she turned and inquired if he had brothers or sisters of his own.

"No," he said shortly. Then, grudgingly, he added, "I was raised in an orphanage." To avoid seeing pity in her eyes, he concentrated on finishing his breakfast. He wouldn't accept pity from anyone—least of all her. Setting the tray aside, he flung the covers off and prepared to rise.

Amanda was right there, leaning over him, her cool hands on his biceps, pressing him back into the pillows. She was thankful when he allowed her to detain him, for she had felt the round mass of muscle beneath her hands leap into hard relief before he decided not to fight her, and she knew she was no match for his strength. "Where do you think you're going?"

"To work, lass. I've overslept as it is."

"Don't be ridiculous, Tristan. You've been ill."

"And now I'm not," he said with fine disregard for the faint throbbing in his temples. It was nothing compared to last night's pain, in any event, and the nausea that had accompanied it was totally absent. He was going to live, after all.

"Your head still hurts, though, doesn't it?" she asked, surprising him. Was she fey, reading his mind that way?

"It's nothing I can't handle," he muttered, but he subsided for the moment when her fingers began their seductive massage of his temples. God, that felt good.

He didn't care to think of himself as a man who categorized people, but he had to admit he'd harbored some misconceptions about dancers before he had actually ever met any. When he had first learned he was to be assigned to this case, he'd been angry. He had made up his mind that male dancers were men of questionable sexuality, and female dancers were perhaps one step above whores.

In some cases, it happened he was correct. But he had met too many dancers since his assignment to continue automatically lumping them all together. Amanda Rose Charles was a case in point.

Closing his eyes and giving in to the pleasure of her ministration, he admitted Amanda was in a class all her own.

From the first, when she had dismissed him with such disdain outside the morgue, he had wanted to believe she was amoral as an alley cat, because he'd taken one look at those long legs and those big blue eyes, with their unusual purple cast, and he had felt a visceral jolt unlike anything he had ever experienced before. And he had ironclad rules governing unbidden attractions to women on the job. Besides, there had been something about the way she had looked down her long, narrow nose at him that had made him want to picture her in the worst conceivable light.

But she wasn't amoral. She was . . . decent. He didn't meet many decent people in the course of his work, but the word seemed appropriate, somehow. Look what she'd done for him last night and this morning. She had cared for him like a mother cares for her child.

She sure doesna kiss decent. The thought popped unbidden from his subconscious. Tristan opened his eyes to stare at her mouth. It was soft and full and desirable, and its taste had lived on in his mind, resurrecting full-blown memories at the most inconvenient moments. He thought about her too damned often.

Decent be damned, his baser self decided. He was going to have her. If she was sexually ripe, he wanted to be the one to benefit. And to hell with his usual rules about mixing business with pleasure. He didn't like the way she was invading his mind, and he was going to work her out in the only way he knew how.

He ignored the voice of reason that questioned the callousness of his decision. It only made him feel guilty and restless and edgy.

"Who's your decorator, MacLaughlin?" Amanda suddenly asked into the silence. "Nautilus?"

Unaware of Tristan's thoughts, she had been looking around the room. Its stark lack of personality made her uneasy. He had taken everything of Maryanne's that Amanda hadn't already packed and had put it away somewhere. She could understand that; Maryanne had decorated with a feminine touch, and he wasn't a man who'd like to be surrounded by frillies. But he had taken it to extremes, stripping the dust ruffle and the fussy comforter from the bed, and he hadn't bothered to replace Maryanne's odds and ends with anything of his own. There was a complete lack of personal effects in the room—in the whole apartment, now that she thought of it. There were no photographs, no keepsakes, no books or magazines, no bits and pieces that gave a clue to the real Tristan MacLaughlin. The only items of an even remotely personal nature were the set of weights and portable bench-press board in the corner, and his gun out in the living room.

She found it difficult to reconcile the sterility of the room with the warmth of the man who had kissed and fondled her with such passion just a few short days ago—the man who had sent flowers to Rhonda. Was she fooling herself? Was she so enamored of his body and the new world of sensation it had unexpectedly opened to hers that she was blinding herself to the essential emptiness of the man? What if he was exactly what she had thought him to be from the beginning —a cold, withdrawn, self-disciplined man with all the natural warmth of a robot? The last thing she needed right now was to get herself involved with a man who was all hormones but essentially an emotional wasteland.

Then, too, there was the question of her own reactions.

She was confused and less than confident about the validity of her judgment. Could you truly trust the discernment of a woman who ran out and bought new lingerie after one encounter with an aggressively sexual man, and then was ready to climb back into her serviceable old cottons after viewing the barrenness of his living conditions? Maybe she had better reign in all this rampant horniness that suddenly had her crawling the walls, and try to think things through. She was asking for nothing but pain and heartache if she leapt blindly into a situation she wasn't one hundred percent certain she was ready for.

Not that he had asked, necessarily. Wouldn't it be the height of conceit if she was agonizing over nothing? He hadn't been knocking himself out to seduce her. She really was getting a fat head. The man was flat on his back with the remnants of a painful migraine, and she was worried that he might try to trick her into bed with him before she was prepared for the consequences. She swung her gaze back down to his face with a sudden, brilliant smile, feeling both a bit foolish and relieved. One session up against a wall with MacLaughlin had obviously given her an inflated opinion of her own desirability.

She looked straight into a molten silver blaze of raw, determined hunger.

The shock of seeing his undisguised desire on the heels of her own mental wanderings sent her heart slamming up against her rib cage. She snatched her hands away from his temples and surged to her feet. Tristan's hand shot out and grabbed her by the wrist. He began to exert pressure that tugged her back to the edge of the bed and forced her to lean over him. Amanda braced her free hand on the mattress next to his shoulder and locked her elbow, stiff-arming herself as far away from him as possible. Desperately, she said, "You're ill."

"Not that ill, lass." His eyes were all over her and his free hand raised to grasp the zipper tab of her sweatshirt, which was fastened to her throat. Slowly, he tugged it down-ward until the sides fell free.

"Stop that!" The morning air felt cool against her exposed skin. Then, as suddenly as he had grasped her, he set her loose, and Amanda straightened shakily. Oh, thank God, he had changed his mind.

Tristan had changed nothing. He skimmed his sweatshirt over his head and flung it aside. Then he rose up and grabbed both sides of Amanda's open velour jacket and whipped it off her shoulders and down her arms, dropping it to the floor at her feet. He picked her up by her rib cage, swung her around, and lowered her to the mattress. As he leaned over her, his grin was lusty, his expression younger and more approachable than any Amanda had yet seen on his normally stern face.

It had been her own stunning smile that had overloaded the scales in Tristan's battle with his conscience, but it was no longer in evidence. Slender dark eyebrows gathered del-icately above her nose and the obvious trepidation in her wide, violet-blue eyes gave him momentary pause. But the honey-toned warmth of the upper slopes of her breasts, rising from the low neckline of her teal-blue chemise, drew him like a magnet, and he lowered his head. One taste, he told himself. One taste, and if she told him to stop, he would. He nuzzled his mouth into the valley between her breasts.

"Oh, please," Amanda whispered, and even in the con-fines of her own mind she wasn't entirely certain whether she was begging him to stop or to continue. His mouth was soft and hot, his jaw was hard and abrasive with stubble, and the total effect devastated her senses. "This isn't why I came down here . . ."

"I know, lass." Tristan slid her shoulder strap down her arm and one large hand reached in the chemise to free her breast. He looked at the weathered darkness of his hand against her pale flesh. Ah, God, it was a beautiful sight. He stroked the resilient fullness, then cupped her weight in his hand and pushed it up, moving his mouth and licking at the tiny beige bead that was her nipple. Amanda arched beneath his mouth.

"I was waiting for you to get home, you see . . ." He tugged her nipple fully into his mouth and Amanda found herself digging her fingers into the bare, warm skin of his wide shoulders and tossing her head back, arching into his touch. Her thighs sprawled apart and he immediately rocked himself into the space she opened up. There was no doubt about the state of his arousal. "Ahh, Tristan, please . . ."

"Aye, darlin', I'd like to please you."

"I was waiting for you to get home," she panted, her body twisting with a life of its own beneath his ministrations. She was tempted to let explanations wait, but she had originally come down here for a very important reason. "Um . . . because I need your advice . . ."

"I advise you to touch me, lass. Ah, Mandy, please." His lips closed around one nipple and drew it to its full extension. He rolled the other with his fingers.

Shuddering, her hands slid down his back, exploring the texture of his skin with tactile appreciation. The muscles beneath her flattened palms were hard, warm, and his spine was long and supple. Her fingertips kept returning to the shallow groove to test the incredible softness there. "Advice about these phone calls I've been receiving . . ."

Suddenly she was sprawled flat on her back on the bed, all alone, with one breast exposed and a throbbing ache in her loins. Tristan towered over her, and his face was as closed and set as the first time they had met. It didn't matter that his upper torso was bare and his hair was tousled, or that his glasses were lightly misted with leftover passion. The forceful lover of a moment ago had disappeared. In his place was the cold-eyed cop.

"What bloody phone calls are you talkin' about?"

CHAPTER
14

The emotion tightening his stomach was so unfamiliar, at first Tristan failed to identify it. But as Amanda slid the drooping satin strap up her arm and covered her breast with the silk chemise, he acknowledged it for what it was: fear, pure and simple, gnawing at his gut with red-hot ferocity and lending a painful throb to his heartbeat.

"Tell me about these phone calls," he demanded roughly once again. Jesus, let it be something unrelated.

Amanda's expression defied description. Staring at her, Tristan experienced a brief sensation of disorientation. It was like watching two images collated into one. He saw her on two levels at once. One level was as a possible witness, or worse yet, a potential victim, having just uttered the words that might link her to his case, and the cop in him reacted instinctively. But at the same time, he related to her as the woman who charged him with sexual energy, no matter where he was or what he was doing, whenever she was near.

Amanda quivered visibly with confusion. Her eyes were hot with a montage of emotions: resentment, embarrassment, bafflement, and a lingering remnant of passion. Her color was high, and her pale hair appeared to have taken on the

energy of her emotions: it was a wild blond cloud around her
head. Yet, even as he waited impatiently for her reply, he
observed the shutters slamming down. She drew her innate
poise around her like a sable cloak. Her chin tilted at a
stubborn angle, and quite pointedly, he thought, she fumbled
with her velour jacket, zipping it up to her neck once again.
Damn her, did she think he had arbitrarily discontinued his
lovemaking? His passion had been killed more swiftly than
a kick in the balls by her husky whisper about phone calls,
and he wasn't exactly thrilled about it himself. His head hurt
and his body ached. If she didn't start talking pretty damn
quick, he was going to grab hold of her and shake until her
orthodontia-perfect, gleaming white teeth rattled. "Lass . . ."

"I received the first call four nights ago." Her cool voice
overrode Tristan's. "A man with a whispery voice, who will
only identify himself as 'a friend,' has called me a total of
three times."

"All in the same night?" Tristan kept his voice carefully
impersonal.

"No. He called the first time the day I had the rehearsal
at my apartment. The day you came up . . ." Amanda's eyes
faltered for a moment, remembering that then, too, Mac-
Laughlin had managed to strip away all her inhibitions with
a minimum of effort. "Technically, I suppose it would be
the next day. It was after midnight—around two-thirty or
three."

"And the next two calls?"

"The following night . . . about the same time, and the
night after that."

"None last night?"

"None that I'm aware of. I hadn't been home long when
I heard you down here, and I came down to ask your advice.
Then . . ." Amanda shrugged, feeling it unnecessary to elab-
orate. He knew the rest.

"What does he say?"

"He . . . admires me. He seems to have this notion that
I'm the last virtuous woman, or at least the last virtuous

dancer." Amanda blushed. She bet MacLaughlin thought that was a hoot. She was never especially virtuous around him.

But MacLaughlin wasn't amused. He was worried. He didn't like the sound of this at all. "Why didn't you call me at the number I gave you?"

"Rhonda said I should," Amanda whispered. He hadn't laughed at her, and the deadly seriousness with which he was treating this was scary. "But I didn't know what to report. The calls are disturbing; I'm not denying that. But they're not obscene or anything, and he never talks long. He's . . . very polite, and each time it's the same. I tell him it's late and I'm tired, and he says good night and hangs up."

"Does he call you by name?"

"Yes."

"Does he appear to know your schedule?"

"Yes," she replied hoarsely. She was beginning to feel frightened. "He called all three times about twenty minutes to half an hour after I arrived home from the last show."

"Has he ever said anything . . . personal? Anything to indicate he knows things about you he shouldna be knowin'?"

"No."

"Does he make reference to your sex life?"

Amanda shook her head.

"What makes him think you're more virtuous than most?"

"I don't know. Maybe because it's become kind of a . . . a joke of sorts that I don't date much. The dance community is very small—you hear everything about everyone, eventually. And for reasons I'd rather not go into, I've always kept my distance, uh, sexually, from the male portion of the dance world. I've acquired a reputation." Amanda studied her fingernails carefully. "It's sort of like being the fastest gun in town. There is always someone new who is challenged by it, who is sure he's got what it takes to turn me around. Once it went so far . . ." She hesitated, not liking to admit this to Tristan. Then she looked up and continued in a carefully level voice, "The guys have a pool going. They place bets about who will be the first to score with me and when.

Not all of them, you understand; the really nice guys, like
David and Pete, didn't want to be involved.'' Her mouth
curled up in a small, tight smile. ''Of course, Pete is gay,
so he had nothing at stake.'' She shook her head impatiently.
''No, that's not fair. Pete is just a decent man. And it's not
that I don't like most of the guys, you understand. But I don't
go to bed with them.''

She looked up at Tristan, standing at the side of the bed,
looking down at her. She tried to gauge his reaction to the
information she had imparted, but his expression was carefully blank. Neither spoke for a moment, and Amanda's
nerves stretched tighter. Finally, she couldn't stand the silence. ''Tristan?'' she murmured in a very small voice. When
his professionally distant eyes met hers fully, she confessed,
''You're frightening me. What are these questions leading
to?''

Tristan reached down and grasped her by the shoulders.
He pulled her off the bed to stand in front of him. His first
inclination was to pull her into his arms—just to hold her
and tell her there was nothing to fear, that he'd take care of
everything. He stood stiffly, staring down at her. That he
could even consider doing something so unprofessional rattled
him badly. Where was his flamin' objectivity now? His tone
was crisp and distant when he replied.

''I don't want you to be frightened, Miss Charles. But at
the same time, you must be made aware that there's a possibility of danger, so you willna be takin' unnecessary
chances.''

Miss Charles? Amanda's eyes narrowed. Was this the same
man who'd had her pinned to his bed not five minutes ago,
taking all sorts of liberties with her body? And now he was
calling her *Miss Charles*? Closely inspecting his stern face,
she couldn't find a single trace of the sexy, playful lover,
and it gave her a horrid sensation of having been toyed with.
Amanda's temper rose and every one of the social defenses
she had learned in her formative years slammed into place.
Her chin rose as she stepped away from him, forcing him to

release his grip on her shoulders. "I don't take unnecessary chances. *Lieutenant* MacLaughlin," she replied, stressing his title. "And if I am in danger, I feel I have a right to know what kind. So, if you could be a little more specific?"

She was as cool and distant as he was and Tristan knew it should have pleased him to be back on a professional footing with her. But somehow, it didn't please him at all. "What do you call wandering around your yard in the middle of the night when there's a madman on the loose, if not takin' an unnecessary chance?" he demanded hotly, stepping closer to her again.

She stepped away. "That was one time! But, I'll have you know, Lieutenant, I haven't been out on my own after dark since that night. I've followed your instructions explicitly— up to and including the installation of outdoor lights—and I've made damn certain that I'm well aware of those around me." Her chin jutted up further yet. "You may like to believe I'm too simpleminded to take care of myself, but I assure you I am not. Now, what sort of danger am I in?"

"Perhaps none," Tristan replied stiffly. "But I want to place a tap and a tape recorder on your phone. Does the name Duke mean anything to you?"

"No."

Tristan was uncharacteristically hesitant to proceed, but there was no avoiding it. He had to inform her of the possible danger. Bluntly, he did so.

Her reaction was exactly what he feared. She paled noticeably, and although she tried to appear calm, he could see she was badly frightened. He had always felt a detached sort of compassion for victims in the past. Amanda's fear he registered in his bones. And worst of all was the way she withdrew from him, erecting a barrier that firmly shut him out. They were on opposite sides of an invisible fence; he could read it in her eyes. She saw herself as a potential statistic and him as an uninvolved cop, interested in her only as it influenced the case. He could hardly complain; he had worked overtime to project that very impression. But he regretted it.

"So . . . what now?" Amanda stared up at Tristan and tried to pretend she was in control. She didn't feel it. "Am I to be the bait?" She hugged herself, feeling suddenly cold, although the room was warm.

"No!" Tristan grasped her upper arms and pulled her against him. Amanda leaned on him, vaguely grateful for his warmth. She wished things were different; she wished she could cling a little and cry out all her fear. He was so big and solid, and she felt safe when he held her, but she knew it was an illusion. She had learned to be a realist over the years, and this was not the time or place to begin fooling herself. He was a professional doing his job, and he neither needed nor wanted a hysterical woman clinging to him, begging for reassurances. Tristan confirmed her assumption when he put some space between them and held her at arm's length. He looked down at her intently.

"There is no way in bloody hell you're going to be used as bait," he told her firmly. "The first thing we do is determine we're not frightening you unnecessarily. For all we know, lass, your caller might be just your garden variety crank." He brushed back several stray tendrils that had fallen over Amanda's forehead. "Which is why we hook your phone to a recorder. Have you ever heard of a spectrograph—a machine that takes voiceprints?"

Amanda shook her head.

"I'm not all that certain of the specifics myself, lass. But basically, each person's voice, like his fingerprints, is unique. With a spectrograph, you take a recording and it's translated into a visual pattern of sounds—a spectrogram. Y'ken?"

"Yes. But what good will it do? You don't keep voiceprints of known criminals on file like you do fingerprints, do you?"

"No. But don't y'see, Amanda, we can at least compare it to those we took of this mon Duke who's been callin' me. If they don't match up, then your caller is not the mon who's been killin' the dancers. We can proceed from there."

"And if it does match up?"

"We proceed from there," Tristan stated flatly. He watched her visibly withdraw again and briefly wished he had tempered his response. But, dammit, if he had sounded like a cop to her, that was probably because he was a cop. It was his life's work and he wouldn't be apologizing for it. They *would* proceed from there, and he *would* make damn certain she came to no harm. He could do no better than that.

There was a knock at the door and Tristan left Amanda standing in the middle of his bedroom while he went to answer it. He opened the door to a visibly worried Rhonda.

"Lieutenant, have you seen Amanda this morning?" She stepped into his apartment and closed the door. "She didn't answer her door, and when I let myself in with my key, I could see her bed hasn't been slept in." She grabbed his arm. "You don't know her very well, but take it from me, MacLaughlin, Amanda doesn't sleep in anyone's bed but her own. She's been getting these weird phone . . ."

"She's here, Miss Smith," Tristan interrupted, and he felt a trace of amusement as he watched Rhonda's mouth drop open. She appeared speechless for once. A wry imp of humor he didn't ordinarily indulge prompted him to add, "She's been here all night."

"Get outta town," Rhonda scoffed. She didn't doubt this big bruiser had the hots for Amanda, but she knew her Mandy. And despite Amanda's attraction for the big cop, Rhonda couldn't picture her blithely tripping down to MacLaughlin's apartment and agreeing to spend the night. She had too many inhibitions. Yet, here he stood, wearing nothing but a pair of low-slung sweatpants, stating that she had. "Seriously?"

"Rhonda?" Amanda poked her head out the bedroom door and Rhonda murmured, "Well, I'll be damned, Mandy Rose . . ."

"Uh, it's not what you think," Tristan belatedly assured her as Amanda's skin flushed a wild rose. Maybe this hadn't been the best of times to let his normally caged-in sense of humor run free. "She came down last night to tell me about the calls she's been receivin' and I was ill, so she stayed to take care of me."

"Uh-huh." There was a world of skepticism in that low-voiced murmur of assent.

"Rhonda!"

"Okay, okay, just kiddin'," Rhonda said, but she gave them a knowing grin. When she turned fully to Tristan, however, all traces of humor had left her eyes. "Lieutenant, what did you think about . . . Well, hi there, Ace." She interrupted herself to squat down and scratch the dog's belly as he flopped over at her feet. She spent a moment satisfying Ace's need for attention, then peered up at Tristan. "What do you think of these calls she's been getting?"

Tristan hesitated. Discussing the details of a case he was working was not something he would ordinarily consider doing. But he knew how close these two women were, and he knew there wasn't a hope in hell Amanda wouldn't tell Rhonda everything anyway. Better if he had some control over the situation. "I want your word you won't be discussin' this with anyone other than ourselves, Miss Smith," he began sternly. "No exceptions, y'ken?"

"Oh, for Pete's sake, Lieutenant," Rhonda snapped. "Call me Rhonda. Miss Smith makes me sound like some old maid schoolteacher." At Tristan's stiff nod, she continued seriously, "As for secrecy, you've got it. I'm not about to say anything that might jeopardize Mandy. She's the best friend I have in this world."

"Aye," he acknowledged, and proceeded to tell her as much as he felt she needed to know. Rhonda Smith, he noted, was one tough lady. She lost a bit of color, and her jaw clenched, but she heard him out in silence, and then took charge of Amanda. She led her over to the couch, sat her down, and picked up Amanda's hands in her own. They began to talk quietly. Tristan narrowed his eyes to conceal his intense interest as he watched them for a moment. Then he turned and walked away.

Holding herself rigid, Amanda turned her head to stare at the long, supple groove of Tristan's spine as he rumbled orders into the phone. She was grateful to Rhonda for providing a hand to clutch, and she sat very still, her lips compressed in a straight line, waiting for Tristan to finish. When he finally went into the bedroom to dress, Amanda let herself go. She allowed herself to cry on Rhonda's shoulder for a while and to verbalize her fear. She apologized for falling apart and then fell apart again. Finally, she straightened and wiped her cheeks with the palms of her hands and scooped up the puddles beneath her eyes with the sides of her fingers. With a shaky laugh, she confessed she'd been wanting to do that ever since Tristan had told her who he thought her caller was.

Emerging from the bedroom and crossing to the couch to retrieve his gun and holster, Tristan subjected Amanda to an intense once-over, but Amanda refused to meet his eyes. He was all buttoned down again in his white shirt and tie, a visual reminder—as if she needed it—that the cop was back with a vengeance. She averted her head when he strapped on the holster and adjusted the fit beneath his arm.

Amanda didn't want to see the professional distance in Tristan's eyes when he began to explain what he expected of her for the rest of the day and what she could expect tonight after the show, so she avoided eye contact entirely. She stared instead at the minuscule piece of toilet paper stuck to his jaw by a drop of blood where he had obviously nicked himself shaving. She inspected the subdued pattern in his tie and watched his Adam's apple slide up and down his throat above its perfect knot. Her gaze dropped to his holster, but the sight of his gun was too disturbing, so quickly she raised it again. She didn't meet his eyes until he suddenly reached out and grasped her upper arms.

"Look at me," he commanded. When her violet eyes snapped up and locked with his, he growled, "Have you heard a bloody word I've said, then?"

"I heard every word you said, Lieutenant," she replied

crisply and repeated it back to him. "I'm to behave as normally as possible at rehearsal. If I don't feel I can accomplish that, then I should make an excuse to stay at home, which you think might be wisest in the long run. I'm to go nowhere alone. Your men will set up their equipment in my apartment this afternoon, and they will be in place by the time I get home. They will be discreet upon entering my apartment. Have I got it all?"

His teeth clenched. "Aye."

"Good." She rolled her shoulders and glared up at him. "Let go of me."

Tristan's grip tightened momentarily, bringing her up on her toes; then, abruptly, he set her loose. "I'll need a key to your apartment."

"You can have mine," Rhonda offered as her gaze flew between Amanda's tense, angry face and Tristan's equally tense but controlled countenance. She'd sure love to know what had gone on here earlier. The air fairly crackled with hostility and sexual electricity. "I'd like to spend the night with her, anyway, as an extra precaution."

Tristan's head snapped around and he stared at Rhonda blankly for a moment. He opened his mouth to speak, but the doorbell rang in that instant. He closed his mouth, ground his teeth, and went to answer it.

"You okay?" Rhonda whispered, and Amanda barely had time to nod before Detective Cash and another man she didn't know entered the room behind Tristan. The remainder of the afternoon was a blur. They went up to her apartment and the policemen checked the strength of the locks on all her windows and door. The new man, whose name was Edwards and whose dramatic good looks made him appear more like a Hollywood leading man than a Reno policeman, took her phones apart and hooked in wires that led to the machines he had set up on her nightstand and on the marble-topped end table in the living room.

She insisted on going to rehearsal, and once there, she made her mind a blank and let the music seep into her bones, concentrating on nothing but the movement of her body. Home again, she cooked dinner for herself and Rhonda and the three detectives, and she watched Rhonda flirt with Edwards. When Rhonda turned her attention to Joe Cash, Amanda ignored the gray eyes burning a hole in her back and talked quietly with Edwards herself until it was time to go back to the Cabaret for the eight o'clock show.

After the two women departed, Tristan paced Amanda's apartment. He prowled from room to room, picking up and examining her possessions, then setting them down again and restlessly moving on until something else caught his eye. He tried to catch up on his paperwork, but he couldn't concentrate, and finally, he tossed the folder he was reading onto the coffee table and stood up. "I'm going out for a while," he informed the two detectives, and, ignoring the looks of relief they exchanged, let himself out of the apartment.

Tristan spent the next couple of hours driving to the places where the four victims had been found. He wondered if the killer ever did the same. It was a peculiarity of serial killers that they often revisited the scenes of their crimes to fantasize about the manner in which they'd killed their victims, and he wondered if Duke was typical.

At eleven-thirty, he found himself in front of the hotel that housed the Cabaret. He drove around to the lot where the dancers parked, left his car, and went into the casino.

Tristan killed ten minutes at a blackjack table, then tipped the dealer with his last chip and bought a ticket to the midnight show. He slipped in just as the house lights went down, ordered a whiskey sour from a cocktail waitress in a skimpy outfit, sat back and watched the curtain rise as music swelled from the orchestra pit.

The dancers opened the show, and Tristan's eyes scanned the lineup until he located Amanda. His eyebrows knit together when he finally spotted her. She looked so different.

Her blond hair was hidden beneath a close-fitting sequined cloche, and with her dark eyebrows, one might be forgiven for assuming she was brunette. The makeup she wore was closer to what he'd expected of a dancer before he had ever actually met one. It was heavy and dramatic, and he didn't care for it much. It changed her appearance, made her look like some damn tart on the town. And her costume, what there was of it, exposed a great deal too much cleavage and sleek, trim butt. He heard the man sitting at the next table, obviously the worse for drink, mumble lewd comments on the various merits of each female dancer's body. Tristan drilled him with a savage look. When the man's head turned in Tristan's direction, his loose, inebriated smile was met head-on with cold rage, and he swallowed the rest of his comments unsaid. Tristan turned his attention back to the stage.

She was a hell of a dancer. Tristan nursed his drink and watched her closely each time she came on. It wasn't hard to tell she loved it; in fact, seeing her up on the stage, it was hard to imagine she had anything even faintly sobering on her mind. All the dancers smiled, but on many of them it was a professional grimace, pasted on for the benefit of the audience. Amanda's smiles were spontaneous and natural, clearly inspired by doing what she loved best. She moved with boneless grace, as though the music were an integral part of her. She glowed up there in a way he had never seen her do before.

Tristan waited around after the show was over, and unobtrusively trailed Amanda and Rhonda back to the lot where Rhonda's car was parked. Once he saw them safely out, he gunned his motor and raced back to the triplex, beating them by a matter of minutes. His engine was still pinging in the cool early morning air when he climbed out of his car to greet them as they pulled up to the curb in front of him. Rhonda expressed pleased surprise at his unexpected appearance, but Amanda merely met his eyes briefly; then, as quickly, she dropped them again. All the joy he had observed when she was dancing was extinguished as thoroughly as if it had never existed outside his imagination.

Once inside, Amanda dropped her purse on the couch and

headed straight for the bathroom. She brushed her teeth and washed her face; then, bracing her hands on the edge of the sink, she raised her still-dripping face and met her apprehensive reflection in the mirror. Tension knotted her stomach. For a short time while she was on stage, she'd been able to put all her anxiety on hold and simply revel in her body's automatic response to the music. But the fear and worry were back now, and she needed to prepare herself to deal calmly with whatever happened. She was determined not to fall apart.

Rhonda handed Amanda a cup of hot chocolate laced with peppermint schnapps when she rejoined the group in the living room a short while later. Amanda sipped at it, but while she was grateful for its spreading warmth, she wondered if it was wise to be drinking alcohol. She was barely hanging on to her composure as it was. God only knew what sort of fool she was likely to make of herself if the liquor further frayed the threadbare restraints she was rigidly imposing on herself.

She stood off by herself, but her eyes were drawn to the three detectives gathered around the coffee table. It was stuffy in her apartment and the men had all removed their jackets. Until she had met Tristan MacLaughlin, she'd never even seen a real gun, and now there were three men in her home, each with a lethal weapon tucked under his arm. It was insane—the men in her world didn't wear guns strapped to their chests. How on earth had she gotten involved in this outlandish situation? Amanda began to tremble.

Stop it! she commanded herself with abrupt fierceness, and slowly she unclenched her muscles. *Just calm down. Having hysterics will accomplish nothing, girl, so get a grip on it. Take a deep breath . . . that's right. Now, slowly, let it out. Good. Now, another. Breathe in . . . hold it . . . let it out.* She shook out her hands and told herself she was going to be fine. *And if fine isn't in the game plan,* she thought grimly, *then at the very least I will not make an absolute ass of myself.*

Feeling calmer and at least marginally in charge, Amanda squared her shoulders and moved to join the others. She didn't even avoid Tristan's sharp eyes when he abruptly looked up and watched her cross the room.

Then, as Amanda was bending down to place her empty cup and saucer on the coffee table, the telephone rang, sounding strident and shrill in the quiet apartment.

Her fragile control splintered.

CHAPTER
15

The cup and saucer fell from fingers gone nerveless, and for a millisecond, Amanda existed in a vacuum as she stared without comprehension at the mess she had made. Her ears rang, her peripheral vision receded, and the object of her scrutiny grew dim and gray. It was like viewing a soundless, flickering, black-and-white television picture through the wrong end of a telescope. Then her peripheral vision returned as abruptly as it had disappeared, color re-emerged and sound and activity suddenly buffeted her from all directions. She was aware of Rhonda's hip gently nudging her aside to clean up the spilled dregs of chocolate and right the tilted cup, and of the warmth of Tristan's hand on her forearm. Joe Cash was moving into her bedroom at MacLaughlin's nod, and Edwards was fiddling with the machine connected to her phone and watching her.

"Do you remember what we discussed earlier, lass?" Tristan's voice was stern and detached, but his eyes were laser-sharp as they passed over Amanda's pale face. Her nod lacked certainty, and he shook her without gentleness. "Look at me!"

Her eyes snapped up, and after a brief struggle they managed to focus on his. "Pick it up on the fourth ring," he commanded her coldly, without regard for her obvious terror. "Joe will pick up the extension in your bedroom at the same time." It should have been his job, Tristan knew, since he was the only other person to have heard Duke's voice first-hand. But he had traded places with Joe when Amanda had shown signs of passing out. He could feel the chill of her flesh beneath her thin blouse, and without realizing what he was doing, his hands rubbed briskly up and down her arms. "Keep him talking as long as you possibly can, lass. Okay, there's the third ring." He released her and stood back where Joe could see him, his arm raised. "Quiet! And four—pick it up, Amanda."

Amanda watched his arm drop as she removed the receiver from its cradle. In the other room the extension was quietly picked up. "Hello?"

"Where were you last night, Amanda?" The whispering voice demanded to know, and Amanda's heart began to thud heavily in her chest. She glanced at Tristan, and a small measure of warmth returned to her extremities. The man on the phone couldn't hurt her as long as MacLaughlin was here.

"Who are you?" She sank onto a cushion of the davenport, clutching the receiver with enough pressure to turn her knuckles white.

"I asked you where you were last night!" There was fury and a cold demand in the disembodied voice, and Amanda rushed to explain, resenting the fear that made her do so.

"I sat up all night with a sick friend." Then, on a small spurt of courage, she demanded, "What business is it of yours, anyway? You won't even tell me your name!"

"I'm your friend, Amanda," the voice said gently. "I worry about you, out at night on your own." He hesitated, then said, "It's dangerous out there."

"Tell me your name," she breathed softly.

"It's not important. What was the matter with your friend?"

"Migraine, I guess. At least a murderous . . ."—*oh, bad*

choice of words, Amanda—"um . . . incapacitating headache and some nausea." *God, had he caught that?* She shook
her head impatiently. "Listen, I don't like this. You seem
to know a great deal about me, but you won't tell me anything
in return."

"You're a good woman, Amanda," the voice said softly,
responding selectively to her end of the conversation. "Beautiful and talented, kind and pure."

Amanda closed her eyes. "Please," she whispered.
"Won't you tell me your name? You call me late each night,
and you . . . you pay me such lovely"—she nearly choked
over the word—"compliments, but you won't say who you
are."

"Good night, Amanda."

"Please! Who are you?"

"Sleep well." The line went dead.

"Damn you!" Amanda screamed and slammed the receiver
back in its cradle. She buried her head in her shaking hands.
Rhonda sat down beside her on the couch and wrapped an
arm around her shoulders, whispering reassurances.

Tristan looked at Edwards, who shook his head. There
hadn't been enough time to run a trace. Joe emerged from
the bedroom. Tristan talked to both men quietly for a moment,
then crossed over to where Amanda was huddled on the
couch. Rhonda moved her legs to make room for him, and
he crouched down in front of Amanda, picking up one of her
limp hands. Stroking his thumb up each of her fingers, he
said with quiet gentleness, "You did verra well, lass."

Amanda shuddered. "He makes me feel so . . . crawly.
Dirty."

"Aye," Tristan agreed. "He's a sick mon. But he'll not
be harmin' you, Amanda."

"Why don't you take a hot bath?" Rhonda suggested as
she stroked Amanda's tumbled hair from her face. "I'll make
you another hot drink so you can sleep."

"Okay." Amanda struggled to her feet. Tristan positioned
himself so he could watch her until she closed the bathroom

door behind her, then he turned to Rhonda and began to speak briskly. Moments later, he let himself out of the apartment and loped down the stairs.

Amanda didn't climb out of her bath until it had quieted completely in the outer rooms of her apartment, and she was reasonably sure that everyone except Rhonda had left. She was grateful not to be left alone tonight, but she really didn't feel up to making small talk.

She dried herself and pulled on a silky nightie. She heard the ping of her microwave timer as she closed the bathroom door behind her and followed the sound into the kitchen.

Tristan was retrieving a cup of chocolate from the appliance's interior, and he turned and extended it to her when she walked in the room. Automatically, she reached for it. "Where's Rhonda?"

Tristan's eyes made one brief pass up and down her body. "I sent her home. I'm staying tonight."

Amanda took a sip of her drink. More schnapps. Then she nodded wearily, eyeing the sheer size of him dwarfing her tiny kitchen as he leaned against the counter a few feet away. Rhonda was a more comfortable person to be around. But the truth was, Amanda felt much safer knowing MacLaughlin would be here.

Something warm and furry touched her foot, and she looked down to see Tristan's homely dog, sprawled in his favorite, immodest position at her feet—spread-eagled on his back with his stubby paws pointed in four different directions. "Oh!" she exclaimed, and gave Tristan a genuine smile. "You brought Ace up to keep us company." She set her cup on the counter and crouched down, rubbing the dog's stomach. Ace's tail thumped against the tiled floor.

Tristan stared down at her. He knew it was warm in here and that she had been expecting Rhonda, rather than him, but he wished she had put on a robe.

It had bothered him all day when she had held herself aloof from him. She had hardly even looked at him if she could help it. He had steamrollered Rhonda into letting him stay here in her stead—not that she had offered any objection. He had assured her that as a policeman, he was much more qualified to protect Amanda, should the need arise, and Rhonda, bless her, had accepted that explanation with a perfectly straight face.

But she had known, as did he, that it wasn't the cop who had insisted on staying. If the cop portion of his persona had been dominant, he would have taken measures to ensure Amanda's safety and then gone home and forgotten her. And it sure as bloody hell wasn't the cop standing here now, rooted in place by a smile meant for his dog, staring down at Amanda's pale topknot, tracing the path of steam-tightened tendrils that escaped along her nape and temples. It was the man who was aware of her skin, flushed from the heat of her bath, and who noticed the way the thin tangerine material of her nightgown pulled tight over her rounded bottom and dipped low between her breasts—breasts whose full, weighted texture his restless hands remembered, whose taste his mouth retained.

"Tristan?" Amanda looked up and caught him staring at her, and the naked need that blazed in his eyes made her skin flush with reciprocal desire. Oh, no. She didn't want to feel this way. It wasn't right that all he had to do was look at her a certain way to make her want him. She forgot the question she had intended to ask him as she climbed slowly to her feet. Staring at him, she backed away.

Despite the sudden lust that pulsed through his veins, Tristan's intention had honestly been only to spend the night guarding her. Want her he might, with a desperation that sometimes seemed to claw at his guts, but he was prepared to do nothing more than hold her, if she wanted, and take care of her the way she had taken care of him last night. Tristan was accustomed to a lifetime of denying his own wants and needs, and this was just one more instance where he was fully prepared to ruthlessly squelch his body's strident demands.

But the excitement that flared in Amanda's violet-blue eyes

when she caught him looking at her, and the unmistakable way her nipples suddenly stood up beneath the silk of her gown, begging to be noticed, conspired to undermine his ironclad control like nothing else in his life had ever been able to do. Almost against his will, he found himself stalking her retreat until she was backed up against a wall.

"Oh," she said in a little voice, and then again as Tristan's head lowered purposefully, "Oh!"

The way he kissed her was every bit as exciting as Amanda remembered. She had wondered if perhaps her memory had exaggerated its impact, but that most definitely wasn't the case.

He had a way of concentrating solely on what he was doing to her that aroused her to a near frenzy, and she began to crave his insistent mouth the way a dieter craves sugar, an alcoholic craves a belt, an addict craves his drug. She didn't close her eyes, and there was something exhilarating about being able to watch him when he wasn't looking. His eyes were closed, his lashes dusky crescents upon the hollows above his cheekbones, and his thick eyebrows furrowed together above his nose. His hands in her hair were almost rough as they clamped her head at the angle he desired, but his mouth, for all its firmness, was soft, his tongue aggressive and hot. Amanda wrapped her arms around his waist and tugged impatiently at his shirt, separating it from his slacks so she could feel his skin beneath her hands. Tristan's breath shuddered hot and ragged between her parted lips as he raised his mouth.

Amanda lifted up on tiptoe in an attempt to follow his departing lips, but Tristan obliged her by bowing his head only long enough to bestow one hard kiss on her swollen mouth. Then he picked her up and carried her to her bedroom, firmly shutting the door on Ace's inquisitive face. He set her on her feet and removed his shoulder holster, setting it aside. He sat down in her slipper chair, and his eyes roved with aggression over her nightie while he removed his shoes and socks. "Take it off." He unbuttoned his shirt cuffs.

A tiny trickle of unease invaded Amanda's feverish arousal. He was ordering her to strip, which she was not accustomed to doing in front of a man. Couldn't he have couched it in pretty words, or helped her do it . . . or something? Her chin raised. "Or what?"

"Or I'm likely to rip it off you." He didn't mean that quite literally, of course; he was simply afraid he'd tear it in his haste, and the garment looked very expensive.

"Oh!" Who did he think he was, some hero in one of those rip 'em and rape 'em novels that graced every bookshelf across the nation? Well, she just wondered how he'd like it if the shoe were on the other foot! Eyes smoldering with intent, Amanda stepped forward. Tristan stood to meet her, but he wasn't prepared when she grasped the tails of his pristine white shirt on either side of the button placket and yanked with all her might. Buttons flew and Tristan's starched collar rasped loudly against his skin when it ripped out from beneath his tie. The shirt dangled off his massive shoulders, but the tie, with its perfect knot still intact, hung down his naked chest as neatly as though it still completed his ensemble.

Tristan stared down at his wrecked shirt with outraged Scottish frugality. "What the bloody hell did y'do that for? This shirt is almost new!"

"Well, my nightie's new, too, and you were going to rip it!"

"Not deliberately, I wasna! What kind of attitude is that, anyway? Do unto others before they can do unto you?"

She shook with reaction at the shambles she had made of this. All because of her damn, fluctuating emotions. One moment she was the world's biggest coward, and the next minute she was Leo the lionhearted, and constantly, it seemed, he made her feel so damn defensive. Now he was mad at her and probably wouldn't make love to her after all.

But she hadn't taken into consideration the natural aggressiveness of an aroused male. "Oh, hell, Amanda!" Tristan concluded irritably and wrapped his big hand around the nape of her neck. He exerted pressure, hauling her onto her toes, demonstrating who was boss. His mouth twisting on hers was violent with the force of his emotions, but when he felt her shiver, it softened slightly. His tongue, however, demanded total capitulation, and it wasn't until she was sagging weakly against him that he raised his mouth again. "Take it off, Mandy," he whispered. "Please, lass. I want to see your body, and my hands are too big and impatient to do the job properly." He held her away from him and brushed the slender straps off her shoulders.

Hesitantly, Amanda tugged the bodice down over her breasts, but when it pooled around her hips and she saw the hot appreciation in Tristan's gray eyes, she grew bolder. If he wanted her to strip, then she would. She'd give him a show in the process he wouldn't soon forget! Rubbing her palms down her thighs, she bunched the material between her fingers, and when she smoothed them up her legs again, the material dragged upward with the motion of her hands until it nearly reached the juncture of her thighs. But then she released it, letting it drop back in place, while she reached up to remove the pins holding her hair. She shook her head, dislodging her pale hair from its precarious knot, and reached once more for her hem. She inched it up, only to let it fall once again.

"Dinna tease me, lass," he whispered hoarsely, and the raw hunger in his voice made Amanda burn with excitement. Tired of the game herself, she hooked her thumbs into the material and pushed the gown over her hips. Once past the rounded curves, it slid down her legs to form a silky tangerine puddle at her feet.

Tristan's breath hissed sharply between his teeth, and impatiently he kicked off the remainder of his own clothing. She barely got a glimpse of his body before he picked her up and set her on the bed. Leaning over her, he pressed her into the pillows.

"God, you're bonny," he said in a raspy voice and sank his mouth into the side of her throat. "So verra, verra bonny."

There was no doubt in Amanda's mind as to who was in charge of their lovemaking. From the first touch of bare skin against bare skin, she knew herself to be totally dominated. It wasn't Tristan's size, or even his vaster experience. It wasn't that he displayed any overt desire to dominate. She simply seemed to lack control whenever she ended up in his arms. All he had to do was kiss her, touch her, and she lost all awareness of place, time, or circumstance.

Tristan dragged his open mouth down the slender column of Amanda's throat. He pushed himself up on one elbow, and his eyes burned a path down her body, missing nothing. His look was so open and bold that Amanda was tempted to shield herself from it, but he so clearly liked what he saw that she lay quietly and let him look his fill. He lifted a hand to trail his fingertips over her collarbone and down her chest to climb the slopes of her breasts. He drew lazy figure eights between them, circling her nipples without actually touching them. "You really are a blonde," he murmured.

Distracted by his actions, Amanda replied, "Well, of course I am." Then, as the meaning of his words sunk in, she surged up on her elbows. "Tristan MacLaughlin! You've been thinking I dye my hair!" She gave his large shoulder an indignant shove, which didn't budge him an inch. He just smiled at her lazily and closed his forefinger and thumb around one nipple, giving it a gentle squeeze. Leaning over, he gently lapped his captured bounty with the flat of his tongue. Amanda's back arched. Her head dropped back and her elbows melted out from under her. When Tristan raised his head, he turned it, staring openly at the sparse blonde stripe of downy curls gracing her mound. "With your eyebrows so dark, I felt you must be lightening your hair." Removing his glasses, he drew a tiny pattern on her stomach with one of the stems. Then he set them aside and raised up to pin her with his eyes. Amanda was held in place by the direct stare, unsoftened by blurring lenses. "But I can see I was wrong, then, wasna I?"

Scalding color burned over her entire body, and something

deep and tight twisted in Tristan's stomach. He couldn't think of another moment in his life when he had felt as alive as he did right now. He was hard and ready for her, but he wasn't in any hurry. He was going to draw this out for as long as he could bear it. Hell, he must have thought of a hundred ways to satisfy her while he lay in his solitary bed at night. Now that he actually had the opportunity, he wouldn't rush —not for anything.

He rolled half on top of her, plunging his fingers into her hair and pulling her up to meet his mouth. He loved kissing her. She reciprocated with a responsiveness that excited him as no other woman ever had. Her lips were soft and full, her tongue was hot and supple, and she tasted of toothpaste and chocolate and something that was ineffably hers. And she clung when he kissed her, her body arching up to press against his, her arms wound tightly around his neck, fingers digging into his skin and scalp.

One of Tristan's hands disengaged itself from her hair and smoothed down her body. It cupped the angle of her jaw and stroked down her throat. It rubbed the long, smooth hollow of her underarm and pressed against the side of her breast. Then it skimmed down her side, over the curve of her hip and along the length of her thigh as far as he could reach. Tristan lifted his mouth away from Amanda's and raised up to watch her as his hand began the upward return journey.

Her eyes blinked open as his fingers moved up the inside of her thigh. They were deep purple and drowsy, staring into his. Her thighs fell apart at the raspy circles he drew, higher and higher, and she gasped and arched up to meet his fingertips when they suddenly separated intimate folds of slippery flesh and slid up and down with exquisite slowness. She clutched at his shoulder with the one arm still wrapped around him and breathed his name, then licked her upper lip and rubbed her free hand down his chest to his abdomen and, lower still, to his rigid belly. Tristan tried to turn aside far enough to evade her reaching fingers, needing to remain untouched to prolong their lovemaking, but he felt her hand wrap around his stiff member just as he slid the tip of a finger inside her and reached higher to separate damp curls so he could ply her with his thumb.

Amanda arched up and her hand released him as it grabbed for his side, digging her fingernails into his skin to anchor herself. Her hips pumped in countermeasure to Tristan's finger, silently begging for completion, but almost immediately, she tried to disengage herself. She retracted her nails from his skin, and with the same hand attempted to push him away, but it was like trying to move stone. "Please," she whispered, staring at the smoldering gray eyes watching her every reaction. "Please, Tristan, you've . . . umm!" Her eyes drifted closed, then reopened. "Oh, God, you've got to stop. I can't hold on, ohpleaseohplease, I'm going to expl . . . I'm going to . . ."

"Come, lassie," he growled, and his finger pressed deep, and his palm flattened, and he hungrily covered Amanda's mouth with his own, swallowing her frantic cries of completion. He held her tightly until the last shudder wracked her body and she went limp in his arms.

Then he set about rebuilding her passion.

Covering her in kisses, he worked his way down her body until his tongue took up residence where only moments ago his finger had lodged. His tongue was slow and gentle, then rough and fast, and not until she was once again straining for satisfaction did he raise his head. Pushing up on his forearms between Amanda's sprawled thighs, Tristan reached for his slacks. Unwilling to forsake contact, he stroked his fingers along her thighs while he one-handedly wrestled his wallet from the back pocket and fished out a condom, impatiently tossing the wallet aside and sitting up. Amanda watched him with blurred vision as his large hands competently unrolled the protection down, down—oh, my—a formidable length. When he looked up at her, she had her arms held up to him.

Tristan's heart slammed up against his rib cage and he

gathered her in his arms, holding her tight, kissing her with unbridled hunger. He captured her right wrist and directed her hand down to where he strained between their two bodies. Amanda wrapped her fingers around him and moved her hand slowly up and down.

"Guide me," he demanded; he begged. And his held breath sharply expelled as he felt her impale him that first inch.

Amanda's body, long unused to such activity, would only yield to him in increments before it nervously closed up again, her thighs gripping his hips to prevent his body's progress into hers. Tristan gritted his teeth and forced himself to be patient, to be still, ruthlessly suppressing his natural inclination to plow into her, regardless of the discomfort she would experience. But what his body denied, his tongue couldn't help but express. Breathing harshly, he kissed her.

"Please, darlin'," his voice whispered in her ear, in her hair, against her mouth, "relax a little, I willna hurt you, I willna . . . Oh, God, yes, like that." His eyes slowly drifted open and he looked down at her. "Take all of me, Amanda . . . please, Mandy, take . . . That's it, darlin'. Oh, God, yes, that's it." And he sank into her as far as a man could go.

Tristan held himself still, deeply imbedded in her, and he felt like he'd come home. For once in his life, joined with a woman, he didn't experience his old familiar, searing loneliness. Usually he felt like a big tomcat searching for a hearth, knowing all the while the most he could hope for was a little transient warmth. With Amanda it was different. God, he had to make it last. Cautiously, he rotated his hips.

Amanda murmured into his shoulder and rotated hers.

Tristan slowly withdrew.

Amanda's soft hands on his hard buttocks pulled him back into her.

He shuddered and arched his pelvis, pinning her to the bed. "Ah, God, you're sweet," he whispered, and his voice had an urgent, sandpaper rasp. Amanda's fingernails flexed in his rump, and with careful intent he began to move inside her.

Amanda swiftly learned that Tristan could not be swayed once he'd developed a plan of action. He was insistent upon loving her with excruciating slowness, and nothing Amanda could do would make him rush. He didn't attempt to be fancy. He just thrust into her, filling her, stretching her, and then withdrew. Thrust and withdrew. Slowly. God, so very, very slowly. It didn't take many moments of careful stroking before Amanda was again hanging on the edge of a climax, but it was an edge he wouldn't let her topple over. When she tried increasing the tempo, he grasped her hips, buried himself deep inside her, and wouldn't resume until she'd once again stilled. Her whispered pleas went unanswered, stifled by his mouth and tongue, making love to her mouth until she was too breathless to beg. He reacted to the pain of her piercing fingernails by slowing down further still, contracting his buttocks and retreating by centimeters until he'd nearly withdrawn, pushing up on his hands until he was poised above her. Once he was satisfied she had settled down, he filled her once again with a slow, sliding plunge, using his entire body, bending his arms until his chest once again rubbed against her breasts. He twisted, rubbing against her like a big, sleek cat, kissing her hard, kissing her softly. But the moment she came close to attaining her satisfaction he stilled once more, waiting for her to cool off before starting the whole process over again.

Amanda went wild. Writhing beneath him, she wound her arms around his neck, head thrown back, tossing restlessly from side to side on the pillow. In order to have more of him, her pelvis tilted and her knees drew back farther and farther until her shins were wedged in the angle of his armpits, his steady rocking causing a soft friction where silky shinbone met tufted hair. But although Tristan emitted a ragged growl at this deeper access to her, he still didn't accelerate the pace of his thrusts. He was thorough and he was silent, except for his harsh breathing, blasting hot against her ear.

Amanda couldn't stand it any longer. She opened her eyes
to beg him please, to make him *stop*, for she simply couldn't
sustain this level of intensity without losing her mind. Oh,
God, she wasn't a robot.

Amanda looked into his face, and she saw that neither was
he.

It was hard to determine where ecstasy left off and agony
began in Tristan's ravaged countenance. Sweat poured from
his body, and his eyes stared straight ahead, tortured and out
of focus. His head was thrown back, his lips drawn back
from clenched teeth, and his Adam's apple rode up and down
the column of his throat as he swallowed convulsively, over
and over again.

He looked like a man viewing a glimpse of heaven from
his own private hell.

"Tristan?" Amanda pressed her lips against his throat. It
was hot and wet, and she dragged her mouth up and down
its length. "Love me a little harder. Please, harder?"

He gripped her head and pulled it back until he could stare
into her eyes. "No," he said adamantly, through clenched
teeth. "Not yet. Soon. Just . . . not yet. Got to . . . make
it . . . last."

"Please," she panted. "I can't . . . Please." She saw
the intent in his face as he lowered it to hers again, and
she snapped her head back into the pillow, shoving at his
shoulders with her hands. "Don't! Dammit, don't you try
to shut me up by kissing me. You're not going to get away
with manipulating me that way, Tristan MacLaughlin. Not
again."

Tristan stared at her blindly and continued his slow,
steady thrusts. "Oh, God," she whispered, lifting her hips
higher. "Oh, God, I love you, Tristan. I love you, oh please
. . ." And he cried out as if she'd suddenly touched electric
wires to his damp skin.

She was as surprised to hear the words issue from her
mouth as he was, but in a long-protected corner of her heart,
she knew she spoke the truth. She didn't know how, she

didn't know why, but she knew with bone-deep certainty that this domineering, taciturn man had somehow burrowed his way into her heart and taken up residence. And the words were magic in more ways than one, because finally—finally! —his iron control broke and his hips began to pump into her with more speed and force, harder and rougher, and those blood-rich nerves deep in her body detonated their withheld sensations like fireworks in a midnight sky, sizzling and flaring, clenching and contracting. "Oh, God, Tristan! Oh, G . . . uhh!"

Grasping a handful of Amanda's hair, Tristan dragged her head back and wrapped his mouth around her lips, swallowing all her frantic cries. Suddenly, he stiffened and cried out also, groaning into her receptive mouth as with one final, powerful surge, he drove into her and let the muscular, milking spasms of the tight sheath gripping him rob him of the remainder of his control.

When the last jump and shudder of Tristan's release died away and he slumped heavily upon her body, Amanda experienced a boneless sort of euphoria. But an instant later the events of the day caught up with her and silently she began to cry. She was exhausted and confused, and she couldn't take much more of this emotional roller coaster that she'd been riding, keeping her sensibilities swooping and soaring from one extreme to the other. In the space of one day, she had experienced just about every emotion imaginable, and it was suddenly too much. Even the exquisite pleasure he had just given her had nearly been more than she could bear.

And dear God, had she really told this harsh, dominating man that she loved him? She was under too much stress to trust any of her emotions. Lord, she didn't actually even know the man! Amanda cried harder.

"Amanda?" As the first scalding tears rolled into the contour of his neck, Tristan raised up and looked down at her. He pushed up on his elbows, and Amanda's arms fell away from his neck, dropping limply onto the mattress. "Was I too rough, lass?" He tried to wipe the tears from her cheeks with his blunt fingers, but they flowed faster than he could handle. He placed kisses about her face and neck. "Shh, now . . . dinna cry. Did I hurt you?"

"No." Amanda's head rolled from side to side on the pillow. He looked so startled and concerned, and she felt like such a fool. "No, it's not you, Tristan. It's . . ." With both hands she attempted to dash the tears from her cheeks. "God, I'm sorry. It's . . . just everything, sort of catching up." The tears finally began to abate and Amanda regarded him with weary trepidation. "Tristan, do you think my caller was that same Duke person who's been calling you?"

He had expected the question earlier; he wasn't prepared for it now. And he knew it was fortunate they were no longer pressed together, chest to breast, for he couldn't control the sudden thump of his heart against his rib cage. He'd had Edwards play the tape for him while Amanda was in her bath, and he was pretty damn certain it was Duke. But, looking down into her exhausted eyes, he assured himself he couldn't be positive. And there was no sense letting her worry about it tonight.

"We won't know until the results of the voiceprints come in from the lab tomorrow," he murmured, and reluctantly disengaged his body from hers. He rolled them both over and wrapped his arms around her, pressing her head into his chest. "Don't worry about it tonight, Mandy." Large, tough fingers gently combed through her hair. "Just go to sleep, love. It's been a long, hard day for you. Rest."

The warmth and strength of his body, wrapped around hers, made her feel secure. Amanda was exhausted, so she let go, and within minutes she did exactly as he'd directed and fell asleep.

For Tristan, holding her and staring into the darkness, sleep was a longer time coming.

CHAPTER
_____ 16 _____

Tristan was aware of the moment Amanda awakened. He felt her eyes on him, but he completed his push-ups before he allowed himself to turn his head and look at her. She was sitting up in the middle of the bed with the sheet chastely tucked under her arms. One corner of Tristan's mouth quirked up as he rolled to a sitting position. He had looked at every inch of her last night, but ridiculously, he enjoyed her modesty. It indicated he had seen what bloody few other men ever had, and that satisfied a deep-seated possessiveness he hadn't even realized he had been harboring. Slowly, Tristan smiled at her. "Good morning, Amanda Rose."

Amanda tried to distance herself from his appeal, feeling a need to steel herself against the inevitable transition from lover back to cop. And if he was enchanted by her modesty, she was dismayed by his lack of it. How could he sit there so casually, wearing only his crooked smile, and not even attempt to shield from her the embryonic stage of what she knew would be a formidable erection? Amanda looked away. She dare not risk letting him slip past her guard again—not if it meant having to watch his transformation back into the imperviously cold-eyed cop afterward. She didn't think she could bear it if he made love to her, slipped on his gun, and called her Miss Charles. "G'morning, Lieutenant," she muttered, defenses slamming into place.

Tristan's smile disappeared and he surged to his feet. Planting one knee on the mattress, he fell across the bed to loom over her with his hands braced on either side of her hips. Amanda had to let go of the sheet and fall back on her elbows in order to avoid touching him. "Lieutenant?" he growled. "What happened to 'I love you, Tristan'?" He observed her stricken expression and realized she'd hoped he wouldn't bring that up. But why the bloody hell had she told him that she loved him if she didn't? God, he'd gone off like a rocket when she had said that last night. A sudden suspicion made his eyes narrow.

Maybe that was the only reason she had said it—to get a little long-awaited satisfaction. God knows, he had gone a wee bit daft last night, trying to string it out past good sense. It was difficult, in the cold light of day, to recapture the exact emotions that had driven him to deny them both ultimate satisfaction. But he remembered the strong feeling of conviction at the time that once he had pleasured her, she would send him away.

But that couldn't actually be the reason, could it? How could she have foreseen the results? He hadn't known himself how badly he'd needed to hear the words from her until she had said them. No, remembering her body's initial difficulty accepting his, he decided it was more than likely a case of something she had felt compelled to say in order to justify the way her hormones stood up and screamed whenever they got within touching distance of each other. A determined light entered Tristan's eyes.

He lowered his head and used his nose to nudge her hair away from her ear. "Say: 'Good morning, Tristan,' " he ordered softly.

"MacLaughlin, don't." But she didn't have the strength

to turn her head away from the warm, wet tongue delicately outlining the whorls of her ear.

"Say it."

"Good morning, Tristan." Her reward was to have him burrow his tongue into her ear with a growl of approval. She shivered helplessly.

Tristan moved his head until their mouths were a hairbreath apart. "Mandy, kiss me proper." He held his breath. She had never once instigated contact between them.

Amanda considered his request, her heart thumping in her chest. *Refuse*, her fine analytical mind demanded. *Tell him to go away*. But her hormones urged a different message, and feeling his warmth, breathing his scent, there was really no contest.

Amanda reached up and framed his face in her hands, rubbing it with appreciative fingertips. It had that special smoothness of the just shaved. "Lieutenant MacLaughlin, there is proper," she whispered softly and pursed her lips, pressing them with cool primness against Tristan's. He tried not to be disappointed with her lukewarm, schoolmarm response. She pulled back, studying his face. "And then there is *proper*," she informed him. And she opened her lips around his and tugged at them with a light, sucking motion in imitation of the way he always kissed her. When his mouth opened, she slipped her tongue between his teeth and thoroughly explored his mouth. Tristan groaned deep in his throat and laid her back among the pillows.

His lovemaking was fast and fierce, displaying little of the determined control he had demonstrated the night before. Amanda met his furious aggression head-on, and she was still quivering with spent passion, tiny inner muscles still clenching him with residual contractions when he pushed up on his elbows and smoothed her tumbled hair back from her face. "Amanda, tell me how your sister Teddy died."

He was silent while she did so, and he kissed away her

tears with a tenderness she had never before seen him display. So it was doubly shocking to Amanda when he spoke. "She sounds a right proper coward," he stated with flat disapproval, and looking at him, Amanda saw what she had feared to see earlier—the gun-metal hard, assessing eyes of the cop.

"How dare you!" Amanda said, and she didn't care if the words were trite. He didn't know the first thing . . . he had no right . . . She shoved at his shoulders, not wanting to be intimately connected to him while he criticized her beloved sister. "She wasn't!"

Tristan refused to move. "The bloody hell she wasn't," he growled, coldly furious on Amanda's behalf. "Where I grew up people were dealt all manner of pain and betrayal. But they bloody well fought to survive, despite everything that was dished out to them. They didna give up at the first setback and settle all their troubles with a handful of pills." He pinned her wrists to the sheet when she continued to struggle with him. "And they sure as bloody hell wouldna have left their little sister to cope with the grief and guilt all alone."

"Shut up!" she panted, shaking her hair out of her face to glare at him. "You don't know anything about her, about me."

"I know that she had more than most. She had youth and wealth and hope for a better future . . . and you. She had you, dammit, but she was too selfish to think beyond her own pain. Well, what about your pain, Amanda? How many nights have you lost sleep, then, blamin' yourself for not bein' able to stop her? There wasna a hope you could have, you know—not once she'd chosen her course."

"I might have! If I'd . . ."

He stopped her words with a fierce kiss. Lifting his head, he said, "You say I dinna know you? Lass, I know everything there *is* to know about you! I know you're loyal and you're strong, and I know you're not a bloody quitter. How old were you when you struck out on your own?"

She regarded him with that mulish slant to her full mouth that made him want to shake her and kiss her at the same time. "How old, Mandy?"

"Eighteen."

"And where did you go, then?"

"New York. What's your point?"

"You have character and you have strength . . ."

"I had financial help." She threw it in his face. He had said he was raised in an orphanage, and from the tone of his words, not in a neighborhood where hope was a ready commodity. Yet he had managed to get himself out of it to where he was today. He obviously set great store on self-reliance.

Tristan went very still. "You took money from this family you profess to scorn?" he demanded in disgust. "You ran away from home, but they still sent you an allowance, is that what you're sayin'?"

"I came into my trust fund on my twenty-fifth birthday." Amanda was very much on her dignity. "Did you think dancing bought this triplex? Guess again. I'm sorry to disillusion you, MacLaughlin, but . . ."

Tristan grabbed her up off the pillows and kissed her roughly. He smiled against her mouth and murmured, "God, you are a prize, then, lass." Sliding off Amanda onto his side, he draped a leg over her and propped himself up on an elbow to study her face while she settled back among the cushions. She was sensuously lethargic as a result of his kiss, but she was also wary, on the alert for his next attack. Tristan refrained from smiling. She was a feisty one, his Amanda. "So, what about the seven years between the time you left home and your twenty-fifth birthday?"

"What about them?"

"Where was your infamous financial help then? How did you pay the rent?"

"I shared with other dancers. I waited tables. I was a bicycle messenger and a not-very-proficient office temp. And, a bit at a time, I got legitimate gypsy work."

He picked up a strand of her hair and rubbed it between his fingers. Looking directly into her eyes, he murmured, "Like I said: strength and character."

Amanda looked up at him, trying to wade through the confusing morass of her mixed emotions. How on earth was she supposed to stay angry if he insisted on being so blessed complimentary? There was so much more to Tristan Mac-Laughlin than she had originally assumed. She had thought this man was so cold, yet underneath the natural reserve there was warmth and fire . . . and even flashes of humor. But he had said such awful things about Teddy. "I loved my sister, Tristan," she whispered fiercely. "And I miss her. I won't let you or anyone else criticize her."

Tristan gave her words careful consideration. He still felt Teddy had been weak and selfish, but she'd been little more than a child when she had opted out of life's problems. He instinctively recognized her suicide to have been a major factor in Amanda's general sexual inactivity, but he couldn't actually regret that Amanda hadn't given herself to a lot of other men. Then, too, he was the first to admit he knew nothing about the love between siblings. What he did know, with gut certainty, was that Amanda would shut him out of her life entirely if he insisted on bucking her loyalty to her dead sister.

"Aye," he finally agreed. "I willna be sayin' no more." His reward was her slow smile and watching her relax. Unable to resist, he lowered his head.

The phone rang, and they both froze. On the third ring, Tristan snatched it up and passed it to Amanda.

"Hello?" she said apprehensively. Then she relaxed fractionally and handed the receiver back to Tristan. "It's for you."

Even stark naked, Amanda was amused to note, Tristan managed to project an impression of absolute authority. But as she listened to his end of the conversation, she grew apprehensive all over again. Her eyes were solemn when he finally hung up and turned back to her. Tristan's were equally serious.

"The voiceprints match, Amanda."

Lightning zigzagged across her stomach. "It's he, then?" she whispered. "The man who killed Maryanne and the others?"

"Aye, it looks that way."

Amanda tossed back the covers, prepared to bolt, mindlessly, without consideration to destination. She was intent only on obeying a primal urge to flee. Her flight was aborted when Tristan's hand reached out and grasped her wrist, staying her. The fingers of his free hand tunneled into her hair and he tipped her face up until she met his eyes. "Don't go panicking on me now, lass."

The fear hazing her eyes ate at him, and Tristan's fingers tightened in Amanda's hair, pulling her head against his chest. He wrapped her in his arms and whispered reassurances and promises he had no guarantee he could keep. Even as he did it, he wondered at his actions. Since he had met her he'd broken damn near every rule by which he had structured his life. But, conscious of her arms clinging tightly to his neck, the warmth of her, he gave a shrug. The hell with it. What was one more transgression at this point?

He felt something for her that he had never felt for another living being in his life. He imagined it was love, but how was he supposed to know? His life hadn't exactly been overburdened by that particular emotion, and before he had met Amanda Rose Charles, he had never really believed in it. In a way, he even halfway hoped what he was feeling wasn't love, because what the flamin' hell kind of future could there be for a cop spawned in the bowels of a Glasgow slum and a dancer of obvious breeding? What did they have in common, aside from a mutual dislike of the accoutrements attached to their respective professions? She quite obviously hated the gun he wore. And he hated the leering drunks who ogled her in her sexy wee stage costumes and garish makeup.

But there was no denying that his feelings for her were stronger than any he had ever known. And come hell or high water, he would keep her safe. He told her as much, and then suggested she take a bath to calm herself, having observed they seemed to be Amanda's version of a tranquilizer.

She surprised him by laughing into the skin of his chest. When she released him and pulled back, determination had replaced the fear in her eyes.

"I've cried so many tears and taken so many baths since the day I identified Maryanne's body, I'm beginning to feel like an overused sponge," Amanda explained in the face of his puzzlement. She climbed out of bed and donned a robe, then turned back to study Tristan's face.

For once, it wasn't studiously blank; she could actually read his frustrated confusion. She wondered if he was having as much trouble as she was reconciling their relationship. Silently, she handed him his slacks, and slinging his shirt over her shoulder, she got down on her hands and knees on the floor and began crawling around in search of scattered buttons.

Tristan's whispered reassurances and the strength of his arms had comforted her greatly; she felt much calmer. But she wasn't proud of the way she had been allowing her emotions to rule her every action lately. It was past time to take stock of the situation and recapture the trust in her own intellect and instincts that she had always relied upon in the past.

Amanda gathered the last button and stood up. Tristan had donned his slacks, socks, and glasses, and was sitting on the side of the bed tying his shoes. When he raised his head to stare at her, she avoided his eyes, opening her fist to show him the buttons, instead. "I'll sew these back on your shirt," she murmured distantly. "I imagine you have to leave for work soon."

Tristan surged to his feet, and in two giant strides, he was towering over her. Amanda found herself staring at his collarbone at close range, but when his hands closed over her upper arms, she tipped her head back to see his face. He was furiously angry.

"Sod the flamin' shirt," he snarled. "And for the moment, sod work, too. You think this is the way I want it to be? You turn me inside out until I don't know up from down, and I'd give my left testicle for this to be a normal situation that allowed us time to learn about each other. Well, we dinna have that luxury, Amanda Rose, and I'm not exactly happy to know you'll be doin' your damnedest to avoid lookin' at me the minute I strap on my gun. But I'll bloody well be damned if you'll get away with actin' like you expected all along that I just wanted to fuck you and forget you." The crude alliteration was deliberate. "Not before I so much as even reach for the flamin' holster . . ."

"I did no such thing!" Color flowed into Amanda's cheeks. "I never said a word about . . . and I'd never say . . . call it . . ."

"Aye, Amanda Charles wouldna sully her mouth usin' crude words, would she? Not when she can use her best party manners to dismiss me like a polite little girl with an unwanted guest . . ."

"That's not fair!" Amanda wrenched out of his hands. She grabbed his wrist and slapped the handful of buttons into his palm. "Here! Sew your own damn buttons on, and then just get out, will you? You're making me crazy! I don't know how I'm expected to act with you. One minute you're my lover . . ."

"Too bloody right I'm your lover! You canna just brush that aside when we're no longer makin' love."

"That wasn't my intention, Tristan MacLaughlin! Quit twisting my words." Amanda made an effort to calm down. She wanted to make her point in a rational manner. "You and I are lovers, yes. But I held my breath this morning, waiting for you to call me Miss Charles again." She saw him wince. "I'm not blind, and it hasn't escaped my attention that you're bothered about being in charge of a case that involves me. It puts you in an untenable position."

"Aye, it is bloody awkward," Tristan interrupted. "I'll
not deny it. But if you really believe I'm capable of informing
you one minute that your caller is the mon who's wanted for
killin' all those lasses and then turning around the next and
trotting off to work, leavin' you to cope on your own, then
we've not made a lick of progress since the day you called
me a robot."

"Oh, Tristan," she whispered. "I think I've come to know
you better than that. I just wanted to make it easier for you
to do your job." Amanda brushed his chest with her fingertips
in a conciliatory gesture, and then slowly looked up until she
was staring directly into his clear gray eyes. "Don't you see?
I can't cling to you. I want to—you don't know how much
I want to. But I realize that you can't be with me every
minute. You have a job to do . . ."

"And I'll do it." Her touch had robbed him of his anger.
And those eyes—God, those beautiful, honest eyes. "Ah,
lass, let's not fight. If we work together, it's possible we'll
come up with something we havena thought of before. Get
dressed. Then we'll sit down and hash this out." He turned
her toward the bathroom and, stroking his hand down her
bottom, gently boosted her on her way.

Amanda was groomed and fixing a pot of coffee in the
kitchen when Tristan used Rhonda's key to let himself back
into the apartment a short while later. She eyed the armful
of clothes he brought with him, but there was a knock on the
door before she had a chance to ask him about it. With Tristan
standing to one side of the door with his hand on the butt of
his gun, Amanda opened it cautiously.

It was Rhonda.

"Good morning, boys and girls," she said cheerfully,
breezing into the apartment. "Or should I say good afternoon?" She eyed the stack of clothes that Tristan had dropped
on the couch in response to her knock. "Well, well, well.
What have we here, my fine big laddie? Moving in?"

"Aye," he agreed shortly, and his eyes, on Amanda, dared
her to disagree. She asked him about provisions for Ace,

instead, and he flashed her one of his rare white smiles and
hooked an arm around her waist, pulling her to him to bestow
a short, hard kiss on her mouth. He left with the dog to get
the rest of their belongings, carefully locking the door behind
him. Amanda, slightly flushed, turned to face Rhonda.

"Well, don't just stand there, kiddo," Rhonda demanded.
"Tell me. Is he as good as he looks?"

"Better."

"Oh, God, I knew it." By the look on Rhonda's face,
Amanda could tell she was gearing up to launch an entire
battery of embarrassing questions. Partly to avoid them, but
mostly because it was uppermost in her mind, Amanda
blurted, "Rhonda, my caller is the Show Girl Slayer."

"No! I mean, are they sure?"

"Yes. The lab called Tristan not too long ago with the
results of the voiceprint, and it matches that of the man who's
been calling him at the station. There is very little room for
doubt."

"Oh, shit, kiddo. What are . . . ?" Rhonda broke off as
Tristan and Ace reentered the apartment. He took one look
at them and carefully lowered the large box in his arms.
Picking Ace's food and water dish off the top, he straightened
and regarded them gravely.

"Let me fill these and put them in the kitchen for Ace,"
he said quietly. "Then we'll sit down and talk about it."

The women trailed him into the kitchen. Tristan filled the
dog's bowls and placed them on the floor out of the way.
Amanda poured coffee and they sat around the small table.
There was an awkward moment of silence while Tristan studied Amanda.

"Do you want to leave town?" The instant he gave her
the option, Tristan felt divided. If it were anyone else, he
would be trying his damnedest to convince her to stay.
Amanda was his first direct link to the killer, and by letting
her leave, he would dramatically reduce his chances of catching the man before he killed again.

But it wasn't anyone else; it was Amanda. And on a purely

emotional level, he wanted her somewhere safe. He balked at the idea of Amanda as bait, knowing better than most that no matter how many precautions the police took, she was still vulnerable. They couldn't make her one hundred percent secure. And historically, serial killers possessed a formidable native intelligence. There were just too many things that could go wrong.

"And go where?"

Lost in his personal conflict, Tristan's head snapped up at the sound of Amanda's voice. He hesitated, thinking of her options. "Your family?"

"No!"

"You could go to my flat in Seattle." The idea made him cringe. If she ever saw the rat hole he occupied there, she'd probably run as fast and as far from him as she could manage. Why the bloody hell had he been so tight-fisted with his money? He could have afforded to fix the place up a bit.

Amanda was thinking furiously. "Tristan, if I did leave, what would happen to your investigation?"

He eyed her warily. "It would continue on as before."

"But it could continue on for months . . . or even years, couldn't it?"

He was silent, tight-jawed, and she pressed. "The Green River killer in Seattle—I've read about him, and that case has been going on for several years now, hasn't it? In fact, don't they now think he may be the same man who is killing those girls in San Diego?"

Sod professional responsibilities. Ignoring her question, Tristan said with quiet force, "I'll not be lettin' you set yourself up as bait, Mandy, if that's what you're thinkin', so just put the idea out of your mind."

Rhonda, who up until then had been silent, agreed vehemently.

Amanda looked at them both with determination. "I'm not exactly thrilled with the prospect myself," she pointed out quietly. "But the alternative is a professional and personal limbo that could last for God alone knows how long. I refuse to put my entire life on hold, waiting until this maniac has been captured.''

Tristan gave her words serious consideration. Much as he wanted her safe, he could understand her feelings. It could be years before it was safe for her to return. And selfishly, he didn't want her to go away and start a new life elsewhere; he wanted her near him. "We'll leave it the way it is—for now," he finally agreed. "As long as Duke limits himself to calls that are admiring in tone, you should be safe enough. But at the first hint of a threat, Amanda Rose, you're gettin' out.''

"Hmm," she said, knowing he assumed her consent. And it wasn't that she harbored a burning desire to flout his authority or set herself up as a madman's target. But for her entire adult life, she'd had no one but herself to depend upon in times of crisis. Now, she had suddenly been thrust in the midst of a situation that was not of her making. And it shook her right down to the ground that she was seriously tempted to forsake her hard-won self-reliance. She had come to the realization earlier this morning that if she did that—if she let her fears and emotions rule her to the extent where someone else was allowed to step in and make all the decisions in her life for her—then she would be enabling a maniac to destroy her mental health as surely as he would attempt to destroy her physically, should he decide to make her his next victim. In all probability, if it came to the crunch, she would follow Tristan's orders, for he knew a great deal more about dealing with this type of situation than she did. But she would not arbitrarily offer a blanket promise to that effect before the fact.

"Will you get yourself a gun, lass? I'll teach you how to use it.''

Amanda's head snapped up. "No!''

The flatly stated, instinctive rejection was like a slap in his face, and Tristan's eyes turned opaque, all expression erased. He shoved his coffee cup aside and rose to his feet.

"Excuse me," he said stiffly. "There are still a few items

downstairs I need to bring up.'' He left the kitchen and a moment later Amanda heard the front door close behind him.

Amanda stared across the table at Rhonda. ''I think I hurt him.''

''Go talk to him, kiddo. Straighten it out.'' Rhonda examined her closely. ''That is . . . if it's a relationship you'd like to see progress?''

Amanda was already rising, and she looked at her friend helplessly across the table. ''I think I love him, Rhonda.''

''I think you do, too, kid. And I think he could use a lot of love. Don't allow a misunderstanding to fester into something more serious. Go straighten it out.'' She sat back in her chair after Amanda left and raised her coffee cup. ''Listen to me. I sound like a Jewish mother.'' But Tristan MacLaughlin had earned himself a special place in her heart, and she wanted to see things work out right for him and Amanda.

Tristan's door was open, and Amanda followed the sounds of activity to his bedroom. She stood in the doorway and watched him slam exercise equipment into an oversized cardboard box. ''Tristan?''

He stiffened and turned slowly. His eyes assessed her with apparent calm indifference.

''I'm sorry,'' she said. ''The idea caught me by surprise.''

Tristan shrugged. ''It was just a suggestion. You didna like it. It's not important.''

''Yes, it is. You think I was rejecting you, but I wasn't.''

''Like hell.'' His eyes focused on something above her head.

''I wasn't, Tristan!'' She stepped up to him, and when his gaze remained fixed above her, she grabbed his tie and gave it a yank, forcing him to look at her. She hated it when he wiped away every trace of expression from his face. She didn't have the first idea what he was thinking as his level gray eyes met hers. ''Don't you see,'' she pleaded for his understanding. ''Guns make me nervous. Before I met you, I had never even seen a real one. But the fact that I'm uncomfortable around them has nothing to do with you, Tristan. I understand your need to wear one.''

''You bloody well don't!'' Tristan's eyes blazed with sudden fire. ''Or you wouldna turn away every time I put mine on!''

''You've had it on since you dressed, and I haven't turned away, have I?'' He hesitated, and Amanda continued insistently, ''I'll admit it took some getting used to, Tristan. But I've accepted it as part of you. But, don't you see, your job requires wearing a gun. If I bought one, I'm scared to death I'd end up shooting you or Rhonda or someone else equally innocent by mistake. You hear of that sort of thing happening all the time.''

The implacable indifference that shielded Tristan's eyes lifted, replaced by determined insistence. ''I could teach you to use it safely, lass. Guns wouldna be makin' you so nervous if you gained some knowledge of them.''

Amanda didn't know why he was so insistent, but apparently it was important to him. It was a new experience for her to give in to someone else's wishes against her own better judgment, and she struggled with it for a moment before she acquiesced. ''All right,'' she ultimately agreed. ''I'm not comfortable with the idea, but I'll try it.''

''Good.'' The muscles in the back of Tristan's neck relaxed. If Amanda learned something about guns, perhaps he would never again have to see that expression in her eyes— that look of repugnant disdain that never failed to set off a chain reaction in his gut. He could tell she didn't understand why it was important to him, but he didn't know how to describe to her the blow his sense of self-worth sustained every time he strapped on his gun and he saw her turn away as if he were suddenly unclean. He was the same man with or without it, but he doubted she would ever truly believe that unless she learned something about the handling and care of firearms. Once she learned even the rudiments, she would see that picking up a gun didn't automatically turn a person into a trigger-happy goon.

Tristan looked at her helplessly. He knew he should try to explain his feelings to her, but he wasn't accustomed to expressing himself to another person, and he didn't know how or where to begin. Instead, he smiled at her and contented himself with saying, "Thank you. You willna be regrettin' it, lass, I promise you."

Amanda looked less than convinced, but she returned his smile gamely. A light began to smolder in Tristan's eyes and he bent down to kiss her, igniting at her instant response. It was immeasurably exciting the way she pressed herself against him and automatically raised her arms up to wrap around his neck. His arms tightened against her back in response, pulling her into him, and he edged her backward until the bed bumped the back of her knees. Before he was able to lay her down on it, however, Joe Cash called to him from the outside doorway, and once again reality intruded into their private world.

Tristan straightened away from her slowly, reluctant to let her go. Were they never going to get two minutes to themselves? He resisted the urge to swear, slam the bedroom door shut, and finish what he had begun. He would do it in a minute, if he thought he could actually get away with it. But he knew better.

Right now, real life called. It was time to get back to work.

CHAPTER
17

Tristan and Amanda weren't able to go on dates like an ordinary couple would. He was afraid she would be put at risk if she were seen in public with him. But tonight they had decided to chance it and had driven to a small Chinese restaurant on the outskirts of town. They were both feeling lighthearted as they flirted across the smoky, flickering flame of the red glass votive candle in the middle of the table.

"Get your chopsticks out of my prawns, MacLaughlin."

Tristan withdrew his chopsticks from Amanda's plate, pretending he didn't notice there was still a nice, fat prawn between them. He got it as far as the edge of her dish and thought he was home free. But then Amanda rapped him across the knuckles with her own chopsticks and the prawn tumbled back onto her plate.

"Ow." He brought his knuckle up to his lips and sucked on the little red spot. "There's no need to turn vicious, lass. I just wanted one little bite. I'm hungry." He attempted to look pathetically underfed—not an easy endeavor for a man who is six feet four inches tall and weighs in excess of two hundred pounds.

"Ah, poor baby." Amanda reached across the restaurant table and picked up his hand. "Let mama kiss it better."

He let her carry it to her lips before he said, "It hurts real bad, Mandy. But a prawn would make it feel immensely less painful."

Amanda's lips curled in an involuntary smile against his knuckles before she loosened his hand and gave him a stern look. "Forget it, Tristan. If you wanted prawns, you should have ordered them yourself."

"Aw, come on, lass! One flamin' little prawn. I offered you part of my oyster ginger beef."

"Yeah, knowing you were perfectly safe doing so. No one in their right mind would eat that stuff."

"Hey, it was good."

"Big recommendation, coming from a man who eats peanut butter straight from the jar with a spoon."

Tristan grinned at her, and for an instant, Amanda stilled. She loved that smile. She would do darn near anything for him when he flashed it, and he probably knew it, too, the rat. When he was hungry, she had discovered, the man was totally lacking in scruples. She struggled to hang on to her principles for almost forty-five seconds. Then she planted her elbow on the table, propped her chin in the palm of her hand, and smiled back at him.

And gave him the prawn.

Amanda lived on the memories of their night out for quite a while. Between her schedule and Tristan's, it was difficult to manage enough time simply to be together, let alone to go out on worry-free dates. And that evening had been so special. But nearly two weeks later, she was beginning to believe their rare night out had been nothing more than a wishful daydream.

She was taking refuge in the bathtub. Again. But it was either that or send Tristan packing, and that she couldn't bring herself to do. Dammit, she had never expected to fall in love. And doing so, she had discovered, wasn't the end-all romance books ritually promised it would be. All it did was heap confusion on an already overburdened and volatile range of emotions. She had found the past few weeks baffling.

Amanda wasn't a romantic. She didn't know of many happy marriages. She had known before she was old enough to articulate the thought that she didn't care to emulate her parents' union, but in the ten years since leaving the high-rent battleground they had called home, she'd only met two couples whose sense of belonging to each other she had envied. Two couples, out of so many. Too few marriages appeared to be blessed. Meantime, all around her she had observed the frenzy of her friends falling in love, but she had judged it an ephemeral emotion, for it never seemed to last.

She had been infatuated three times in her twenty-eight years, but even in the deepest throes of attraction, Amanda hadn't once mistaken her feelings for love. She had therefore not been prepared for the strength of the emotions Tristan MacLaughlin unleashed in her. Even upon first making love, when she had told him that she loved him, she had suspected that it was the sex more than the man that held her enthralled. It was quite a jolt to discover she wasn't the cool and fastidious woman she had always believed herself to be. And professing her love, she had feared, was merely a justification to beautify the fact that Tristan, with the slightest touch, could reduce her to such a basic and primitive level, that she no longer even recognized herself.

Sexual enslavement. She rolled the taste of it around her mind the way a connoisseur might test a fine wine on his tongue. It tasted quite nice . . . and convenient. It would let her off the hook for that embarrassing demand that Tristan discard his ubiquitous condoms. It still made her squirm to remember the way she had taken one away from him and tossed it in the wastebasket one day, telling him that as much as she appreciated his sense of responsibility, she had dusted off her old diaphragm and had gone in to have the fit checked, and she really didn't want to feel anything between them again. They were bold words from a heretofore sexual coward, and if she could just convince herself that Tristan had her sexually enthralled, then she wouldn't have to accept responsibility for them.

Not that Tristan had appeared to object, necessarily. Actually, for some odd reason, he seemed to get a kick out of it whenever she acted bold. And enslavement was such a hard word to swallow, when used in relation to oneself. For a woman of her temperament, it held connotations she found it near impossible to live with.

Besides, sexual enslavement alone didn't explain the flash of pure joy that had surged through her veins when Tristan had announced he intended to move in with her. Since the day she could afford to, Amanda had jealously guarded her privacy. It had been a relief to finally have a place of her own again where she would no longer be at the mercy of a roommate's whim or personality. But it was entirely different in Tristan's case. She liked him living here. No, the truth was, until about two hours ago, she had loved it, pure and simple.

She was content to simply talk to him for hours on end. And it astounded her how many things Tristan had to say to her. It was almost as if he had been storing up conversations all his life, just waiting for the right person to come along and listen to him. He had a wide range of knowledge—much wider than her own, actually—and when he was relaxed and they were alone, he could be so interesting and funny and playful.

That he possessed a sense of humor at all still amazed and delighted her. She had been so sure he did not before she had come to know him. But not only did he possess a dry wit, a lighthearted side to his personality was beginning to emerge. He was turning out to be something of a tease.

Besides, if all she wanted was continued sexual gratification, why did she need to know everything about him? Why was she harboring this latent desire to make a home for him to help atone for what she suspected was a barren childhood and lonely adult life? Why did she watch him with his homely mutt and wonder what he'd be like with a baby? She'd never before considered such a thing; it had never even occurred to her to do so. Have a child? It would have meant not dancing for too many months.

If this was only sexual infatuation, why were her favorite moments spent curled up in his lap, just being held quietly, head pressed to his chest, listening to the surge of his blood through his veins? Why couldn't she stop telling him she loved him every time he made love to her? She didn't say it to drive him into a sexual frenzy. That was merely a bonus.

No, some things you can't go on denying forever. This was love.

But there was nothing simple about it. These weren't simple times.

In a perfect world, she and Tristan would have had time to adjust to their new feelings. Not that she was certain Tristan's feelings for her matched her own for him; he had never actually said so. But she decided to assume he cared for her as much as she cared for him until such time as he said otherwise. In any event, in a perfect world, a woman would have time to explore and test her new feelings. She wouldn't have to contend with phone calls from a psychotic killer.

Duke continued to call at irregular intervals in the early morning hours, and Amanda thought it was a measure of the general insanity of her life these days that his brief conversations no longer had the power to reduce her to jelly. It just went to show that one could become accustomed to anything, eventually. She didn't contend that the calls had lost all power to disturb, but Tristan's large and comforting (if sometimes infuriating) presence in her life had lessened the impact, which had originally driven her into a panic.

But the calls were a constant reminder that hers wasn't an ordinary situation. And then, of course, there was the gun.

Amanda intensely disliked what her newly purchased gun represented.

In the gun shop with Tristan on the day he had moved into her apartment, she had instinctively put her hands behind her back when he had held out the pistol for her to try. It wasn't until that hated blank mask had settled over Tristan's stern countenance that she had ultimately reached for it. As her hand had sagged beneath the gun's unexpected weight, she'd felt a flash of resentment for the emotions that bonded her to this complex man. It was ridiculous the lengths to which she would go to prevent that unadulterated lack of expression from establishing permanent residence on MacLaughlin's face. She had no business owning a gun. She was a dancer, not Annie Oakley.

Every opportunity he could devise, Tristan had driven her into the hills outside town for target practice. Amanda admitted she was becoming quite comfortable handling her pistol, cleaning it, and loading it. And knowing herself to be a woman who liked to excel at anything she tried, she even enjoyed growing more proficient at hitting the bull's-eye target. With a minimum of effort, she could almost pretend it was only a game, or a new challenge to be mastered. But then today, without warning, Tristan had substituted a police-issue target for the bull's-eye, and Amanda had refused to pretend any longer—not when the new target was a life-sized outline of a man.

Tristan turned back from pinning the target on the tree and watched Amanda as she unloaded the gun she had loaded only moments before.

"Amanda?"

She looked up at him, and he knew he was in for a battle when he spotted the mulish slant that hardened her soft mouth, the defiance in her violet-blue eyes. "I'm not shooting at that, MacLaughlin."

"It's just a target, darlin'—same as the bull's-eye."

"Baloney. It's a man. You want me to learn to shoot a man."

"What I flamin' want," he snapped as he closed the distance between them and took the gun from her hand, "is to teach you to defend yourself." He reloaded the weapon and extended it to her. "You think if Duke comes callin' you're gonna be able to politely rebuff him with words? A posh accent's not going to affect that bleeder's heart. Take the bloody gun and practice on the target."

Amanda averted her face and her right hand remained stubbornly at her side.

"Take it, Amanda."

She turned her head and looked him squarely in the eye. "No."

Tristan drew in a deep breath and silently counted to ten while he exhaled it. "I could hit you, lass. I could bloody beat you to a pulp. And there isn't a thing you could do to stop me."

Spontaneously, a smile flashed across Amanda's face, diluting her anger. "No, you couldn't," she replied with complete confidence.

"No, you're right. I couldna." He tucked her gun in his waistband. Without warning, his right had whipped out and secured both of her wrists while his left hand, despite her enraged attempt to stop him, easily divested her of her jeans and panties. One large foot swept her feet out from under her, and before she could regain the breath that her sudden descent into the dust had knocked from her lungs, he was on top of her, ruthlessly spreading her legs and pinning her to the hard ground with his weight, unmindful of the painful bits of brush and rock that dug into her exposed backside. "But Duke would." His voice was cold and clipped. "Duke would rape you, beat you, bite you—fucking kill you. If he got the chance."

"Get off me, you limey bastard." Tears swam in Amanda's eyes, but she stared at him without blinking, willing them not to fall.

"I'm not English, Amanda. I'm an American." Tristan rose to his feet and leaned over to extend a hand. Amanda ignored it and scrambled to the spot a few feet away where her panties and jeans lay. He watched her as she picked an embedded pebble out of her hip and brushed herself off. "But, just for the record," he continued quietly, "my lack of parentage originates in Scotland." He waited until she was dressed and extended the gun to her once again.

Amanda snatched it from his hand and spent the following hour in grim silence, taking aim at the target. She wasn't half bad, and Tristan wryly wondered if that was because she was pretending it was him.

When she still wouldn't talk to him on the ride back to town, Tristan began to worry. He tried several conversational gambits; she ignored them all. With every mile that passed in tight-lipped silence, grim specters of Amanda stomping into her apartment, packing his gear, and telling him to hit the road rose to haunt him. But although she tried her best to bounce the front door off his forehead, the word eviction wasn't uttered when they arrived home. Instead, she locked herself in the bathroom and took one of her eternal baths. Tristan sank into the couch and pondered the methods that women use to make men sweat.

Ace climbed up on his lap, and Tristan stroked him absently. Until today, he had soft-pedaled the threat of Duke to Amanda, but the truth was, Tristan had been growing increasingly uneasy. Duke had terminated his calls to Tristan at the time of Joy Frede's death. At the very least, Tristan had expected him to call to gloat. But the killer's silence had been sudden and complete. About the same time, the calls to Amanda had begun.

The tone of Duke's conversations with Amanda were odd. Tristan had no way of knowing for sure, but Joy Frede's roommate had said she was under the distinct impression that the phone calls that Frede had received had been of a threatening nature. Duke's calls to Amanda were anything but. And calling to admire Amanda at irregular intervals seemed to pacify the man, for there hadn't been any outbreaks of violence in the past few weeks. But how long would it last?

Tristan had his men working around the clock, but so far, the results had been negligible. He wanted the sod behind bars, but Duke was typical of his breed—he was intelligent and crafty.

Tristan picked up Ace and placed him gently on the floor. He walked over to the bathroom and stood for a moment. Was she going to stay in there until it was time for her to go to work? Tristan's hand raised to knock, but settled lightly against the woodwork instead. Turning away, he walked into the bedroom and sat down on the bed to wait, idly fingering a department store sack that rested next to his hip.

Twenty minutes later he heard the bathroom door open and close, and Tristan sat up straight. But Amanda walked past the bedroom doorway without glancing in.

This had bloody well gone far enough. He pushed off the bed, prepared to follow her and have it out, but he hadn't taken more than three steps across the carpet before she strolled into the room, carrying her gun. She didn't look his way as she crossed to the nightstand, unloaded the weapon, and placed the gun and bullets in the drawer. She knew it drove him daft that she refused to keep it loaded. What the bloody hell good was it going to do her without the bullets? He didn't, however, think this was a prudent time to resurrect that particular argument. Tristan sat down on the bed again. Paper crackled beneath him and he raised his left hip to slide the department store bag out from under him.

"You ever going to talk to me again, lass?"

Amanda paused with her hand in her lingerie drawer and glanced at him over her shoulder. "Eventually."

He watched her pull the pins from her hair and shake it loose. Remembering his error in believing she dyed her hair, he had once remarked how pretty her hair was, and wasn't she lucky then to have naturally curly hair. She had smiled at him so sweetly and then said, "Thanks, MacLaughlin. It's permed." God. Women and their beauty secrets. Who could keep up with them?

His mouth went dry when Amanda dropped her robe on the slipper chair, and he bolted upright. "Now, that's not fair! Y'canna be givin' me the cold shoulder, then go flauntin' yourself in front of me.'' She didn't even glance his way, but a small smile curled her lips.

"Come on, lass. I'm that sorry I made you mad. But I'll not be flamin' apologizing for gettin' you to practice on the target. I'd bloody well do it all over again, if it meant makin' you more capable of defendin' yourself should the need arise." His eyes ate up every movement she made as she stepped into a minuscule pair of silken panties, pulling them up her long legs and smoothing them over her hips, and as she shook her full breasts into a matching bra. Without once taking his eyes off her, he pulled his glasses off, pinched the bridge of his nose, and reseated them.

Amanda leaned into the mirror and brushed her hair with hard strokes. Deftly, she twisted it up off her neck. Her eyes met his in the mirror. "I bought you something," she said. "It's in that sack you sat on." Dropping her eyes, she scouted around the top of the dressing table for hairpins.

Dead silence greeted her remark, and Amanda glanced up at his reflection in the mirror. He was staring at the bag and she was arrested by the expression on his face. She turned to face him fully.

"This is for me?" he asked.

"Yes." For once he hadn't been stone-faced, and she had been enjoying his frustration. Besides, she figured he deserved to squirm a little after dumping her in the dirt and scaring the bejesus out of her. His action had driven home her vulnerability against a man's greater strength, but she would be damned before she'd admit that maybe he had a point when he insisted that she learn to use the gun with some degree of accuracy. His method still made her furious. As it was, Charlie was going to have a cow if she couldn't disguise the spot that was turning purple high up on her thigh. And if she had fallen wrong, she could have been put out of commission entirely.

But the look on his face now as he fingered the sack made

a lump rise in her throat. Hadn't anyone ever bought him anything before? "Open it, Tristan. It's a present."

He looked up at her. Then he lowered his head and slowly opened the bag. He drew out a pair of stone-washed jeans.

"I thought you could wear them when we go up in the hills," she explained anxiously when he didn't say anything. "Or when you're off duty." She watched him fiddle with the tags. "I didn't get a chance to wrap it, and I know it isn't much . . ."

Tristan lurched up off the bed and was across the room in two giant strides, the jeans still clutched in one big fist. He jerked her to her feet and pulled her against him with his free arm, burying his face in her hair. "I love you, Amanda, lass. God, how I love you!" He pulled her head back and rocked his mouth over hers, thrusting his tongue deep with a desperate kind of urgency.

Amanda felt her heart explode. She wrapped her arms around his neck and stood on tiptoe, kissing him back for all she was worth. Not even the jeans' scratchy cardboard tags, digging into her bare back, or the butt of his gun, gouging her right breast, could mar her joy. He'd said it! *Oh, thank you, God, thank you. Tristan MacLaughlin loves me.*

Tristan raised his head. "Thank you for the present, Mandy." He gave her another quick, hard kiss and released her to look the jeans over once again.

"Try them on." Amanda grinned. The spellbound expression on his face as he examined his present made her feel like Santa Claus. "The first day we met you, Rhonda said all you needed was a pair of jeans to look like a hairy version of the Soloflex hunk."

Tristan's brows knit above his nose. "The what hunk?"

"Soloflex. It's an advertisement for body-building equipment. It features this guy with a really nice body, wearing a pair of jeans—and nothing else," she added with relish. "Try them on."

Tristan shucked out of his slacks and dragged the new jeans

up his long legs. He tucked in his white shirt and did up the fly. Then he squatted and stood up. "The fit is bloody perfect. How'd you do it?"

"I'm a genius." She patted his rear with feminine appreciation. "You look good. I wish I had more time . . ."

"Well, if you hadna spent an hour in the tub," Tristan growled.

"If I hadn't spent an hour in the bathtub, MacLaughlin, you'd probably be back downstairs in your own apartment right now."

"Aye. I kept expectin' to be evicted the entire ride back to town."

The doorbell rang. "Rats," Amanda muttered and grabbed up her robe. She whipped it around her body and tied the belt. "That's got to be Rhonda. C'mon out and show her your pants."

With his customary caution, Tristan stayed out of sight until he verified the identity of Amanda's visitor. The fewer people who knew he was living here, the safer she would be. She had said the dance world was a small one, and he didn't want word of their relationship making the rounds. He didn't know where the connection lay—if Duke was actually a dancer, like Rhonda believed, or just some kind of dweller on the fringes, but one way or another, it appeared he was definitely tapped into the dance community.

"Hey, kiddo, get your clothes on," he heard Rhonda say the instant the door opened. "It's time to roll."

Amanda listened to Rhonda rave over the fit of Tristan's new jeans as she dressed, and, taking pity on him, she hurried. In the past few weeks, she had discovered, to her amazement, that Tristan was actually quite shy around women if he wasn't dealing with them in a professional capacity. For the most part, he was comfortable in Rhonda's company—more so than that of most women. But her unapologetic, insouciant sexuality occasionally baffled him. How was he supposed to respond to half of the things she said? he had asked Amanda one day. Usually, when he ran across a woman who talked and acted like Rhonda did, he was in the process of slapping cuffs on her and throwing her into the wagon to be taken downtown and booked.

The slight flush staining Tristan's neck and face confirmed Amanda's intuition when she emerged from the bedroom moments later. He was standing with his shoulders hunched, big hands stuffed into the front pockets of his new jeans, and his professional mask firmly in place as he listened to Rhonda rattle on. Amanda patted his rump, raised up on her toes to kiss him good-bye, and went off to work, happier than she had any right to be.

She wasn't so cheerful by the time she left the Cabaret after the last show. Damn the real world for butting into her happiness. And damn Randy Baker in particular.

"He's not about to accept any responsibility for his own actions," she snarled at Rhonda on the ride home. "My God, he's immature. Five'll get you ten he carries a picture of his car in his wallet."

Amanda had been running late because she'd had to spend time layering makeup on her bruise, to camouflage the result of Tristan's graphic demonstration this afternoon. The Cabaret's costumes were skimpy in the extreme, and Charlie had a tendency to become very peevish indeed if a mark on one of his dancers marred the total effect. Charlie's opinions were widely known—you could knock yourself black and blue . . . it made no difference to him. But it had better not show.

Halfway down the hall, she had heard angry voices coming from the little alcove where hall met backstage. She hadn't been crazy about the idea of being an unwilling witness to someone's argument, but her options had been severely limited. It was five minutes until the dancers opened the show, and the only route to the wings lay down the hall.

". . . hands on me again and I'll chop them off at the wrists!"

Amanda had come close to being bowled over by the furious redhead who had burst out of the alcove. It had been Sherry, Maryanne's replacement, and although Amanda's curiosity had been piqued, she really hadn't had the time to do more than wonder who she'd been talking to. She'd picked up her pace.

Without warning, a rough hand on her forearm had jerked her to a standstill. Startled, she had looked up into Randy Baker's angry face. "You friggin' bitch!" he'd snarled. "I hope you're pleased with yourself. You've been tellin' lies about me right and left."

Amanda had been stunned by the attack, but anger had quickly replaced astonishment. She'd pried Randy's fingers from her arm. "Been sneaking feels again, Randy?"

Red color had mottled his cheeks. "What'd you tell her about me?"

"Oh, Randy, for God's sake, grow up," she'd snapped back. "I didn't say a word to Sherry. I didn't have to. It's your tendency to put your hands where they don't belong, not my mouth, that's getting you into trouble. Keep your mitts to yourself and you won't have a problem." She had turned away with apparent indifference, but impotent fury at his adolescent disregard for anyone's feelings but his own weighed coldly in her stomach, and she felt it still. His venomous, low-voiced verbal attack as he'd trailed her to the wings had merely been the icing on the cake.

"You're such a frigid bitch. You think you're so much better than anybody. Maybe if you had a little attention from a real man, you wouldn't be so goddamn snooty." In the car with Rhonda, Amanda mimicked his parting shot. "Well, baby, someday you're gonna get yours." She shook her head in disgust. "I told him I'd had a real man, which was what had taught me to know the difference when I was confronted with a punk kid."

Rhonda had been laughing, but now she sobered. "I don't know, kiddo. What with everything else, I don't like the sound of this." She pulled up to a light and looked over at Amanda's profile as her friend morosely stared out the window. "And I don't even like to contemplate what Mac-Laughlin's gonna have to say about it."

Amanda's head snapped around. "MacLaughlin's not gonna say anything, because MacLaughlin's not going to hear about it. I don't need Tristan to fight my battles for me."

"Mandy Rose, you've been receiving telephone calls from a murderer. Randy Baker threatened you. Don't you think Tristan would wanna know?"

"You weren't there, Rhonda; you didn't hear Randy. He's a twenty-four-year-old man with a high school stud mentality. It's his damn immaturity that makes me want to scream. His saying you'll get yours is like saying your mama wears combat boots. He's no killer."

"All the same, kiddo . . ."

"I'll say something tomorrow, okay? But for what's left of tonight, I'd just like to forget about it and pretend Tristan and I are a regular couple without any special problems."

"Fair enough." They parted at the stairs and Amanda let herself into her apartment.

"Tristan?"

"In here." She followed the sound of his soft voice into the bedroom. All the moisture left her mouth as she stopped dead in the doorway and stared at him. He had obviously just taken a shower, for he was sitting on the side of the bed with a towel over his head, briskly rubbing his hair. He was wearing his new jeans—and nothing else. Drops of water glistened here and there on his wide, muscled shoulders and long, strong back, and Amanda wanted to crawl all over him, licking them off.

"I found the slip in the bag." Tristan's voice was slightly muffled by the towel. "Sixty dollars is a lot of money for a pair of jeans, lass."

"I thought you said you were an American, MacLaughlin." Amanda inched nearer and studied every exposed inch of Tristan's body. "Any true-blue American knows the value of a pair of jeans. You can wear a pair of jeans every day for two years straight, and they just keep on looking better and getting more comfortable."

"Bet they'd smell bloody awful, though."

"You wash them between wearings, you idiot." She was standing directly in front of him. "God, Tristan, you look so hot."

Tristan dropped the towel around his neck and looked up at her. "Oh, aye? Show me, lass."

"I'm all sweaty." He was peeling her out of her shirt.

"Aye, so you are, darlin'. I like you that way."

He was perfectly serious. Amanda had always thought being bathed and perfumed was a prerequisite to making love, but although Tristan made love to her when she was squeaky clean and sweet, he wasn't fastidious about her state of hygiene. It had shocked her a bit at first, but his lovemaking was as honest and unaffected as a healthy animal's out in the wild, and she had ultimately decided if he didn't mind her a little bit musky, then she wasn't going to let her own self-consciousness interfere with their pleasure either.

"Y'smell like a woman." Tristan buried his face between her breasts and Amanda bowed her body around him. She pushed at his shoulders until he was sprawled out on his back across the bed. Then she did what she had wanted to do since walking through the bedroom door. She planted kisses from the center of his strong chin, down the smooth column of his throat, across both his shoulders, and down his chest. With her tongue and teeth, she worried the flat brown disk of his nipple beneath its light mat of hair. Slowly she moved downward, licking up errant drops of water, stringing kisses and light bites along the hard ridges that defined his muscular stomach. Her hands raced ahead to unfasten his jeans and push them down to his knees.

With a growl, Tristan shoved up on his elbows as her long, capable fingers wrapped around his erection. He watched her descending mouth. "Ah, God, Amanda, you're not goin' to . . . ahh, God, lass!" She was and she did.

Amanda reveled in her sudden power over him. She had never dominated him sexually. She was usually too thoroughly dominated herself to make the attempt. But this time it was his thighs that sprawled wide, and his hips that arched in silent plea, and his hands that buried themselves in her hair, molding the delicate bones of her skull as reverently as though he were holding a priceless golden chalice. She glanced up and found him watching her, and she purred with self-satisfied contentment. He groaned, his fingers clenching against her scalp.

The phone rang shrilly, and Tristan's hands dropped leadenly to his sides. Amanda raised her head and rested her forehead against the rigid muscles of his abdomen. Fury exploded. "Damn him! Damn him!" She leaned across Tristan's legs and snatched up the receiver. "Not now," she snapped. "I am sick and tired of getting calls at this hour of the morning from a man who won't even identify himself. Tomorrow I'm calling the police and getting an unlisted number!" She slammed the receiver back in its cradle. For good measure, she unplugged it. Then she burst into tears.

Tristan didn't tell her she was better off receiving the telephone calls than not. It was the only means they had for keeping even the weakest of tabs on Duke's movements. Time enough in the morning to tell her that she wasn't getting an unlisted number. He gathered her in his arms and rocked her. "Shh, Mandy, shh, now. Don't let the sod get to you. Besides, it was a timely interruption. There's been something I've been wantin' desperately . . ."

She wiped her eyes against the swell of his pectorals and looked up at him. "I thought that was what I was just doing."

Laughter rumbled from deep in Tristan's chest and she pulled back a little in order to see his white, crooked-tooth grin. "Oh, darlin', that you were. But even more than that, I've been dyin' to hear you say that you love me just once when you're not all hot for my lovin'."

Amanda forgot her anger. She hugged Tristan hard. "Well, shoot. I thought you were going to ask for something terribly difficult." She pulled back until she could look into his eyes. "I love you, Tristan MacLaughlin. I have never in my life said that to another man. You're my very first."

His tone was peremptory. "I'm your flamin' last."

"Yes. I believe you are." Her mouth was very solemn but a smile lurked in her eyes. "I do love you."

He rolled her onto the sheets. "Ah, Mandy, lass. I love you, too. I've not said that to another woman either." His teeth nipped her lower lip and tugged on it. "I love you." The tip of his tongue moistened her lip when he pronounced his l's. "I love you. I love . . ."

It was very late, and Tristan was feeling boneless with satiated exhaustion by the time he finally groped around the floor and found the plug for the telephone. Yawning, he plugged it back in.

CHAPTER
18

It seemed to Tristan that he had just fallen asleep when a strident ringing dragged him back to the edge of consciousness. He pried an eyelid open, but the prickles of grit irritating the sleep-starved membranes prompted its immediate reclosure. Had he turned on the alarm last night? No. He knew he hadn't. Wrapping the down-filled pillow around his ears, Tristan burrowed into the mattress.

An instant later he swore and flung the pillow aside. Amanda must have set the thing, for the bloody ringing wasn't letting up. Tristan ran a thickened tongue over dry lips and fumbled blindly for the alarm.

He had slapped at the button on top of the clock twice before it occurred to him that the sound might not be the alarm. He forced open an eye that felt as if it had been liberally sprinkled with sand. Umm. The bloody phone was ringing. Patting Amanda's hip placatively as she mumbled in somnolent irritation, he leaned over her and groped for the phone. Holding the receiver under his chin, he flopped back onto the mattress. "H'lo." He covered the mouthpiece with his palm and yawned widely.

Silence greeted his salutation, and suddenly Tristan was

wide awake and cold as ice with the knowledge that he had
made the biggest mistake of his life—of Amanda's life. Of
all the unforgivable, irresponsible . . . *Bluff, MacLaughlin.
Bluff like you've never bloody bluffed before.*

"Hello," he repeated with crisp authority. "Speak up. This
is Lieutenant MacLaughlin of the Reno police. Miss Charles
called us a few hours ago to lodge a complaint. Said she was
the recipient of annoying phone calls. If you are the party responsible for harassing Miss Charles, you are under advise-
ment that a tap has been placed on the phone, and . . ."

"I thought she was different," Duke's hoarse voice cut
across Tristan's improvised cover-up. "But she's a worthless
whore, just like all the rest." For an instant, there was only
the disturbed sound of his breathing. Finally, he whispered,
"She's a dead woman, MacPrick. I'm really going to enjoy
taking care of her. I'll make it extra special, now that I know
she's your woman."

The phone went dead.

Tristan swore and replaced the phone on the nightstand.
He climbed out of bed and pulled on his new jeans; then he
stood for a moment, staring down at Amanda as she slept.
How could he have done something so idiotic? He was supposed to be a bloody professional. *God, lass, I'm so sorry.*

He picked up the telephone and placed two calls in rapid
succession. He used up an additional fifteen minutes show-
ering, shaving, and dressing in his customary suit and tie.
Then, dreading it, but knowing in all good conscience he
couldn't postpone it any longer, he woke Amanda.

Amanda watched Tristan's retreating back as he loped
down the steps. He didn't look back. Turing to Rhonda, she
said coldly, "You can leave, too."

Rhonda studied her friend's face in silence for a moment.
Then she nodded, and her expression was a contradictory
mixture of concern and disgust. "Fine," she replied. "I'm
outta here. Call if you need me." The next moment she, too,
was gone.

Softly, Amanda closed the door and stood a moment, staring at the blank expanse of wood. Then, in frustration, she slapped the solid door with the flat of her hand and whirled away. Ignoring the curious glance of her watchdog as he glanced up from his book, she stalked into the kitchen.

She was numb with fear, but more than that, she was angry—with fate. With Tristan. With Rhonda. With the faceless man who had the ability to terrorize her. Oh, hell. Mostly with herself.

She had sworn, both to Tristan and to herself, that she wouldn't cling to him or interfere with his work in any way. But dammit, she *knew*, with a stomach-twisting certainty, that Randy Baker wasn't the man responsible for killing Maryanne and those other three women. Or for the disturbing phone calls. But would Tristan take her word for it? He would not.

"It's not that I'm discountin' women's intuition, lass," he had said when she'd called him a pigheaded, thick-skinned, stubborn Scot. "You women are usually better than men at getting at the truth. But I also have a healthy regard for the law, Amanda. And I'll not be ignorin' Baker's threats to you. Or the scratches on his arm that Rhonda told me about, either." Then he had wrapped his hand around the nape of her neck and pulled her up on her toes. "And it's an American I am, Amanda Rose. Y'canna seem to remember it." He had kissed her hard, and moments later he was gone.

But not before she had accused him of leaving her to the mercies of the real killer and had begged him to stay.

Not before she had said if you really love me, you won't leave me with only Dogface to protect me.

Amanda pulled out her blender and went to the refrigerator for chili peppers, lemon juice, and onion. She didn't know why she was making guacamole at eight o'clock in the morning, except it was a way to keep her hands and mind occupied. Maybe then she could erase the image of wounded fury that had flashed across Tristan's eyes before he had rapidly assembled his features into cool, detached, professional indifference. She looked blankly at the two avocados in her hand and wished she had kept her mouth shut. Even Rhonda had looked shocked—and disappointed in her.

Amanda chopped the stems off the chilies, cut the onion in small slices, measured the lemon juice, and threw everything in the blender. She remembered tomato and went to the fridge.

Rhonda had no business being disappointed in her. Let her be pulled out of a warm bed at six o'clock in the morning after too few hours of sleep, to be told her life had been threatened. Let her be left alone with a strange and silent watchdog while the one man who could keep her safe went chasing after a wild goose. Or, more aptly, an immature turkey. It was Rhonda who had convinced Tristan of the need to bring Randy in for questioning in the first place. If she hadn't remembered seeing those cat scratches on his arm the day the fourth dancer's body had been discovered, and if she hadn't told Tristan about Randy accosting Amanda in the alcove near the wings last night, he would be here with her now, instead of leaving her with that silent, bulldog-faced man in her living room.

Amanda paused in the act of fitting the lid on the blender and stared blindly at the wall. No, that wasn't exactly fair. Rhonda had only been acting out of concern for her. And she sure as hell had no one but herself to blame for the rotten way she had spoken to Tristan.

She pried the lid back off, glowered at the mess in the blender, and reached for the pepper mill. Dammit, why was she cursed with this inconvenient sense of fair play? She wasn't in the mood to be reasonable. She was at extreme risk. She was all but immobilized with fear, and just once, she wanted to throw a tantrum like a spoiled child. Then she wanted to crawl into MacLaughlin's strong arms and be held there while she cried out all the poisons that built up when a woman's life was removed from her control by the actions of a madman. And she didn't want to take a step from his side until the killer was behind bars.

She wanted to be safe, and to lead a normal, regular, everyday kind of life with that big, stubborn, Scottish—no, *American*—cop.

Amanda punched a button on the blender, and it whirred to clamorous, noisy life just as the doorbell rang.

Was that so much to ask?

Detective Cash and Lieutenant MacLaughlin were playing Good Guy/Bad Guy. Tristan had assumed the bad guy role, and he thought it was a damn good thing. He didn't think he'd have a prayer, where Randy Baker was concerned, of sustaining Joe's role of nice cop. For the first time ever in all his years on the force, he had a burning urge to get seriously, viciously physical with a taxpayer.

Tristan closed the door behind the lab man as he left with a tape of Baker's voice to be rushed through the spectrograph. He crossed to the table where the young dancer sat. "Tell us what you know about Amanda Charles."

Randy's head snapped up. "Is that what this is all about? That whoring bitch came whining to you, didn't she?"

Randy jumped when Tristan's large hands slammed down on the table in front of him. The giant cop was leaning over the table, his face only inches away, and Randy's head reared back with an instinctive need to put distance between himself and the raw, malignant emotion that emanated from the silver-gray eyes. The cop's face was impassive, a frozen wasteland. But, Jesus, his eyes . . .

"Is that how you think of women, Baker?" Tristan's voice was a low, hoarse rumble. "Are they all bitches to you? Whores? Is that what you call them when you're rapin' them, when you're beatin' them to an unrecognizable pulp?" Tristan wrapped one meaty fist in the soft material of Baker's T-shirt and twisted, pulling the dancer from his chair, forcing him to lean awkwardly over the table. "You sick son of a bi . . ."

"That's enough, Lieutenant!" Detective Cash separated Baker's shirt from Tristan's fist, and Randy sank into his chair as if his legs refused to hold him any longer. "Ya gotta cool down, man . . ."

"Give me five minutes alone with him, Joe," Tristan said to Cash, but his eyes never left Baker. "Five minutes. I guarantee you results. The boy might not look so pretty, and he might not dance so pretty, but he'll be ready to tell us the truth. I promise you."

Randy's bowels threatened to give way, and he stared at Detective Cash as if he were a savior when he returned from leading MacLaughlin over to the window, having murmured something that apparently had appeased the angry man. Randy accepted the cigarette Detective Cash shook out of a pack and extended to him, but he kept a wary eye on MacLaughlin's harsh profile as he smoked it. The cop's interest was focused on something outside the window. Randy blew out a stream of smoke and brushed the hair off his forehead. He looked up at Joe.

"That guy's crazy."

"Yeah, I hope I can keep him off your back. But last night you told his lady she was gonna get hers. A few hours later he gets a phone call saying Amanda Charles is a dead woman. If you have anything to say for yourself, Baker, I'd speak up fast, if I were you. MacLaughlin outranks me. All he's gotta do, kid, is order me outta the room."

Randy paled. "Jesus H. Christ, you think I'm the Show Girl Slayer? That's nuts, man! I ain't never hurt a woman in my life!" His voice rose with each word.

Tristan turned from the window. "You just feel the lassies up, is that what you'll be havin' us believe?"

"Yes!"

"Y'just cop a feel here, cop a feel there, but nobody gets hurt, right? Grab a little tit, pat a little ass, who's to care. Is that what you're sayin'?"

"Yes, yes!"

Tristan surged away from the wall and crossed to tower over Baker once again, hands planted on the scarred wood of the tabletop. "The lassies care! The lassies have told you, more than once, and more than one of them, to knock it the hell off, but y'havena, then, have you?'' Suddenly, he straightened. He stared down his nose at the seated young man. ''There were scratches all over your arm the day Joy Frede's body was discovered in a dumpster. Did she object a wee bit too hard to bein' felt up by the likes of you? Is that why you raped her and then killed her?'' The words were rapped out hard and fast, and sweat streamed from every pore on Randy's body.

''It was a cat! A cat made those scratches. Jesus, you gotta believe me! I ain't never hit no woman in my life. Please, Lieutenant! I'm sorry I touched your girlfriend, but I wouldn't hurt her. I swear. Does Amanda think I'd do that? I'll apologize; I'll never touch another woman without her permission as long as I live. I'll do anything, but you gotta believe me.''

''Amanda's soft. She insisted it couldna be you. She says you're more punk kid than killer.''

''God, man, listen to her!''

Trisan was beginning to think he should have. When they had first dragged Baker out of bed and told him to get dressed to come downtown with them for questioning, Randy had been as arrogant as the favored son of a small town's richest man. He hadn't even asked why; his attitude as he had accompanied them had been cocky and insolent. A cold rage had burned through Tristan's veins at the thought of this young punk putting his hands on Amanda, and it had taken a little longer than it should have before it sank in that, despite the little sod's smug opinion of himself, Baker wasn't acting in the accepted manner of a serial killer. He hadn't attempted to control the interview, and his air of superiority had evaporated quicker than spit in the desert the moment he'd realized where the questions were leading.

Tristan reached over and picked up the phone.

He hung up a few moments later and ran both hands over his face in a scrubbing motion. He looked up at Joe. ''They haven't got the results yet.'' He turned to Baker. ''Is there anyone who can verify that you were scratched by a cat?''

"How the hell would I . . ." Randy saw the look in MacLaughlin's eyes and immediately modified his tone of voice. "I didn't see anyone. Someone could have been looking out their window, though."

"We can send someone out to check with your neighbors." Giving in to a faint feeling of unease, Tristan turned to Joe. "Take over. I'm going to call Amanda."

As he dialed the number, Tristan heard Joe ask about an alibi for any of the dates when the other three victims were murdered. He wasn't paying close attention, frowning as Amanda's phone rang and rang and rang, but by the rising hysteria in Baker's voice, he assumed the kid couldn't automatically provide one. A moment later, he slammed down the receiver and jumped to his feet, grabbing his coat.

"Let him go." Turning to Baker, he snapped, "Don't leave town, lad." Then he was gone, slamming the door behind him.

When Joe got to the parking lot, it was in time to see Tristan's car reversing out of its parking slot in a tight, fast U-turn. He raced over and ripped open the passenger door, diving headfirst into the car just as Tristan slammed the gearshift into first. "What the hell is goin' on?"

Tristan took off with a smoking screech of rubber before Joe had a chance to close the door behind him. He hit the street already doing forty.

"Nobody answered the bloody phone."

Amanda lifted her finger from the blender and listened. Then, out of sorts, she shook her head and turned the blender on again. Typical. Every time she ran the vacuum cleaner she thought she heard the phone ringing. Now the blender was making her hear doorbells.

Amanda frowned and raised her finger once again. The appliance whirred into silence. She had used this blender a hundred times before and she'd never noticed that particular phenomenon. It was probably nothing, but to be on the safe side, she'd check in with the watchdog.

"Sergeant Kalowski?" She walked into the living room. His book was open, facedown on the coffee table, but he wasn't sitting in the chair where she had last seen him. She poked her head in the dining room. It, too, was empty. "Sergeant?"

Maybe he'd had to use the bathroom. She headed there, passing the open doorway to the kitchen on her way. She glanced in. If necessary, she'd pound on the bathroom door, if that's what it took to determine his whereabouts. She tried not to think of the embarrassment to both of them if he was simply obeying a sudden call of nature. He may simply have failed to hear her call.

Her feet hesitated a few steps beyond the kitchen doorway. Something wasn't right. Her mind's eye had belatedly registered an aberration in the kitchen. There had been a long shadow bisecting the tiled floor, and she couldn't think of a thing that could account for it.

It had looked almost like that of a man.

Shivers tightened her scalp and raced along her spine, leaving a wash of goose bumps to rise up in their wake. Her heart surged up her throat, then dropped with a sickening swoop and began to pound against her rib cage. She had half-turned toward the kitchen. Now she spun on her heel, prepared to run for the bedroom.

Visions of the lock on the door, the phone, the gun, all shattered beneath the sudden agony that detonated in her skull. Steel fingers gripped her hair, and Amanda was swung around by the froth of curls escaping her banana clip until she crashed up against the wall just inside the kitchen. Pain exploded in her cheekbone from an unseen fist, and she felt a rush of cooler air upon her heated skin as her blouse was ripped open. Vicious fingers tore at her bra, gouging the vulnerable skin. Blinking through tears of pain and against the brightness of the kitchen following the hall's gloom, she peered at her assailant.

And recognized him.

"Dean?" Her voice cracked in the middle of the one-syllable name, and for a moment, his hands quit tearing at her clothes. He grabbed her by the shoulders and slammed her back against the wall. Pain erupted in the back of her head where it struck the hard surface, and then she bent double and choked when he buried his fist in her stomach. He dragged her upright again.

"That's right, Amanda." She looked up through pain-fogged eyes at a face stripped of civilization and into eyes that gleamed with a lust for blood. "It's ol' Dean. Happy to see me?"

"Why?" she whispered, but he didn't appear to hear her. He seemed to be looking inward, gloating over something only he could see.

"Where's Kalowski?" she asked hoarsely. "What have you done with him?"

"Sent him to that ol' pigsty in the sky," he replied, and then he laughed. Chills ran up and down Amanda's spine. "It was perfect, Amanda," he told her confidentially. "They made it almost too easy. The dumb shit didn't even ask who was there. He just stuck his head out the door and . . ." He made a sound like cracking bones. "Now he's permanently looking over his shoulder."

Amanda couldn't stifle her small moan of terror.

Dean's mouth stretched in a parody of a grin. "They're all stupid," he informed her. "All of them." Then his eyes got a faraway look, a little frown puckered his brow, and he murmured to himself, "I thought that Scottish bastard was crammin' Rhonda Smith . . ."

"Rhonda!" Amanda couldn't stop herself from exclaiming. "Then it *was* you in that parking lot . . ."

"She gets herself talked about, you know. Word has it she was dirty dancing with him at some party, and I was going to get to him through her. He's the one I've got to show. I figured . . . But it didn't turn out exactly the way I had planned." His face twisted; then, slowly, he focused on Amanda again.

"You know, it really is too bad you know who I am," he

whispered and brushed the hair out of her face in a grisly travesty of tenderness. Then he backhanded her with vicious strength. "It woulda been kind of fun to just splinter all your bones, slice up this pretty face"—the backs of his fingers trailed down her cheekbone to her jaw—"and leave you here for MacPrick to find." He giggled. "It would be worse than death for you, wouldn't it, Amanda? That's what I want for you, you see—whatever will destroy you most completely. I thought you were different; I thought you were pure." His hand closed over her windpipe and squeezed with increasing strength, cutting off her air. "But you're worse than all those other cunts put together. Yeah, I really wish I could leave you alive. MacPrick wouldn't have any use for you—not once he saw I'd used every orifice in your body." He released her and Amanda sagged against the wall, gasping for breath. "Not after he saw the face I'd leave you with. And you wouldn't be able to dance—ever again, Amanda." He giggled once more. "Oh shit, it'd be great. It's almost as much fun to destroy a dancer's career as it is to kill. I discovered that when I pushed that fag Schriber in front of the truck."

"Pete?" she whispered. "You pushed Pete?"

"Yeah. I wanted to dance for the Cabaret. Hell, you saw me audition; you know how superior I am to the rest of those lead-footed hoofers. But Charlie said there weren't any positions available." He shrugged, unconcerned. "So I opened one up."

Amanda felt something very cold take possession of her emotions. It encased her, numbing her terror. Okay. Fine. She was all alone. And he was crazy. But she was going to get out of this.

By herself, as usual.

She had always known, in a far-flung corner of her mind, that only one person could ever be held accountable for her safekeeping, and that person was she. All of her life, it seemed, she had taken care of herself. She had learned not to depend on other people to look out for her, and she knew now that it had been a mistake of gargantuan proportions to count on Tristan for her safety, because he was nowhere around when it really counted, was he? Once again, she was on her own.

Dean was still gloating over his cleverness when Amanda slammed her knee into his crotch. With a dancer's quick reflex, he deflected most of the blow, but she knocked him to his knees nonetheless. He fell across the doorway, blocking her planned avenue of escape, so Amanda ran for the drawer where she kept the knives. She pulled it open, but Dean rolled across the floor and to his feet, throwing himself at her back and slamming her forward, and her stomach shoved it closed again. The force of his tackle bent her over the counter, and her wide-flung arms knocked the container off the blender. It skittered along the counter, and Amanda made a grab for it just as Dean punched her in the kidney. Still clutching it, she fell to the floor, rolling away from the foot that he aimed at her face. It glanced off her ear. She pried off the rubber cap and plunged her fingers down into the chunky liquid at the bottom.

Dean kicked the container out of her hands, stomped flat-footed on her forearm, grabbed her left wrist and jerked it. Amanda screamed as the delicate bone snapped.

Breathing heavily, Dean hooked his fingers in the waistband of Amanda's pants and dragged her to her feet. She moaned as her broken arm flopped against her side and pain pulsed through her with red-hot agony. In her ear his voice muttered a litany of obscenities, interspersed with self-satisfied assertions of his own superior intellect. Shoving her against the wall, he kept her upright by planting a hand flat against her chest. He cocked back his fist.

Amanda reached for his eyes with her right hand, and Dean screamed when her fingers, with their coating of lemon juice, pureed onion, and chili pepper came into contact with the membranes of his eyelids. He let her go and clutched at his eyes.

Left arm hanging uselessly at her side, Amanda ran for the bedroom. She slammed the door and slid the bolt, knowing it wouldn't hold him for long. Pulling out the drawer of her nightstand, she cursed the squeamishness that had caused her to insist on keeping the gun unloaded. An hour ago, she would have been willing to swear she was constitutionally incapable of pointing a gun at another human being and pulling the trigger—would have *sworn* she couldn't do it, regardless of provocation.

Well, wasn't it amazing how naive she had been an hour ago? It was a hell of a lot easier to be idealistic when you have never been attacked, when you've never felt firsthand the kind of pain that could be inflicted by a madman, she decided coldly as she sat on the side of the bed with the gun tucked between her knees, stuffing bullets into their chambers. A number of bullets fell to the floor. Idealism, she was learning the hard way, was subjective. She set the gun down for a moment and snatched up the phone.

Damn him to an eternity in hell. It was dead.

Putting more bullets in her pocket, she grabbed up a scarf and tried to fashion a sling, but it was impossible to tie a knot one-handed. And he was at the door.

When the door bowed inward with the force of his weight, Amanda pulled the trigger. He howled, but an instant later there was another thud. She fired again, her mind working coldly, remembering everything MacLaughlin had taught her. But he must have stood back to kick it that time, for he didn't make a sound to indicate he had been hit. The door bowed inward again. Then it flew open, smashing against the wall and bouncing back until it almost closed again.

"Come on, you sick bastard," Amanda whispered, "come on."

There was silence from the other side. Amanda sat on the edge of the bed, training the gun on the door, her broken arm cradled in her lap. Oh, God, she hurt so bad. She could barely see for the pain, and it didn't help that her right eye was swelling shut from the blow to her cheekbone. The sudden cessation of noise unnerved her. What was he doing?

Ten minutes passed, then twenty. Still he didn't make a

move. Twice, music blared out of her stereo system in the living room. The first time, Amanda fired her gun at the door in sheer reaction. The second time, she merely jerked convulsively, then sat quivering with nerves until he turned it off again. She rested her gun hand on the bed, but she didn't take her eyes off the door. She tried telling herself the longer he waited the better were her chances, for Rhonda surely must have heard the gunshots and called the police.

But what if he had taken care of Rhonda, the way he had taken care of Kalowski, before he even came down here? And with every moment that ticked by, it grew harder to ignore the pain that radiated along her nerve endings, pulsing fresh agony with every heartbeat. Another ten minutes crawled by.

Then Ace began to cry.

Oh, God, what was he doing to the dog? Every few minutes Ace began to howl. Then the howls would fade to whimpers before they suddenly escalated again into pained yelps. Amanda's nerves stretched closer and closer to the breaking point. The tiny bit of hope she had still harbored that Tristan would somehow get here in time to help her splintered beyond repair, and she became a being of pure instinct, embracing the corroding effects of hatred.

Suddenly, something hurtled through the doorway. Amanda screamed and fired off a shot that went wild. She watched in horror as the object rolled across the carpet, spewing flames. It was some sort of handmade Molotov cocktail —a jar of flammable liquid with a length of cloth for a wick. Only the thickness of her rug prevented it from shattering. As it was, the liquid splashed out and caught fire to a pillow lying on the floor, and she was forced to tuck the gun in her waistband and grab her heavy wool poncho to beat out the flames.

That was when Dean dove through the door. Amanda screeched and threw her poncho at him. It wrapped around his head and she struggled to extricate the gun from her waistband. She was cold and clammy and rapidly losing strength. Her hand trembled badly and the gun wobbled precariously as he rose to his feet and came at her, brandishing one of her kitchen knives. He had another knife tucked into his belt, and the edges gleamed with a fresh sharpening. She took a deep breath and pulled the trigger.

Dean staggered and a new patch of red bloomed beneath his collarbone, but to Amanda's horror, he kept coming. She didn't think she could lift the gun one more time, and he was only four feet away.

She shot him in the foot, then let the gun hang uselessly by her side and watched him take another step toward her, dragging it. Her eyes closed as he raised his arm, the knife clenched in his fist. It was silent in the room, except for the labored rasp of their combined breathing.

The front door crashed open. "Amanda!" Tristan's voice roared through the apartment.

"You fucking bitch!" Dean snarled, and Amanda smiled with cold malice, finding the strength to raise the gun one last time and aim it at him with lethal intent. He lunged at her with his knife.

A shot rang out, and Amanda watched dumbly as finally, *finally*, Dean crumpled to the floor and was still.

"Noooo!" she wailed, and the attenuated word was an anguished, animalistic cry. Tristan had shot him—*Tristan had*. Dammit, he was *hers*. It was up to her to . . . she wanted to kill him. She wanted . . .

She met Tristan's eyes across the room and a look of revulsion twisted Amanda's already misshapen features. Breaking eye contact, she regarded the gun in her hand with horror and flung it away. Oh God, what had he turned her into? What had that monster . . . ?

Everything went black.

CHAPTER
19

". . . hospital states her condition as satisfactory."

Tristan snapped off the television and looked down at the bed where Amanda slept. Satisfactory. That was one way of looking at it.

It was true that her arm would mend and her bruises would fade. None of the injuries was permanent, and thank God for that. Tristan only wished he could feel as confident about the healing powers of her spirit.

Slumped on his tailbone on the chair next to her bed, he watched over her. From the other side of the closed door, he could hear the muted sounds of a hospital settling for the night and the occasional creak of a chair, when the man who had been posted outside the door to keep the media away shifted position. Rubber-soled shoes squeaked on linoleum as nurses made their rounds, and down in the emergency entrance, a siren moaned into silence. But here in the room it was dim and quiet. Tristan chewed the skin around his index fingernail and regarded Amanda with unwavering intensity.

He tried to convince himself that his pessimism was premature. He was probably expecting too much too soon. Hell,

Amanda had been through an ordeal this morning that most people couldn't even imagine. Undoubtedly it would take some time for her to accept the reality of being safe.

But his captain in Seattle had been fond of saying "don't kid a kidder," and the phrase had been running through his head all day long. It was hard to fool himself—he was worried. He had seen many victims during his years on the force, but he had never seen eyes that had changed as much as Amanda's had. Her beautiful eyes—those warm, honest, confident eyes—had learned not to trust. They now regarded everyone—friend, lover, and stranger alike—with a cold wariness. Someone he didn't recognize looked out of Amanda's familiar face, and it scared the living daylights out of him.

Her account of her ordeal had been unemotional to the point of eeriness. There hadn't been a trace of color in her face, except for its various contusions—the bruised-pansy purple of her left eye and the changing hues of her swollen-shut right eye. As white as the plaster on her left arm, she had sat up in her hospital bed, and with a total lack of expression had recited the details of her encounter and had dispassionately answered questions—coldly and precisely, without tremors, tears, or hysteria.

Tristan rubbed a weary hand over his face. He would have welcomed an emotional display, but Amanda, whose expression was usually so easily read, had been impassively stoic.

Only once in this entire long day had she seemed like herself, and then only for the briefest moment. It was right before they had brought her to the hospital. As the paramedics had been carrying her out to the ambulance, Rhonda had raced up, breathless and nearly incoherent, trying to simultaneously elicit information about Amanda's condition and explain her frantic search for a telephone.

Apparently, Dean had disabled Rhonda's car. She told them she had banged on doors all over the neighborhood before she had finally given up and started running for a convenience store about a mile away. Once there, she said

she'd had to practically climb over the counter to convince
the high school boy manning it to let her use the telephone.
She was still quivering with reaction as she hovered over
Amanda like a distraught mother over her only child, reassuring
herself that Amanda really was alive and relatively whole.

Amanda had clutched Rhonda's arm with her good hand,
begging her to find Ace and make sure he was all right. For
just an instant, life had flared in her eyes. But as soon as she
had obtained Rhonda's promise to take care of him, to see
that he was attended to by a veterinarian, the wary stranger
had returned, snuffing out the light of concern in her eyes.
Tristan hadn't seen a trace of the old Amanda since that
moment. He didn't even attempt to fool himself into believing
it was the painkillers the doctors had prescribed that accounted
for her cold control. It didn't take a wizard to see that Amanda
had locked herself in a place where she couldn't be reached,
and he just had to hope that she would come out of it again
once she had a chance to realize she truly was out of danger.

Amanda stirred. Tristan stood up and leaned over her ex-
pectantly, but she merely shifted her cast-encased arm a fraction of an inch. Her legs moved restlessly, looking for a more
comfortable position, and she whimpered softly when she
didn't find one before lapsing deeper into sleep. Tenderly,
Tristan pulled the sheet up over her shoulders and whispered
a kiss across her mouth. When he straightened, he pulled his
glasses off and ground the heels of his hands into his scorched
eye sockets, massaging the pounding in his forehead and
temples with his long fingers. He felt ten years older than he
had this time last night.

He had killed a man today, and he was finding it difficult
to come to terms with his reactions.

Unlike their counterparts on television, real policemen
don't have shoot-outs on a weekly basis. And when they were
forced to draw their guns and shoot, there were damn few
who were ever able to view taking a life lightly. Dean Eggars
was a cold-blooded murderer who deserved to die, he tried
to reassure himself. But Tristan experienced a sick regret all

the same that it was by his hand the man had done so. Yet, as he looked at the damage Eggars had done to his Mandy, he felt a vengeful desire to have him alive once again and at his mercy, to experience the pleasure of beating the man, if not to death, then to within an inch of his life.

Guilt and self-recrimination, in the form of a relentless leaden weight in his stomach, had been constant companions all day long as he had tried to balance his obligations as a policeman and his emotions as the victim's lover. For the first time since he had joined the force, he had resented his duty to his badge. Even though Amanda apparently had no use or need for him, it had torn him in two to be dragged away from her hospital bed for the better part of the day while he collected evidence at Eggar's apartment, cleaned up loose ends, and dealt with the media.

He had left her this morning when she had begged him to stay, and her accusation, which had so angered and hurt him at the time, had come true. While he was interrogating the wrong man, the killer had managed to get to Amanda. Kalowski had been a minimal deterrent at best; they had found his body in the shadowy alcove next to Amanda's front door. Tristan had felt responsible and he hadn't wanted to leave her bedside. Only years of self-discipline had been able to pry him away.

It didn't alleviate his guilt to remember the look of loathing Amanda had given him or to keep hearing her demented cry when she'd realized he had killed Eggars. He didn't understand it. From her own account of the events, she had tried her damnedest to kill the man herself, yet she had regarded Tristan with a revulsion he couldn't erase from his mind. For just an instant, she had looked at him as if she hated him. And since that moment, she had treated him like a stranger.

He felt as if he were caught up in the middle of a nightmare. Hadn't he feared all along that his gun would somehow be instrumental in the ruination of their relationship? God, he would give anything not to have used it, for the look in Amanda's eyes said their relationship was shattered. And he had an ugly suspicion that even if he could somehow gather together all the scattered pieces, he wasn't going to be able to piece it back together again.

Light spilled into the room as the door whispered open. Tristan exchanged quiet greetings with the nurse and watched her as she monitored Amanda's vital signs. When she finished, she looked Tristan over and a faint frown drew her brows together. "Miss Charles is going to sleep through the night," she whispered. "Why don't you go home and get some rest. You look as though you could use it."

"Aye," he agreed wearily, his massive shoulders sagging with defeat. "Not much sense in stayin', I guess."

Tristan left shortly thereafter and drove straight home. He wandered around Amanda's apartment for a while, picking up and discarding her possessions, before he finally went into the bedroom. It smelled of scorched wool, and Tristan made a mental note to have the carpet cleaned or replaced before Amanda came home from the hospital. Staring down at the empty bed as he peeled out of his clothes, he thought it was unlikely he'd be able to sleep without her here beside him. But the moment his head touched the pillow, he was out.

The phone ringing the next morning awakened him, and for just an instant, remembering yesterday's events, he was hesitant to pick it up. Then, shaking his head impatiently, he reach for the receiver. It might be Amanda or the hospital.

It was Captain Weller, in Seattle. He congratulated Tristan, and discussed at length the abundance of evidence that had been unearthed in Dean Eggars's apartment, marveling at the twisted mind that would keep a souvenir of the murder of each of his victims.

"He had a flamin' shrine in there," Tristan said, sitting up and reaching for his jeans. "There was a portrait of a young, pretty lass on the dresser in his bedroom. It had the most elaborate frame I've ever seen, and it was surrounded by a semicircle of candles. At its foot, like some bleedin' sacrificial virgin, was this damned bundle of unopened letters, bloody gift-wrapped in a red ribbon. They were all stamped

Return to Sender and addressed to a Marsha Cranston, who, it turns out, was Eggars's sister. That was his real name, incidentally: Dean Eggars Cranston." Tristan ran his hand over the rough stubble on his cheek. "Anyway, N.Y.P.D. contacted her for us. They said she didn't sound at all surprised to hear about her brother. Seems she's been waitin' for something of this nature to occur for some time now. Said her brother's always been dead odd."

"There's odd," Weller growled. "And then there's flat-out crazy. Sounds to me like her brother was a helluva lot closer to crazy."

"Aye, well." Tristan shrugged. "She claims Eggars was often kicked about as a child by their mother's various lovers. Mum was an exotic dancer in some dive, when she worked. Seems she had a wee fondness for the bottle."

"Do tell."

"Miss Cranston said she, herself, was a fragile child, often sick, and she was spared a great deal of the abuse her brother received." Tristan began to speak quickly, anxious to wrap this up and get off the line. He wanted to go see Amanda.

"To make a long story short, Eggars apparently idolized his sister. She was enrolled in dance classes to build her strength, and more to be with her than for any other reason, Eggars joined, too, which is how he got his own start as a dancer, I suppose. He called her his little Madonna. But one day when she was twenty and he was twenty-two, he caught his little Madonna in bed with a neighborhood tough. He roughed her up pretty badly. Stopped short of killin' her, though. He was, in fact, the one to bring her to the hospital. While she was recovering, he convinced himself that she must have been forced against her will. But although he was prepared to forgive her, she wasn't feelin' equally as generous toward him. She said she was scared to death of him from that point on, and refused to have anything further to do with him. She dropped out of two different dance companies when he joined them in order to be with her, and finally went underground. Eggars never stopped trying to contact her, if the letters we found are any indication. They were all addressed to her, in care of their mother.''

"Which may or may not be the basis for this guy's sick obsession," Weller stated without any apparent interest. Who would ever know or care? Eggars had destroyed too many lives for Weller to feel pain at this late date for his childhood traumas. He came to the point of his call. "So, how long's it gonna take you to tie up the loose ends?"

Tristan hesitated, running his hand through his hair. It was obvious, from Weller's abrupt change of tone, that he wanted Tristan back in Seattle, and Tristan was in no hurry to return. "It's hard to say," he finally replied. "Too many of those souvenirs didn't belong to the four victims whose names we know. I've got bulletins out to other cities that employ dancers. Atlantic City responded to our earlier requests for information, so we're clearin' a couple of their cases off the books, but the rest are going to take a wee bit of time."

"Let someone else handle it," Weller stated with callous unconcern. "I need you back here."

"I'm not ready to return."

There was a moment of silence. "Is this the same man who didn't want to go to Reno in the first place?" Weller finally asked.

"Aye. I've . . . become involved. With Amanda Charles. I can't be leavin' her now."

Weller swore softly under his breath at the tone of finality in Tristan's voice. They both knew he could order Tristan back to Seattle. If he chose, Weller could place Tristan's entire career on the line.

"Two weeks, MacLaughlin," he finally ordered. "Two weeks, and then I want to see your ass back up here where it belongs." The connection was severed.

Tristan replaced the receiver, threw back the covers, and climbed out of bed. He rubbed his heavy morning stubble again. Two weeks. He'd better shave and hit the road. He didn't have a lot of time.

* * *

Amanda ignored her breakfast tray. At its best, other than being nutritionally balanced, hospital fare had little to recommend it. Besides, she wasn't hungry.

She was numb. In part, that could be attributed to the two white pills the nurse had given her earlier. They masked the pain from her broken arm and other contusions, which still throbbed between medications. But mostly, her lack of feeling had its origin elsewhere. She counted the holes that marched in regimented lines across the acoustical ceiling and refused to analyze what that something else was. She was safer and happier if she didn't examine it too closely. It didn't matter, anyway, for she was content in her lack of sensation. The numbness formed a shell around emotions that were too painful to face.

Amanda pulled her gaze from the ceiling when the door swished open. She frowned. MacLaughlin stood in the doorway with a small bunch of violets bunched incongruously in his large fist.

"How are you feelin', lass?" He stepped into the room.

"Fine." She really wished he hadn't come. Whenever he was around, her desensitized state was imperiled. She didn't want to feel, and only his presence had the power to threaten her carefully balanced emotions. She looked back up at the ceiling.

A small frown pulled Tristan's thick eyebrows together. He had hoped a good night's sleep might restore the old Amanda, but it was the new, indifferent stranger who was so studiously ignoring him now. He thrust the flowers at her. "These are for you."

She barely glanced at them. "Thank you."

Tristan tried to rein in his frustration. He put the flowers in a drinking glass and splashed in some water. "When are they releasing you?"

"After lunch," she replied without looking at him. She wondered how to ask him to vacate her apartment. When she left here, she just wanted to go home and be alone. She didn't want the effort of having to share anything of herself with him—with anyone.

"My captain in Seattle called," Tristan said. Amanda didn't reply, and he began to worry in earnest. Her lack of response was scaring him. Hoping to shake her out of the fog of indifference that seemed to surround her, he continued, "He wants me to come back to Seattle. Right away." *Be outraged, Mandy. Please. Say it's too soon. Demand that I stay.*

Amanda felt an undefined emotion agitate for attention deep inside, and she firmly stamped it out. Her unharmed eye, big and round, assessed him coolly. "I think that's a good idea," she stated agreeably. "I was going to ask you to move out of my apartment anyway. This simplifies matters."

Tristan felt as if she'd gut-punched him. "This simplifies nothing!" He braced his hands on either side of her hips on the hospital bed, towering over her with angry menace. He didn't know what he hoped to accomplish, but she sat quietly without reaction. That was the whole bloody problem. She didn't react to him at all. She just sat there and patiently waited for him to leave her alone. He felt the optimism with which he had left the apartment shrivel and die. All the moisture left his mouth and he licked his lips with a tongue gone dry. Slowly, he straightened.

"I love you," he said, and he realized he was pleading. It was a new experience for him, but this was too important to let pride stand in the way. "I want to marry you."

Amanda flinched. "It wouldn't work."

"We could make it work!"

She didn't point out that his job was in Seattle, while her work tied her to Reno. She knew him well enough to realize he would somehow work around the obstacles, and she didn't want him to do that. She wanted him to leave her and her deadened emotions alone. Instead, her reply was short, to the point, and utterly final. "No."

Tristan leaned over and kissed her with a fierceness that

pushed her head back into the pillows. Her mouth beneath his remained cool and unresponsive. Finally, he straightened and stood looking down at her, breathing heavily. His skin itched; his stomach was jagged with raging nerves; and he had a rampant thirst. He also felt perilously close to tears— a condition he hadn't experienced since he was eight or nine years old.

"You're safe now, Amanda Rose," he assured her, hoping against hope that hearing the words would make her accept the truth of them. "Dean Eggars is dead, and he'll not be hurtin' you or anyone else ever again." She looked at him without blinking, and he exhaled wearily. "Ah, lass. Don't let him steal your life away even in death. That'd be givin' the mon power he doesna deserve."

Tristan's words beat at something deep inside her, so Amanda deliberately scrambled them in her mind until they were nonsensical. She watched him without expression, and when he showed no signs of giving up, she sighed. "Go away, MacLaughlin. Please."

Tristan's determination caved in and he sighed also. "Aye. I'll leave. I'm going back to Seattle." His eyes met hers, and they were silver with the intensity of his emotions. "When you discover your safe little world is a lonely one, I want you to come and get me. I'll leave an address with Rhonda, and lass, I'll be waitin' for as long as it takes." He walked to the door, then paused. Without turning back to her, he said to the door, "Take care of Ace for me."

Then he was gone.

Amanda resumed counting the holes in the ceiling. When Rhonda picked her up, she thought she'd ask her to stop on the way home so she could pick up a new nightgown.

A nice cotton one.

CHAPTER
20

Rhonda looked at Amanda in her prim white cotton nightie as she sat on the couch watching television. She was watching a game show—a game show, for the love of God! Amanda, who hardly watched TV at all, aside from the news and an occasional videotaped episode of "China Beach" was staring at this mindless pap as if she found it interesting. It didn't even have the distinction of being one of the intelligent ones that demanded a bit of thinking in order to be entertaining.

Disgusted, Rhonda walked over and snapped the set off. Amanda just blinked at her with blank patience. Seeing Amanda's bright, inquisitive mind suspended in a deliberate state of limbo made something in Rhonda snap.

She had been patient, dammit. She'd waited for Amanda to emerge from her fog. She hadn't pushed. She had even bitten her tongue while she'd watched Amanda pack away all of her pretty new silk and satin bits of lingerie and climb into those damn Victorian cotton shrouds she'd taken to wearing. Rhonda had even let her avoid the subject of Tristan when the poor man was eating his heart out for her up in Seattle.

Well, no more. Amanda wasn't making the slightest effort to get back to normal on her own, and watching her vegetate in front of the tube finally pushed Rhonda beyond her level of tolerance.

She stood in front of Amanda, fists planted on her shapely hips. "When do you plan to get up off your butt and get on with your life?" she demanded.

"My life is progressing just fine," Amanda replied calmly.

"You call just sitting around for hours, watching shit like this on television, living? Oh, that's just dandy, Amanda. You haven't made the slightest attempt to get your life back in order since you came home from the hospital. You've let yourself go. Hell, look at you! You haven't shaved your legs in nearly a month, and your fingernails are a mess. You don't want to see your friends; you don't want to leave the apartment. My Gawd, never mind the screw-up of the century, which was when you sent Tristan away. He's only the best thing that's ever happened to you, but hey, no big deal— good men are a dime a dozen, right? That's practically small potatoes anyhow, compared to what really scares me: since you've felt better, you haven't even tried to dance!"

Amanda shrugged, and the indifference that caused a constant veil to shutter her eyes made Rhonda furious. She bent down and scooped Ace out of Amanda's lap and set him aside on the couch. Then, grasping Amanda's good arm, she hauled her to her feet.

Amanda wrenched her arm free, and the look that flashed across her face made Rhonda pause. For just an instant, she caught a glimpse of the expression that must have been on Amanda's face when she was fighting Dean Eggars for her life, and it was frightening. But if she simply let Amanda go back to stagnating in front of the television set, then Eggars might just as well have killed her that day, for she was dying by inches anyway. She hadn't shown a spark of interest in anything in several weeks. Rhonda reached for Amanda's arm once again.

Amanda backed away. "Keep your hands to yourself,

Rhonda,'' she hissed angrily, and Rhonda was encouraged by the first real show of emotion Amanda had displayed. ''Just leave me alone.''

''Oh, that's right,'' Rhonda crooned. ''We're all supposed to tiptoe around poor Amanda, because she's had a real scary experience. Well, I'm sorry as can be that Eggars picked you to terrorize, Mandy Rose. And I'm sorrier still that you were hurt.'' She was totally sincere. She wished more than anything in the world that it hadn't happened to Amanda. But her tone was deliberately sarcastic, and she watched the fury build in Amanda's eyes. Good. Better a show of temper than that rotten indifference. ''Well, baby, at least you're still alive. That's one hell of an improvement over Maryanne and those other dancers. Jeez Marie, I bet they would spin in their collective graves if they could see your zombie routine in these damn Victorian virgin jammies . . .'' She tweaked the voluminous folds of Amanda's nightgown.

Amanda's violet-blue eyes blazed and she snatched the material out of Rhonda's grasp. ''Better a Victorian virgin,'' she retorted flatly, ''than a slut.''

It was like being blindsided out of the blue, and Rhonda shook her head as if she'd sustained an actual blow. ''What?'' she whispered.

''A slut,'' Amanda repeated with precise enunciation. ''A woman who spreads her legs for any man to hit the horizon. Ring a bell?''

''Are you saying that's what I am, Amanda?'' Rhonda blinked fiercely to hold back tears. ''A slut?'' God, Amanda had always made her feel so special. But now she was saying . . .

Amanda shrugged. ''If the diaphragm fits . . .'' She examined her fingernails and frowned. They really were a mess—all ragged and dirty—and it upset her that it had been necessary to have it pointed out to her. God, if Rhonda was right about her letting herself go, then perhaps she was right about the other things she'd said also. Suddenly, the cush-

ioning state of numbness that she had been carefully culti-
vating was rent in two.

Damn that black-haired bitch. Damn her! The sudden unwelcome, returning rush of feeling to her frostbitten emotions
was excruciatingly painful, and Amanda struck out blindly,
wanting Rhonda, the cause of it, to hurt as much as she did.
With calculated cruelty Amanda said, "At least Victorian
virgins know how to keep their knees together, so they don't
run the risk of contracting infectious social diseases."

Amanda looked up just as Rhonda was whirling away, but
she was in time to see her friend's tears overflow and splash
down her cheeks. Shame and remorse slammed through her,
painful in their intensity, and she took a step forward to
apologize, to stop her friend from leaving. But before she
could do so, Rhonda's voice sliced through her and hit a vital
hidden nerve.

"Victorian virgins don't run risks, period. Isn't that the
point of this whole charade?" She indicated the now-dark
television set, Amanda's general scruffiness, and her messy
apartment. "What a pitiful farce. Well, I hope you enjoy
your chaste little world, Mandy Rose," she said in a hoarse
voice and then added flatly, "and don't worry about Tristan.
We both know what a sexual man he is. I'm sure he's found
someone to replace you by now."

She left, closing the door quietly behind her. Amanda sank
back down on the couch and buried her head in her hands.
Then, for the first time since Dean Eggars had tried to kill
her, she began to cry.

Amanda wrapped a plastic produce bag around her cast
and stepped into the shower, turning to keep her injured arm
out of the spray. Twenty minutes later she stepped out again,
scrubbed, shampooed, and shaved.

She dried her hair, clipped and filed her fingernails, and
sat down at her dressing table to apply a light coat of makeup.
Then, dropping her towel to the floor, she padded naked from

her dresser drawers to her closet and back to her dresser again. Finally, she turned and looked at the bed. Walking over to it, she got down on her knees and awkwardly retrieved the cardboard storage box from beneath it. Sitting back on her heels, she opened the carton cautiously.

Looking inside was almost anticlimactic. For a moment, she just gazed at the contents within. Then she pulled out a pair of teal-blue satin panties and the matching chemise that rested on the top of the stack of lingerie in the box. After donning the underwear, she carried the rest over to the dresser and pulled open her lingerie drawer. For several moments she stood looking down at the three white, carefully folded cotton nightgowns she had purchased on the way home from the hospital.

Then she scooped them up and dropped them on the floor, kicking them aside with her bare foot while she refilled the empty drawer with her scraps of satin, silk, and lace.

The hardest part of pulling her life together again, Amanda discovered, was facing what had happened that day in her apartment and learning to forgive herself for not responding to the situation with the perfect grace and style that she had been raised to project. She acknowledged that—in her case, at least—no matter how far or how fast she tried to flee, she had never really outrun the parental dictates that were drummed into her head as a child. She still hated admitting that she was far from perfect.

She relived that day in bits and pieces as she dusted and vacuumed and did what chores she could manage with one good arm. And at first all she could think was *I should have done this*, or *I should have done that* or *If only I had* . . .

Well, she hadn't. But she had survived. And if her pristine manners had become just a little bit sullied in the process, well, that was just tough shit, as MacLaughlin would say.

Amanda went very still in the midst of chasing down dust balls along the hardwood floor under her antique sideboard.

She bowed her head, leaned her chin on the wooden handle of the dust mop, and closed her eyes. *Oh, God. Tristan.*

Little by little, she was coming to terms with her own human frailties. She had always been quick to forgive the sins of others; she was now learning to forgive her own. They weren't more scarlet than anybody else's, regardless of what Mother and Father had raised her to believe. Just because she failed to live up to their sterling standards didn't mean she didn't have a value of her own. She wasn't perfect, she never would be perfect, and she was simply going to have to learn to live with that, instead of beating herself black and blue over her failure to be what nobody else was, either.

So, she was making strides, learning to accept at age twenty-eight what most people knew by the time they were five.

But she wasn't sure that she was ready to face the dilemma of Tristan MacLaughlin just yet. Probably the smart thing to do was just leave it well enough alone and get on with the rest of her life.

But a secret corner of her mind wanted to know: *Had* he found someone to replace her?

Slowly, she began to swipe the dust mop back and forth beneath the sideboard once again. She told herself it was probably for the best if he had.

But the thought hurt.

God. It hurt so much.

Amanda almost lost her nerve. Over the past few days, she had managed to come to terms with her own myriad faults. She had resolved heretofore unresolved feelings for her parents and sister Teddy. Those were the toughies, so why was her nerve failing her now? But it was. And consequently, her tap on the door was administered with such a light hand, it was doubtful it could be heard three paces away. She waited a scant count of three and then turned away.

The door behind her opened.

Slowly, she turned around again. Rhonda stood in her doorway. "How are you?" she asked, quietly formal.

"I'm okay . . . fine." For a woman who had been trained to be poised and articulate in any situation, Amanda was at a dead loss. She hugged her plaster cast to her stomach, and shifted her weight from one foot to the other. Finally, she blurted, "Rhonda, I am so sorry about those things I said to you!"

Rhonda regarded the distressed blonde on her doorstep with dispassionate eyes. Finally, she stepped back from the doorway. "Come on in, Amanda."

Amanda followed her into her living room. The furnishings warmed her, for they were pure Rhonda—bright and eclectic and cluttered. She watched as Rhonda picked her cat out of an overstuffed chair and dumped him on the floor. Her expression shuttered, Rhonda glanced at Amanda over her shoulder. "Have a seat. Do you want something to drink?"

"No." Amanda sat down, perching uneasily on the edge of her chair. She avoided Rhonda's eyes for a few heartbeats, looking down at her newly manicured fingernails instead. But, finally, she looked up and met Rhonda's eyes. "I didn't mean what I said, Rhonda. I didn't." She tried not to cry, but her emotions had been fluctuating wildly these past few days and the tears began to fall, despite her best attempts to stem the flow. "The things you were telling me made me feel emotions I had been doing my damnedest to avoid feeling, and it hurt. God, it hurt, and I wanted to make you hurt, too."

There was silence in the apartment for a moment, and Amanda began to wonder if Rhonda had heard a word she said. Finally, she stirred. She looked Amanda straight in the eye and whispered fiercely, "I am not Teddy, Amanda Rose."

Amanda's head jerked in shock. "What?"

"I said, I am not your precious sister Teddy."

"I know that."

"Do you? Do you, really? Or have you just convinced

yourself that I'm the next best thing to having her back alive? Rhonda's an okay substitute," she mimicked with some bitterness. "A slut, of course, and not nearly as good as Teddy was, but better than nothing."

"No!" Amanda jumped to her feet. Knuckling the tears from her eyes, she rushed over to squat down in front of Rhonda's chair. Peering earnestly up into her friend's face, she saw the pain there, only partly disguised behind Rhonda's indignation.

"I love you for *you*," she said flatly. "And you are not a slut. I told you I only said that to hurt you, and it looks like I did a pretty good job of it."

Amanda grasped Rhonda's hands in her own. "It's true that what first drew me to you is the fact that you are a lot like Teddy. But you are a much stronger woman than she was. Trist . . ." She choked in the middle of his name. "Um, Tristan once said Teddy was a coward." She shook her head and laughed bitterly. "God, I hated hearing him say that, but maybe he was right. I've given it a lot of thought since I last saw you, and I know that I've had a tendency to idealize Teddy since her death. Well, it's a fact that I will always love her, and she will always have a special place in my heart. But the truth is, she should have come out fighting, instead of taking Mother's pills. That's what you would have done, Rhonda." Amanda's deep-blue eyes drilled into her friend's brown ones. "You are so many things that I am not, and you possess qualities that I don't—qualities I admire. You're more lighthearted, and you're friendlier, and people are automatically at ease with you. You accept things for what they are instead of trying to analyze them to death, the way I do. And you're brave. You don't give a damn what people say about you."

Rhonda's hands jerked in Amanda's grasp. "Everyone cares what people say about them, Amanda."

"But you always laugh when anyone says anything the least bit critical."

"Well, okay. The opinions of some of those idiots we

know are hard to take seriously. But I want to be liked, just like everybody else. There's probably not a person alive who doesn't crave approval from someone at one time or another.'' Rhonda stared down into Amanda's round, earnest eyes. ''When you came along, you were like manna from heaven, Amanda. Sure, there were people who said, 'Rhonda Smith? Yeah, she's a lot of fun. Let's give her a call.' I had about a million acquaintances to knock around with, but not one really close friend. It was like a special gift from God the way you and I just clicked—as if we'd known each other forever. You are the least judgmental person I know, and you've always made me feel that no matter what I did, you would always like me. That's why, for you to say . . .''

Amanda squeezed her hands. ''Will you please believe that I only said what I did to strike back at you?'' she interrupted. ''You made me feel things that were painful, Rhonda, and I was damned if I was going to hurt alone. But I'm sorry—so sorry. God, don't let something I said in the heat of the moment ruin our relationship.'' She found herself squeezing Rhonda's fingers with increasing strength and forced herself to loosen her grasp. ''Please, Rhonda. I *hate* being alienated from you.''

''Well, I really should make you sweat,'' Rhonda said, and then she smiled at Amanda—a real smile, from the heart. ''But, what the hell. Deep down in my heart of hearts, I know you'll be eaten up with guilt for the next six months anyhow, so one way or the other, I'll have my revenge.''

Amanda laughed, thinking that no matter how much she resolved to change her ways, Rhonda was most likely right. It was difficult to reverse a habit developed over a lifetime. She raised up on her knees and Rhonda met her halfway. They clung to one another. Sweet relief flowed through Amanda's veins at having her friend back again. With reluctance, she loosened her hold when Rhonda pulled back to look in Amanda's eyes.

''What are you going to do about Tristan, Amanda?''

''Nothing.'' Amanda couldn't look her in the eye. ''I don't

know." She got up from her crouched position and resumed her seat on the chair across from Rhonda's, eyeing her friend uncertainly. "You said he's probably found someone to replace me."

"And you believed that bullshit? Jeez Marie, kid, I guess I've already had my revenge." Rhonda studied Amanda's face. "I'm sorry, Mandy. I told you that for the same reason you called me a slut, I guess—because I was angry and I wanted to hit you right where you live. You must know it's not true. That man loves you."

"Maybe. But maybe he's forgotten all about me. I haven't heard a word from him since he left."

"And whose fault is that? You didn't exactly leave him with a whole lot of hope, kiddo. You literally told him to leave town and get out of your life."

Rhonda knew a number of things about Tristan that she could have told Amanda, but she decided against it. This was one decision Amanda would have to make on nothing more than her own gut feelings. So, instead, Rhonda told her friend what she believed in her heart to be true. "The next step has to be yours."

"I guess," Amanda agreed. But she was afraid she lacked the courage to take that step.

CHAPTER
21

"MacLaughlin!"
Tristan looked up from his desk as Sergeant Talbot walked over to him. "I'll take over for you here. There's a real hot-lookin' honey who's been waiting almost two hours to see you. Had to put her in the roll call room when it looked like the guys' drooling was going to cause a health hazard on my nice clean floors."

Tristan smiled slightly, informed Talbot of the charges against his prisoner, and walked away. He pushed his glasses up on his nose. The "hot-looking honey" was most likely Julie, a recently acquired informant. She was a hooker out on Highway 99 near the airport, and her flashy attire generally exposed a great deal of leg and cleavage. For her to show up here, she must have something good—maybe something on the Hunter case. Usually, she just called to have him meet her in a dimly lighted dive on Pacific Highway South. He opened the door to the roll call room and froze in the doorway.

"Hello, Tristan," said Amanda, rising to her feet, and she smiled hesitantly. Her heart was beating so hard she could barely breathe. His face was as expressionless as the first time she had seen him. Had she left it too late? She swallowed drily and forced herself to continue. "My safe little world got lonely, just like you said it would."

"Mandy? Oh, Jesus, lass, Mandy?" He crossed the room in two giant strides and his arms swallowed her up, crushing her to him. Blindly, dipping his head, his mouth sought hers and the old familiar heat exploded between them. Mouths and bodies clung. He waltzed her backward until he had her pressed against the wall, and his hands were everywhere. It wasn't until he had dragged her skirt up around her waist and slid his wide-splayed fingers beneath her silky panties to grip her bare bottom that he remembered where they were. Laughing shakily, he stepped back and helped her rearrange her clothes, reaching out to brush the light curls of her bangs away from her dark eyebrows. His eyes couldn't get enough of her. "God, darlin'. I canna believe you're really here."

Amanda searched his face. "You don't mind that I've come here, then? I was going to go to your apartment, but Joe said you'd probably be easier to track down at work."

"Are you serious?"

Looking closely, he could see that she was. Her diminished confidence was a legacy from Dean Eggars, just one more thing for which the bloody beggar would never be called to account.

"No." Tristan's voice was emphatic as he reassured her. "Lord, lass, no." He pulled her into his arms again and laughed, feeling wonderful. "Would I kiss you like that and try to climb into your pants in the middle of the roll call room if I minded? No one else has ever had the ability to make me forget where I am the way you do. I love you, Amanda Rose. Never doubt it."

"I love you so much, Tristan," she whispered and began to cry. "I was so afraid I had ruined everything between us for good. I was such a mess when you left, and I didn't know if you'd even want me anymore, but I had to come here and find out." She brushed at the tears on her cheeks. "I'm sorry, MacLaughlin. I'm so sorry about everyth . . ."

"Hush, lass. Shh, now." He held her tight and rubbed his

jaw against her hair. "Y'needn't be apologizin' to me. And I wasna giving up, y'know. I was comin' after you."

Amanda tilted her head back to look at him. Her eyes were solemn and full of hope. "You were?"

"Oh, aye. I wasna about to let you go without a fight. I'm being transferred to the Reno Police Department, Amanda— permanently. Captain Weller helped me make the arrangements."

Amanda's sudden smile was radiant. "Oh, Tristan, honestly? How? When? Oh, God, this is wonderful."

Tristan smiled at her excitement. He felt so good. He had thought he would have to work his way back into her life in gradual stages, but here she was. She had come to him. He led her over to a chair and waited until she was settled. Whipping another chair around, he pulled it up close to face hers, straddled it, and crossed his arms over the back.

"I was angry about havin' to return to Seattle," he explained. "I thought that maybe if I hadn't been under pressure to return, I could have figured a way to work things out with you." One shoulder hunched up toward his ear. "That theory might not've been grounded in any sort of reality, but it was the way I was feeling when I got back to Seattle. First thing I did was storm into the captain's office and tell him I was quitting to move to Reno. Captain Weller pointed out that I was only three and a half years short of bein' eligible for my pension. He insisted I had invested too many years to flush it all down the loo, but I didn't care. I've never been in love before, and I couldn't see a way to work out our differences if I had to do it long distance."

He was silent for a few moments as he sat facing her, running his eyes up and down her frame, searching for changes. He reached out and touched the softness of her skin. "You know I'm not much good at sharin' my feelings, but I had to talk to someone, so I ended up spillin' my guts all over his office. Mandy, I've been thinkin' the captain's a bit of a sod, but he's been dead grand about this. He said I always was a hardnose, and it was almost worth losin' a good

cop to see me knocked on my ass by love. And he pr⟨ ⟩
to do his damnedest to get me transferred with my pension
intact if I'd just keep my shirt on and promise him two months
in return to train my replacement and help tie up some loose
ends." Tristan grinned at her. "He bloody well did it, too.
He made the arrangements with the brass in Reno. I've got
a week left here and then I've got some accrued vacation
time comin'. We can use it for a honeymoon. I don't have
t'report to the Reno PD until the fifteenth of October."

Amanda had been listening to Tristan's account with enjoyment, but one word made her eyes widen, and she gave
him a slight smile. "Honeymoon? Are we getting married,
then, MacLaughlin?"

"Oh, aye, lass; that we are. As soon as we get back to
Reno. I've got it all planned. We'll find a real church, not
one of those bloody little chapels, and Rhonda and Joe will
stand up for us. They've agreed. We've just been waitin' on
you, then."

It didn't occur to Tristan that she might find it arrogant of
him to have arranged for attendants before he had even asked
her to marry him. Briefly, Amanda considered pointing it out
to him, but upon consideration, she left the words unsaid.
She had come to Seattle not knowing what her reception
would be, but fearing in her heart that sending him away in
order to preserve her foggy world of numbness might have
cost her his love entirely. She had treated him shabbily to
protect her own frayed emotions, but he had been making
plans to get back to her all along. It would take a woman
with more brass than she possessed to criticize his methods.

Instead, she asked mildly, "You've been in touch with
Rhonda since you left?" Rhonda had lounged on her bed and
listened to Amanda worry about Tristan's reaction to having
her show up unannounced, and she hadn't uttered a single
word to alleviate her tension. She probably thought I deserved
to stew, Amanda decided. "Did she tell you I was coming?"

"No." Tristan hitched his chair closer to Amanda's. "She
let me know that there were no complications with Ace, and

he was doing all right. She also let me know how you were doing.'' He reached out and picked Amanda's left hand out of her lap. He inspected her forearm, which was a little thinner and paler than the right. Without raising his eyes, he continued, ''She told me the cast came off two days ago. And that even though Charlie was foaming at the mouth, he was an opportunist above all else, so he didn't dare replace the woman who had escaped the Show Girl Slayer. She informed me that he's holdin' your place at the Cabaret until you're ready to come back, and that he'll probably blazon it across the marquee when you do, for the sheer publicity value.''

Amanda stared at the top of his head as he gave all of his attention to her once-broken arm. She wished he would look at her. ''Rhonda told me a lot of things, Amanda,'' he continued. ''She advised me to give you time, promised me that you would come to your senses. She told me that—oh, hell, how did she put it? Oh, yeah, that way down deep, in your heart of hearts, you loved me.'' He raised his head suddenly and his steady, serious eyes were nearly pewter with the intensity of his thoughts. For several heartbeats he was silent as he stared at her. ''But she didna tell me you were coming to me,'' he finally ground out in a voice made rough by suppressed emotion. ''She didna tell me that.''

''Rhonda is the best friend I have—probably a better friend than I deserve,'' Amanda said softly. ''I said some awful things to her after you left.''

Amanda told Tristan about the confrontation the day Rhonda had removed the kid gloves. ''I still can't believe I said those things to her,'' Amanda whispered, staring at Tristan. ''I'm so ashamed of myself. Rhonda's talk is more promiscuous than she is—'' She correctly interpreted Tristan's skeptical look. ''Okay. Rhonda is every bit as promiscuous as her talk. But that's Rhonda, and it's her business. I mean, isn't that the whole point of being someone's friend? Aren't you supposed to accept them for the person they are and not expect them to be an exact replica of yourself? And I knew even as I was spitting the words in her face that she's always been cautious about her sexual encounters.''

Tristan found it hard to visualize Amanda being deliberately hurtful. Usually, Miss Manners could learn a thing or two from her. ''Did you apologize, lass?''

''Yes. As soon as I pulled myself together, but that's not the point. I never should have said those things in the first place: I didn't believe the stuff I said, even as I was spewing it out. Rhonda held up a mirror and wouldn't let me ignore the unflattering image of what I was letting myself become, and it hurt. God, Tristan, it hurt so damn much that all I could think about was hitting back. Well, I did a bang-up job. Do you know, in all the time that I've known Rhonda, I had never seen her cry? It still twists my stomach in knots to know that I deliberately picked the very words that could make her do so.''

Tristan picked up her hand and fiddled with her slender fingers. ''I'm not sayin' it was a nice thing to do, Mandy,'' he said quietly. ''But y'canna go beatin' yourself over the head with it forever, either. Did you not care about her sayin' I'd be findin' someone else to replace you in my bed?''

A flush darkened Amanda's cheeks. ''I told myself I didn't care. For the next two weeks, while I was getting my life back together, I told myself it would be for the best if you did. But, oh God, Tristan, I was so jealous at the thought, it was like some malignant thing inside me, eating me alive.''

''Well, then, Rhonda got in some licks of her own, didn't she? Have you not forgiven her for that?''

''Yes, of course. She swore she only said it because she was hurt and angry.''

''Lass, you can't keep hugging the guilt of your mistakes to your chest forever. You have a tendency to do that, y'know—to set impossible standards for yourself and then whip yourself over your failure to attain them. If you've forgiven her for sayin' something hurtful, isn't it reasonable to assume that she's forgiven you also?''

"Yes." Amanda's smile lit up the room. "Yes, that is reasonable. I've said as much to myself, but somehow, it's more valid coming from you. Oh, I do love you, Tristan MacLaughlin. How'd you get to be so smart?"

"I'm a college graduate, darlin'. I can think circles around a dancer with a paltry high school education." His tone was perfectly serious, but the glance that accompanied the words was sly, and Amanda grinned at him. A teasing MacLaughlin was a man few people ever saw. Even as she watched, Tristan grew sober again.

"Mandy, why did you hate me for killing Eggars?"

She was perplexed and shocked. "What are you talking about? I didn't hate you!"

"I'll not soon forget the look you gave me when I shot the mon, Amanda Rose. It was as if I'd turned into something disgustingly repugnant right before your eyes. I recognize hate when I see it, lass, and I need to know why. I know you never liked my gun. Was that it? Or was it because I convinced you to get a weapon?" He had been living with the questions for seven weeks now.

"No!" Amanda's stomach knotted as she thought of the moment in question. "Tristan, it only had to do with you peripherally. Honest. I didn't hate you. I couldn't." Seeing that he was prepared to argue, she looked around the bleak room. "Could we go someplace else to talk?"

Tristan glanced at his watch, surprised at how much time had passed. He led her from the room, but it was quite a while before they were able to leave the station. Several people approached. A few of them needed questions answered, but most just wanted an introduction to the woman who had managed to change MacLaughlin so dramatically. By the time he was able to sign out the shift had changed, and that meant even more people wanting to meet Amanda.

"Don't expect much," Tristan warned her as he unlocked his apartment door some time later. "I've been packing to move." He didn't add that the apartment hadn't been noticeably better before.

Amanda looked around with interest. She had wondered what his place looked like. It was so stark at this juncture in his packing that it was difficult to tell what it must have looked like with a few decorations. It was stripped of all personal effects, except for a picture of her on an empty nightstand in his bedroom. The photo was a framed snapshot, one that she remembered Rhonda having taken about a year ago. She picked it up and smiled at him. ''Where did you get this?''

''Rhonda let me have it when I left to come back here. That picture has kept me goin', lass.'' He took it from her hands and replaced it on the stand. Seeing in his eyes what was coming, she started to turn away, but he reached out and turned her back to face him.

''Are you the one who taught Ace the trick with the quarter?'' she asked him with some desperation. Anything to postpone the moment of truth.

''What?'' He shook his head, clearly thrown off balance.

''The trick with the quarter.''

''I don't know what you're talkin' about, lass.''

''Well, Ace has this great new trick. I discovered it by accident when I spilled my wallet one day, and I thought perhaps you had taught it to him. See, out of all the coins that had spilled, he snatched up this one quarter like it was his long-lost mother or something, and he refused to give it back. He would back away from me about five or six feet and then drop the coin on the floor, only it was merely a tease, you see, because whenever I tried to pick it up, he'd snatch it up and back away a few more feet and drop it again. It really was quite tricky. I figured if we ever had a cash-flow problem, we could always hire him out to one of the casinos. It would make a great come-on for the customers. I think he'd be a terrific barker. Get it? Bark . . .'' Her voice trailed away at the resigned patience in Tristan's eyes. One look was enough to let her know that he had let her stall her last. Her time had come; he was through waiting.

''Tell me how I was only—what did you call it?—pe-

ripherally included in the hate you felt when I shot Eggars,''
he said, glad that she had finally wound down. It set his teeth
on edge to watch so much false gaiety when she was clearly
running on nerves alone. ''Amanda, you looked at me as if
you loathed me, and if I could take back killing him, I swear
I would, because it wrecked everything between us.''

Amanda placed her hand over his mouth. ''I hated *me*,''
she cried. She'd give anything not to have to confess this,
but she couldn't bear to see him blame himself. ''Not you,
Tristan, me! When you shot him . . .'' Her hand dropped to
her side and she shook her head. ''I've always had a problem
with admitting that I have faults. I've told you about my up-
bringing—how I was groomed to be my parents' little social
asset.'' Taking a deep breath, she confessed, ''Over the years,
I've taken the easy way out by blaming my parents for my
own inability to confront my imperfections. After all,'' she
said in a brittle voice, ''didn't I constantly have it drummed
into my head that a Charles must always be socially impeccable?'' She was silent for a moment. Then, in a low voice,
avoiding eye contact, she continued, ''But I'm the worst kind
of hypocrite there is, Tristan. Because, after a certain point
in your life, you have to accept responsibility for your own
actions. You can't just keep shoving the blame off onto someone else. I've made choices in my life. And while I've been
busy resenting my parents for making me feel that mistakes
are unforgivable, I've continued to try my damnedest to live
up to their image of what I should be.''

''That's bullshit, Amanda. You're making yourself out to
be neurotic, and you're not. That's more your parents' prov-
ince.''

''It's not bullshit. You've said it yourself: I set impossible
standards and then flay myself alive when I fail to attain
them. It's okay for someone else to mess up, but Amanda
Rose Charles has a lofty position to maintain on her pedestal.''

She paused for a moment, then her mouth twisted bitterly.
''Besides, you wanted to know why I looked at you the way

I did. It wasn't a result of anything you did, Tristan. I swear to God. None of it was your fault. I was the one to go to pieces . . .''

Amanda's voice trailed away and she sat on the edge of the mattress, rubbing her hands up and down her arms. She stared at the tiny water spot on the wall, until Tristan reached out and touched her arm. She clutched herself a little bit harder, in an attempt to control the fine tremors that rippled just beneath her skin and glanced over at him. ''Where was I? Oh, yeah, upon my august perch. Well, when I finally fell from my little pedestal, I really fell long and hard, didn't I? I was such a righteous little prig until the day Eggars walked into my home and killed Kalowski and terrorized me. God, I have never in my life experienced emotions even remotely similar to those I experienced that day. I simply *burned* to be the one to kill him, and it sickened me afterward. I couldn't live with that image of myself. Where were my much-vaunted manners then? When you wanted to teach me to handle a gun, I was so damn smug, so certain that no matter what the provocation, I could never shoot another human being. But that was before I learned how it felt to hate.'' She hugged herself and looked up at him. ''Dean Eggars taught me to hate, MacLaughlin, and God, it was a lesson I learned so well. It absorbed all my emotions. I hated him like I've never hated anything or anyone in my life. I wanted him dead. I didn't care if it was right or wrong. I just wanted him dead. Tristan, I tried so hard to kill him''—her voice began to rise—''but he just kept coming at me and *coming* at me, no matter how many times I shot him. Then, when *you* were the one to kill him, when he finally went down and stayed down, I was consumed with rage. I felt like something had been taken away from me. I can't forget the way I felt—like some mindless animal scenting blood, then being denied its prey. And God, it sickened me to realize how quickly I could be reduced to such savagery.''

The memory still retained the power to make her entire body quake with rage and shame, and Tristan reached out and pulled her into his arms, surrounding her with his strength and wrapping her in his warmth until she calmed.

"Ah, lass. My beautiful, brave lass. You canna go on blamin' yourself for feelings you had no way of controlling." He held her tight, smoothing her hair with one large hand. "It's not exactly an everyday event to have a crazed killer doin' his damnedest to inflict pain on you."

"I know," she mumbled into his chest. "He was an animal. And he turned me into an animal right along with him. I've had a lot of time to come to terms with all that these past few weeks. And intellectually, I realize I probably reacted exactly like anyone else in my situation would. But, Tristan." She looked up at him. "Emotions don't have a thing to do with logic. And the feelings from that day still tend to resurrect themselves at odd moments." The calm she had attained began to splinter. "They come out of the blue, and it's as though no time has passed at all since that day. I'm so filled with hatred and rage again: for him, for me. It just swells, until I feel like I'm going to burst with it. And I'm so damn scared, Tristan."

He tightened his grip on her, nuzzling his face into her hair, her cheek, the contour of her neck. "Shh, now," he murmured. "It's okay. I've got you, darlin'. You're safe now. Nothin' is ever going to hurt you again."

He held her and whispered reassurances. Then the soothing words and comforting kisses changed, suddenly became demanding and hungry and hot. Breathing grew harsh, clothing dissolved, and the next time Amanda had a moment for coherent thought, the chenille bedspread was twisted beneath her back, imprinting its pattern into her bare skin. Tristan was a heavy weight bearing her down into the mattress, and her body hummed with satiated pleasure.

Shivering beneath the postcoital kisses he pressed along her throat and shoulders, flushed with the words of love he murmured, Amanda held Tristan tightly and blessed the love she had never expected to find. She was a realist, and she knew that, given their personalities and respective professions, their marriage would not always be a smooth or easy one. He had shed light into a world she hadn't even realized was cast in shadow, but she knew her MacLaughlin. She knew for a certainty that there were going to be times in the future when Tristan himself would thunder all over her bright new world. Both of them had spent the majority of their adult lives alone, and there would be times when they would find it difficult to adjust to each other's needs. Each was stubborn, and they would struggle with their allotment of adversity. Their marriage was never going to match up to June and Ward Cleaver's, any more than her own parents' union had. But it didn't matter.

Tristan began to laugh deep in his chest. "Barker!" he said and hugged her hard. "So, you're goin' to put Ace to work, eh?"

"Oh, sure, now you laugh," she muttered. "Where were you when I was trying to avoid the issue?"

"I wanted to get everything out in the open," he replied into her neck. "I made a lot of mistakes of my own, darlin'. I mismanaged that case practically from the word go."

"No, you didn't!"

"Oh, aye. I did. I let my involvement with you color too many of my professional decisions, and . . ."

"And everything turned out fine! If you had remained an uninvolved cop, then I never would have gotten to know the real Tristan MacLaughlin. I never would have fallen in love with you."

"Ah, God, I'm happy you're here, lass," he murmured, pushing up on his elbows to look at her with eyes filled with masculine satisfaction. "I missed you somethin' dreadful." He smiled at her, obviously content. His hands were never still—stroking her hair, touching her face, reassuring himself of her presence and conveying his love.

Amanda practically purred. "Oh, Tristan, I missed you, too." She dug her fingernails into his hard buttocks and shifted her legs, feeling him begin to harden inside her once again. A smile lit her face.

Let the future bring its worst, for somehow, when they were together, she felt they were both better people. He was more open and humorous; she was less concerned with presenting a faultless image of herself to the world. When Tristan was with her, she wouldn't allow him to hide his emotions behind a mask. And, spending any length of time with him, the value of speaking plainly and directly, instead of hiding behind a shield of good manners, was bound to rub off on her.

No matter what else happened in their lives, they would always have this: a consuming love, respect, and passion for each other.

And she knew deep down in her heart of hearts, as Rhonda was so fond of saying, that as long as they had that, the rest would work itself out.

GET LOVESTRUCK!

AND GET STRIKING ROMANCES FROM POPULAR LIBRARY'S BELOVED AUTHORS

Watch for these exciting romances in the months to come:

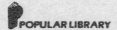

POPULAR LIBRARY